Deep Fried And Pickled

A Novel
by
Paisley Ray

Copyright ©2012 by Paisley Ray
Cover Art by Chantal deFelice

ISBN: 1500685046
ISBN 13:9781500685041
Library of Congress Control Number: TXU001835116

This novel is a work of fiction. Names, characters, places, and incidents are either the product of the author's imagination or are used fictitiously. Any resemblance to actual persons, living or dead, or to actual events or locales is entirely coincidental.

The Rachael O'Brien Chronicles
by
Paisley Ray

"There are no good girls gone wrong,
just bad girls found out."
~Mae West

Prologue

My four-year plan included getting an art history degree, losing my virginity, and partying—hopefully not in that order.

However bucket lists don't always unfold the way you envision. Admittedly, the wealth of knowledge I obtained from my nine-month south-of-the-Mason-Dixon-Line experience at North Carolina College wasn't overly focused on academics. Instead, I followed a nagging feeling about a painting that turned into a full-blown compulsion to uncover a fake. The little voice inside my head kept warning me, but I didn't pay much attention until it was too late.

August 1986

1

Grogan Hall

"DEEP FRIED AND PICKLED," my dad said as he parked the car in front of Grogan Hall at North Carolina College. "That's the way they like things down here."

I would have preferred driving the 436 miles from Canton, Ohio, to Greensboro, North Carolina, in a subtler, neutral-colored vehicle, but Dad liked the idea of free advertising. Before the sun had risen we'd packed his work van, a cherry-bomb-red-and-cobalt-blue block-letter billboard that read, *How's Your Art? O'Brien's Fine Painting and Furniture Restoration.*

The apple hadn't fallen far from the tree as I was here for an art history degree. Half asleep, I'd casually mentioned the trip's purpose—settling me into my dorm, not finding commissions for his business. My innocent comment had morphed him into Captain Buzzkill. "Young lady," he lectured, "who do you think is paying your out-of-state tuition?" He droned on about that one from our driveway until we crossed the Virginia state line.

1

College campus move-in day mirrored a directionally challenged, lawless rush hour, with drivers blatantly ignoring one-way streets and no parking zones. Boiling frustration and a herding mentality short-circuited my dad's normal rule-abiding modus operandi. Outside of Grogan Hall he wedged the van between a row of triple-parked vehicles.

When I slid the van door open, heat waves bounced off the asphalt and collided with the arctic blast that escaped its air-conditioned interior. Squinting to block the light from the unrelenting sun, I positioned my hand like a sailor looking for land and leaned against the painted logo on the sliding door.

Figuring we were sitting ducks for a parking violation, I rushed to unload my belongings and heaped them in a pile on the curb. Everyone had the same idea, and the sidewalk in front of the tower dorm looked like a flea market that had exploded.

Back inside the van, I climbed past a hanging clothes rack onto a mountain of essential stuff and couldn't help overhear a mom and daughter two cars down in the throes of a blowout over who forgot to pack bedding. Through the open van doors, I glimpsed a man clutching a floor lamp. With his free hand, he picked up a box of my toiletries that had merged into an adjacent pile.

"Dad," I shouted out the back, "my bathroom supplies are walking away."

Near the bottom of a flight of stone steps, he caught up with the perpetrator. Mom and I watched him retrieve my six-month supply of toothpaste and tampons.

Rings of sweat stained Dad's armpits, and he snapped, "Rachael, only unload what you can carry."

"She was just unpacking. It's not her fault," Mom said.

"Maeve, come down to earth and help carry something."

Mom and Dad had bickered in the car the entire road trip and hadn't stopped, even though we'd arrived. *Weird.* It was the longest-running disagreement I'd ever witnessed between my parents. Until today, my PUs—parental units—had functioned as a united front, not crossing the other in front of me. Under an asinine banner of "We know what's best," they had managed to ruin my teenage social life with a barrage of ridiculous rules and regulations about vehicles and boys. Having a 10:00 p.m. curfew and minimal car access had crushed any hopes I'd had of dating and, by default, losing my virginity. After we unpacked, the PUs would be driving home without me, and I planned to make up for lost time.

At six feet tall, my dad wore size eleven laced suede shoes. His hair had more salt than pepper and was overdue for a cut. Reaching behind the van seat, he handed me a worn leather-bound Bible. "Thessalonians is a good read. I marked it for you."

Dad abided by a strict Catholic code and was a regular holy day and early Sunday Mass patron. Mom and I exuded less zeal. A Bible wasn't the sort of book that I'd browse through in my free time. He was testing me? That was the only explanation. If I refused the book he handed me, he'd probably go parental, forgoing the nonrefundable tuition he'd already paid and haul my ass back to the Buckeye State. I drilled my pupils into his and concentrated on vaporizing him, but I couldn't muster any superpowers.

Awaiting a response, he smiled at me. I knew how to can this conversation. Years of teenage experience had sharpened my silent treatment skills. Biting my lip, I swallowed my annoyance and tucked the tattered book into one of my duffel bags while mumbling a less than ecstatic, "Thanks."

The air inside the van hung motionless. Mom rested against the bumper and blotted her neck with her scarf. Hearing Dad's mention of the Bible, she closed her eyes and kept them shut. Herbal tea and meditating were the newest accessories she'd added to her arsenal. Dad or I could be midsentence and Mom would go into "the zone." She signaled this by pinching her index finger and thumb together. After recharging, she'd make herself a cup of ginkgo biloba tea—her brain tonic. I once made the mistake of sticking my nose into the tin of Gypsy brand tea leaves. It stank like an ode to dried cat piss, and I passed whenever she offered me a cup.

Until now, I'd only seen her trance out in the privacy of our home. While Dad ignored her, I felt embarrassed by her homage to the sixties and shouted, "Mom!"

Her eyelids flew open, and she ran a hand through the waves that the humidity had unraveled in her Dorothy Hamill haircut. Flapping her shirttails, she turned toward Dad, "Rachael's eighteen. Do you really think that a Bible is going to keep her in on Friday nights?" She didn't bother to whisper.

Mom's words weren't meant for discussion. She refocused and began unpacking a cardboard box full of homemade lemon squares, chocolate everything cookies, and iced brownies. Dad snuck one and midbite, I heard him grumble, "It's always good to have a Bible."

Moving to the passenger side of the van, Mom fumbled inside her purse and unlatched a compact case mirror. Seeing for herself how the southern humidity had transformed her hair, she chucked it back into her handbag. Before zipping it closed, she clutched a wrapped book-sized gift. Fiddling with the bow, she turned toward me. "I also have a book of sorts for you."

My parents had already spent a fortune on supplies and new clothes, and their gifts surprised me, not that a used Bible counts. "You shouldn't have," I said, and clumsily reached between the seats to hug her. I let go, but she didn't. With her embrace lingering, I asked, "Should I open it or wait?"

She released me and smiled with distant eyes, "Why don't you save it until you're settled in?"

Despite sauna temperatures and short-fused temperments, attending college far from home put me in a euphoria that was ten times better than a pan of double-chocolate brownies, powdered with sugar and rinsed down with a cold glass of milk. Since the PUs' irritation level was already high, I concentrated on hiding the bounce in my step and tried not to gloat. Being an only child, I guessed Mom and Dad would go down Emotional Lane when they pulled away from campus without me.

TOWER DORM SOUNDED FANCY, Grogan was not. A high-rise, all-girl dorm, it lacked two crucial comforts not noted in the brochure: carpet and air conditioning. Inside the elevator, Pine-Sol air clung to my skin as sweat gathered behind my ears, in the small of my back, and ten paces directly south.

I'd left the PUs on the curb. Dad's van idled while he waited to move, and Mom guarded my pile by sitting on it. Rubbing my thumb over the notches of my room key, I ignored the duffel bags slipping off my shoulders and the cardboard box full of sunbaked confectionaries in my hands and focused on finding my room.

I spied into every open door I passed by, glimpsing power strips overloaded with mini home appliances, stockpiles of Ramen noodles, and unmade, gray-striped twin bed mattresses piled high with luggage.

Seven-hundred-seventeen had to be next. Like a can of shaken soda, the pressure inside me was ready to burst. The hallway bustled with students, siblings, parents, and grandparents; their voices seeped through my foam headphones and garbled into the Depeche Mode cassette playing in my Sport Walkman. The lid on the baked-goods box edged off, and I secured it with my chin.

Weaving around a cluster of bodies, I used tunnel vision to count down the room numbers. In a blink, something zunged my ankles and jerked my feet from under me. My teeth clipped the edge of my tongue, and I involuntarily lobbed the box of lemon bars and brownie bits toward the ceiling. In a domino effect, I toppled into two bystanders, and the three of us nosedived until we made intimate contact with the green-and-white linoleum floor.

My headphones had twisted, and one pirated my left eye. In a tangle of limbs and snarled hangers, an uncradled telephone receiver rested between my thighs and a voice called out, "Katie Lee?"

Nobody spoke until a red-polished index finger propelled into the air, and a New York accent near my ear clipped, "God damn it, I broke a nail."

In this twisteresque body snarl a moaning noise reverberated. An unshaven leg the color of chocolate syrup rose an inch off my shoulders before clunking a bedazzled canvas slip-on back down. "With cussin' like that, it's no wonder we've been stricken down. The Lord is sayin' somethin'. That mouth is going to send us all into the eternal inferno."

The New Yorker wiggled below me. "Don't Bible-belt me. I've been assaulted with baked goods."

This was not how I envisioned meeting new friends in the dorm.

A medium-built brunette, who smelled as though she'd bathed in Lauren perfume, peered down at the three of us. Her bob haircut cradled her face. Like a page out of *The Preppy Handbook*, the green madras Bermuda shorts and pink polo she wore gave the appearance of a slice of watermelon with its collar up. Sucking wind, she gasped and, with linguistic precision, spoke in rhythm to her exhale. "Y'all dropped like a spare. I don't see blood. Are all y'all okay?"

As far as I could tell, the only things injured were Mom's homemade baked goods and the bathroom supplies that littered the hallway outside the dorm room I'd yet to see.

"You still there?" the idle phone chirped.

The standing southerner stared at the phone between my legs. "Pardon me," she said and tugged at its cord. Sandwiching the telephone between her earlobe and neck, she whispered, "Gotta go," and hung up.

The girl in the sparkly shoes propped herself up on her elbows. Under her breath, she garbled, "P-shwank. Do you have a license to talk and walk?"

Focusing on Sparkle Shoes, the girl with the phone said, "Where are my manners? I'm Katie Lee Brown. I didn't catch your name."

"Francine Battle."

Katie Lee busied herself collecting the panty liners that had exploded from someone's wash bag. Delicately pointing at Francine's left breast, she shielded a side of her mouth and offered the liners. "You're leaking lemon curd."

After using her thumb to wipe yellow glop from her chest, Francine said, "Lord, girl, I'm not a mini kind of woman. Those don't belong to me."

The New Yorker, still on the floor, opened her palm, and Katie Lee handed over the stack of feminine care pads. "I was talkin' with my boyfriend. Nash and I are missin' each other somethin' terrible. I heard voices out here and thought one of you might be my roommate, Rachael O'Brien."

The New Yorker stood, brushed off some crumbs, then raised her chin to the ceiling and mouthed, "Thank you! You got the wrong girl. I'm Macy Stephen."

I pushed to my feet, stepped out of the remnants of the confectionary cyclone, and offered my hand to my assigned roommate. "I'm Rachael O'Brien."

Swaddling me in a hug, Katie Lee swooned, "So glad to finally meet you." Releasing me she held onto my wrists and swung my arms. "This year is going to be amazing."

Francine moaned, "Um-hmm," and massaged her lower back.

Katie Lee let go of me to lend a hand to Francine. I rescued an antique gilded frame from the floor and blew crumbs off a black-and-white photo of a toddler in cornrows. The child's plump fingers clutched the hand of a gray-haired woman in a plain cotton dress. Francine snatched the frame from my grip; her stare softened as she became lost in the memory she held. Meeting my eyes, she spoke under a light breath. "My great-memaw. She's an artist, you know. She's the one who pushed me to get the education she never had."

Macy leaned her head in toward us. "I'm hopeful that this is the start to nine months that'll make *Animal House* look like a fucking retirement home."

Wiping the humidity from my hairline, I twisted my head to make sure my PUs hadn't appeared. "Me, too."

NOTE TO SELF
Getting rid of the PUs—glorious.

2

Twenty-One-Year-Old Freshman

I'd been away at school for one week. My body hadn't adjusted to the southern climate's secret double whammy: heat 'n humidity. Between classes, I skirted into the shadows cast by campus buildings. During peak heat I conserved words, not responding when a head nod sufficed. A newly purchased minielectric fan rested on my desk shelf, blasting recirculated hot air onto my face. It dried the sweat off my eyebrows, but my thighs still stuck to my shorts and my t-shirt to my back. The broiling temperatures that started the day I'd arrived stuck on campus without any sign of relief.

Early Wednesday morning, I was still in bed when there was a knock on our door. Katie Lee asked, "Who is it?"

"It's Macy. Come out here, quick."

I threw off the cotton sheet and followed Katie Lee into the hallway.

"What's going on?" I asked.

Macy nodded her head toward Francine's door, and Katie Lee gasped.

Spray-painted letters that spelled DAN dripped down her doorway.

"Who's Dan?" I asked

Macy rolled her eyes. "It's no ex-boyfriend."

Before Katie Lee knocked on Francine's door, she whispered, "It's an abbreviation: 'Dumb-ass-nigger.'"

The only thing mixed in Canton, Ohio, was the bicolor corn that grew in the fields, and I almost didn't believe what Katie Lee told me until Francine opened her door. Her hand flew to her mouth, and the corners of her eyes became glossy.

Macy put an arm around Francine's shoulder and guided her back into her room.

"Do you have any Windex?" I asked. "I think we can wipe it off."

"No," Macy said, "don't touch it. Call campus security."

Across the hall our phone rang, and Katie Lee dashed off to answer it.

I sat on Francine's unmade bed while she fumbled to find the number for campus security. Like Macy, Francine had a single room, smaller than the one Katie Lee and I shared. She had chosen lavender for her bedding, desk cushion, and rug. A shelf above her bed displayed framed photos of big smiles and equally big hugs. At an outdoor picnic, an older man in a boat held an overgrown whiskered catfish, and I noticed the photo of Francine and her great-memaw that I'd rescued from the hallway pileup.

Francine's voice rasped as she spoke into her phone. "This is Francine Battle, Grogan Hall, seventh floor. Racial graffiti has been spray-painted on my dorm door."

The conversation was brief and as Francine hung up, Katie Lee shouted, "Rachael, it's your daddy on our phone."

Mom and Dad had arranged to ring me on Sunday mornings. They referred to it as a weekly social call, but I knew better. It was a make-sure-you're-not-partying-too-hard-Saturday-night-since-you'll-be-hearing-from-us-early-Sunday call. I'd been away for less than a week and besides Francine's drama, nothing was new. I almost asked Katie Lee to tell a fib and say that I'd dashed off to class, but then thought better of it.

"Rachael, are you all right?" Dad asked.

"Of course I am," I said, keeping my voice sharp so I'd pass his sneaky surprise inspection. I watched Katie Lee leave the room with a towel and shampoo caddy. She said something about showering before campus security showed up.

"Your mother has walked out after twenty years of marriage." His words resonated like a winter whiteout, and my head went blank.

She'd never leave my dad. He must have done something. I wondered if he'd cheated and asked, "Why would she do that?"

Dad cleared his throat. "She scribbled a note on a piece of planetary stationery. Your mother left to be with a group of healing psychics. Says she's gone to find her 'inner channel.'"

My ears tuned out the hallway chatter, and an icy chill froze my insides. I went into lockdown. "Mother? Psychic? Since when?" *She never knew I borrowed that twenty out of her purse or that I forged her name so I didn't have to dissect a frog in biology. Did she?*

"Rachael, I didn't phone until I was certain that this wasn't a hoax. I hired an investigator who has proof that your mom is staying at a private residence in Sedona, Arizona."

"Arizona? We've never been to Arizona. Does this PI have a license? Why did she go there? What if she was kidnapped or drugged?"

The phone went silent. "Dad, are you okay?"

"Bear with me," he said, his tone sounding small and distant. "What I'm about to tell you falls under the category of mumbo jumbo. I've done some research. The red rock that surrounds the town is known in certain circles for its vortex, ancient mystical frequencies, and healing power. There, I said it."

"This is ridiculous. Have you called her? When are you going to bring her back?"

"Rachael, there are no phones, and the property is surrounded by high walls and a guarded gate."

"Are you sure the Moonies or the Mormons don't have her?"

Dad sighed, and I heard ice cubes clank. To deliver this news, I guessed he'd upgraded from beer to something stronger.

"I'm sure. I thought about marching out there to bring her back until I consulted a lawyer. He said if I did, I'd probably be arrested. She has to come home on her own. Hopefully this craziness will wear off and she'll call one of us."

After exhausting every explanation we could think of, our conversation dead-ended over Mom's newfound calling. When I hung up the phone, my core rattled with an emptiness I'd never felt. Manic emotions floated inside me, and I didn't know which to pick: anger, guilt, fear. Disbelief of her abandonment fermented. It seemed so bizarre; my parents were diehard Sunday Mass patrons, and we never even owned a Ouija board.

Lying on my bed, I listened to voices in the hallway. Someone from campus security named Tuke introduced himself to Francine. My mind fixated on the words Dad had spoken, and I didn't have an ounce of extra capacity to delve into the vandalism.

Quietly I shut my door and contemplated my mom. Why did she leave? Did I miss the signs? *Obviously.* Mom and Dad didn't seem unhappy. *Freakin' psychic?* The only thing psychic about my mom was her ability to read my moods. But that was Mom 101 stuff. She'd started meditating. I thought that was just a stress relief thing. Except for the ride down and the Bible-burst moment, I couldn't even remember them fighting. Was that it? They didn't care enough to fight?

I never dreamed the day she and Dad moved me into the dorm would be the last time I'd see her. The hug she gave me in the van, our last embrace. Then I remembered the gift I'd forgotten to open and ran to my closet to find the present. I untied the bow and removed the silver wrapping paper. It was a journal and pen combo. Tipping the ink pen upside down, I stared at gold moons and silver stars bob in a sea of glitter. My back crept down a wall, and as I sank to the floor, I mindlessly fanned blank pages. The second to last had a note in Mom's handwriting: "Be true to yourself."

What did that mean? How long had she been planning to go? I had lots of questions, but no answers. I wished I'd said how much I was going to miss her and all the nice things she did for me. Clean-sheet

Mondays, homemade mac 'n' cheese, buying me the ninety-dollar Gloria Vanderbilt jeans on the condition I didn't tell Dad. I loved those jeans but would've returned them in exchange for Mom in a heartbeat. It was too late. She'd left, and I didn't know how to get her back.

WHEN KATIE LEE RETURNED from the shower, voices in the hallway rose. Leaning against my open door, I batted my eyelids as fast as hummingbird wings to keep the stinging tears from forming. Crossed-armed, Francine watched a man from the campus police take Polaroid photos of her door. The red stitched name embroidered on his shirt read *Tuke Walson*. Wearing the kind of uniform that you see on security guards, dental assistants, and electricians, navy blue and snug, I pegged him as older than a graduate student, but younger than my dad.

"Looks like Dan has left his mark. How long you been datin' this boy?"

"Ah, Tuke," Macy said. "Dan's not a guy. It's a racial slur abbreviation."

Tuke's shoulders stiffened as he processed the letters like an indecipherable crossword.

Francine asked, "You southern?"

"Born and raised," he said, and the meaning registered. A tsk slid off his tongue as he shook his head. He touched the paint with a finger. Still wet, it smeared. "Any you ladies hear early morning noises?"

Macy, Katie Lee, and I shook our heads.

Tuke walked the hallway, checked the staircases, and questioned our neighbors about last night. As the morning's drama unfolded, I was thankful that Francine's door distracted Katie Lee and Macy from noticing the turmoil I kept to myself. Like Francine, I'd had a jolt, but unlike her nemesis who hid behind a can of spray paint, I knew the face of the person who rejected me.

A replacement door arrived sometime later, and Tuke left after he installed it. Macy, Katie Lee, and Francine had classes, but I stayed behind. Keeping the blinds shut, I buried my head in my pillow. I wanted to believe that the news about Mom was wrong. There could have been an emergency, a miscommunication, but I couldn't fathom a reasonable alternative explanation.

The phone rang again, and I wondered if my mother had received a cosmic signal to call me. No matter her reason, I just wanted to know that she was okay.

"O'Brien," Katie Lee said. "Get over here. We saved you a spot."

My head hovered in a sticky emotional web. "Where are you?"

"The nastyteria, waiting for you."

I TRUDGED ACROSS CAMPUS DRIVE feeling strung out, unable to remember or care if I'd brushed my hair or locked the dorm door. I couldn't be bothered. This was all wrong. I was the one who was supposed to go away to find myself, not Mom.

A burnt stink of charred frying oil suffocated the entire cafeteria, even the table in the back where Katie Lee and Macy had saved me a seat. Somewhere in the kitchen, someone was having a lousy day, and I could relate. I didn't know why I'd agreed to meet them. Curled under the covers in my dark room, brooding about Mom was where I wanted to be. *Why couldn't she be normal and just have an affair?*

The numbness that pressed inside my chest overpowered my appetite. I did little more than pick at the edges of the meat and cheese layers in my Italian sub. I wondered if I should go home to be with Dad, but staring at him wouldn't bring Mom back. Besides, what if she tried to call me at school?

Rubbing her thumb across her blood-red nail polish, Macy randomly clicked the underside of her nails. "There isn't shit going on. This place sucks."

Katie Lee dipped a hush puppy into soft butter. "Y'all, I hear a decent crowd turns up at the Holiday Inn bar. We could go this Friday."

Macy huffed a throaty guffaw. "You have to be kidding. Partying at the Holiday Inn?"

"This sounds made up," I said. "Where did you get this tip?"

"I overheard two cute guys talking by the elevator."

Arranging fries in a puddle of ketchup, I scoffed. "Holiday Inn? As in the cheap hotel with the bathtub-sized swimming pool and vending machines as meal service?"

Katie Lee's eyes roamed the cafeteria. "It's going on week two," she reminded us, "and I'm tired of staring at our dorm walls."

"We've got one problem," Macy said. "The drinking age is twenty-one."

Considering consequences, I ranked the humiliation of being arrested and thrown in the clinker for underage drinking at the Holiday Inn a worse offense than flunking out. "We can't get in," I told the girls. "They'll card us."

Chewing on her bottom lip roused Katie Lee's inner magic fairy. In an aha moment, she zipped her index finger in the air, which sparked extra twinkle from her lagoon-blue eyes. "We can go to the registration office. Tell them we've lost our school IDs."

I pushed my tray aside. "What good will that do? Unless we get our birth date changed."

Katie Lee winked while Macy stopped her annoying nail clicking long enough to ask, "Who's going first?"

My mom, it seemed, had pretended to love my dad and me. Raw emotion grappled my insides and I professed, "I hate fakes and scams. Besides, what bar would let us in with doctored student IDs?"

As much as I thought I wanted to party and meet "The Guy," I didn't want to get busted in the process. I did my best to squash the idea, hoping we'd discover some place less illegal to drink and some other way to do it.

Something with apples and cinnamon was baking in the ovens and began to overpower the charred smell. "Come on, Rach," Katie Lee said. "No one will check."

I tried to reason with the two. "If we get caught forging an official document, chances are we'll get kicked out of school."

Ignoring my objections, Katie Lee stood and walked toward the kitchen. Moments later she returned with three warm apple strudel tarts. She sank a fork into one. "Y'all, I'll go first."

NOTE TO SELF
Fake ID: the ultimate ticket to a more meaningful university experience? TBD.

3

Blood, Drugs, and Forgery

The afternoon heat sweltered, and everything but the humming cicadas stood still. Like the locked heat index, my mind stuck on Mom. I'd been away at school four days before my parents' relationship collapsed. Dad had gone into crisis mode for two days before he called me with news. He didn't say it, but he had to have been freaking out. I was, and knew it had to be ten times worse for him. When I returned from my afternoon classes, I called to make sure he was eating, sleeping, and not doing anything stupid.

"I've had a haircut, and I'm staying busy," he assured me. "I've accepted a commission to refurbish six Clementine Hunter paintings for her hundredth birthday celebration."

"That's cool. Museum or private collector?"

His voice filled with glee. "New Orleans Museum of Art."

"Who do you know in the South that recommended you?"

I thought I detected gloating when he said, "The artists granddaughter noticed the van in Greensboro and contacted the museum currator. Once we talked, they checked my references and awarded me the commission."

Pride swelled inside of me. Although Dad's personal life hung in chaotic uncertainty, professionally he'd worked hard to attain a reputation for his meticulous attention to detail. This was a big deal, and my chest weighed heavy knowing neither Mom nor I was home to help him celebrate. I still couldn't believe she'd run off. Mindlessly, I twirled the phone cord around my finger and stared out the window at Campus Drive, waiting for someone to say "April Fools!" or "Gotcha!"—something to shake the reality of Mom's unexpected departure. But none came, and before I found heartfelt words, Katie Lee flung our door open and distracted me. In full peacock strut, she parade-marched the length of our nine-by-twelve cell while waving her rectangular card in the air. Making an excuse, I hung up, then snatched her prized possession. "Let me see that."

Katie Lee's two-by-three-and-a-half-inch university photo ID card was still warm from the laminate machine. Under the university seal, she was a twenty-one-year-old freshman. She'd secured her golden ticket to a night of drunken bliss.

A milkshake of emotional anxiety and boredom can warp one's perspective of fun. After thumbing through my wallet, I handed Katie Lee my ID and said, "Hide this."

"Why?"

"So I can say I lost mine and get a new one with a clear conscience."

AN OVERLYING SCENT OF formaldehyde hung in the windowless basement of the humanities and science building. The woman behind the flip-top wooden counter of the registrar's office styled her Clairol medium-blonde locks in a bouffant and wore a shift dress with billowy sleeves. "I've lost my ID," I said.

Curling her lips in a glum frown, she handed me a form to fill out. After a ten-minute wait, I paid a twenty-dollar replacement fee and left with my new card.

I wasn't proud that I'd lied about my birth date on an official form. You weren't supposed to do that until you turned thirty. Knowing my mom had hit the road with a group of traveling head cases and spending all my free time in the company of books while living in mock prison quarters was a recipe for emotional turmoil. If I got busted, I figured I could plead insanity.

Not lingering around, I headed to class. Finally I had plans. I'd be spending Friday night at the Holiday Inn. Since I hadn't found any cute, witty guys on campus, I hoped that this was where they were hiding. Drinking and dating weren't approved activities under Mom and Dad's roof. But I wasn't living with either one anymore.

PROFESSOR'S WEREN'T SHY ABOUT assigning heavy loads of reading reaquirement and after a late dinner, and some library time, I was back at the dorm, but avoided my room. Katie Lee's hometown boyfriend, Nash, was nocturnal and always called after eleven. They'd dated for two years in high school, and she professed to anyone who'd listen that she'd found her soul mate. Trying to pace myself on the personal information intake, I ended up across the hall, in Macy's beanbag, and hoped my roommate's phone conversation would be brief so I could get some sleep.

Being a Greek New Yorker, Macy embodied more oompa than the average eighteen-year-old. At least more than any I'd ever met. Unpeeling my late night snack, I offered her half of my Slim Jim.

Fluttering her hand in front of her crinkled nose, she squeaked, "Eugh," which I took as a "no thanks."

"I'm a strict vegetarian," she reminded me.

Despite her meat abstinence, she spewed animal magnetism when she danced with her laundry to the B-52's. She folded a towel or t-shirt during the pauses and slow parts of the songs. Every piece of clothing she pulled from the basket was black, gray, or blue, except her panties and bras. Those were bright colors constructed from lacy fabrics. Macy's physique resembled a roller coaster, and her bras, easily two cup sizes larger than mine, gave me feelings of inadequacy. When she opened her underwear drawer, I was transfixed by the discovery of what could only be a tunnel into Candyland. The neatly folded stacks of intimate apparel drew my eye and gave me a sense that each piece could provide a wealth of information that probably wasn't decent.

When the late night news ended, Macy's door swayed open and clunked against the gray plastic wall bumper. The TV provided the only illumination in the room and cast a luminescent glow around Katie Lee's shadowy figure as her slipper sock feet made a whisk-whisk noise across the floor. Macy clicked on her study light, and we both watched Katie Lee's curled fists window-wash mascara and tears into raccoon rings around her eyes.

Turning the TV off, Macy wrapped her arm around Katie Lee's shoulders. "You're a mess."

I softened my voice. "What's going on? Did you have a fight with Nash?"

I didn't mean to send her over an emotional waterfall, but my question opened her tear ducts, and by the time she calmed down she'd filled the garbage can to the rim with tissues.

"Nash was in a car accident. I should be with him, but I'm stuck here. Y'all, it happened in New Bern, near my house."

"When was this?" I asked.

"Yesterday. Late afternoon."

Macy guided Katie Lee to her twin bed and offered her a pillow. "What happened?"

"To miss an oncoming vehicle, his Chevy truck lurched into a ditch, and he knocked his head into the steering wheel." She sniffled and blew her nose. "His windshield broke, and glass cut his hands and face. He probably had a slight concussion but managed to walk over to our house to lie down."

Macy sat upright. "Why didn't he call sooner?"

Katie Lee's voice cracked. "He passed out in my bedroom and didn't feel well enough to call me until now."

Holding the beanbag to my backside, I moved closer to the bed. "Wait a minute. Your dad's a doctor. Did he examine Nash's injuries?"

"Mama and Daddy are attendin' a medical conference in Beaufort. They aren't due back until this evenin'."

"How did Nash get in your house?" I asked.

Crimping her eyebrows at my questioning, she enlightened me. "Southerners don't lock doors."

"For real?" I asked, and Katie Lee brushed over my astonishment. My father was a lock addict. He added dead bolts to doors and even locked his toolbox that he kept in the latched cabinet behind the padlocked garage. At my house, we always locked doors.

"Nash called some friends. They came over to give him a tow and help get him home."

"Is he okay now?" Macy asked.

"He says so, but his voice sounds weak. I think he's keepin' some details of his injuries from me so I won't worry. I should be home takin' care of him."

FRIDAY, I AWOKE TO a dull ache behind my eyeballs and a knot in my stomach. I'd stayed up consoling Katie Lee, but tonight I might be the one who needed solace. If I was caught using my fake student ID, my dad might get a call from the police to bail my ass out of jail. The thought made me queasy, and I reached for the Pepto-Bismol. Normally I didn't touch the stuff, but I had a morning lecture to sit through, so I chugged from the bottle.

The phone cord snaked into the hallway and I guessed she'd been out there most of the night. Knowing Katie Lee worried about Nash, I speculated that she'd leave for the weekend to be with him. Her boyfriend woes were my only nonwussy excuse for bailing out on the planned outing at the Holiday Inn. As I sharpened my pencils and arranged them from tallest to shortest, I asked, "Did you talk to Nash this morning? Are you going home to see him?"

"He's doing better. I don't have a ride home, and he convinced me to stay. It'll do me some good to get off campus for a drink."

My stomach corkscrewed. "Do you think there's a chance we'll get busted?"

Katie Lee spritzed perfume above her head and walked underneath. "It's just a night out. The worst thing that'll happen is they'll turn us away."

She pulled a robe and a plastic basket of shower essentials from her closet, and I asked, "Why did you put on perfume if you're going to shower?"

"It reminds me of Nash," she said and headed down the hall toward the communal bathrooms.

I stayed in bed. Her words didn't subdue my skittish stomach. Thoughts of drinking illegally triggered a hiccup, a nervous habit I'd developed as a kid. I knew the best way to stop them. Holding my breath, I sucked water from a straw and let a drizzle down my throat. I imagined the meadow behind my home in Canton. The blades of the wild grasses, the notches on the lily pads in the stream-fed pond. The serene thoughts cleared my mind of the potential negatives of underage drinking, like eating hot dogs and burnt grilled cheese for the rest of my life at the women's correctional facility. That last thought was not helpful, and as I breathed deeply to erase it, the phone rang.

"Rachael, Mrs. Brown here. Put Katie Lee on, will you?"

"She went to the shower."

"Be a dear and fetch her. It's important."

My roommate had grown up in a small town along the North Carolina coast. Before college began, she and I had spoken long distance a couple of times. Over the phone, she'd told me, "Last year was my debutante party at the New Bern Country Club. We live on the historical side of town. My girlfriends come over all the time and hang out on our screened-in porch that overlooks the Trent River."

Katie Lee's life had sounded like one continuous party. I had the only parents I knew of who enforced curfews to the minute, kept car usage to a minimum, and made sure that the money from my low-wage after-school job at my dad's restoration shop went into the bank.

A minute ago, I would've swapped my life for hers, but as I fast-walked to find her I had second thoughts.

I didn't mean to eavesdrop, but as I dressed for class I could hear Mrs. Brown's voice clearly transmitted from New Bern and was thankful that the phone wasn't on my ear.

"There's been trouble at the house."

Katie Lee squeaked water out of her loose ends, and bubbles stuck to her fingers. "What do you mean, Mama?"

"We didn't get home until dinnertime last night. When your daddy pulled up to the mailbox, he found an empty whisky bottle tucked in with the bills and letters. We headed up the driveway and could see beer cans scattered around the magnolia trees. We became alarmed when we noticed the open garage doors."

Our room's cement block walls trapped suffocating air, and I opened a window. Hearing Mrs. Brown's voice rise an octave, I scrambled to gather my books for morning class.

"Inside the house, I found dried blood on the carpet, bed linens crumpled, and wine missing from the cellar. You know how your father feels about cigarettes. The smell inside our house makes The Split Happens bowling alley seem like a perfumery. Do you have any idea who could have done this?"

Katie Lee and I locked eyes. I hadn't met Nash Wilson, but a picture of him in an orange jumpsuit with shackles on his ankles sprang to mind. I hoped he'd be like my second cousin on my mother's side who lived with some indigenous tribe in the South Pacific. I'd never met him and never would. Placing my bottle of Pepto-Bismol next to Katie Lee, I whispered, "See you when I get back."

THE WIND CONTINUED TO kick through campus, and by late afternoon I'd resorted to fastening my tousled brunette shoulder-length hair in a messy ponytail. Intermittent gusts had broken the stagnant heat and invigorated me. Five hours had passed since I'd left my room. My stomach had settled, and I'd sat through my lecture without incident. I'd even eaten a light lunch and hung out in the library to start a psych paper on paralleling codependent relationships and addiction.

I wondered what awaited me in my room. Perhaps Katie Lee had taken a bus home? If that were the case, I could tell Macy it didn't feel right going without Katie Lee since it was her idea in the first place. This would postpone the attempt at entry into the Holiday Inn, and hopefully we'd find another way to meet cute guys.

A Webster's dictionary held our door open, as gusty winds from the window swept my desk papers into disarray. Still wearing her robe, Katie Lee lay with the back of her head hanging off the foot of her bed. Four Pepsi cans that had missed the garbage can littered the floor.

"What's going on?"

"I just hung up with my dad. He says the New Bern police questioned Nash for forgery."

She ambushed me with that piece of information. "Forgery? For what? Where's he now?"

"Valium. I don't know. I can't find him."

"How can you forge Valium? Start from the beginning. Tell me what your dad said."

Her soapy hair hadn't styled well, and blotchy, red patches created a highway that ran south of her eyes to just north of her collarbone. She held a cold compress in her hand. "Honestly, Rach, I've never heard Daddy yell so loud. Not even the time I sailed the Sunfish out with a pony keg and nearly sank her because I forgot to plug the bottom."

I shut the window. "Start from the beginning."

"'Do you know who I just finished talking to?' Daddy asked." Katie Lee exhaled her frustration. "Like how would I?"

Dropping my book satchel, I perched on top of my desk. "Who was your dad talking to?"

Katie Lee sat up and blew her nose. "Ray Saunders. Apparently he's some kind of detective with the New Bern Police Department. He told Daddy that Nash attempted to fill a prescription at the pharmacy in town for Valium, written on Dad's prescription pad. The pharmacist, Kitty Klum, recognized Nash and called to verify the prescription."

"Holy shit. Was it Nash?"

"Couldn't have been."

"So why is Nash a suspect?"

"Dad's receptionist told Kitty that Daddy was in Beaufort and had been for two days."

Unsure where this story was going, I was curious enough to keep listening.

"I tried to tell Daddy everyone thinks teenagers all look the same. The pharmacist probably saw someone who resembled Nash, but he talked over me."

"Like who?"

"Rachael, that's not the point. He just blasted my ear. Said, 'I didn't write any prescriptions and certainly none for Nash.'"

Speechless, I shifted my seat.

"It gets worse. Daddy got all negative about Nash and gloated, 'Unfortunately for your boyfriend, Kitty stalled and called the police.'"

Pulling two Pepsis from our mini refrigerator, she tossed one to me. "By the time the sheriff arrived at the pharmacy, Nash—or his impersonator—had left."

She popped the top and slurped with her eyes closed as if she wished she were drinking something stronger. "Daddy railed on me. Said he's mad as hell at that boy. I asked if he was sure about all this. I think he was drinking. I heard him drain a glass. He told me a patrol car caught up with Nash at the 7-Eleven. With an expired license plate and refusing to answer questions, the deputies took my boyfriend to the station."

Not wanting to make Katie Lee feel worse, I told her, "If Nash didn't forge the prescription, they'll have to let him go."

Lying down, she covered her eyes with a wet washcloth. "Daddy said Detective Saunders know Nash and I date. That detective wanted to know if Daddy could shed some light on the situation."

"Did he?" I asked.

Katie Lee sat up. "Daddy's wiring short-circuited over the phone. 'Katie Lee,' he raged, 'I don't have any light to shed. Do you?'"

I searched the library in my head for comforting words. My card catalogue opened on "your boyfriend is an idiot." Keeping quiet, I hoped that a sympathetic gaze would suffice.

Peeling the washcloth off her face, she rolled on her side. "Daddy's tongue went all kinetic. 'That boy is on a path of self-destruction. Nash Wilson is tarnishing the Brown family name.' His temper was barely below ballistic when he said he's deciding whether to press charges for trespassing and forgery. I've been so upset I'm skipping all my Friday classes."

Katie Lee moped in a puddle of turmoil, but managed to confide her father's final words as she struggled to dam the drips that overflowed her eyes. "Daddy warned me, 'That boy is trouble, and I don't want you having anything to do with him. You hear me?'"

"He forbid you to see Nash?"

She nodded.

EARLY THAT EVENING, NASH called Katie Lee. He'd been released from the police station without being charged. Katie Lee confronted him about trashing her parents' home, and he modified his story from the previous day. He now claimed a concussion had erased portions of his postaccident memory.

I'd only spoken to him a few times via phone, and my experience with a boyfriend was zero, but I was fairly certain that I could find one less prone to trouble.

Around dinnertime, I heard Katie Lee speaking to her mother. "He did a stupid thing, and he admits it. Mama, Nash didn't have the upbringing that you and Daddy gave me. Give him another chance. He's really a good person." The conversation lowered into a whisper zone until she hung up.

"Maybe we should stay in tonight?" I suggested.

"Like hell. I need a drink."

NOTE TO SELF
Suffocating in the stickiness of the Carolina heat and humidity. Find myself lingering in the air-conditioned non-dorm buildings. A tricky ploy to get the students to spend more time in an academic setting. I'm not fooled.

Macy's underwear intimidates me.

Nash Wilson is not someone I ever need to meet.

4

Holiday Inn

Roaming the empty halls at the Holiday Inn with Macy and Katie Lee, I found myself thinking about my aunt Gert. She had a personality like pistachio ice cream, out of the ordinary, and tolerated by few. The air in her cluttered house, a concoction of gardenia carpet powder and pipe tobacco, was a replica of the motel's. Pushing those thoughts aside, I decided to concentrate on the positive possibilities. The Holiday Inn could be a secret hot spot, and this could be the night I become a woman with experience.

We stopped at a corridor near an ice machine. Macy's New York banter vacuumed me out of my head fog. "Don't tell me, there isn't a bar in here."

Since dinner, Katie Lee had contained her emotional tsunami. We'd worn the topic of Nash out and hadn't discussed him for nearly an hour. Springing into action, she said, "Y'all sit tight. I'll ask at the desk."

"We'd better wait outside," I whispered. "Don't want to look like we're casing out a room to rob."

Initially I'd been nervous. Not about the flaming shots and relentless flirting, but about the logistical specifics of how to get into a bar with my student ID. Fast-talking myself into an opportunity or out of a predicament had never been a strength. A soft night breeze cleared my hesitations. I determined I'd be fine once I held a drink. This was college life. I was supposed to get my party fix. In four years, I could leave my wild ways behind to become a responsible adult and contributor to society, or some bullshit like that.

After tucking her red bra strap under her black shirt, Macy hooked her arm around mine. "I've got something in my purse to occupy us."

My tongue skirted over my crooked eyetooth. "You scare me when you say things like that."

She unzipped her Gucci. "Cigarette?"

"I'm not a smoker."

"Take one. It'll relax you."

Outside the lobby doors, Macy and I huddled near a raised planter window box where I flicked ashes into the overgrown ivy that choked pink geraniums.

"For God's sake, Rachael, you're in tobacco country. Don't mock them. At least make an attempt to smoke it."

Up until now, I'd only inhaled secondhand smoke at Aunt Gert's. Trying to save face from additional verbal scolding, I sucked hard on the white filter until I gagged and hacked like an old man dislodging a lugie.

Emerging from the revolving glass door, Katie Lee pinched the cigarette from my fingers for a drag. "Y'all know these things will kill you."

"Thanks for the news flash. Where's the bar?"

"There isn't access from the hotel. The entrance is around the corner."

A NARROW CEMENT STAIRCASE led down to a lime-colored neon sign. We were just a few feet away from the entrance of "The Lounge," and my heart palpitated in a synchronized rhythm with my flip-flops. A cue ball head bouncer who wore clip-on shades positioned one leg on the ground and the other on the crossbar of a barstool. Max, according to his pin-on nametag, bore a resemblance to a neighbor in Canton. The one who turned his lights off and blocked his front door with garbage cans every Halloween. *Would I be denied access to this drinking hole?* Holding my breath, I kept my feet moving, but before I passed, he stuck out an arm. Not bothering to look up from his crossword puzzle, he asked, "Who wrote *A Clockwork Orange?*"

This had to be a trick question.

"Anthony Burgess," Macy said.

"Thanks."

We were in.

With a name like "The Lounge," I expected mirrored walls and purple velvet high-back booths. My mind threw a complete miss. The subterranean drinking establishment was tricked out in hunter green and mauve jungle décor.

Katie Lee's drama had spilled into my psyche, and I'd worked up a thirst for drinks garnished with fruit, and although thankful to be in a bar, the ease of entry had me wondering why I'd parted with a twenty for a new ID.

Macy and I followed Katie Lee past a window air-conditioner that hummed as it sent beads of rust-tinted water down the tropical wallpaper. Musty air smelled of fermented yeast, and oak veneer tables dotted half of the dimly lit room. In the far corner, a dance floor, smaller than my dorm room, meekly beckoned for company other than the jukebox that flashed SOS signals.

Slapping her purse on the counter top, Macy said, "This place is a dump, and it's empty."

A bartender wearing a straw fedora planted one foot on a keg and fiddled with a TV remote, eventually settling on stock car racing. Over his shoulder, he asked, "Ladies, what'll it be?"

I whispered to the girls, "Is that a canary on his shoulder?"

"That's not a canary, that's a stuffed cockatoo," Macy said.

"What's your bird's name?" Katie Lee asked.

The bartender moved toward us. His nametag read *Stone R.* Stroking the still feathers, he leaned toward me. "Give Lolita a pet. She's friendly."

I used one finger to touch the taxidermy bird.

He smiled. "Your order?"

As long as the bartender didn't stir my drink with a feather plume, I was happy to ignore the winged accessory he'd fastened to his shoulder.

Katie Lee straightened the edges of a napkin pile and picked up a handful of snack mix. "Three Fireflies with pink lemonade and a lemon twist."

"What the hell is Firefly?" Macy asked, making me feel less amateur.

"Trust me. You're gonna love this drink."

"Is it a green flaming shot? 'Cause I'm not comfortable swallowing fire."

Macy strummed her nails against the bar. "With the right attitude, you can swallow just about anything."

Dipping into a roll of quarters from my laundry money I bought the first round. We settled around a high bistro table, where my feet dangled from the pleather-upholstered stools. The sweet drink gradually warmed my face from the inside out. I traced the darkened water stains on the tabletop with my finger while the three of us hashed out the pros and cons of our freshman classes.

Macy's stool faced the door. Clunking an empty glass down, she asked, "Where is everyone?"

"I don't know," I said, thinking the entire student body vanished on weekends. None of us had cars, but it seemed the rest of the students did.

Resting her elbows on the tabletop, Katie Lee slurred, "Y'all, boyfriend or no boyfriend, this is not a fast start to experiencing freedom and intermingling with coeds."

Stone delivered a round on the house, and Katie Lee quizzed the bird-loving bartender. "Why the fascination with cockatoos?"

Sliding a stool up to our table, he said, "I'm studying to be an ornithologist. The US needs to ramp up security in airports and at border crossings to stop the illegal bird trade."

Macy placed her hand on top of his. "You're wearing a dead cockatoo. That doesn't exactly set a righteous example."

"Lolita brings about curiosity. Curiosity sparks conversation—the beginnings of awareness."

The phone under the bar rang, and he left to answer it.

Having listened to a bunch of bird talk from a guy who had a fixation with feathers, I plunged into a buzzed funk, dismayed at yet another uneventful weekend. The truth serum disguised as Firefly freed my lips, and I confessed, "This is not the college life I envisioned. I've never been with a guy and at this rate never will." I threw my arms up in the air and clonked my forehead onto the table. "I feel cheated. Almost an entire month—and nothing. No obsessions, chance encounters, or drunken romps. Zip, zilch, zero. Not even a sniff of romance." About to throw the towel in for the night, I felt Macy's nail tips pinch my forearm. "Ouch."

"I think those are students coming in past Max."

We watched a steady stream of underage students surge in. The jukebox fired up, and the night didn't seem entirely lost.

In less than fifteen minutes, the bar had filled with late night revelers. I'd been happily sipping my drink and darting my eyes around the room as we ranked all the guys that had piled in. Macy startled us with a warning. "Oh no. Don't look, but here comes a blond guy, cowboy boots—redneck looking. So not my type."

If you tell someone not to look, it actually means look, but carefully. I needed to see this one for myself. As I rotated my body, some klutz from behind knocked my elbow, propelling my arm forward. The cocktail I'd been enjoying launched out of my hand. "I wasn't finished with that," I said to the schlub behind me, before I caught sight of a tall, soggy redhead who, thanks to me, was plucking ice cubes from her cleavage.

Standing a few feet from me, the buxom redhead snarled, "Bitch!"

I turned and looked behind me. No one else faced my direction.

Under normal circumstances, I would've just apologized for my clumsiness and hoped the situation would go away. Unfortunately,

Katie Lee didn't share the same etiquette philosophy. Energized with liquid courage, she leapt off her barstool. Gripping my arm, she anchored me to her hip, puffed out her chest, and delivered a scolding. "Back off. It was an accident."

"I'll show you an accident," the redhead replied.

In disbelief, I watched this stranger close the gap and concentrate on aligning her palm with Katie Lee's face.

An inner panic paralyzed my limbs. Trapped in a duh moment, the only word of warning I uttered was an involuntary hiccup. If I'd blinked, I would've missed seeing Katie Lee duck. Despite the noisy bar, a *whap* noise echoed, and the cowboy guy Macy wanted to avoid became the owner of a left cheek slap.

Eyes wide with surprise, he shook off the blow.

Already unsteady on her feet, post-slap momentum whirled the redheaded she-devil into a stumble that landed her on the sticky indoor-outdoor carpet floor, and she was lost below the heaving mass of drinkers.

Macy confirmed, "It's over. The Amazonian is down."

The guy whose name we didn't know introduced himself. "Hey, I'm Hugh Bass. Y'all like a drink?"

Seeing Macy's eyes roll, I turned my head to suppress a giggle, and my attention strayed to the far corner where I glinted upon a hallelujah moment. Mentally I concentrated on a tall, undeniably attractive man feeding the jukebox. As he laughed, his smile creased the corners of his eyes, intoxicating me into a dizzying trance. He wore a tent-green jacket that almost camouflaged him into the banana-leaf-themed wallpaper.

My focus became sidetracked when Hugh offered his hand to help the girl who'd slapped him.

Swaying to her feet, a devilish spark filled her marbled topaz eyes and crept downward until it curled the corners of her sealed glossy-pink lips. Shaking out her hair, she straightened her shoulders and then began edging two fingers over Hugh's brass eagle belt buckle. She tugged it in a teasing manner, which amused him.

Her boldness embarrassed me, and I wondered if she had a habit of using men's pants to steady herself. I didn't think I should be watching this intimate exchange, but it was better than HBO.

Playfully prying the cold beer out of his grasp, she took a sip, then dumped the remainder down his pants and tossed the plastic cup on the floor. *Did women always treat him this poorly?*

Hugh jiggled his leg before biting his lip on a garble of choice phrases. Being more polite than she deserved, he asked, "Now why did you go and do that?"

"You psychopath bitch," Miss Manners, a.k.a. Katie Lee, said as she stomped her foot on one of She-Devil's open toe, strappy sandals.

From behind me, a freckled brunette delivered a premeditated Vulcan pinch into my shoulder, and I dropped to my knees to squirm out of the grip. Stitches split on my favorite gingham shirt while I suffocated in a cloud of ground-in aged yeast that clung to the floor. Peering up, I saw a hand reach for Macy's neck. She dodged the invader's grip and slammed her own knuckles under her attacker's delicate chin.

It was an ambush, courtesy of She-Devil's friends. As far as I could tell, there were four of them and three of us. We were outnumbered, and the intruders left me no choice but to open my can of whoop ass. I bit the bare leg in front of my face and it jolted backward. From my line of sight, the space we'd claimed had become infiltrated with moving Keds, ballet flats, and an outdated pair of jelly shoes. I pondered where to flee or whom to fight when some unexpected company dropped to my level. Curled in a ball, Hugh cupped his wet crotch with both hands.

"Ouch," I sympathetically mouthed, guessing that one of the girls had sandwiched his peanut butter and jelly.

Straining to speak, he squeaked, "Just clipped the edge."

Motioning for me to follow him in a crawl, he led the way under a nearby table and out of the mayhem until we popped up at the bar. Looking back, I saw that Katie Lee had somehow managed to climb on top of the bistro table, and like a lion tamer, she pushed a barstool against She-Devil's chest. Hands tugged on her ankles, and we watched her leap into the crowd. Failing at an attempt to body surf, she ate it and bowled down two male student types with her.

"Damn," Hugh shouted.

I cringed.

Katie Lee shot up, rubbing her forehead. Her limbs seemed to be working, and I didn't see blood, so I focused on locating Macy.

Back at the table, Macy was clutching the neck of an upside down Heineken bottle high in the air, and there was open space around her.

Stone and Max had abandoned their posts. In a struggle against knees and nails, each chose a girl to secure in Operation Straightjacket, and after two trips they'd shoveled the invaders out the door. But She-Devil held her ground. She worked her purse above her head like a lasso until the hot guy I'd seen wearing the tent-green jacket tucked her under his arm. *What was I thinking? Lusting after someone who had a relationship with a lunatic.*

Fantasy Man hauled She-Devil on a path through the crowd that I realized would cross mine. In an astral body experience, I reached behind the bar and gripped the nozzle of the hose control for soda. With a single nod of his head, Hugh gave me a "go on" look of consent and stood to conceal me. As they passed by, I stretched the tubing under Hugh's armpit and power washed She-Devil's ass with Diet Coke.

Hugh gave me a high five. "Damn good shot. I'd think twice about taking you to a rifle range. Might tarnish my standin'."

Despite the purple turnip on Katie Lee's forehead, she made it safely back to the table, and Macy, I noticed, had surrendered her empty Heineken.

Powdering her forehead, Katie Lee assured Stone and Max of our innocence. "Y'all, we've never seen them before. Those girls attacked us from nowhere, for no reason. We're certainly not the type to go looking for trouble."

Hugh backed up Katie Lee's claim and pointed to his wet front, which convinced them we were the victims.

Stone smoothed Lolita's feathers. "Y'all can stay, but no more well drinks."

In hopes of drying out, Hugh stood. With skinny hips and wide shoulders, he carried a cowboy physique. He was a likeable guy, but I wasn't attracted to him in an "I want to rip your clothes off" kind of way. My bells chimed for something taller that wore a green jacket and rescued crazed redheads.

Macy leaned toward my ear. "I don't want to hang out with Cowboy Hugh. He'll ruin our chances of meeting other guys."

I had to agree, so we went to the ladies room, smoked a cigarette outside, and strolled the perimeter of the room, twice. Macy didn't find anyone to pursue, and I was devastated that Mr. Green Jacket hadn't returned.

Back at our table, a girl I'd never seen before had seated herself on my barstool. With Maybelline looks and a bra size comparable to Macy's, she flicked her highlighted hair. Katie Lee made a round of introductions. "Rachael's my roommate. And this is Macy. Y'all, this is Bridget. She lives in Grogan too and is studying nursing."

Bridget batted her eyelashes. "I recognized Katie Lee from across the room."

"She saw my rough landing and came over to check on me."

Turning to Hugh, Bridget asked, "Are you from around here?"

"I'm a South Florida transplant. My dad lives in Wilmington, and my mom's in Fort Myers."

Bridget lifted a camera from around her neck. Instructing us to squeeze together, she snapped a photo. "Which one of you is Katie Lee's roommate?"

I guessed she hadn't heard Katie Lee a second ago, so I wiggled my fingers.

Bridget put the lens cap back on. "You're so lucky. Katie Lee is the sweetest person I've met on campus. My roommate's a sophomore. I never see her."

"Don't worry," Katie Lee said. "You can hang out with us anytime."

I half listened to Bridget talk about growing up in Columbia, South Carolina. The She-Devil altercation and the hot guy sighting had fueled an overdose of adrenaline, and I had the attention span of a new puppy learning to sit. Intermittently my schizoid gaze locked with Hugh's mustache. He must have thought Macy and I were hot for him. Repositioning himself between us, he asked Macy "W" questions. "What dorm do you live in? Where is that darling accent from?"

Holding her body in a rigid, I-am-not-interested stance, she barely acknowledged his presence. I had trouble deciding if this was a drunken Macy, a New York standoffish Macy, or a you-have-no-chance-in-hell Macy. Cocktail courage numbed his rejection antenna, and he continued his one-way discussion with her, occasionally tossing me a polite consolation question.

Although Macy wasn't interested in him, Bridget giggled at every syllable he uttered. Flashing a come-hither pouty smile, she rattled her ice cubes, to which he fetched her a drink. When he returned, she slid her hand across his to retrieve it. Sadly, I realized I was a complete novice when it came to men. I needed to find an opportunity for some hands-on training.

NOTE TO SELF
The Holiday Inn turned out to be better than expected, minus my drink blunder, minus ripping my favorite shirt in a fight, and minus the man of my dreams leaving with She-Devil under his arm.

Girl fighting, sport or art? Katie Lee and Macy undoubtedly have experience.

Should've asked the PUs for an extra roll of quarters. If they let us back in the Holiday Inn, I'll definitely run out of laundry money before Thanksgiving.

September 1986

5

Welcome to The Bern

Katie Lee woke up with an impressive welt on her head, making the raw scab directly under my bra strap look like a mere shrapnel scratch. Figuring the Bar Brawl Bitches would seek revenge, we mutually agreed to avoid the Holiday Inn for a few weekends. The bar scene had given me a party fix with an ending I didn't want to repeat. We planned to search for another venue, where I hoped I'd have another sighting of the guy in the green jacket. I'm the kind of girl who preps for tests and picks out clothes the night before class. On the off-chance of an encounter, I jotted down one-liner ice breakers that ranged in topic from "I'm lost" directional-type questions to compliments on shoes.

Saturday afternoon I hadn't found the strength to shower and nursed an ice water from a straw. The only energy I mustered came from shifting my butt so it didn't go completely numb in Macy's black beanbag. Katie

Lee lounged in her floral robe and debriefed us on the latest in the Nash-car-accident-turned-trespassing-prescription-forgery saga.

"Y'all, Daddy's not pressin' charges. Nash went over to our house and apologized. He's goin' to wash and wax our cars and boats to pay for the grief and minor damage he caused at the house. The entire misunderstanding has been forgotten."

I stared at Katie Lee in wonderment. *Did she make this stuff up?* A car wreck that involved detectives from the police department, patrol cars at the 7-Eleven, a pharmacist, and Dr. Brown's office receptionist. How could Katie Lee and her parents brush the incident aside?

When Katie Lee's updates wound down, my eyes hung on her in a hypnotic stare. I wasn't sure of an appropriate response, and an uncomfortable silence clouded Macy's room.

Macy drenched a cotton ball with polish remover and offered her two cents of insightful feedback. "That's fucked up."

I laid my head back and closed my eyes. "You need to find another boyfriend."

I LAUNDERED MY BEDDING every Monday, whereas Katie Lee was of the do-laundry-when-you-run-out-of-clean-underwear mind-set. She hadn't developed a relationship with the basement washing machines and electric dryers since we arrived, and her closet floor held an avalanche of clothes. I suspected she regarded her underwear as reversible.

Frustrated that I wasn't in a regular party scene and hadn't met any available guys, except Hugh, I slumped around our dorm room and smoked cigarettes. After squaring the corners of my freshly laundered sheet, I sprawled on my bed and told Katie Lee, "Waves of guilt wash over me regarding my newly acquired habit of nicotine consumption."

Huddled over her notebook with her back to me, Katie Lee wrapped her ankles around her desk chair legs. "Fortunately your memory becomes a blank slate when you pick up a lighter."

I bent a row of matches back before I ripped one out. "The nagging conscience I possess is the kind that only extremely crafty PUs are capable of instilling in their children, even though they are physically hundreds of miles away."

"Come on, Rachael. You feel guilty even though your mother's in Sedona? She hasn't even called. Her behavior doesn't exactly set an example."

"Maybe the guilt is from my mom being gone. Like I should be the model student, perfectly behaved, otherwise I'll end up like her—chasing illusions." Pretending to have a spasm, I dropped to the floor and winced. "PTT—parental telepathy transmission—coming through."

The slim white filter I placed between my lips bobbed like a teeter-totter as I spoke. Two identical transmissions. One from Ohio and another, from Arizona."

Without glancing up from the love letter she penned to Nash, Katie Lee asked, "What're they telling ya?"

"It's not words. More of an image. I'm being escorted by the earlobe into the Order of the Nuns of Perpetual Silence for permanent residence to refurbish Bibles—forever."

Capping the pen, Katie Lee licked the back of a lavender envelope. "Damn, Rachael, where do you come up with this stuff?"

I didn't have an answer.

She relocated her backside on the edge of my desk and bummed a Benson & Hedges slim cigarette from the open pack. "Next weekend is New Bern's high school homecoming football game. Wanna come? All my girl-friends will be there. It'll be a blast, and I've found someone to drive us."

"Who?" I asked.

"Hugh."

"The guy from the Holiday Inn who wore the beer down his pants?"

She nodded. "He's headed to his dad's house in Wilmington, and he'll drop us off along the way. My mom will pick us up from Warsaw."

More than once, Katie Lee had droned on about how her home-town on the coast was "an official historic North Carolina tourist loca-tion, founded in 1710." I'd already memorized her rambling verbatim.

"New Bern is the second-oldest town in North Carolina, with over one hundred fifty landmarks—some dating to the eighteenth century." She also swore it was a hell of a place to party.

Katie Lee liked drama—her boyfriend was proof—and she had a tendency to exaggerate. I suspected she added umph to New Bern's fun factor attributes, but it didn't matter. I kept my expectations low. Going away for a relaxing weekend, eating normal food, and getting ahead on my studies were my only requirements. "I'd love to visit New Bern," I told her and meant it.

IT WAS ONE OF THOSE weeks that went on forever. When Friday arrived, I could barely contain my excitement to leave town. That is until I took a good look at the students behind me in my psych lecture. Katie Lee and I were meeting Hugh in half an hour. My head was in the clouds, and I'd dawdled outside my class feeling bittersweet. Wait until I told the girls. Mystery man has been behind my back, literally, since day one. The lecture hall I'd left had over two hundred students, and I always sat near the front of the auditorium, away from the arctic air-conditioning vents. Plus, I liked to decipher the scribbly notes the professor etched on the board in case they ended up on a test. Today I'd had a *Where's Waldo* sighting. The hot guy in the green jacket I'd spotted at the Holiday Inn freakin' sat in the nosebleed section. On the plus side, I hadn't seen any tall, blue-eyed redheads near him. Maybe someone had the foresight to lock her in a padded room. Now I just had to figure out if Hot Guy and She-Devil were involved.

HUGH DROVE HIS POOP-COLORED rusted Datsun hatchback well below the speed limit the entire trip. He and Katie Lee carried on a conversation in the front seats of the car, which I couldn't hear above the busted muffler that hummed in my ears. Shifting in my seat, I leaned forward to avoid the cracked plaid plastic upholstery stuffing that pricked at my shoulder and the underside of my bare knees. The gray duct tape that held the passenger door together had lost its money-back-guaranteed adhesive stick, and I listened to shredded strips flap like a flag in high winds. Driving above fifty would've left generous mementos, in the form of vital engine parts, on North Carolina highways across the state, so neither Katie Lee nor I grumbled about Granny-Snail-Speed behind the wheel.

By the time Mrs. Brown picked us up, an hour outside of New Bern, daylight had succumbed to dusk. The trip across the state took four excruciating hours, and Katie Lee complained, "As sweet as Hugh is, his car is a dump. We're lucky we made it to meet my mom."

Mrs. Brown had a heavy foot, and in no time, her headlights reflected neatly aligned magnolia trees that led to a detached garage. I stepped out of the car and inhaled a pine tree woodsy smell. Clustered like matchsticks, the dried needles formed a carpet along the berm that framed the driveway. Soft churns of rippling water lapped against the shore I couldn't see, and a night owl called.

"Come on, y'all," Mrs. Brown said. "Let's get inside."

Following Katie Lee, I paused. Gas porch lights flickered on a two-story brick home. Moss baskets draped with beech ferns and vinca vine hung between half a dozen columns on an elevated porch. Rushing past a pair of high-back plantation rocking chairs, Katie Lee vanished through the front door. I admired the handmade needlepoint bolster pillows and watched the rockers sway in harmony with the night breeze. Mrs. Brown rested her hand on my shoulder. "Late at night, I sit here to rest my bare feet on the floorboards and ponder. It's my favorite spot."

I turned to her. "If I take one of these chairs for a test rock, I may never go back to school."

"Hey, Daddy!" Katie Lee shouted above hound howls. Past the entry in a room tucked in the back, Dr. Brown sat resting his neck against a soft leather recliner. I guessed the two furry companions with droopy ears had been keeping his feet warm until we arrived. She wrapped her arms around him from behind and planted a kiss on the peak of his graying hair before cooing at the dogs that stuck their wet noses into her knees. "Okay, Uncle, okay, Sims. Settle down."

Folding what looked like a medical periodical, Dr. Brown stood and hugged Katie Lee. I'd briefly met him the first day on campus, and he was dressed exactly the same in khaki pants with pressed creases down the center. He probably rotated between dark polo shirts in the winter and bright ones in the summer. Tucking the paper between the arm of the chair and the cushion, he greeted me, "Well hey there, Rachael. How are your classes going?"

"It just basic classes for now. I may fit an art history course in next semester."

"Y'all must be hungry," Mrs. Brown said. "Come on into the kitchen. I have crab cakes and slaw waiting."

Mrs. Brown liked decorative plates, and Dr. Brown killed furry things. Both their tastes merged in a display on the high shelf that wrapped around the eat-in kitchen.

"Mama, you shouldn't have gone to so much trouble. I hope you don't mind, but we have to eat and run, otherwise we'll miss the game."

Pulling the crab cakes from a warming drawer, Mrs. Brown set them on a lazy Susan. She offered me a clear ketchup bottle with pink sauce. "It's my secret recipe. Puts kick in your crab cakes."

"Daddy, I still get the van tonight, right?" Katie Lee confirmed. She'd told me that her dad was particular about who drove the car and normally only used the vehicle for special occasions and on road trips. Tonight Katie Lee had volunteered to chauffeur. She told her parents, "I'm picking up a few friends, and there's more room in the cruiser."

Mrs. Brown lowered her red-rimmed glasses down the bridge of her nose. "What friends, exactly, are y'all drivin'?"

"The usual. Patsy, Shelby, Addie, and some others."

With piercing eyes, Dr. Brown told Katie Lee, "No Nash. Understood?"

"Oh, Daddy, he's old business."

That was news to me.

"All right then," Dr. Brown said. "Drive safe, and don't be too late."

A PLASTIC ODOR CLUNG to the van interior, and a light dust coated the dashboard. Clicking the power window switch, I let river air subdue the upholstery smell, and settled into the passenger seat. "We'll pick up Patsy first. You've probably heard me talk about her. We've been friends since the fourth grade. She's a senior at New Bern High."

Riding around in a van full of girls didn't hold much promise for meeting guys and partying. I figured we'd go to the football game and then end up on someone's porch, shooting the shit. I guessed I'd shadow Katie Lee as she caught up with her high school buddies. I'd try not to be the clingy roommate, but not knowing anyone in New Bern, that could prove to be a challenge. Not my idea of a killer night, but still a better option than staring at dorm room walls.

A mile from her house, Katie Lee eased off the gas and glided into an oyster-shell-covered driveway that popped and cracked under the Michelins. Headlights illuminated wisps of honey-streaked hair fashioned behind a silk scarf headband. Patsy McCoy's patchwork denim skirt had been several pairs of Levi's in a prior life. She leaned on a mermaid mailbox while she tapped her flip-flopped foot. As we pulled up alongside, she uncrossed her arms, uncovering the peace sign logo on a tie-dye tee.

"Patsy," Katie Lee said. "Rachael."

Patsy slammed the slider door shut. "Y'all are late. What happened?"

Katie Lee had never fully depressed the brake, and the van lurched when shifted into reverse. "Lord, Patsy, our ride, as sweet as he was, drove below the speed limit the entire way home is what happened. Then Mama went and made crab cakes. The table was set. We couldn't leave."

Holding her hand on her heart, Patsy gaped. "With the pink sauce?"

"Rachael and I are wrecked. The trip took an hour 'n' twenty longer than it should've. Hugh's car isn't road trip safe. We're not ridin' with him on Sunday."

"How are we going to get back?"

"You just leave that to me."

Patsy unzipped her purse and pulled out a pack of cigarettes. "Pick up Shelby next. Leslie is over at Addie's. I told Trish, Sarah, and Delany we'd be there in twenty."

"No smoking in the van. If Daddy smells tobacco, he'll make us look at x-rays of lung cancer patients again."

Katie Lee may as well have driven an oversized yellow bus. Lost in a maze of names and conversations, I decided to stop paying attention to the body count at the fifth driveway. I knew there were enough girls in the back to clear a drugstore's shelves of lip gloss and hair spray in a single sweep. With the van seating at capacity, Katie Lee pulled into the 7-Eleven.

Positioning an unlit cigarette in her mouth, Patsy held out her free hand. "Everyone who wants BJs, pitch in a five."

"Sounds good. I'm in," voices mumbled.

Handing five singles to the back of the van, I thought BJ didn't sound right. I'd lived in North Carolina for a month and still found myself confused when a southerner spewed slang, tall tales, colloquialisms, or idioms. "So," I asked Katie Lee, "they're getting BJs?"

"And cigarettes," she told me.

I still didn't have a clue what my five-dollar donation would be purchasing.

Two girls climbed out, and moments later, a rap, rap, rap noise startled me. They climbed back in and emptied paper bags in the middle of the seats. Patsy handed me a green glass bottle with a silver label. "You like Bartles & Jaymes wine coolers, right?"

Katie Lee spun the driver seat around. "Y'all, listen up. I'm drinking tonight, so who's gonna drive?"

Silence lingered between whispers. Without a volunteer, we were stuck at the 7-Eleven until I heard Patsy grumble about already having missed the first half of the football game. Yielding her wine cooler to an open hand, she called out, "Move over," and clambered her way into the driver seat. Turning the ignition over, she twisted her head to the passengers. "Ladies, next stop, the football field."

Sitting in the front with Patsy, I listened to gossip and guy-scoop from Chapel Hill, Meredith College, and NC State, but if tested on who said what, I'd fail miserably. Katie Lee relaxed her no cigarette rule, as long as the girls exhaled out the window.

A hand from behind passed a makeup bag forward. "This is for Patsy."

Stuffing the small case between her legs, she unzipped it with one hand and pulled out a bowl, a palm-sized baggie of weed, and a stubby metal pipe. Using her gift of ambidexterity, she alternated steering with her left then right while she packed the bowl. For an encore, she lifted both hands off the steering wheel and drove with her knees so she could light up.

"Are you okay there?" I asked.

Patsy sucked the pipe and ballooned the sweet smoke in her lungs. She exhaled out the open window. "I'm great. Want some?"

I found it curious that Katie Lee wouldn't drink and drive, but it was okay for Patsy to inhale and drive. I'd never smoked weed. It was on my "to-do" list, but I thought it best not to stink up the Browns' van. I didn't want Dr. Brown lecturing me on the hazards of inhaling. "Naw, I'm good."

Patsy's post-pot driver foot powered through three yellows. Beneath the traffic lights, she licked two fingers and stuck them onto the carpeted roof above her head.

"What's the saliva finger thing all about?"

She informed me, "It's good luck to lick and stick under a yellow light."

When we entered a residential neighborhood, she executed two stop sign roll bys. I would've been more comfortable in the back where I couldn't see Patsy's navigational finesse flash before my eyes. Since I was trapped in the cockpit, I reached behind the visor flap and familiarized myself with state maps. When I looked up, oak trees framed the underside of an illuminated stadium, and autumn leaves had gathered between the parked cars. Patsy drove up and down the aisles looking for an open spot. "Crap, y'all, we're late and there's no parkin'."

Turning a fast, not-wide-enough left, we heard a CRUNCH-SMASH noise, and Patsy locked her eyes with mine.

"Shit, y'all," someone shouted. "Was that a fender bender?"

Another voice sent a news flash. "I see a hunk of metal lying on the ground back there."

The hairs on my arms stood straight, and I thought three lick and sticks had been overkill. The third one had probably jinxed us. Midway down the aisle, Patsy put the van in park, and everyone piled out. As we assessed the situation, we saw that no one seemed to be around, and the noise from the cheering crowd stayed contained inside the stadium. After a pause, the consensus of our huddled group became: What crunch? What noise? Fender? I don't see a fender lying in the parking lot without a car attached to it.

In a serious tone Katie Lee professed, "Y'all, what just happened, didn't happen."

My internal bells and whistles blared an urgent PTT—parental telepathy transmission—but not wanting to create a confrontation or add to the drama, I quickly rationalized: *It's their town. It's Katie Lee's van. These girls must know what they're doing.*

The dozen girls from inside the van who'd been witnesses were eager to move away from the accident and scattered like fiddler crabs beneath the rising tide. Patsy, Katie Lee, and I found a distant parking spot and examined the van under the haze of a street lamp.

From the curb, Patsy and I watched Katie Lee pace. "There're a few nicks along the side," she said to herself. "No big dents or missing parts. When the van is in the garage, the scratches will face the wall. No one will notice."

Katie Lee had mentioned that New Bern was a hell of a place to party, and I found myself wondering if she meant to say, "New Bern is a hell of a place to get arrested." Her "No one will notice" proclamation seemed an ostrich-head-in-the-sand fantasy. Someone could go to jail. It had better not be me.

NOTE TO SELF
Katie Lee's home is over-the-top southern. If I were from New Bern, I'd brag about it.

BJ. Get your mind out of the gutter. It's a wine cooler brand.

Hit 'n' run—imagine it never happened. My gut tells me that's highly unlikely.

6

Deer Steaks and Bathtub Dew, Who Knew?

From under the tiered bleacher seats a lanky man with short, wavy brown hair strode toward us. His faded jeans were torn on one knee, and his NASCAR t-shirt looked vintage. He locked eyes with Katie Lee, and she waved.

Patsy leaned into my ear. Under her breath she informed me, "Finding the right guy in New Bern is about as likely as finding a hen with teeth."

Luckily I wasn't looking to hook up in New Bern. I had my sights set on the guy who sat in the back of my psych class.

Katie Lee squealed, "Nash," and kissed him like he was a sailor who's home on leave. Before she made introductions, he wrapped his arm around her shoulder, and the two disappeared into the shadows.

In front of the concession stand, Patsy and I shared a warm pretzel, which I thought was a lot like her personality, hard and a little salty on the outside, yet sweet and complex underneath. When she'd crunched the fender I'd glimpsed the soft spot inside of her that had vulnerability.

We watched twenty minutes of the game before it ended. New Bern was crushed by two touchdowns, and disappointed locals flooded out of the metal stands. The girls from the carpool gathered around. One of them suggested, "Let's get a move on and go on over to Billy Ray's."

"Before the kegs run dry," another blurted.

Shielding her eyes from the stadium lighting, Patsy stood on top of a picnic table and scanned the crowd. "Y'all, Katie Lee's gone missin' with Nash."

Nash and Katie Lee were knotted in a tight emotional bond that I didn't get. I could blame my inexperience with men, but from all I knew about her boyfriend, experience wasn't necessary to categorize him in the do-not-date bracket. The cosmic vibe he had transmitted during my short encounter had flashed PROCEED WITH CAUTION in blinking red, not yellow.

Anxious to leave, the gaggle of us stood next to an empty stadium while we smoked cigarettes. I worked myself into a slice of irked, iced with panic.

One of the carpool girls summed up the million-dollar question. "Damn it. Where's Katie Lee?"

Asking around, Patsy finally spoke to Lisa, who'd seen Joe B, who said, "Nash and Katie Lee drove off in a white Chevy before the game ended. They were headed to Billy Ray's."

After relaying this news flash, Patsy pulled a baby-blue Tar Heel key chain from one of her pockets. "Let's get goin'. I'm thirsty."

BY DEFAULT, I FOUND myself in the front passenger seat again. I made sure the seat belt buckle locked securely, double-checking the tightness on my waist. Patsy reassured me that we'd find Katie Lee—eventually. Driving to Billy Ray's in the Browns' van without Katie Lee made me uneasy. Since she'd disappeared, what choice did I have?

Being in a new town and not knowing anyone, I had recently witnessed—and was an accomplice to—a hit and run. Now my host, who dou-
bled as my roommate, had vanished. The night had turned into a buzzkill
and squashed my party mood. I considered asking Patsy to drop me off at
the Browns' house, but it was still early, and they'd ask questions. As much
as Katie Lee peeved me, I didn't want to snitch on her. We were roommates, and the year had just begun. I couldn't show up alone at her house.

I slipped my feet out of my sandals and rested them on the dash.
Preferring not to look at the landscape that flew past my window, I
asked Patsy, "What does Nash have that is so attractive to Katie Lee?"

"If I knew, I'd bottle and sell it. All I see is a can of messed up."

"So you don't have any insight?"

Patsy fumbled with the cellophane on a pack of cigarettes and
handed it to me to open. "Hell no. And it's no use talking to her. She
listens, tells me I'm right, then goes back to him every time. Mostly I'm
able to ignore the butthead, but I'd be lying if I told you his relationship resiliency with her didn't grate on me."

"How long has Nash been trying to get arrested?"

Above the girl chatter, Patsy told me, "Since he learned to walk. Katie
Lee is one of my best friends, and she's great until Nash appears. He casts
a spell of stupid over her that eradicates sensibility. If I hadn't known her
since grade school I'd have disowned her by now for dating him."

"Will she ever get tired of him?"

"Once he lands in Craven Correctional. Maybe then she'll meet
someone else."

An arm reached between Patsy and me, pushing a Joe Walsh cassette in the tape deck. Patsy cranked the volume, and the girls began
singing, "My Maserati does one-eighty-five; I lost my license, now I
don't drive." Although my personal musical taste veered toward alternative punk, I knew better than to suggest another tape. The song added weight to Patsy's gas foot, and waking up tomorrow morning became
a top priority of mine, so I silently said a little prayer:

Please, Lord,
Let me live through the night with these
CRAZY-ASS southern girls.
AMEN

We rode through the outskirts of New Bern on narrow roads without traffic lights or stop signs for Patsy to ignore. I imagined a police report in the local paper: *Despite deep lacerations, bruises, and broken bones, Rachael O'Brien bravely led the search team through the kudzu-tangled tree line, down a steep slope into the mosquito-infested, stagnant swamp where Dr. Brown's half-submerged cruiser van sank. The rescue team recovered twelve unconscious girls, all currently in intensive care at New Bern Medical.*

When someone in the van shouted, "Don't miss the turn past old man Wright's," it snapped my focus to the present and my chest constricted. *What kind of party could be near old man Wright's?*

The road tapered to a single lane, and Patsy shouted above the music, "Where the hell is Wright's place?"

I stopped daydreaming and sincerely worried that we were lost in back country where there was a high probability of a Sasquatch sighting.

Mumbling profanity with a drawl, Patsy maneuvered a tight left. The reflection in my side mirror cast a muted red glow over the hailstorm of pebbles and dirt clumps that pelted the tire wells like a salvo of BBs.

"Damn, it's dark," she said, easing her foot off the accelerator and fumbling with the bright beam switch. My odometer of concern rose when Patsy drove into a plowed field. Planting my feet on the floor mat, I braced myself with hands on the dash. After cutting the engine, Patsy swiveled her seat backward, and in a raspy drawl she announced, "We're here, y'all."

Here? Where? As far as I could see there were parked cars, and beyond the field we'd landed in, floodlights illuminated a modest-sized ranch house and a prairie barn. The girls spilled out of the back of the van. I'd underestimated Billy Ray's party. "This is an impressive turnout."

"It's a small town. Word gets around, and everyone shows up."

"Who is Billy Ray, anyway?"

Patsy flexed her dimples. "He's a local we've grown up with. His daddy grows a fair amount of tobacco—among other crops."

She'd baited me, and I wanted to hear more, but a familiar voice called, "Hey, y'all, what took so long?"

Standing a few feet from the van, Katie Lee sipped out of a blue plastic cup with Nash at her side. Not bothering to shut the driver door, Patsy hopped out. She zoomed in front of Katie Lee and dangled the key chain in the air. Katie Lee opened her palm, and Patsy released her grip.

"You're worse than a bitch in heat for leavin' us without a word."

Hearing Patsy, Nash blew a high-pitched whistle.

Stunned by her directness, I realized I couldn't recycle her cunning line, for I am incapable of the sentence speed and inflection that she possessed as a God-given gift.

"Thanks for abandoning me," I scolded, secretly thankful that I'd found my roommate.

She slipped her arms around Patsy and me and squeezed. "I'm sorry if I worried y'all. It's just that Daddy said no Nash in the van, so I rode over with him. Patsy had the van keys, and I told Jen to tell y'all to meet us at Billy Ray's, and here we are. Don't be mad. I didn't mean any harm."

Nash launched a dried corn husk with the toe of his hiking boot. In an earthy drawl, he said, "So you're Rachael O'Brien. Katie Lee says you're a pretty cool roommate considerin' you're studying one of those dead-end flouncy degrees."

Receiving a compliment as well as an insult in the same sentence peeved me, and I told Nash, "Screw you. Art is big business."

Patsy barked a chortle and offered me a cigarette. Nash wiggled the fingers of his open palm, and she begrudgingly sacrificed one to him too. Before I asked for a match, Nash cupped his hand near my face and flicked a silver butane lighter. I needed the night air and the nicotine fix to center myself. Hoisting my backside onto a tailgate, I began to relax as I listened to Patsy talk about some guy named Rex. "Lord, he's all hat and no cattle."

"Can you translate?" I asked.

"Rex...is...full...of...himself," she said, moron slow.

Next time, I'd remember to interpret her southern inside my head.

Katie Lee swirled the liquid in her cup. "I hear Jessie Ann Jones is claiming she's carryin'. And Drent is the responsible party."

Patsy puffed her cheeks and mimicked an explosion. "If they ate supper before it was dinnertime, there's gonna be trouble."

Nash kicked at a rock in the dirt. Neither of us struck up much conversation, and I suspected we had psychoanalyzed one another, forming those first, often lasting impressions. Knowing he had the capacity for the kind of trouble I didn't want, I mobilized my force field.

THE FOUR OF US MOVED away from a barbecue-smoke-filled air current that blew across the field. We walked toward a muffled beat that drummed near the house, and I realized my premonition about tonight was a complete miss. A sea of sixteen- to twentysomething-year-olds infested Billy Ray's property and hovered near a seen better days wood-stained barn. *Maybe I would meet someone of interest in The Bern.*

"Is there livestock in that barn?" I asked.

With sincerity Nash said, "Are you kiddin'? Cows produce more milk when they hear music. The Rays got federal funding to put up those amps."

Katie Lee gave his arm a shove. "Nash, stop teasin.' Rachael is going to get the wrong impression of southerners."

Walking through double-sided sliding doors, we skirted around John Deere tractors and an assortment of giant metal attachments, like the ones I'd seen plowing and harvesting in Ohio cornfields. Near the back, past stacked hay bales, I spotted a Mustang covered in dust, a torn-apart Ford Falcon, and a mint condition Model A. Patsy led us to the center of the barn where six kegs and one garbage-bag-lined trash bin rested. A buff guy in a Tulane baseball cap held chew in his bottom lip while he ladled a lime-green drink from the garbage can into plastic cups.

I slid my hands into my pockets and leaned over the liquid in the can. "What's the concoction?"

"That's Bathtub Dew," Katie Lee said. "Around here, the Rays are famous for distilling grain alcohol. But be careful. It goes down easy, but will seriously knock you on your ass."

His warning sounded exaggerated. The libation that lurked in the garbage can intrigued me, and I asked Patsy, "Are you having one?"

Patsy motioned with her fingers. "Hey, Bubba, two dews." Clinking her cup to mine, she toasted, "Welcome to The Bern."

Nash passed on the Bathtub Dew, so I asked, "Why aren't you having one?"

Pinching a grin, he said, "Too sweet for my likin,' but don't let me stop y'all. Drink up."

The Bathtub Dew had the kind of kick that could stimulate chest hair to sprout under a bra. I managed to sip mine without drawing extra attention to myself, but when Patsy swallowed a gulp, she puckered her face into a wince and let out the biggest holler I'd ever heard. Her yell gathered momentum, and others in the barn shouted their own hoots and yips. My ears rang, and I couldn't help but link the howling to a coyote cry after a fresh kill. I elbowed Katie Lee. "What's Patsy doing?"

"Haven't ya ever heard a rebel yell?"

Patsy slapped my back. "Let it out, darlin'."

Down here, a need to scream was considered party etiquette, so I released my vocal cords and belted out a "yip-yip, yeahhhh-haw." It felt damn good.

Nash shook his head. "Nice coonhound imitation."

Katie Lee winked. "You carried that clear outta Craven County."

Patsy roosted on the tire wheel of a tractor, and I joined her. She pointed out who dated whom and who had slept with whom. As far as I could tell, New Bern was an exceptionally active town, sexually speaking. I hoped it would increase my chances of meeting someone as hot as the guy in my psych class. I didn't tell Patsy my mission but inquired about potential availability of a few cute guys at the party. "Come on. I'll introduce you around."

"What about Katie Lee and Nash?"

She draped her arm around my neck. "They'll catch up."

Patsy talked to some friends about the crushing football game. Eventually we relocated to a pair of metal folding lounge chairs in a strip of mowed yard between the house and barn. A steady stream of introductions acquainted me with most of the town.

"Whatcha got on that plate?" Patsy asked someone.

"Billy Ray's grillin,'" was the reply.

Midsip, Patsy swatted my arm. "Come with me and say hey to one of The Bern's finest. I guarantee you'll never meet anyone like him."

NOTE TO SELF
Patsy McCoy masterfully expresses the English language in ways I never dreamed possible.

Alcohol referenced as "Bathtub Dew" is deceitful. It didn't taste at all like Mr. Bubble.

Redneck yell—completely therapeutic.

Drinking in the middle of no-man's-land eliminates the worry of getting into trouble with the law.

7

Shag, Not a Carpet

I didn't have a reason not to go with her, but as we tromped through the high grass, Patsy's unprovoked giggles made me think this wasn't the best idea. Walking made me dizzy, and I wished I'd stayed in the lounge chair. Stopping at the commercial-sized barbecues, she tapped some guy on his shoulder. The smoke erupting from the grill stung my eyes and stirred light-headedness. Above the music, she shouted, "Hey, Billy Ray, I want you to meet Rachael, Katie Lee's roommate."

Closing the grill cover, Billy Ray turned around, and I guessed his age to be a smidge below thirty. He styled his thick hair in a ponytail and wore a small gold loop earring in his left lobe. The missing sleeves from his untucked pink oxford showed off his t-shirt tan. I'd never seen a guy wear a bowtie as a choker before now. Below the waist, he lost all formality with turquoise plaid Bermuda shorts and drugstore flip-flops.

I'd drunk a few BJs, a Bathtub Dew, and inhaled waves of nicotine. I checked my feet, making sure they stayed on earth before taking a hard look at this man. I pegged him as having been raised by a fussy mother who'd wished she'd had a girl and a father who snuck around trying to undo all the soft and delicate things his mother taught him. Pressing my fingertips to my mouth, I jump-started my words. "Nice to meet you, Billy Ray."

Billy Ray's thin lips pursed, and his smile reminded me of the Joker. He reopened the grill before reaching inside a beat-up Igloo cooler. Placing bright red meat steaks without any visible veins of fat onto the metal grates, he asked, "You ladies hungry?"

I gripped Patsy's arm to steady myself. "What are those?"

"Deer steaks, darlin.' Shot the buck myself, weekend before last."

He continued telling us the specifics of the two rifle shots he fired to kill the deer, how long it took him to butcher and clean the animal, and how he carried the carnage for ten miles back to his truck. I eat meat, but I don't have a need to know how it gets to my plate. The conversation sent my stomach into a queasy zone.

After the animal slaughter details, awkwardness hovered over the conversation, and I watched Billy Ray reposition his grilling spatula in his left hand so he could drain a beer with his right. With bent knees and an arched back he made a show of aligning the bottom of his plastic cup to the starry sky. When he carelessly crunched the cup and tossed it into the thicket of trees, I was ready to leave. Unfortunately my exit wasn't quick enough. He slipped his fingers around mine. With a firm hold he kissed the back of my hand, dead center, between my fingers and my wrist. I noticed his dirty fingernails splattered with bright-colored paint. He was the last person I'd peg as an artist and figured he got his kicks detailing hot rod flames on one of the cars in the barn.

Billy Ray's donut eyes appeared glazed, and he spoke in a slur, barely recognizable as English. I turned my ear toward his mouth and strained to understand him. "It's my sincerest pleasure to meet you, Razzle."

I pulled back, but he continued holding my hand as though steadying me on a patch of ice. "Rachael. My name is Rachael."

Flexing his operatic aria, Billy Ray sang, "Razzle dazzle, I love your pizazzle."

Trapped between a smoking barbecue and Billy Ray drunk off his ass, I turned my head and mouthed "help" to Patsy's backside. In my moment of need she was flirting with someone I didn't know. My level of attraction to Billy Ray hovered below frosty. I needed an exit strategy and settled on the tried-and-true "I have to use the bathroom." Lightly placing my free hand on his arm, mostly for balance, I said, "You'll have to excuse me, I—"

"No excuses, Raz," he said, and led me to a clearing. "Let's show 'em how it's done."

Before I had a chance to bolt, Billy Ray slid an available arm around my waist. "Rrrrazzle," he growled, stretching his tongue across the single *r* as if it had multiplied. Stiffening to a bullfighter stance, he advised, "Get your shag on."

I had no idea what he meant by shag. Wangling out of his grip, I made my excuse. "I'm really not a carpet kind of girl."

Billy Ray folded into a knee-bender laugh. "You're funnier than Raid on a cockroach." Standing back up, he created a scene by twirling the spatula over his head before he bowed. "May I have this dance?"

Before I'd agreed, he'd positioned his feet in a one, two, three prancing step and started without me. With catcalls echoing around us, what was a girl to do? The host of this shindig had enlisted me in his two-person parade. I considered construing a story about a dodgeball kneecap mishap and planned to hobble away, but Billy Ray took me for a spin before I had a chance to limp. With an audience circling, I did the only thing I could. Pretended I knew what I was doing and followed his lead.

For a husky man, he was surprisingly light in his flip-flops. Working moves that impressed me, Billy Ray turned out to be an expert shagger. With his accent thick and the music loud, I didn't understand a word he spoke. "So, Razzle," he asked, "u ike ew ern?" Pretending comprehension, I nodded and concentrated on my footwork.

When the song ended, he led me back to the grill. After rubbing his sweaty forehead with the wrist of his spatula hand, he flipped a piece of meat onto a paper plate. "Thanks for the shag."

Out of breath and a little stunned, I murmured some "much obliged, thank you" rubbish and carried the deer steak toward Patsy, who sat on a nearby tree stump enjoying a cigarette. "Why did you introduce me to Billy Ray? You could have pointed him out from a distance."

She stubbed out her smoke and put the butt in her empty glass. "Razzle, no trip to The Bern is complete without meeting Billy Ray."

"Would you stop with the Razzle?"

"The name suits you. Razzle O'Brien, I reckon we need another drink to wash down the steak."

Not wanting to look available for another shag, I focused my eyes forward and followed Patsy toward the kegs.

A FLURRY OF FLYING INSECTS circled the floodlights above a deck as large as the footprint of the house. Shagging with Billy Ray had disrupted my inner harmony. I eyed a garden hose and considered rinsing the cooties his meaty hands had passed to mine. Settling my backside against a deck rail, I held two beers while Patsy sawed at the slab of meat with a plastic knife.

"How can you eat that?"

"What?" Patsy asked. "It's a steak."

"You know the details of how it was killed and cleaned. And did you notice Billy Ray's hands? He had deer goo under his nails. Doesn't that ruin your appetite?"

A smartass reply didn't make it out of her mouth. Raised voices began a shouting match, and Patsy corked her head toward a dispute that had erupted behind our backs. I turned to look, too. Yelling grew heated, and two guys closed the space between their faces. To be clear, it wasn't the "yee-ha" call-out I'd experienced earlier, but more of an "I'm gonna kick your face in" kind of shout.

Dropping her paper plate, Patsy grabbed my arm. "Oh shit. It's Stewart and Kent. They're goin' at it like ducks on a june bug."

Two sets of fists turned into a pile-up of bodies on top of contorted aluminum lawn furniture. Bloody faces and ripped shirts escalated into pure pandemonium. Patsy tugged my elbow, and the beers I held sloshed. "Come with me." She led me into the yard, away from the full-on brawl that had exploded below the deck.

Billy Ray and two others came out of the barn holding rifles in the air. When Patsy and I heard CRACK-CRACK noises ricochet, we concentrated on running. The barn, the house, and the yard emptied as a stampede of partygoers dashed to their cars, blazing the darkened field with headlights that moved in all directions. Tires grinding the dried earth drowned out the cricket chirps. Not wanting to become causalities of a stray bullet, Patsy and I stumbled across uneven ground looking for the parked van. With our arms linked, I asked, "Is firing a rifle a southern goodnight, time to go home signal?"

"These bumpkin buffoons need to keep the ammo under lock and key. Somebody could get hurt." Skidding to a stop, she squatted between two cars. "Cover me, Raz."

"Patsy. Bullets are flying. This is no time to tinkle."

She lowered herself to the ground. "I'm meeting cotton. It's safer out here than the house. Like hell I'm trekkin' back to use porcelain."

For privacy's sake I tried to block any view of her, but my legs swayed like a blowing curtain. "Damn Bathtub Dew," I cursed, regretting the cup I'd washed down with a few beers.

After straightening her skirt, Patsy hooked her arm back in mine. The two of us blundered around the field for an amount of time I was unable to measure. With only a handful of cars left, I finally asked, "Where's the van, Katie Lee, and all the girls we came with?"

"I...don'...know," Patsy said before she nosedived for a closer inspection of the trampled alfalfa.

From my aerial view, I called out, "Patsy? Patsy?" I didn't bend down to assist. If I had, we'd both have been down.

Attempting to rouse her, I nudged my toes into her side and took to shouting her name. When she garbled a marble-mouth dialect, I began to worry that Katie Lee would be fretting over our disappearance. I felt a hiccup stir and swallowed against it.

From nowhere, "Hey, y'all," floated through the night. Patsy rolled onto her back. Placing her hand to her forehead, she saluted and said, "Reporting for duty," then released a tee-hee snicker at the wit that oozed off her tongue. Two guys I didn't know stood by me. From the ground, wide-eyed Patsy looked at us through finger-hole binoculars. "Is that y'all, Mitch McCoy and Josh Jenkins?"

The shorter of the two, an AC/DC fan, wore a black t-shirt with a lightning bolt on it. He pulled his hands out of his pockets and extended one to Patsy. "It's not ladylike to roll around in the dirt in your Sunday clothes."

Patsy was as pliable as taffy, and Josh struggled to raise her to her feet. She fell into him and whispered, "I won't tell if you won't."

The taller of the two twitched his neck to flick bangs the color of dried wheat bleached from the sun out of his eyes. He mischievously smiled. "I don't believe we've met."

Patsy turned her skirt right way around while Josh brushed dirt and grass blades from her back. "Mitch, quit flirting. This is Katie Lee's roommate, Raz."

I estimated Mitch to be six feet tall. Under the starry sky, his tousled hair gleamed, and his java eyes were shadowed like hidden passages in a cave. Quietly I centered my mind and had a little talk with myself. *Stop thinking you want to fool around with Patsy's brother.* A roommate's friend's brother was too close a link, practically incestuous. The Bathtub Dew sent unholy thoughts swirling inside me regarding Mitch McCoy.

Patsy swayed. "Have you seen Katie Lee? We need to get home."

Josh steadied her straight. "I hate to tell y'all, but Katie Lee and Nash drove off in the van hours ago."

"We're stranded?" I asked no one in particular.

Mitch placed a hand on my back. "Afraid so. But turns out you ladies got buzzards' luck. Josh and I can take y'all home."

"Josh," Patsy said, "you can't drive. You don't have a license."

He reached into his back pocket and pulled out a Velcro wallet. "Do now," he said, handing Patsy his five-day-old State of North Carolina driver's license.

"Nice photo," she teased.

"Come on," Josh said. "We'll get you damsels in distress on home."

With no other option, Patsy and I went with the two across the plowed field. I asked Mitch, "What time is it, anyway?"

Turning his wrist palm-side up, he read the glow-in-the-dark hands on his watch. "Midnight. Approaching the witchin' hour. Watch your feet," he said and escorted my disoriented limbs in the direction of Josh's car.

While guiding Patsy, Josh asked, "What are ya doin'?"

She made a show of balancing on one leg, like an ice skater before a leap. "Wait for it—wait for it," she said, then flung her airborne leg forward, launching her sandal into the dark until it thudded to the ground out of sight.

"Patsy," Josh said, "why'd you go and do that? I can't keep ya standing if I have to help you fetch your shoe."

Patsy kept straying from Josh. For every step he walked forward, she took two or three backward, sideways, or any combination of the two.

"The car's ahead, not behind," Josh instructed her.

In my woozy state, it was a comfort to have Mitch, not Patsy, guiding me.

A CARDBOARD PINE TREE dangled from the rearview mirror of the minivan Josh had borrowed from his mom. It permeated the interior with a manufactured alkaline scent that smelled nothing like Christmas. Cutting the ignition, he switched the headlights off. "As promised, I've delivered you safe 'n' sound."

I swallowed hard. I hadn't seen Katie Lee for hours and hoped that she was back at the house; otherwise, how would I get inside? Sticking our heads out the back windows, Patsy looked for any sign of her while I inhaled nonscented air.

"Nope, don't see her," Patsy abruptly said and ducked back inside.

She'd hardly searched. Not the kind of partner you'd choose in a scavenger hunt. Patsy had the attention span of a tick, and she couldn't resist tousling the back of Josh's head. "Josh Jenkins, your hair's as soft as a chinchilla."

He removed her hands. "Gee, Patsy, you sure know how to charm the dew off a honeysuckle."

"Could the van be in the garage?" I asked.

"That thing's a beast," Patsy said. "It takes a spotter and a driver to park. It could be in there, but I doubt it."

Staring at the front seat headrests, I felt my throat constrict, and a round of hiccups ignited. I dropped my head between my knees. "Patsy, will you come with me to check the garage?"

My voice startled her, and in a feat of slow-motion gymnastic wizardry, Patsy fell off the back seat. Attempting to catch herself, she gripped the door handle on her descent to the floor mats. I heard the click of the door as it glided open, and watched her spill onto the driveway like oatmeal—slow and lumpy.

Mitch peered over the headrest. "Damn, there she goes all cattywampus."

Huddled in a ball, it took a few beats for her to flinch. I was worried until she sat up and said, "Y'all, I swallowed something with wings."

Being in a strange town, having witnessed a hit 'n' run, and uncertain of Katie Lee's whereabouts, I wanted to cry, but my tears were stubborn and refused to spill. Wedging my shoulders between the front seats, I stretched my arms along the plastic cup holders. In between hiccups, I posed a question. "How am I going to get into the house without Katie Lee?"

"Come on, Raz," Mitch said. "I'll check the garage with you."

In no position to argue my new nickname, I gave up the Razzle battle.

Mitch unlatched my door and offered his hand. "Nothing exciting ever happens around here. Trust me, you'll be fine."

Josh scooped Patsy back into the car. Through her open window, she shouted, "Use the side door. It's always open."

When we stopped crunching gravel under our shoes, I could hear dried sea oats rustle in the still night. The detached three-car garage was a miniature version of the Browns' brick home. A covered breezeway connected the two. My warm cheeks flushed, and I lifted my hair off my neck to let any hint of airflow cool my skin. Resting my back against the garage, I procrastinated going inside. Closing my eyes, I inhaled the river perfume.

"What are you doing?" Mitch asked.

I kept my eyes shut and only moved my lips. "Gathering any wits available for use."

"While you check your eyelids for holes, I'll just take a peek inside the garage."

I barely knew the Browns, but I liked them and wanted them to like me. If they caught me sneaking into the house without Katie Lee, there'd be questioning. Telling them the van was in a fender bender, that I got drunk on Bathtub Dew, caught a ride back from a farm field in a minivan, and lost their daughter—although I was fairly certain her whereabouts were in proximity to Nash—didn't sound likeable. As I was trying to think of a positive spin on the night's events, something soft rubbed against my leg, and a shrill scream propelled out of my lungs.

"It's just Bacon," Mitch said, stroking Katie Lee's tabby.

Stabilizing my heart with my hand, I asked, "Did you see anything in there?"

"Two new Yamaha Jet Skis with packaging still wrapped around the steering wheels. Dr. Brown must be prescribing lots of meds these days. I'm gonna have to talk to Katie Lee about a test drive."

"That's it? No van?"

Placing his hands on my shoulders, he squeezed lightly. "Looks like you're the first bird back to the nest."

"Mitch McCoy," Patsy shouted from the driveway, "could we get goin' before I turn forty?"

He walked me under the breezeway and opened the back door. "Don't be a stranger."

Seven hours in The Bern had wrecked me. I needed it to be tomorrow. Listening to my temples pound and feeling my head spin, I leaned my elbows against the kitchen sink. Ducking my head under the running faucet, I gulped hard to keep the contents of my stomach from visiting my mouth.

A tapping noise like a ticking clock crept up behind me. A throaty *grrrrrr*, deep and low, vibrated until it gathered enough momentum to wake the neighbors. Uncle and Sims, Dr. Brown's hounds, slept indoors and probably chased squirrels when they weren't flushing something feathery out of the thicket or guarding the kitchen from late night visitors.

"Shush, Uncle, shush, Sims," I whispered to quiet their serenade. My head spun and I tasted bile on the inside of my throat. Pursing my lips, I sealed them with my hand and darted through an open door, where I hurled into the top-loading Maytag. Uncle and Sims clipped at my heels, and I was too busy holding my head between the agitator and the drum to shoo them away. The last thing I remember was closing the lid and pressing my cheek against the cool metal while two moist noses sniffed at me from behind.

NOTE TO SELF
Shag has nothing to do with carpeting.

Deer steaks—eugh. May convert to vegetarianism.

Katie Lee and Nash. Gag worthy.

Patsy McCoy. Have never met anyone like her, and probably never will. As for her brother... Never mind. He's her brother.

8

Agitators

Wrapped like a burrito in the arms of a green jacket, I dreamt we rode through a car wash. He was about to kiss me when Katie Lee interrupted, "Rach, you okay? I brought you water."

Unwilling to leave the portal before the kiss, I squeezed my eyelids and puckered my lips tight, hoping that Katie Lee would leave me alone. When I heard Dr. Brown say, "Well, lookie what we have here," it was over. Their voices pulled me from dreamland, and I couldn't get back in.

Shoes clacked against the slate floor, and I squinted up at Mrs. Brown holding an armful of dirty towels. "Oh my Lord, Hayden, is she hurt?"

Dr. Brown cleaned his glasses with his sweater vest then slipped them on his nose. "She's alive. I'm guessing she drank more than the apostles at the last supper."

Hearing the Browns discuss my condition, I decided it was best to pretend I was asleep until something warm and wet licked my left eye and brow. It tickled in a good way, and I meekly brushed my hand into a tongue and whiskers.

"Would you look at Uncle?" Katie Lee said.

"Hayden," Mrs. Brown quipped, "that's not right. Call him over here."

"He won't do her any harm," Dr. Brown chuckled.

I opened my eyes. In the far corner of the laundry room, Uncle and I spooned on his flannel dog bed while he dutifully washed away my party funk.

"Did you sleep down here all night?" Mrs. Brown asked.

It was all I could do to rest my head on Uncle. "I'm not sure."

Dr. Brown dug in a closet and pulled out a golf bag. He slipped a fancy looking bottle of Woodford Reserve bourbon into the side zipper pocket, and Mrs. Brown gave him a questioning look.

"It's for Husk. He won last weekend."

"Katie Lee," Mrs. Brown asked, "what happened last night?"

"We were at Billy Ray's. Rachael drank the Bathtub Dew."

Golf clubs encased beneath blue-knitted socks rested in a leather bag. Dr. Brown removed a cover and inspected the wood driver. "The Rays still make that? I thought the sheriff closed Ray Senior's still down."

Mrs. Brown rotated her head from her husband to me, then tilted her nose down and her eyes up. "Apparently they didn't."

"One thing's for sure. Rachael won't be drinking from the bathtub anytime soon," Dr. Brown said.

Katie Lee assisted me up to her bedroom. In a comatose state, I groaned, "Damn Bathtub Dew."

"I warned you," she said.

I moaned some more.

From the hallway, I could hear the Browns talking. Mrs. Brown worried that I'd contracted alcohol poisoning and advised her husband to take a blood sample. He assured her, "She'll be fine."

Refocusing her concern, she made a fuss about the distilled green drink. "Hayden, you need to report the Rays."

"I'll see Sheriff Henderson on the golf course this afternoon and mention it."

Katie Lee concentrated on the bright pink polish that she painted her toenails.

"I was worried about you. Where did you disappear to?"

In hushed tones, she said, "Sorry, Rachael. You must think I'm so rude for leaving you. I was with," she stopped before she whispered, "Nash. We lost track of time."

"Come over here."

"Why?"

"So I can kick your ass."

"Rachael, you're too hung over to swing anything. It won't happen again. I promise. How did you get back?"

"Patsy's older brother Mitch and his friend Josh dropped me off."

"Mitch is Patsy's younger brother," she corrected.

"Where's the van?" I whispered.

"Nash helped me park it in the garage last night."

"Did he sleep over?"

She shook her head. "We drove in separate cars."

Pessimism bubbled inside of me. "Don't you think your dad is going to notice the scratches?"

"Naw. They're barely visible."

"Katie Lee," Dr. Brown shouted up the stairs. "Where are the van keys? I want to get it washed before my golf game."

IT WASN'T UNTIL THE SUN descended behind the river late Saturday that humanlike qualities returned back inside me. At dinnertime, we met Patsy in a downtown New Bern café called The Red Cabbage. The interior was cozy with ceramic pendant vegetable lights hanging above purple-and-red-striped vinyl booths.

I shuffled my way toward Patsy, who'd saved us seats. It had taken a major effort to get out of bed and shower, but I knew a hot meal and a quiet evening would help diminish the cringe-worthy events of last night.

"Raz, you don't look so good."

"Thanks. Neither do you."

"Raz? Where did that name come from?" Katie Lee asked.

Patsy and I looked at each other then at Katie Lee. In unison we said, "Billy Ray."

She smacked her palm to her forehead. "Lord Almighty. Please don't tell me you fooled around with Billy Ray."

Her suggestion offended me, but I didn't have time to voice an objection before Patsy blurted, "She shagged with him."

"What? When did this happen?" Katie Lee asked.

"After I downed the Bathtub Dew."

"I'm sorry I missed that."

I sipped sweet tea out of a mason jar, and the two insisted I order a pulled pork sandwich with slaw under the bun. Over dinner, Patsy and Katie Lee worked through an endless web of tall tales and hearsay. They filled their sentences with "hankering this" and "tarnation that."

The sandwich was a work of culinary art, and it gave me strength to revel in the previous night's highlights. I prodded Katie Lee. "You left the party early."

"That's a lot of together with Nash," Patsy said before both of us stared her down, waiting for the blanks to be filled in.

Sliding her plate aside, she conceded. "First you have to promise that what I'm about to tell you stays at this table."

"Promise," I said.

Katie Lee waited.

Stretching an arm across the back of the booth, Patsy shrugged. "I'm good for it."

"Nash and I wanted some alone-time."

Patsy rolled her eyes. "Jesus, Katie Lee, I don't want the play by play. Just tell us what happened."

"He and I drove the van from Billy Ray's party to a piece of deserted land where the Neuse River meets the Trent. We were fooling around when headlights in the distance flashed."

"A patrol car?" I asked.

Katie Lee shook her head. "That's what I thought. But Nash said he recognized the truck and left. I stayed behind and buttoned my blouse. I figured some of his friends were night fishing."

She went on to tell us, "I lost sight of him and watched the truck pull away. I would've followed, but Nash had the keys. I called for him, but the grass was high and the mosquitos thick, so I stayed in the van."

Patsy blew bubbles in her sweet tea, and I wondered if she'd heard a similar story before.

"I was beside myself. It was another twenty minutes before I spotted him in a side mirror. He hustled toward the van carrying two plastic suitcases."

I wished she'd been bullshitting, but that wasn't Katie Lee's style. Scooting to the edge of my seat, I chewed jagged edges in the straw. "What'd you do?"

"Locked him out of the van and pitched a fit through the window. My voice went hoarse from yelling."

My mind raced. "What was in the cases?"

Patsy slammed a palm on the table. "He's runnin' snow."

Katie Lee shook her head. "I asked him if he was moving hooch or blow. He acted like dealing drugs was the dumbest idea in the world. Told me, 'that's small-time shit.'"

"Do you believe him?" I asked.

"Y'all, I know it sounds crazy—" she started to say.

"Jesus Christ," Patsy blurted, "whatever he told you is bullshit. Your boyfriend is about as honest as a snake oil salesman and as useful as a white crayon."

"I'd know if he lied. He's up to something, but not drugs."

"I'm with Patsy. You need to lose him."

Katie Lee ripped her paper napkin into pieces until it was confetti.

"What else happened?" Patsy asked.

Could there actually be more?

"We fought for hours. I slapped him once and broke up with him at least twice. I grabbed one of the carriers, but Nash pulled it out of my hands."

"That's out of control," I said.

She shrugged me off. "He fessed up. Told me business documents were inside."

"And you believe that?" Patsy asked.

"The cases were slim, like art portfolios. What else could it be? When we left we made a stop and dropped them off."

"Where?" I asked.

"At Billy Ray's. When we got there, everyone was gone."

NOTE TO SELF
My guess is the same as Patsy's: Nash is a train wreck.

New Bern injected some South into my northern veins. I'm in love with a pulled pork and red slaw sandwich.

9

Divinity Needed

Sunday morning, I felt like an heirloom rose bush on a hot afternoon: tangled, wilted, and thirsty. My eyelids were Krazy Glued shut until the hum of a lawn mower rattled my brain. I pried one eye open to glance at Katie Lee and was startled by Mrs. Brown's yellow damask skirt and matching sweater. Her clothing signaled caution. "Y'all need to get dressed for the nine o'clock service at Saint Anthony."

"Mama, why are you wakin' us so early? It's supposed to be a relaxing, do-nothing weekend at home."

Mrs. Brown slipped her arms into a crossed pretzel. "Proper ladies are bound to duty."

She wasn't moving until we did.

Katie Lee peeled her cover off, "All right, Mama. We'll be down in fifteen."

Not entirely awake, I wondered if I'd heard Katie Lee's reference to the weekend as "relaxing" correctly. In my short experience, the Friday night yet-to-be-discovered hit and run, as well as Katie Lee disappearing, twice, were recipes for high-drama-inducing anxiety, but mere mishaps compared to the secret she swore Patsy and me to keep.

As I dressed for church, disturbing thoughts about Nash orbited my head. "Katie Lee," I said, "I'm having a hard time believing Nash 'happened' to pick up those suitcases last night."

"Hush," she told me. "We'll talk later."

Besides being hung over all day Saturday, I felt guilty about more things than I could remember. New Bern was not a place to chill, and the sooner we met Hugh to drive back home, the better.

"Do you think your dad noticed the scratches when he had the van washed?" I whispered.

She zipped her new Lilly Pulitzer pineapple-motif pants. "He hasn't said anything."

"Maybe we should call Hugh and get an early start."

"Rachael, relax. Nothing bad is going to happen."

"I feel like crap, and I'm completely embarrassed that I threw up in your washing machine. Your parents must think I'm a complete doof."

"Mom feels horrible that you got sick on your first visit here and was worried about you all day Saturday."

"And your dad?"

Katie Lee checked herself in the mirror behind the door. "He says that life is a road trip, and we make a lot of wrong turns. At the end of the trip, we'll forget the mundane highway drives, but remember the wrong turns."

"He thinks I'm a wrong turn?"

"Anyone that spends the night on the floor with his hunting hounds rates high. After church, we'll go out for breakfast. You'll feel better once you eat something."

As the weekend wound down, my paranoia heightened. Dr. Brown had to have noticed the dings in the paint, and I wondered if he'd be philosophical about a literal wrong turn. The chances of getting back to campus without someone leaking the story of the van incident had to be nil. My guilt bells chimed with a long list of newly acquired social habits, unladylike thoughts, unlawful behavior, and a growing set of four-letter expletives I frequently placed in my sentences. A transmission from my PUs said, "Rachael O'Brien, get to church."

A MAÎTRE D' DRESSED IN a white sport coat pulled out a chair, placed a napkin on my lap, and slid me under the table. Outside the country club's floor-to-ceiling windows, we had a view of twenty-two-foot Capri sailboats racing against a headwind on the Trent River. Having attended Sunday service and now ordering a stack of pancakes, I felt like my old self—before I'd arrived in New Bern. Sitting quietly in a wooden pew had helped me to realize that the right thing to do was have Katie Lee fess up to her parents, once we were back at school. The blow on both parties would be easier from a distance. Morning service had shed a divine light on my turmoil, and after a stack of flapjacks my stomach would be equally gratified. Until Katie Lee opened her mouth and ruined my inner peace.

"Mama, Daddy," she said, very businesslike. "I'd like to drive the blue Olds back to Greensboro this afternoon and keep it there."

Silently I cursed her for choosing the topic of automobiles.

"We've been over this before. Your mother and I think it's best if you wait until next year to have a car at college."

"Daddy, what if Rachael or I get sick or hurt? I'd hate to rely on public transportation to get to the hospital."

The Browns were generous and treated me like family. I wasn't happy that she referenced my name in reason number one. I didn't want them to think I was unappreciative and feared that siding with her would give that impression. When the waiter refilled my orange juice, I asked, "Do the sailboats race every Sunday?"

With bloodhound persistence, Katie Lee talked over me. "Mama, when I want to come home, you won't have to fetch me."

Having humiliated myself in the laundry room, I didn't need any more red Xs on my scorecard. I sat in my chair and acted like Switzerland until Katie Lee kicked me under the table. "Rachael can attest. The food in the cafeteria is horrible. Isn't it?"

"Well, yah. They don't serve crab cakes with pink sauce."

"We need to make grocery runs, and the Piggly Wiggly isn't within walking distance."

My roommate possessed nerve like none I'd encountered. Without a thought regarding the damage on the cruiser van, she gathered momentum, pleading her case for the blue Olds. *Drop it*, I mentally transmitted, but she'd blocked my signal.

"Y'all, I can pack myself up at the end of the year."

Mrs. Brown blew on her coffee.

Lifting a spoonful of grits, Dr. Brown cracked a grin.

"Katie Lee," Mrs. Brown said, "that's silly. It took three of us four hours to unload you."

In a last ditch effort, Katie Lee dug deep and teetered on the bullshit fence line. "Mama, I was considerin' volunteering at the local children's hospital."

I busied myself by arranging pieces of my pancake into a smiley face mosaic. The table fell silent as I ate the nose.

Dr. Brown looked at Katie Lee then at Mrs. Brown. *Holy shit, he was caving.* I knew Katie Lee's number one reason for wanting the car. His name began with *N* and ended in *ash*. Sisterly protectiveness welled inside of me, and I didn't want either of us to have contact with him.

After scraping the last of his grits off his bowl, Dr. Brown asked, "Where are you going to park the car on campus?"

AN ORANGE SPAGHETTI-STRAP sundress accentuated tanned arms that Patsy waved at us from the dock. Crossing her feet at the ankle, she leaned against the Browns' covered Bayliner ski boat and waited for Katie Lee and me to walk down the path. "I wanted to say good-bye before y'all head back."

The river slurped against the rocks, playing hide-and-seek with the shoreline. The three of us dangled our feet over the edge of the dock. Staring into the cyclical ripples she created with her toes, Patsy asked, "Have they noticed anything?"

"Like what?" Katie Lee asked.

"Stop messin' with me. Have your parents seen the van?"

Katie Lee stood up and leaned her back on a piling as tall as she. "Y'all, there's nothing to notice."

Y'all? I didn't bring up the subject and was irritated by the insinuation. Unable to clear my head of Nash's "special pickup" the night before, worrying about the van took lower priority. Katie Lee needed to ditch her boyfriend, and I needed to convince her.

Baitfish darted under the shadows of my legs. I didn't like being responsible for their short-term safety and pulled my feet out of the water. "What are you going to do about Nash?"

Staring across the river, she didn't answer.

The tide was low, and Patsy stripped empty barnacle shells from the underside of a dock plank. "I'm telling you this as a friend. The kind who looks out for ya. Word is Rays are purchasing old man Wright's place. Billy just pulled a permit to break ground on a huge home. We're coming out of a summer drought, and the economy is moving into a recession, but it's raining cash at the Rays. If Nash is dealing with that lot, sooner or later, someone's gonna end up with a turd in their punchbowl."

"Y'all are making a fuss over nothing. Nash just moved some business papers around is all."

"Come on, Katie Lee," Patsy said.

I tipped my head back and let sunshine warm my neck. "Nash isn't being honest with you."

Katie Lee turned on her heel. "Y'all can kiss my ass."

NOTE TO SELF
Persistence is critical to a successful wear-'em-down. Katie Lee secured the keys to the blue Olds.

Five weeks in and my roommate and I aren't speaking—going to be difficult to convince her to fess up to her PUs about the van.

October 1986

10

Don't Mess With Mama

Humidity indexes had dropped, the days grew shorter, and the murmur of cicadas now hummed later in the afternoon. Fall had arrived. I'd finished stringing paper bats and jack-o'-lanterns above our dorm beds and began decorating the flat surfaces with speckled gourds and cheese-wheel pumpkins.

Katie Lee had secured the blue Oldsmobile and a gas card from her parents. On the ride back from The Bern, our sentences had been short and without substance. I knew she held a grudge, and I was doing my best to ignore the knots it put in my stomach. If she was looking for an apology, she'd have a long wait. When I'd told her to lose Nash, I'd meant it. The little I knew about the black cases was more than enough to make me nervous. I didn't want to be linked, in any way, to her boyfriend.

Leaving our door open, Katie Lee had strayed down the hall to nuke a bag of popcorn. Nibbling candy corn can make you thirsty, and I had a craving for fresh apple cider. Improvising, I crumbled a cinnamon stick in the coffee machine filter and brewed apple juice that

I'd smuggled from the cafeteria self-serve station. It needed something more, so I added a shot of mandarin-flavored wine cooler I borrowed from Macy. Sipping the warm apple bite, I concentrated on chapter eight in my psych book. I'd just read, *The winner of a mind game is the person that returns to the adult-ego stage first* when I heard shouting from across the hall.

Seated at my desk, I had a panoramic view of two other open doors and noticed Francine's shadow sashay into Macy's room. Separated by a cement block wall, normally the two stayed away from each other. The catalyst for their dislike had grown from something seemingly small, a fingernail and a picture frame. When the three of us landed on the floor that first day, both chipped. Macy had blamed Francine's clumsiness as the reason we toppled, and Francine had accused Macy's abusive mouth of sending down bad karma.

Two months into freshman year and they loathed each other. It wasn't black versus white distaste. I knew this since the graffiti on Francine's door had infuriated Macy. The bristly animosity stemmed from equally strong temperaments that clashed from depths beneath the skin. Francine eyed Macy as though she were foreign food, masterfully donning an array of contorted facial expressions in the form of high arched brows and exorcist-rolling eyeballs. Macy countered her arsenal with an extensive assortment of finger, wrist, and arm signals.

From behind my desk, I stood and pretended to search for a missing book. Tapping a pink furry-slippered foot, Francine shouted, "Turn that whiney music down."

Relaxing on her bed, Macy wore men's plaid boxers and a wife beater tank top. A contraption that looked like brass knuckles, only Styrofoam, separated her toes. She capped a bottle of polish, most likely her signature color—Smok'n in Havana—before adjusting an oscillating fan. "Francine, go back to your cave."

On tiptoes, Francine stood five feet tall max. Being short in stature made her voluptuous curves all the more intimidating. She wore a permanent scowl and didn't walk, but strutted in a motion that mimicked the swish-swish of maracas in a samba. Francine grew up Baptist on the Louisiana Bayou and used ragin' Cajun when she threw out insults.

Marching back to her room, she returned to the hall with her boom box on a long extension cord. Strategically aiming the speaker at Macy's open door, she pushed play. The speakers thumped a gospel choir musical selection, "Take Me to the River," which rhythmically conflicted with the B-52's "Rock Lobster" playing on Macy's stereo.

I considered shutting my door but became mesmerized as the two moved the dispute into the common corridor.

Macy, apparently unable to control herself, poked Francine in the shoulder, which began round one of verbal assault Ping-Pong. "I'll listen to whatever I want."

Batting Macy's hand aside, Francine growled, "Don't poke me with those hooker nails."

Shoving and jabbing evolved into an amateur-wrestling match that rivaled the sneaky moves of Hulk Hogan versus The Undertaker.

The two landed in my room, and from under Francine's armpit Macy squeaked, "Help?"

"Francine. Let go of her."

"Rachael, keep your gumbo out of this. Miss Filth Mouth needs a lesson in respect."

Knotted together, Macy hooked her leg around Francine's ankle and repeatedly tried to throw her off balance. Momentum moved them backward into the built-in dresser, capsizing Katie Lee's perfume bottles and my cosmetic containers.

I jumped on my bed and warned, "Someone's going to get hurt."

Grappling out of the elbow hold, Macy paused to catch her breath while Francine rested her hands on her knees.

"Truce?" I pleaded.

Macy positioned her hip sideways and extended her butt. "Listen here, Mama," she said then paused long enough to slap her ass with a whack sharp enough to send any four-legged animal into a gallop. She told Francine, "You can kiss this."

"Your Crisco's gone rancid!" Francine shouted.

I was born with the nonconfrontational gene and vehemently avoided situations where mental or physical injury seemed likely. I would've bolted, but Francine blocked the doorway when she bulldozed Macy into my desk. I leapt from my bed to Katie Lee's side of the room and cringed when my mug of cider tipped over onto my psych book before puddling to the floor. "See what you've done," I spat on deaf ears.

In a defensive countermaneuver, Macy launched gourds and pumpkins at Francine. One ricocheted off her chest, causing her to wince and take refuge behind Katie Lee's closet door. It provided temporary cover from exploding squash grenades and a trail of seedy pulp mush.

When Macy ran out of ammo, Francine came out of hiding. "So that's how you want to play?"

The two circled each other in a game of chicken. "Rach," Macy said, "back me up."

Not exactly sure what she expected me to do, I crouched an arm's length away, dodging and shuffling around them in a caveman dance.

Francine's Louisiana drawl misted the air with every *s* sound she uttered. "You are pissing me off, and I am going to report your biscuit ass and get it kicked outta here."

They were destroying my room, and I tried to think of something to diffuse their tempers. Before anything appropriate popped into my head, Macy flipped a double-fisted bird. Her painted nails glowed like sparkling roman candles, and she told Francine, "Smoke these."

Macy turned to give me a wink, leaving Francine an in to snatch her ponytail and yank. "Listen, you *merde*. Out of consideration to your neighbors you need to control your volume."

I stood in shock at this brazen assault while Macy reached to rescue her hair.

Chucking the scrunchie into the hallway, Francine spat out, "Dumbass," before storming off and slamming her door.

The neck of Macy's tank top had stretched, and her hair had taken on a bedhead-esque style. "I'm gonna kill her."

Clutching her arm, I said, "Leave it."

Hearing the click of a lock enraged Macy. She shook loose and pounded her fists on Francine's oak veneer door, careful not to damage her nails.

"Come on, Macy," I said, tugging her arm again.

I smelled popcorn before I saw Katie Lee and Bridget. "What's all the yelling? What's goin' on?" they asked.

I signaled with my thumb at Macy, and we all watched her press her lips into the seal of the doorframe. "Mama, get your bayou butt out here. I'm not finished with you!"

"Mama?" Katie Lee mouthed.

The three of us huddled around Macy and forcefully escorted her into her room.

Katie Lee, Bridget, and I mowed through the bag of popcorn while Macy spewed insults that referenced the inbreeding of Francine and her extended family.

"You need to calm down," Katie Lee said.

To settle Macy's nerves, I left to brew an apple bite in my room. As the coffee maker sputtered, I picked up pieces of broken pumpkin and squashed gourd. Sticky goo had smeared down Katie Lee's closet, and I opened her wardrobe to give the door a wipe. Under a stack of sweater bags I noticed a black suitcase I'd never seen before. I didn't think much of it until I glimpsed dried paint on the handle. My mind rewound to the diner in New Bern where Katie Lee told Patsy and me about her fight with Nash. I worked hard to convince myself—it couldn't be.

Behind my back, Katie Lee asked, "What are you doing in my closet?"

Like a hound flushing out a quail, I dug deep to contain my nervous energy. Stiffening my stance, I pointed. "Is that Nash's?"

She didn't even look at me when she said, "I don't know what you're talking about."

It wasn't my business, but I couldn't stop myself. I was furious that she hid something for him in our room. For all I knew, he was a serial killer and body parts were fermenting in a hidden corner of our room. Before she could slam the door, I pulled on the suitcase, tumbling the plastic zip bags that rested on top into a heap.

She grabbed the side handle and snapped at me, "What are you doing?"

"I'm opening it."

She hung on. "It's not yours to open."

In a tug of war, I yanked then let go. Katie Lee toppled to the floor and clunked her head on a desk leg.

Macy appeared in the doorway. Not sure how much she'd seen, I didn't care. My roommate wasn't bleeding, and even if she were, I wouldn't have noticed. I was obsessed with the case that lay equidistant between us.

Dropping to my knees, I applied pressure to the lock until it clicked. Katie Lee sat on the floor and shot me a look of pissed-off defeat.

Macy didn't interfere or pick sides, but closed in behind my back.

Turning the heavy case to face me, I slid the zipper around the track and opened the flap.

Macy pitched a shrill whistle.

Bridget joined the gawking audience and yelled, "Holy shit."

Seeing all the twenties neatly stacked and bound by rubber bands, I told Katie Lee, "This is a problem."

NOTE TO SELF

Apple Bite: One-third mandarin wine cooler and two-thirds apple juice brewed through a coffee maker. Can crumble cinnamon stick in the filter. Warning: more than two mugs will put you to sleep when studying.

Studying in the dorm is not an option as long as Macy's subwoofer is in operation.

Katie Lee is hiding a stash of cash—accessory to a crime?

11

Dirty Green

Autumn air from Big Blue's open window fanned my face. Katie Lee fumbled with the radio dial as she drove down I-40 East. "Franklin Street is completely crazy on Halloween. Chapel Hill is one of the best party places in the state."

Katie Lee had invited Bridget, Macy, and me to spend the ghoulish holiday at UNC-Chapel Hill. Not wanting to stay on campus alone, I had accepted her peace-offering invite. Maybe getting away was what I needed to forget about the insane amount of money in my room-mate's closet and about the fantasy guy that sat thirty rows behind me every Friday in psych class. He and I hadn't exchanged actual words. Sneaking glances when I arrived and left was as brave as I'd been. I didn't know his name, what dorm he lived in, or if he was single. My crush was like the one I had with the Hardy Boys TV series as a kid, only ten times worse. Two months at university, and I hadn't fooled around. This weekend, I counted on my luck changing.

Claiming susceptibility to carsickness, Bridget rode in the front. She had styled her blonde hair in a flawless ponytail and wrapped one strand of hair around the rubber band. Tall and busty, her makeup made her eyes sultry and her lips plump and rosy. When she smiled, I found myself self-consciously stretching my tongue over my crooked eyetooth.

Lately Katie Lee mostly hung out in Bridget's room. I didn't take it personally. I liked Bridget. Besides, someone to distract her from Nash would keep us all out of trouble.

"Katie Lee, did you remember to lock our door?"

"I remembered."

Macy blew a pink bubble and pinched it between her teeth. "If anyone breaks into your room, it'd be as good as hitting the lotto."

Katie Lee turned up the radio. "Can we talk about something else?"

For high school graduation, Mom had given me gold-rimmed Ray-Ban sunglasses. The lenses were algae colored and oversized. Everything about them spoke vintage cool. My mother told me she'd worn them at the Ohio State Fair the day she met Dad. Despite my father's fear of heights, the two had soared in a hot air balloon. I hadn't heard from her since she'd flown the coop with a bunch of wannabe psychics to find her inner tarot card. Despite my annoyance with Mom's irresponsibility, I still treasured the glasses. From under them, I surveyed the moving sky. They dulled the brightness and softened the edges of the landscape. Maybe if I'd worn them when I opened the suitcase, the contents wouldn't have seemed so illegal.

Macy whispered from across the backseat, "Did you or Katie Lee touch any of the money?"

"I didn't. I'm not sure about Katie Lee. Why?"

Macy mouthed, "Fingerprints."

I felt sickish about Katie Lee's judgment. She'd told herself and worked hard to convince me that the little favor she was doing for Nash was no biggie. Like hiding a suitcase full of currency happened every now and then. Katie Lee was book smart and boyfriend challenged. I wondered how long she was going to continue to involve herself in something that was sure to spiral into the ground.

"What's your friend's name?" Bridget asked.

"Meredith McGee. Rachael met her at Billy Ray's."

"I met so many people that night. I'm not sure I remember her."

"She remembers seeing you shag with Billy Ray."

I cringed at the memory.

Katie Lee merged into the slow lane and followed the sign to Hwy 54 West/Chapel Hill.

Glancing at me, Macy cracked a smile. "What's the plan?"

"We'll pre-party at McIver Hall, head to State Street, then over to fraternity row for the battle of the bands," Katie Lee said.

Bridget flipped the visor down. "Do you need me to look at a map?"

"I had four years of family visits when my sister went here. I know my way around."

Navigating past one-way streets lined with ivy-clad buildings, Katie Lee parallel parked in a metered spot off Franklin. A tight fit, she maneuvered the Olds carefully, barely tapping the bumper on the car in front, twice. Across the street, a restaurant with a red neon sign read *Hector's. Always Open.*

I asked Katie Lee, "Is Meredith cool with all of us sleeping in her dorm?"

"Of course."

SLIDING INTO A RED plastic booth, Macy contorted her neck at an unnatural angle to stare at a waiter dressed in chaps, a western shirt, and a cowboy hat. "I'd like to saddle him."

Katie Lee tipped her head. "Look at that GI Joe behind the counter."

Her comment surprised me, and I wondered if her relationship had begun to crumble. "You have Nash. Since when do you admire other butts?"

"The opinions I provide are from the goodness of my heart, to help steer you away from any assholes."

Bridget giggled. "Around here, there's sure to be plenty of butts to fall in love with."

"Fuck falling in love. I just want sex with someone hot."

"Macy," Bridget teased.

I kept quiet, not admitting that I wanted sex too, but with the romance part.

"Order me a sweet tea," Katie Lee said, before she left to get change for the parking meter.

Tilting forward, Bridget asked, "Everything patched up between you two?"

"We're not in agreement about Nash, but we're speaking."

"There had to be ten thousand dollars in there," Macy said.

Bridget toyed with her straw. "If that much money was stashed in my room, I'd do some serious shopping."

"That loot is funny money skimmed off something. It won't buy anything but headaches." I gazed out the window at Katie Lee. "I want it gone."

"Is it drug money?" Bridget asked.

"What else could it be?" Macy said.

I pulled out a pack of Rolaids. "That's my guess."

"Has she confronted him?" Bridget asked.

With all the time she and Katie Lee spent together, I thought she'd have more insight than I did. "She called him. He said he didn't know the contents. He was just keeping it safe for someone."

Macy corrected me. "You mean Katie Lee's keeping it safe for someone."

I popped two antacids, then a third.

Macy examined the wrapper. "Since when do you take Rolaids?"

"Since I met Katie Lee."

The cowboy waiter dropped off four ice waters. Bridget waited for him to leave our table before she asked, "When is Nash coming to get it?"

"I don't know the exact plan, just that she promised she'd move the green out of our room."

"Like where?" Macy asked.

"I don't care. I just want it gone."

Katie Lee took off her denim jacket and slid into the booth next to Bridget. "Bring on the goons and goblins. I can't think of a better place or better Halloween company to be with this holiday."

NOTE TO SELF
Spending Halloween on a campus of eighteen thousand students. That can't be bad.

Can you become addicted to Rolaids?

12

Scouts' Honor

cIver Hall's architecture dripped old southern. The three-story Brunswick redbrick exterior sprawled across a freshly mowed lawn. Formal white columns that held up a portico provided a sense of syrupy *Gone With The Wind* romantic ambiance. Before we left Greensboro, I had borrowed half a dozen condoms from Macy. A few extras in case any malfunctioned. Tonight, I had a clear mission. I was getting de-virginized.

Tromping through doublewide entrance doors, Katie Lee veered past the front desk and headed left toward a staircase. Reapplying lip gloss, Bridget followed while Macy and I trailed behind. On the second floor, Katie Lee walked through an open door. A kaleidoscope of olive-green, mustard-yellow, and orange peace signs leapt from Meredith's twin comforter. Egg-shaped swivel chairs on metallic silver bases perched on either side of a two-seater faux fur sofa. Macy leaned into my ear. "It looks like Brady Bunch throw-up in here."

Katie Lee made introductions. "This is Bridget, Macy, and—"

"Hey, Raz," Meredith greeted me.

There was no use correcting her. Thanks to Billy Ray, the nickname stuck to me like a new freckle. Since she wasn't privy to the "van incident," I made a mental note to keep quiet. Tonight we'd be on foot, so I didn't have to worry about alcohol-induced driving mishaps.

Meredith wore low-rise hot pants and love beads, and had a peace sign painted on her cheek. "Everyone will be completely outrageous on State Street. What are y'all's costumes?"

Settling into one of the egg chairs, Katie Lee gestured a three-finger salute. "Girl Scout troop three forty-six reporting for collegiate mayhem."

Meredith giggled. "I'm friends with some guys in Alpha Delta. The bands they've lined up are local."

Bridget began separating pieces of Katie Lee's pencil-straight, shoulder-length mousy brown hair. "Why don't I French braid your hair? It'll add authenticity to your scout image," she suggested as she danced her fingers down the back of Katie Lee's head. Admiring her work, she pulled a ponytail holder out of her hair and twisted it into Katie Lee's.

"Rach," Katie Lee said, "have Bridget do something with yours."

"I'm susceptible to hair headache. A ponytail is as much confinement as I can tolerate. Meredith, is the Ackland Art Museum within walking distance? I want to see the exhibit they're running on Paul Cézanne."

"Is he a male entertainer?" Macy asked.

"Sort of. He was a nineteenth-century abstract artist. Into cubism. One of his landscapes came through my dad's shop a few years ago. I want to see which paintings the museum has on display."

"It's just off Franklin. You can borrow my ID to get in free."

Meredith was tall and had a head full of curls. Even though I looked nothing like her, she assured me that they never checked, and I slipped her ID in my pocket. "Thanks, I'll swing by before we leave."

Macy settled next to me on the faux fur sofa and lit a cigarette. Her ash grew like a weed, and I held an empty beer can under her ciggy to collect the charred tobacco remains before they landed on my lap. "Try not to set anything on fire tonight."

"Can't guarantee that," Macy said. "Some lucky guy is going to need an extinguisher when I finish with him."

WE WALKED ACROSS CAMPUS with guys that Meredith knew. One of them held a clear plastic funnel normally used to pour oil into the engine of a Mack truck. Gray duct tape adhered it to a long, clear tube. "Anyone want a turn?" he asked.

On campus, Bridget always acted so southern: polite, pulled together, apologetic. When she stopped to snap open a beer can and volunteered to hose, I realized I'd misjudged her.

As a kid, my mom and I played a game in line at the grocery store, labeling people as the food they most resembled. Before we arrived, I'd pegged Bridget as orange Jell-O—a refreshingly sweet treat that can be molded or served with a whipped topping. You can add fruit or serve it plain, and it has the flexibility to be a salad or dessert. Seeing her gulp an entire can of beer without choking, I decided there was an unexpected tart lying beneath, and I made a mental note—lime, not orange.

I declined to guzzle from the communal funnel. Certain customs, like drinking beer from a can, shouldn't be broken. Besides, someone wearing a fly-fishing vest over a plaid shirt caught my eye, and I needed some semblance of control so I'd remember tonight, or at least the good parts.

Travis introduced himself. *Yay for me.* Suddenly things looked promising for Camp Rachael. The night had just begun, and I felt an instant connection. Something from inside jolted me, and I just knew he and I would end up being more than acquaintances.

Crowds thickened as we neared Franklin Street. I'd never been in a mob before, but could now check it off my list. Bodies engulfed Chapel Hill's main drag and pulsed down side streets. I didn't own a purse. Never carried one. My Girl Scout dress didn't have pockets, and Macy had given me a handful of condoms, so tonight I had made an exception. I had stashed the foil wrappers, a lip gloss, ID, and twenty bucks in a Thin Mint cookie box on a string.

Travis asked, "Where are you from?"

"I grew up in Canton, Ohio. What about you?"

He leaned against a tree trunk and rested a camel-colored suede boot against the bark. Even his shoes oozed a manly magnetism that drew me in. "Just outside of Lexington. What's your major?"

I was lost in the dimples that had appeared when he finished his reply, but managed to answer, "Art history."

With trepidation, Katie Lee shouted back to us, "Stay to the left. Some perverts with stockings on their heads are buttin' their faces into girls' behinds."

"The costumes tonight are something," he said.

Not a lot in the way of human exhibition surprises someone from New York, but Macy stopped to gawk at a hot-pink spandex unitard that walked by. "Please tell me why a man's black leather shoe is tied to her head."

"She's bubble gum under a sole," someone shouted.

The Hubba Bubba gum took off running, and I heard her shout, "Get that sperm away from me."

In this crowd, if someone yelled fire, we'd all get our bazookas trampled. Meredith must have felt my sentiment. "I can barely move. Let's get a cold beer at Alpha Delta."

Offering a hand, Travis guided me through the bodies. His palm was soft yet firm, and I found myself pondering if he leaned more toward sweet: seven-layer chocolate cake, gooey and decadent. Or savory: like my mom's homemade stuffing of finely chopped French bread and sautéed mirepoix lightly tossed with nuts and oysters before being baked to perfection.

Travis scanned the students we pressed through and asked, "What brought you to North Carolina?"

I struggled to articulate an answer, partly because I couldn't think of anything that wasn't cliché and partly because the tuft of chest hair escaping from the neck of his faded t-shirt led my eye to his beard stubble. The combination was making me crazy. I gave my cookie purse a lucky tap, and the bottom broke, freeing the contents. Travis bent down and handed me my ID. I picked up the lip gloss and the twenty and tried ignoring the condom packages. My cheeks glowed hot as unembarrassed Travis picked them up. Raising his manicured eyebrows, he said, "I see you take the Girl Scout motto seriously."

NOTE TO SELF
Finally hanging out with a cute guy and feeling a connection. Hallelujah.

13

Beefcakes and Suitcases

The porches and lawns of majestic mansions were littered with students who trampled everything not attached to a trunk. Ivy vines partially bronzed from cooling temperatures blanketed brick exteriors. None of the houses on fraternity row had purple exteriors with lime-green trim or showcased decrepit porches as I'd imagined. Above a raucous drumbeat, I asked Travis, "Are these frat houses?"

He pointed to letters above the Alpha Delta porch. "Some have been around since the late nineteenth century. There's a historical society in Chapel Hill. The frats and sororities adhere to architectural compliances."

"Do you belong to a frat?"

Throwing his head back, he laughed, and creases appeared around his eyes. Letting my gaze linger, I found myself lost in his subtleties. I was still enthralled with the guy in psych I hadn't met back in Greensboro, but my odds of getting some experience were better with someone I spoke with. I'd known him for less than two hours, but had decided he was everything I wanted in my first lover.

Stepping onto the lawn, Meredith moved toward a group of people she knew. I didn't notice a garden gnome cemented in a flowerbed until I tripped on it, spilling half the beer from the open can Macy had handed me. I'd been drinking steadily since we'd arrived. Before I took another sip, it was emergency potty time. "Anyone have to go?" I whispered.

Katie Lee shook her head.

"I'm fine," Bridget said.

Their bladders must be made of steel.

Macy pinched my arm. "I'll come."

Walking away, I overheard Bridget ask Travis, "How do you stay so fit?" Knowing she had stealthlike hookup capabilities, my heart skipped a beat. I needed to be quick.

A thudding drum roar from the battle of the bands energized the partygoers that Macy and I wove through. She pressed a cold can of beer onto her neck. "I'm hot for Ryder Ridgemont."

"What movie is he in?"

"He's the dark-haired guy with the chiseled jaw that I've been standing beside."

I registered a blank stare.

"The one I've been trying to sell my cookies to."

My hand reached for the front door handle on the Alpha Delta porch. "Point him out when we get back."

Before I fully twisted the knob, someone said, "It's locked."

"Back door," I whispered.

The side of the house was less congested. Macy hiked up her camp dress and stepped over a low picket fence, but I took it like a hurdle. Fumbling the landing, I barely managed to keep a foot on the ground. "Travis, the fly-tie guy, is hot."

"Is he the one you'll always remember?"

"Maybe."

At the back door entrance, I pushed on the handle. "Locked."

"Of course it is. Look at all these people. They want to keep the riffraff out."

"We may need to go au naturel."

"Forget it," Macy chirped. "I need toilet paper."

I lifted the doormat, then ran my hand around a windowsill.

"What are you doing?"

"Looking for a key."

"Oh please. That is so Ohioesque."

The window near the door seemed the most logical spot. I felt around until my finger slid across the metal key cutouts tucked underneath the sill. I dangled my find in her face, and she threw her arms in the air.

Since we used a key, I rationalized we weren't trespassing, and I bellowed a friendly hello. Inside the kitchen, I waited for an answer, but all I heard was a vertical blind slat clunk against the screen of an open window.

From outside, the property didn't look like a frat house, but inside it met all my expectations. A globe fixture above the metal farmhouse sink emitted yellow light, and a rancid smell stirred with the draft that crept in the open window. Dirt and grime had added a layer to the thick glass pane windows. Cabinet doors were unhinged or missing. Muddy cleats, engine parts, and a dissembled amplifier cluttered the counter tops. I'd cook a TV dinner with a hair dryer before I warmed it up in this kitchen oven.

Leaning on Macy, I pried a foot up to look at what variety of stick had collected on my soles. Throwing me off balance, she clenched my arm and screamed.

"What?"

"Something furry scampered behind the bowl of Wheaties."

"Where?"

She pointed. "Over there. Next to the sink. It was licking the pile of dishes. This place is a fucking dump."

We'd made it inside, and despite the health ordinance warning that should've been posted, I didn't want to waste time trying a different frat or sorority. "Don't touch anything. This is an in-and-out potty mission. Tinkle and bolt."

Off the hallway that led to the front door, we peeked into a common room with chunky crown molding and distressed wood floors. Mismatched sofas lined the perimeter, and above the pool table, a ceiling medallion encircled a Budweiser chandelier.

"Are you nervous about having sex?" Macy asked.

"If you keep bringing it up, I will be. Not to mention the more we discuss it, the less likely it'll happen."

"Why?"

"You'll jinx me and possibly yourself."

"Wouldn't want to do that."

The music from outside stopped.

"Where is everyone?"

Macy gestured. "Outside."

Halloween decorations weren't required to give this house the creep factor. Except for the kitchen, hallway, and rec room, all the first-floor rooms were dead-bolted. The peeling paint, missing floorboards, and stale urine smell beckoned us to leave. We'd been inside longer than we should've, giving Bridget time to charm Travis. The thought pressed on my bladder.

"Up or down?" I asked.

Macy pointed at a staircase. "Up is always better than down."

When we reached the top, I gripped the wobbly railing, making the mistake of touching something.

A beefcake appeared from behind a corner. "Outside, ladies. This house is closed off to non-Kappa."

About to blow my bladder, I crossed my legs. "It's an emergency!" I pleaded.

Macy, always thinking, put on a come-hither look and managed to strain her C cups against the snaps of her camp dress.

The beefcake caved and led us down a hallway where he unlocked a bathroom. The frat boy teased Macy about the badges on her sash.

She whispered, "I can wait."

I didn't argue with her bladder control. Leaving the two, I dashed inside.

A new band with an infectious beat began to play and I found myself bobbing my head, while I used my fingers as make-believe drumsticks. When it was too late to make provisions, I discovered there wasn't toilet paper. Not even an empty cardboard roll. "Macy," I called, but she didn't answer. The shower curtain was cloth, not plastic, and I broke the rule of not touching anything a second time.

With vigor, I washed my hands, adjusted my sash, and reapplied lip gloss. As I eyed myself in the medicine cabinet mirror, I wondered—what do a bunch of guys keep in there? Old Spice? Jock itch cream? I opened it, and my sight aligned with the middle shelf where a nasty hair clump swam in a pool of gelatinous soap had cemented a crumpled beer can. A Bic lighter and baby oil with the label peeled off sat below. I shut the mirror, realizing that I'd touched yet another thing. *That'll teach me*, I thought and washed my hands again.

Ready to secure quality alone-time with Travis, I stood in the empty hall. "Macy?" I called out. Apparently she'd been distracted and had forgotten that this was supposed to be a drive-thru, not a leisurely visit. Listening for her voice, I couldn't stop my hips swaying to the music from outside, where I should be.

Macy's sex drive was like a corked bottle of champagne. I guessed she was still in the house and likely to catch something that penicillin wouldn't correct. She didn't respond to my calls, and I didn't see any sign of her, so I marched down the stairs. An all-out search could result in interrupting something that would cost a lot of money to have removed from my memory. My extracurricular activity waited outside, and I'd dinked around this furry petri dish long enough.

With one hand on the kitchen door, I wanted to leave. But guilt, an ingenious parental weapon that I theorized to be genetically bred, pricked from inside. As much as I wanted to flirt with Travis, I needed to know Macy was safe.

Reaching into the sink, I retrieved a barbecue fork on a long wooden stick. I'd seen the Freddy Krueger movie, and this house would suit his taste. To be on the safe side, I carried the meat prodder. If she needed rescuing, I figured I'd give the beefcake a skewer.

First I checked the rec room sofas and under the pool table. Moving through the house, I listened for yelling or moaning, but the band beat was all I could hear. By now, Bridget and Travis were probably making out, and I seethed. On the second floor, behind a pocket door, I discovered a staircase. I considered Macy's ankle boot on the step a clue and lifted it with the barbecue fork.

A thick cloud of marijuana smoke hung in the stairwell. Macy was a precocious Girl Scout, and the beefcake had lured her into his attic.

Inside the loft, the visual of giraffes in a game of tongue twister greeted me. I cleared my throat and sang, "Hell-o." When they didn't acknowledge my presence, I propelled the boot off the skewer. It nailed the beefcake in the back. Macy unsuctioned her face and ran a hand through her hair.

I held the grilling utensil high in case the beefcake needed to be convinced to detach himself from Macy. "It's your turn to use the bathroom."

"Racharoni," she laughed. "Stewart wanted to—um—show me something."

"I've got to check on things outside. Are you coming?"

"I'll be down."

Leaning against the wood paneling, a mothering instinct gnawed inside of me. If I left, the chances of her reconnecting with us, or finding McIver, were slim.

Stewart had entered a new galaxy and spoke of a super nova in his solar system. Rocking forward, he gave Macy an exaggerated wink. Standing up, he fell back down, and then tried again, this time somehow managing to get to the stairs without killing himself. "I'll get even better stuff," he giggled.

A lava lamp and the flame under a boiling bong provided the only illumination in the windowless room. I watched the back of the beefcake disappear and waited three seconds. "Macy, I'm leaving."

"Let's go," she said.

"Really?"

She curled her pinky. "He's too stoned."

I offered a hand and pulled her from the futon. We skirted out of the loft and through the house. "I hope you're not mad at me for interrupting, but I was worried about leaving you behind."

Macy hugged me. "I'm not mad. But you shouldn't have worried. Stewart's from New Bern. Hayes is his last name. He knows Katie Lee and Meredith."

"That's a hell of a coincidence."

We raced out the kitchen door and didn't bother to lock it. Before we jumped the fence she locked her feet. "I forgot my jacket."

"You're shitting me."

Macy shook her head. In an apologetic tone, she said, "My wallet and keys are inside the pocket."

"I'm not losing you again. Stay here, I'll get it," I said and went inside before she could protest.

Where were all the frat boys? Then again, if I lived in this house, I'd sleep in the library and shower at the gym. Midway up the stairs, I hesitated. Stewart might be in the loft. I didn't have time for long-winded explanations. I just wanted to fetch Macy's jacket and get back outside to flirt with Travis. If I bumped into the beefcake, I decided I'd tell him Macy got sick on herself.

The corner lamp bubbled red gelatinous globs, creating abstract shadows on the walls. Macy's jacket lay crumpled under a homemade coffee table. When I picked it up, I couldn't help but notice the shiny zipper of a bulging art portfolio case.

Pot air tickled my throat, and I started to cough. Sitting on the futon, I patted my chest. Something lacy tickled my bare thigh, and I pinched a pair of bunched-up purple panties. "Eugh." I flung them to the floor. After the panty discovery, I should've rushed out of there to wash my hands, but I'd fostered a new hobby and slid the flat artist carrier out from under the makeshift table.

I'd pegged Stewart as an outdoorsman. The kind who would sit in a tree all day to shoot a turkey. It was inappropriate of me to snoop, but I needed to satisfy a nagging curiosity.

The case had a tricky set of closures. I had to unbuckle a clasp under the handle before I could unzip the leather bifold. I guessed he stored rifles or a bow inside.

Stewart was no hunter. As my fingers glided along a row of canvases, I was dumbfounded. The frat guy whose shoulders practically touched his ears, an art connoisseur? Using my heel, I pushed the wood pallet coffee table aside and began to spread out paintings. Peeling back heavy cling film that separated the artwork, I recognized some sixteenth- and seventeenth-century French artists, a few postmodern pieces, and some early Americana folk art.

No original would be in the hands of a frat boy. The thought was insane and I half-laughed. I guessed these were varnished prints, but I needed decent lighting to be sure. My father restored art, and I'd grown up in his studio. I stared at two notable paintings. An Italian piece by Giovanna Garzoni—baroque era. She had specialized in still life. And work by another Italian eighteenth-century painter, Rosalba Carriera. I'd seen both in the Cleveland Museum the week before school started and these looked remarkable.

A third painting at the bottom of the stack hardened a surge inside me. The typed label on the back read *Clementine Hunter*. Over the phone, Dad had said that he'd received a commission to restore some of her pieces. *These had to be reproductions.* Running my finger over her signature, I whispered, "Why would paintings be in a frat house?"

Someone in the room stirred, and I heard a clunk. From behind the futon, Stewart slurred, "Hey, Macy. Whatcha doing?"

NOTE TO SELF
A key under a window sill is as American as apple pie.

Always carry a few sheets of toilet paper.

Have developed a suitcase-opening fetish.

14

Does Anyone Know a Good Therapist?

Dropping to the floor, I pretended I was in a game of freeze tag, except no one had tagged me. Huddling into a child-like crouch, I flashed back to the time I locked myself in my room with my mom's red lipstick. If I stayed quiet, maybe I'd go unnoticed.

I didn't dare breathe as my eyes darted in search of Stewart's voice. Was I hearing things or losing my mind? I'd been inhaling pot-loft air for more than a minute, so either was a possibility. Above my pounding heart, I heard him again. From behind the futon, he mumbled, "Come over here sweet stuff." He was so far gone that I doubted he'd be leaving the floor anytime soon.

Smoothing my camp dress, I adjusted my sash and looked heavenward. I began to mouth "Thank—" but feet stomped up the stairs, and I didn't get to the "you."

"What the hell is taking so long?"

I pointed at Stewart. "Shish."

"Figures. What's in your hand?"

I pressed my fingers to my lips in an effort to get Macy to show some discretion.

"What?" she loudly asked.

"There's artwork in that black portfolio."

"You're going through his stuff?"

"That's not the point. Don't you get it? A black case? New Bern?"

"Get what? A case of artwork? So what. We don't even know if it's his."

Interrupting my Nancy Drew explanation, Stewart gasped and chewed air in a symphonic compilation that ended with a shrill whistle-snore. Picking her jacket off the end of the futon, Macy slid her hand into the pocket and held a tube of lip gloss.

"No," I mouthed.

She took one look at me, and I knew I couldn't stop her. As she applied pink shimmer to Stewart's lips, we lost all semblance of quiet and burst into uncontrollable giggles.

Before we left, I put the artwork away, and Macy stuffed the lacy purple panties from the floor into her pocket.

After locking the back door, I returned the key under the windowsill. We scurried to the front of the house and stood on the sidewalk where costume-clad goons and goblins surrounded us. A guy with a sculpted jaw stepped next to Macy. He noticed the snaps on the front of her dress threatening to pop open and curled his lips in a smile. "Hey there, Ryder," she purred.

"Where is everyone?" I asked.

"What am I, hamburger?"

Macy batted her lashes. "I wouldn't know."

Her pre-frat house lust interest, who had walked across campus with us, wasn't my thing, but he certainly had her attention. She was a busy Girl Scout, and I didn't care to know what badge she was working on.

Ryder jerked his neck to feather his hair. "Meredith went to check out Kappa Phi."

"What about Katie Lee and Bridget?" I asked.

"Some guy came over, and they left with him."

"What guy?" Macy asked.

"I think his name was Nash."

The noise around my head went momentarily silent. It couldn't be. Katie Lee would've mentioned something. Could Ryder be mistaken? I leaned against a fire hydrant. If he were here, there'd be trouble. I had to find Katie Lee and make sure she didn't disappear with Nash.

"Keeping everyone together," Ryder said, "is like herding cats." Macy purred and meowed. I was in no mood to play kitty. If I didn't find Katie Lee, lip gloss, a twenty, and condoms weren't going to get me back to Greensboro.

Students packed the lawn like pickle spears in a jar. An elevated stage had been erected in front of a detached garage. The closer you stood to the stage, the less wiggle room. While I gauged how panicked I should be, Travis appeared. "Thirsty?" he asked and handed me a beer.

With his Kentucky outdoorsman good looks, he rated high on my cute-odometer—the sort of distraction I needed to forget about my inconsiderate roommate, her trouble-prone boyfriend, and the fraternity house search-rescue-snoop operation.

"So, art history major and business minor. What's your plan?"

I blew the froth off the top of my cup and decided the evening wasn't entirely wasted. "My family owns an art and furniture restoration business. I grew up knowing who Henri Matisse and Raoul Dufy were before Scooby Doo and Mr. Magoo. Someday, I want to own a gallery. What about you? What's your major?"

"Mortuary science."

"And you want to?"

"Open a funeral home."

"You like to dissect things?"

"I'm fascinated with anatomy."

The fly-ties attached to his vest were like feathery charms that swayed with his motion. "Do you dissect things with legs or do you prefer fins and scales?"

"So far, I've had a go at a frog and a crawdad in high school biology."

"Where did the funeral home fascination come from?"

"As a kid, I always buried pets."

"Were they dead?"

He pushed my shoulder. "Yes."

"That's funky."

"Cats, birds, hamsters. I said words of solace and laid them to rest."

Travis tilted his head toward the stage. "What do you think of the band?"

I glanced above the heads that ebbed in front of us. "They're pretty good." Sipping my beer, I looked again. For a split second the drummer stood, and I had a déjà vu. I'd seen him before. Scanning negatives inside my head, a revelation paralyzed my throat muscles. I spit the beer from my mouth onto Travis's shoes. "His picture is pasted all over my roommate's bulletin board."

Travis shook his suede boots. "Are you okay?"

Katie Lee mentioned Nash a lot. As the one and only member of his fan club, she claimed he was a semiprofessional drummer, had a natural gift to fix anything mechanical, was an expert shooter, wrote romantic poetry, and had half a dozen other talents that I'd tossed in my head trash. But Nash attended Carolina East, not Chapel Hill. "I bet she stumbled upon him and was pissed."

"Who?" Travis asked.

"The drummer is my roommate's boyfriend," I said and scanned the area for Macy. I needed to tell her, but quickly spotted her and Ryder in a lip-lock. I didn't know how, but Nash had to be involved with Stewart Hayes and the frat house artwork. Why else would he be here? What were they doing with canvases? They couldn't have stolen the art, they were just college students. Besides, if masterpieces had been heisted, it would've made national news.

THE BAND'S SET ENDED as I drained my third cup of beer. Nash jumped off the back of the stage, and I caught sight of Katie Lee and Bridget making their way to the edge of the stage, eventually disappearing behind speaker stands. With everyone accounted for, I asked myself, *Do I care who Katie Lee parties with?* On another night, in a different location, maybe. But it was Halloween, and I was getting drunk with a hot guy. Being irritated with my roommate and speculating about her boyfriend's unlawful hobbies would be self-sabotage. I needed to focus. Tonight was the night.

Meredith never returned from Kappa Phi. Macy and Ryder came down with the munchies—for one another—and left. Once the crowd thinned, Travis and I walked across campus until we ended up standing next to the old well. "Take a drink."

Suspiciously, I eyed the water fountain under the dome. "Is it safe?"

"Of course. Legend says that if you drink from the well on the first day of classes, you'll have good luck all year. Where are you staying tonight?"

Adhering to tradition, I sipped the H_2O and hoped the Tar Heel good fortune spilled over to finding romance on Halloween. "McIver. If I can find anyone to let me in."

He clutched my hand, and we zagged around campus buildings that cast shadows under a harvest moonlit sky. I'd lost track of time and directional aptitude, but remembered McIver's entrance, and knew the door Travis held open was not the same door. My internal organs, the important ones, pulsed. Travis had definite plans, and I looked forward to when he revealed them. I received a faint PTT—parental telepathy transmission—regarding the inappropriateness of fooling around with someone I'd met only hours ago. Since I had years of experience with these pesky annoyances, I scrambled the signal.

I broke out in a sweat, and my head felt woozy from the Travis-'n'-alcohol potion I'd been consuming. At the top of two flights of stairs, he pushed a dorm door open. Light from the hallway gleamed on two bodies. Tucked under a red comforter, Macy's wavy head of hair lay nestled next to Ryder's perfectly feathered bangs.

"Ryder's your roommate?"

"I thought you knew that."

My stomach gurgled. "They look like cannolis covered in a ragu sauce. Are they naked?"

He laughed, "I'm not checking, but you're more than welcome."

"Psst. Macy."

She didn't answer.

Slipping his waterproof fishing vest off, he hung it over the back of a desk chair. "Dorm doors lock at eleven. Unless you have a key, you won't get into McIver."

I detected an additional body slumbering in a top bunk at the far corner. "How many roommates do you have?"

"Three."

This dorm room reminded me of summer camp cabin. On the walk back, I'd worked up my nerve and had been ready to conquer, but now my plan had logistical issues. What guy would want to have sex in a room full of people? That thought suddenly worried me. As much as I was attracted to Travis, I didn't want to provide the center attraction.

Travis untied his shoes, "You might as well crash here."

The inner me nodded her head up and down. Triumphant to be spending the night with a cute guy, I nestled into his bottom bunk. With my back against the cold cement wall, I watched him unfasten two shirt buttons through their eyeholes. Deciding not to bother with the others, he tugged the rumpled fabric over his head and shot it into a far corner. Travis moved toward the lower bunk clothed in his red-marled t-shirt and Duck Head khakis. Tucking in, he drew his flannel comforter over us, and I imagined him kissing me goodnight well into the morning, but he positioned himself on his side with his back toward me. A fan hummed somewhere in the room. He may have been tired, but I wasn't. My fingers began an exploration of the southern territory around his navel and then below. Suddenly he gripped my hand. I wasn't sure what that meant and bent forward to kiss his neck.

"Rach, don't," he whispered.

"Do I need a mint?"

He turned on his back, "You don't need a mint. You're perfect."

"Do you have a girlfriend?"

Some students shouted in the hallway, and a distant door slammed. "No. It's just that, I'm not the guy you think I am."

The moment wasn't going well. I sat up, awkwardly craning my head under the top bunk. Looking into the shadow of his face, I searched for an explanation. Wondering what I was doing wrong, I wished that Macy was available for a consultation. I swallowed against the sandpaper in my throat. "What are you saying?"

In barely a whisper, he said, "I'm gay."

I plopped on my back. "I'm cursed."

He pushed the hair from my eyes. "I'm sorry. I didn't realize we'd end up in bed. I mean I thought we'd pass out."

"You don't have anything to be sorry about. You're a great guy. The best one I've found."

He kissed my forehead, "You're the best girl I've ever found."

"If you want to experiment."

He put his hand on my mouth. "Goodnight."

Travis fell asleep, but I couldn't. I hadn't seen this one coming, obviously. He'd rejected me, and I questioned the validity of his claim. *Gay or faking it?* I'll admit a hesitation swirled inside me when I realized his room was full of people. But that wasn't the point. Women were supposed to have the option of rejecting a man's sexual advances, not vice versa. I'd need to schedule therapy sessions when I got back to Greensboro campus and decided I'd send Travis the bill.

Dozing in and out of consciousness, I dwelled on the disturbingly high number of students that sleep on flimsy dorm mattresses. I never slumbered into the dreamy REM stage, and by midmorning, my headache had grown to the size of Texas. Trying to connect dots around last night, my mind couldn't draw more than a scribble. Artwork in a frat house? Was disappearing Katie Lee's and Nash's turn on? And most importantly, how had Macy managed to fool around with two guys in one night while I bunked with one who was gay?

I stared at the frame on the underside of the upper mattress as sun began to streak through the miniblinds and warm my face. By the time I heard muffled voices from the hallway, my aching back felt like I'd slept in a tent, and I was sure I smelled outdoorsy. If I stuck around, conversation with Travis was bound to be awkward, so I climbed over him until my hair caught in the underside of the top bunk springs. I mouthed "shit" and reached to rescue my hair.

Travis opened his eyes. "Where're ya headed?"

Straddling him with one foot on the floor and a knee still on the bed, I craned a wonky smile. "Couldn't sleep."

He helped unhook my hair, and I planted both my feet on the floor.

"Let's get some breakfast. My treat."

Unable to think of an excuse, I scribbled on a Post-it, *Out for breakfast, meet you at McIver.* Using fairy godmotherlike fingers, I adhered the sticky note to Macy's forehead.

"I was hoping to stop by the Ackland Museum."

Travis held the door for me. "For a class?"

"Research to spot a fake."

"How do you tell if something's a fake or the real deal?"

"You have to train yourself not to miss the clues."

NOTE TO SELF
Getting D-V'd is proving to be complicated.

The Bern, suitcases, money, and art. Something is going on.

15

Everyone Accounted For?

Across a lawn dotted with aged oaks, I glimpsed McIver. "Thanks for breakfast," I told Travis, "and for going with me to the Ackland."

Travis rubbed his hands together in a quick burst, like he was starting a fire. "If I hadn't met you, I'd never have gone in there. I'm sorry you didn't find what you were looking for."

"They were really sweet to let us search the encyclopedia of paintings for Clementine Hunter." I hadn't told Travis about the paintings I found in the frat house. I'd just acted as though I had a fascination with folk art.

It bummed me out that I didn't get to see an original Clementine Hunter. I'd locked the image of her signature in my head and wanted to compare. Maybe my hunch was way off, but I'd become consumed with a need to know. Now I'd have to wait for another opportunity to study the likeness. As we neared McIver, I yanked Travis behind a broad oak tree trunk.

"Am I missing something here?" he asked.

I pointed to a parking lot and whispered, "Nash."

"Who's Nash?"

"Katie Lee's boyfriend."

"The one who's running drugs?"

Nudging the back of my hand against Travis's shoulder, I reminded him, "Act natural, and don't mention my suspicion."

"Got it."

"Look, his tailgate's down."

"Is that code for something?" he asked.

"As a forensic scientist, aren't you supposed to pay attention to the details?"

"Now Rachael, play nice."

"Sorry. Look, that's Bridget."

"I thought you said Katie Lee was his girlfriend."

"She is."

Travis raised his sunglasses onto his forehead. "Well then, this just got interesting."

My hand pressed against fleecy moss, and I leaned around the right of the trunk, while Travis crouched to the left. We watched Nash light two cigarettes. Bridget's hair hung down her back, and her legs dangled in a soft swing off the edge of his flatbed. Pinching a cigarette from Nash's grip, she inhaled.

"Do you see Katie Lee?" I whispered.

"Around the corner. Holding the fast food bag?"

"Bingo."

Travis tipped his head back behind the tree. "Remind me what we're spying on?"

"We're not spying, we're sightseeing."

"Right."

I tugged his arm. "Come on. Let's find out what's going on. Remember, act normal."

"Rachael," Katie Lee called out as she waved her arm in the air. "I'm glad you turned up. Sorry we lost you last night."

Not sorry enough to try and find me. "You remember Travis?"

Bridget toyed with a piece of hair near her face and pushed it aside. "Of course."

Under a breath of irritation, I asked, "Where did you go?"

Leaning her head on Nash's shoulder, Katie Lee said, "Look who's in town."

As if I hadn't noticed.

Grinning, he nodded his chin at us. I interpreted the silent gesture as hello, nice to see you again.

"Did you see Nash playing drums last night?" Bridget asked.

I hopped onto the tailgate beside Bridget, and she patted a spot on her other side for Travis.

"I didn't know you were in a band," I said.

Red veins covered the whites of Nash's eyes, and darkened circles shaded the paper-thin skin below his lashes. He yawned. "This gig came up last minute."

Wrapping Katie Lee in a bear hug, Nash kissed her cheek. "I'm heading out."

We hopped off the tailgate, and Travis slammed it shut. Katie Lee scurried to Nash's side to share private words and collect a second good-bye kiss. "Call me."

I meandered near Katie Lee, and with the driver door open, I had a view of the truck's interior. I did a double take when I caught sight of a suitcase identical to the one that I'd found in Katie Lee's closet.

My gaping mouth reflected in the polished chrome trim. Nash locked eyes with me. I didn't want to be involved and tried to keep the discovery off my face. "Nice truck, but I thought you drove a Chevy."

"Traded it in," he said, pleased I noticed.

Travis nodded approval. "Custom chrome wheels, kick steps. You must play a lot of gigs."

Hopping into the driver seat, he pulled a lighter out of the console. "It was a demo. Got a killer deal."

Katie Lee's boyfriend had more layers of bullshit than the mystery casserole served on Fridays at the cafeteria. Turning over the ignition, he reached out the open window and patted the door with his palm. "See y'all around," he said and burnt rubber skid marks across the parking lot on his way out. My connection with the suitcase, although brief, was over.

"Any idea where Macy is?" Katie Lee asked.

Travis looked at me. "We know her coordinates."

KATIE LEE SHOUTED INTO the oversized burger intercom, "Four large Pepsis."

From the front seat of Big Blue, Bridget handed Macy and me sodas. "Nash oozes potential. He is an awesome drummer. He so carried the band last night."

Macy pressed the wax-coated plastic cup to her forehead. "Lower your decibels."

Flipping the visor down to reapply blush, Bridget winced. "Sorry, Macy. Don't Katie Lee and Nash make a cute couple?" Laying her hand on Katie Lee's shoulder, she sighed. "He's lucky to be in a relationship with you."

Eyelids closed, Macy asked, "Why did you two smoke screen us? For all we knew, you were dead."

My pounding head whirled with opposing emotions. Like Macy, I was miffed at Katie Lee and Bridget for taking off, but relieved that the suitcase had found its owner.

"I didn't mean to blow y'all off. It's just that I spotted Nash before his set and flipped out. I didn't know he'd be here, and I reamed his ass. Once I calmed down, he explained that the drummin' gig was spur of the moment. Bridget joined me by the stage to hear him play, and we ended up hanging with the band. The guys wanted to grab a bite to eat, and when we came back, frat row was deserted. I looked for y'all, but never found ya."

The corner of my eye spotted Macy. "Someone found a distraction in the frat house."

"That weed I smoked with Stewart inside Alpha Delta baked me."

Katie Lee glared into the rearview mirror. "Wait a minute, Stewart Hayes?"

"Yeah, that's him," Macy said. "Said he knew you and Meredith."

Signaling left, Katie Lee said, "He'd be a catch. His daddy runs an exporting company. I'm surprised he smoked. I thought he steered straight."

"Never mind the pot," Bridget said. "Anything else happen?"

"Not really," Macy said, and I made a mental note to remind her to get a penicillin injection. She'd subjected herself to way more contaminants than I had inside that frat house.

"Did you sleep with him?" I whispered.

She whispered back, "Which one?"

I pried Macy's eyes open. "Dish it out."

"He was cute. The attraction was mutual. We had sex."

Bridget cocked her head. "With Stewart?"

Macy closed her eyes. "Ryder."

Katie Lee squealed. "How was it? I mean with a name like Ride-her Ridgemont, one would have a lot of expectations."

Pulverizing a piece of ice from her to-go cup, Macy garbled, "Good enough. He was creative with the..." She paused. "Study pillow."

I looked from Bridget to Macy. "What are you talking about?"

Bridget enlightened me. "Study pillows prop you up."

"Sure did," Macy whispered.

"Oh," was all I could think of to reply as my imagination flashed through the logistic possibilities.

"What happened with Travis?" Macy asked.

Travis, sexually speaking, was confusing. I'd found the dessert with all my favorite ingredients, but it wasn't available. Embarrassed at my judgment, I decided I'd keep that story, or lack of, to myself and refocus on the men on campus. "Nothing happened."

"Come on, Raz," Katie Lee said, "you can tell us. Was it the night?"

NOTE TO SELF

I'm attracted to a gay man. Hopefully a fluke.

Expect Houdini, i.e., Katie Lee, to disappear when off campus.

November 1986

16

Planetary Disturbances

On my way across the parking lot, bright sunlight pounded my head. Ghoulish drinking, high drama, and a lack of sleep had me shattered. The duffel bag I carried weighed on my shoulder, and against an unearthly gravitational pull, my feet clonked up the dorm steps. The girls went to the cafeteria, but my stomach squirmed and I'd passed.

Always hopeful for some sort of care package or letter, I keyed open my lobby mailbox. Empty.

Dad and I checked in with each other every Sunday afternoon, and I hurried off the elevator toward my room. When he called I'd ask all the usual questions, was he eating right, getting out of the house, and staying busy—my cryptic way of making sure that he didn't obsess about Mom.

We'd never been emotionally bonded. Conversations were discussions of facts, not feelings. My relationship with him was less problematic if I told him what I thought he wanted to hear. It was a functionally dysfunctional relationship that had worked, but my mother's new physic calling had disrupted the mechanics we'd spent years perfecting.

He didn't spell it out, but I knew Mom's abrupt departure had devastated him. Being away at school distanced me from reality. Back at home he endured physical reminders of her. The Quaker bench she'd refurbished, clothes still hanging in her closet, and framed photos—a flash through time—all reminders of a life no longer. I sympathized, knowing I'd escaped the tangible memory triggers he awoke to every day.

We were survivors and had a new bond. He was the sane parent who cared enough to keep in touch with me. Our relationship hadn't vortexed to discussions of personal business—I wouldn't be asking his take on the Travis thing. But he and I now trod on unsurveyed territory, and I didn't mind catching up with him each Sunday.

A hallway roadblock blinded me. Francine, a.k.a. Mama, was dressed like a pastel spin art explosion. Sauntering in the direction of the communal bathroom, she wore a cotton lavender robe and adorned her feet in furry, egg-blue slippers. *Celebrating Easter early? Like a Christmas in July thing?* She must've had plans, because under a shower cap, she had her hair rolled against her scalp in pink foam curlers. Next to her thigh, she swung a basket of beauty essentials.

Since she and Macy had tried to kill one another, we'd only exchanged one or two neutral words. Macy was a good friend, and I didn't want to miff her by becoming chummy with the enemy.

Stopping dead center in the hallway, Francine flexed a territorial maneuver that created a moment of hesitation between us. Halloween had turned my head loopy. Even though Easter was months away, I said, "Hey, Francine, big night with Roger Rabbit?"

She broke her vexing glare, shook her head, and began swatting imaginary flies. "Rachael O'Brien," she said, "you're a corked bottle of crazy, and I admire you for it."

Before I thought of a rebuttal, I heard the shrill ring tone I recognized, and I raced past her. "That's for me."

Fumbling to unlock my door, I jumped to answer the phone.

"You sound out of breath. Is everything okay?" Mom asked.

The stagnant air in my dorm room suffocated my brain. I distanced the phone as far away from my face as my arm would stretch. In a state of disbelief, I fought a natural instinct to drop it and run. "Rachael, are you there?" she called.

Mothers have remarkable powers. Their voices are engrained in children's memories, and when they speak, they can extract compassion even when they don't deserve any. I reminded myself that I'd become a responsible adult, living on my own. What if she was calling to say she was in trouble, or that she'd made a mistake? "Hi, Mom."

"Rachael, it's good to hear your voice."

"Are you okay?"

"I'm fine. How is your freshman year going?"

There was an uncomfortable silence. "Why haven't you called Dad or me?"

"I know you must think I'm horrible for leaving."

The minifridge motor hummed. I didn't want to say anything to make what she'd done okay.

"Channeling is something I was called to act upon. When I met Betts, everything clicked. And with you off at college, well…"

Dad and I had worried, lost a lot of sleep fretting over her physical and mental well-being. Her lame excuse, if that's what it was, fueled an incinerator of anger inside me. "Betts? Who's Betts?"

"Oh, she's marvelous. Betts is the most seasoned trance medium in our celestial cluster. She's helped me to understand that there isn't one creator, but an omnipotent God. We're all living in a multilayered dimension of consciousness and—"

"You're kidding," I said, irritated that she was more interested in converting me than finding out how I was adjusting to being away from home and dealing with her disappearance.

"I couldn't be more serious. It took me months to work up the courage to follow the inner me. If I hadn't, I would've ended up with regrets. And regrets are missed opportunities—harder to live with than mistakes."

"Is this some sort of midlife thing or have you lost it?"

She sighed. "Betts suggested I wait to call until Orion moves southward. The planets under your star aren't in alignment."

"In case you've forgotten it's me, your daughter, and I'm not interested in your extrasensory planetary bullshit. I liked my old mom, the one that raised me. If you find her, will you tell her to give me a call?" I hung up. In my fury, I hadn't noticed Katie Lee. Before she asked, I said, "Mom."

Katie Lee hugged me. "What did she say?"

Forgetting my annoyance with her for ditching me last night, I vented, "A bunch of clairvoyant crap. I'd feel better if I knew she was on drugs or hypnotized. She wanted to tell me all about the multidimension and some Betts person who's a master at transcending through the light and fluffy phyllo dough layers of the other side."

"Is Betts a pastry chef or her boyfriend?"

"Neither. Betts is a she. The head crazy."

"I take it the conversation was short."

My head spun. Sitting on my bed, I hid my face in my hands. "Katie Lee, my mom's orbiting her own planet."

"Are you going to tell your dad she called?"

"She hasn't changed her mind. She didn't say she missed either of us. Telling him won't accomplish anything."

A LIBRARY CHAIR IS one of the best places for head time. Staring at a plastic-coated, three-sided cubicle provided controlled quiet and anonymity. Inhaling musty paper and bound-leather-scented air, I neatly sorted and shelved the emotional leftovers that lingered. The conversation with my trippy mother hadn't delivered a meaningful prophecy, so I rolled our chat into a tight ball, tucked it into a dusty corner of my inner closet, and slammed the door shut.

I had an overly active memory. Mom and Dad said it was a gift, but I didn't always agree. I could recall images of symbols and names, the details of the loop size, any ink stains or drags of the pen with exact accuracy. I still had to read to learn stuff, but my ease with recalling information made fill-in-the-dot tests a breeze. Once other kids found out, they treated me like a toy that they expected to recite answers to the questions they asked, especially homework. After learning the hard way, I kept my head camera to myself.

Penning a plot summary of Shakespeare's *Twelfth Night*, I read over my notes. Olivia, enamored by Cesaro, doesn't realize that he is really Viola. In an emotional irony, Olivia falls for a female impersonating a male. Studying the Bard of Avon has a way of prying at inner closets, and mine crept open, clouding my focus. Did my mom truly believe she had extrasensory abilities, or was she bluffing? What was Stewart Hayes doing with eighteenth- and nineteenth-century canvas oils in a fraternity house? He was from New Bern, so was Nash. Maybe Stewart and Nash were entrepreneurs who transported drugs inside of reproduction canvases? Last night—how could I have been ready to sleep with someone who wasn't what he seemed? Laying my head down on the library desktop, I wondered: *Had I missed a life lesson on faking it?*

A student threw a backpack down in the cubicle next to mine. Opening one eyeball, I held my Swatch in front of my flattened face. My neck was cramped, and drool had puddled under my cheek. It was nearly five thirty. I'd slept for two and a half hours. Coming out of a dead sleep, I stood to stretch my stiff neck, and the plot summary stuck to my cheek. Peeling the paper from my face, I stared down an aisle of ceiling-height gray metal bookshelves. A green jacket moved toward me. It was the guy who sat in the nosebleed section of my psych class. The one who'd rescued She-Devil. He exited the section labeled *900–950, History and Geography*, two topics I'd like to explore with him. He saw me staring and said, "Hey."

Like a discus champion, I swiveled to see if anyone else was around. I was alone, and by the time I spun back around, he'd disappeared between another set of shelves. I wiped saliva off my chin and ran a hand through my hair. "Please let this one be heterosexual."

NOTE TO SELF
Checked Katie Lee's closet and under her bed. No black suitcase.

Parent = sensible. My mother ≠ sensible.

Green jacket is smoking hot. There's probably a BBQ sauce named after him. Would love to marinate in that.

17

Uh-Oh

I lingered on the last sentence of the phone call with Dad. He had been evasive when he said, "I've invited someone over for Thanksgiving that I'd like you to meet."

The thought of my dad and me alone for the holiday was depressing. The possibility of him setting me up, frightening. With the break two weeks away, I didn't want to go home, but I didn't have any other offers or plausible excuses to skip.

Hugh's voice lured me across the hall and into Macy's room. He lounged on top of her chenille bed throw and picked at one of the decorative jewel-tone flower appliqués. Her grandmother had hand sewn the quilt. My grandparents had passed before I was old enough to remember them, and my mother left after eighteen years. I was tempted to wallow in melancholy, but there was no chance with Hugh around.

"You're going to stretch that out," Macy shouted as she rescued her silk eye mask that he wore as a headband.

Under the false pretense of studying, Katie Lee held a book as a prop in her lap. "This weekend was social suicide. We spent the entire time investigating nonhappening, hearsay parties."

"We're not in the know," I said.

We all heard Francine clear her throat at the doorway.

Hugh fished through Macy's plastic case that held polishes and nail gadgetry. He found a pair of clippers large enough to contour troll nails and slipped his boot off. Scissoring the clippers through the air, he asked Francine, "Can I help you?"

Anxious to begin exercising her courtroom intimidation tactics before she had her law degree, Francine announced, "Visiting hours are over."

Macy grabbed her nail case from Hugh. "Francine, don't you have anything better to do than play policewoman?"

"I'd like to play with a policewoman," Hugh said.

"You need to be locked up," Francine said.

Hugh looked from Francine to Macy. "That sounds like somethin' pent up."

Macy escorted Hugh by the arm to her door. "Out."

Inflating her chest, Francine motioned her arm as a directional exit guide for him to follow.

He wiped a fake tear and sniffled. "It's cruel to tease me with talk of locking me up only to send me packin'."

A shrill ring echoed from the hall, and in a blur, Katie Lee brushed past him.

"Is that a curfew bell?" Hugh asked.

Katie Lee had turned the phone volume on high. "That's our ring tone," I said.

Hugh's blond eyebrows were bushy like furry willow tips against his tanned face. He raised and lowered them with an air of mischief. Lazily thumbing a corner of his mustache he said, "If I hear of any extracurricular activities, I'll be sure to call."

Francine retreated to her room, and I shut Macy's door before settling into the beanbag. "There's a magnetism that you and Hugh exert like a competitive sport. You're going to sleep with him, aren't you?"

Macy shivered. "I can't get past the hair growing above his lip."

"Ask him to shave it off."

She sorted her nail supplies into plastic compartments. "I think he's hiding something under there. Besides, if he shaved it off for me, I'd be obligated to screw him, and I prefer to keep the power. Why don't you have a go with him?"

We both knew I was the one who needed the deflowering thing behind me. "You have a valid suggestion. The problem is, I'm obsessed with the guy in psych class, and anyone else will disappoint."

Macy's door handle twisted, and we stopped talking. Katie Lee let herself in. She carried her arms like Lurch of the Addams Family. Standing at the foot of Macy's bed, she tipped face first into the chenille quilt.

I held the beanbag to my backside, stood, and shuffled toward Katie Lee. Parking myself back down, I asked, "What's Nash done?"

She rolled onto her back. "It's not Nash, he's fine. But I'm not. That phone call was from Mama and Daddy. Two police officers were at the house askin' about a hit 'n' run."

"Shit." After homecoming weekend, I never got around to convincing Katie Lee to fess up.

Shutting the nail case, Macy moved toward her underwear drawer. "I'll get the cigarettes."

Katie Lee's voice crackled. "A police report had been filed back in September."

Macy and I joined her on the bed. We waited as she stared at the popcorn ceiling and blinked tears. "The bumperless car belonged to a student, and word of the damaged vehicle Patsy hit spread around New Bern High. Recently, an anonymous witness came forward."

Macy reached for a box of tissues, and I fetched the garbage can. Wondering how much trouble we were in, I asked, "What did your parents say?"

She blew her nose. "They told the officers they had no idea what they were talkin' about." Katie Lee deepened her voice to mimic her father. "Daddy told the officers, 'Surely if there had been an accident, we'd have known about it.'"

Macy pitched a scoff. "Your parents must be pissed," which sent Katie Lee into rolling sobs. The kind where your nose reddens and runs like a broken pipe.

I swatted Macy's back and speculated about whether being an accomplice would put the incident on my permanent record. Placing an arm around Katie Lee, I gave a light squeeze. "Tell us what happened."

She dabbed her tear ducts. "Our family generously supports the department with a donation each year, so of course he cooperated. Mama fetched the van keys, and Daddy told the police that it hadn't been driven since the last time I was home."

Moaning a long, low sigh, I deduced this was not good, and I wasn't sure I wanted to hear the rest.

"Nash's expert parking didn't impress Daddy. When he had to crawl from the passenger side to get to the driver's seat, he figured something was up."

"Wait a minute. Didn't your dad get the van washed before his golf game when we were in town?"

Katie Lee shook her head. "He never got around to it."

My teeth locked. "Did they notice anything?"

"They noticed. Dad blew a gasket over the phone, and Mama said they're mortified at my lack of sense for not reporting the accident. I figured you two heard them in here."

"What did you say?" Macy asked.

"I zoned out while they were yelling. My mind flipped through strategies, and I was about to choose one, but held off when Dad mentioned two empty condom wrappers he found in the back of the van."

Macy chortled, "Now they know you're not a virgin."

Katie Lee picked at Macy's throw. "I said they were Rachael's."

"You did not!"

"Settle down. Daddy was more upset about the roach in the ashtray than the condom wrappers."

"I hope you didn't tell them that was mine."

"Did you sell Patsy out?" Macy asked.

Katie Lee stood and walked to the window.

"I didn't sell Raz or Patsy out. I told them I left the van unlocked at Billy Ray's. The condom and the roach could have been anybody's."

Macy laughed.

"Theoretically that's true," Katie Lee rebutted.

"Freakin' golden excuse," I said. "And that, Katie Lee Brown, is what scares me about you."

"What did you say about the scratches?" Macy asked.

"Mostly the conversation went one way. They knew, so I confessed."

Macy and I clung to the inflection she placed on the word *confessed*, waiting for the clincher.

"I told them what happened, including the part that Patsy drove— filtering the cigarette and alcohol consumption."

"And the part about the Nash delivery to Billy Ray?" I asked.

She launched a stink-eye in my direction.

How much trouble was she in? How much trouble was I in? Would the Browns call my dad and tell him what a bad influence I was on their daughter?

Katie Lee liked the sound her words made when they entered the atmosphere. Somehow, the conversation took a turn from car wreck ramifications to kitchen recipes. "Mama pulled a blueberry crumble out of the oven for the officers. Her recipe is amazing, and she won't share it with anyone. She says I can have it when I get married—"

Like using flares to guide a jet into an airport gate, I crisscrossed my arms for her attention. "Are you, Patsy, or any of us going to be prosecuted for a hit and run?"

"No," she said.

"Is your driver's license going to be revoked?" Macy asked.

She twisted her face. "No."

"Are your parents coming up here to take the big blue Olds away? Make you transfer to the local community college while you live at home until you get your act together?"

"Rach, that's a bit dramatic."

My voice grew small. "That's what would happen to me."

"So, are you off the hook?" Macy asked.

At the window, Katie Lee made eye contact with a distant light post as if it were a long lost friend.

"Katie Lee," I said. "What's going to happen?"

"Daddy's agreed to cover the damages. So no one's pressin' any charges."

"You just got yelled at?" Macy asked.

She spun around on her sock feet. "Patsy and I have to clean the Jet Skis, the Sunfish, and the Bayliner."

Macy and I fish-eyed each other, waiting for her to fill in the blank—her real rap on the knuckles.

"Top and bottom," she emphasized. "Inside and out."

"No, really. What's the punishment?" I asked again.

"Daddy wants all the water vehicles looking brand new. He's serious. Do you know how hard it is to muck barnacles off fiberglass? I'll have to get the scuba gear on and swim underneath. It'll take Patsy and me a solid day."

Macy ran her fingers through her wavy hair, not quite catching all the pieces in a ponytail. "Now let me get this straight. Homecoming football game weekend, a dozen drunken girls drove around New Bern in the family van. Patsy—buzzed—whacks off some car's fender, keeps going, parks, and everyone scatters."

"You make it sound so irresponsible," Katie Lee said. "It was an accident."

Macy signaled silence. "Two months later, give or take, the cops show up at your parents' house, and to everyone's surprise there are scratches on the van. The police, with your parents' assistance, connect the dots to you."

"For the record, which Rachael can attest, they were nicks. Barely recognizable."

Macy paused her recap long enough to file a jagged nail. "You fess up, and your punishment for all this is cleaning the boats with Patsy? Fucking put some sunscreen on, you dodged a bullet."

Katie Lee leaned her arms out of Macy's window and lit a cigarette. She inhaled then passed it to me before saying, "Mama and Daddy are flying to Aspen for some early season skiing. I'm planning a small get-together at my house. Are y'all up for a road trip to The Bern?"

NOTE TO SELF
Hugh and Macy? There's electricity.

Francine and Macy. Hopefully nothing will happen.

Can't decide if Katie Lee is lucky as hell or unlucky as hell.

18

One More for the Road?

I pressed my nose to the rear passenger window and fogged Big Blue's glass. The setting sun painted golden-yellow and burnt-orange streaks on plowed cornstalks and tobacco. The dirt-rooted crops in the red-clay earth blended like hummingbird Bundt cake batter.

With a population just over twenty thousand, New Bern, North Carolina, sits on a junction in Craven County where the Trent River meets the Neuse River. Katie Lee rambled about her hometown being low key and quaint with its trendy boutique shops and Lowcountry-inspired restaurants. Thirty miles outside of New Bern proper, she sped east across a two-lane road without stop signs, traffic signals, or other vehicles.

The girls I'd met on my last visit had perfected the finer points of partying. Of them all, Patsy McCoy, still a senior in high school, was the seasoned pro. I'd had a fabulous time minus Katie Lee disappearing, the hit and run, shagging a three-step with Billy Ray, being in proximity to falling artillery, and losing my Bathtub Dew in the Browns' Maytag. Tonight Katie Lee had arranged a small get-together and assured me the libations she served would not be green or contain grain alcohol. A giddy anticipation simmered inside of me. Drinking a few beers, sleeping soundly on a bed with a box spring mattress, and not sharing a bathroom with fifty girls would be a welcome change.

I leaned into the front seat. "What if your parents had a change of plans? They could be at the house."

Katie Lee cracked her gum. "They called me from their ski villa before we set off. It's snowing. They're stoked for fresh powder. Patsy and Mitch will show up. Meredith's comin' home, plus Nash and a few others. Tonight you can let Raz out."

Initially, the name Raz brought up images of deer steaks and Billy Ray, which I'd only narrowly survived. Lately, though, I've grown to like Raz. She shows up as weekends approach and departs when the Monday morning alarm beeps.

Weather permitting, Katie Lee said we'd cruise the Intracoastal Waterway in the ski boat, but mostly just relax with a few of her friends. I envisioned sipping sweet tea from a mason jar, and I knew which rocking chair I'd claim. Since the party would be at Katie Lee's house, I didn't have to concern myself with her disappearing. The weekend plans sounded perfect.

Beside me in the backseat, Macy dozed. Midway along US-70 East, she opened her eyes and straightened her back. "Are we lost?"

"No," Katie Lee said, "we're not lost."

"There's nothing around. How do people make a living?"

Bridget had given up on the FM dial, and Katie Lee took the task of finding a better station of static. "Most people in The Bern work in the medical industry, cater to tourists, or build for Hatteras."

"Hatteras? As in yachts?" Bridget asked.

Katie Lee grinned. "Big money passes through these parts. Movie stars, moguls, and sheiks all want a Hatteras. It's the Cadillac of yachts."

Bridget rested her arm across the back of the front seat. "Do you think we'll see anyone famous?"

"It's a possibility. Yacht buyers come down here all the time. They like to watch their bank accounts being launched into the Atlantic. Once they pour a bottle of champagne over their new girlfriend's hull, stroke her instruments, and give her a nickname, they charter her to their port."

"I'm surprised you wanted to come home," I said.

"Weekends on campus are so dead. I thought we all could use a breath of fresh air."

"Even after the phone call from your parents?" Macy asked.

"That's all settled," Katie Lee said.

Across the industrial-gray seat fabric, I stared at Macy's square-tipped, polished nails that fanned ten cards. "Your turn," she said.

Macy was a card shark, and I'd cut her too many slices of my humble pie in more hands of gin rummy than I cared to count. I selected a queen of hearts from the discard pile and, in a ploy to distract her, said, "It's November, and my shrink wrap is still intact."

Reorganizing her hand, she threw one facedown and knocked on the armrest. Signaling gin, she laid her matching sets for me to see.

In between heckling the cards I chose and loudly tallying the score-card, she asked, "Did you see any cute guys on your last visit?"

"New Bern has potential," I told her.

She tapped a pink plastic case that rested inside a pocket of her Gucci purse. "Glad I remembered to pack this."

"An orthodontic retainer?"

"It's a diaphragm."

Macy was confident about getting lucky. I wasn't so sure. Shifting backward, I rearranged a new hand of cards. I was desperate to win, but it would have to wait. Passing the magnolia trees that lined her driveway, Katie Lee pulled in behind a black Dodge that blocked the carport and shifted into park. "Make yourselves at home. Beer is in the downstairs refrigerator, and I'll order pizza."

As I opened my door, it rocked on its hinge. A drawn out "Hey y'all" greeted us. Nash held a can of Coors and pinched a cardboard carton of wine coolers in his other hand. He moved toward the car with a couple of friends trailing behind and asked, "Anyone thirsty?"

I didn't want to like Nash, but his welcome offering scrambled my intuitive sensibilities.

"Thanks, Nash," I said, opening a wine cooler.

"You rock," Macy said, distracted by his shirtless, shoeless friend.

I recognized those bare feet, and I knew Macy had familiarized herself with most things above Stewart Hayes's ankles. Standing in Katie Lee's driveway was the beefcake from the Chapel Hill frat house who'd unlocked the bathroom for me. He and Macy had smoked weed before I found them, and Macy claimed that the pot gave her amnesia. Seeing her eat Stewart up with her eyes, I theorized she remembered more than she'd told me.

Katie Lee made the introductions. "Nash, Stewart, Clive, meet my roommate, Raz, and my girlfriends Bridget and Macy."

"Ladies," Nash said in a flirty, singsong voice, "we are delighted to be in your company this evening."

"I believe we've met," Stewart said.

"I'm not sure," Bridget replied.

Macy stepped forward. "Do you prefer Thin Mints or Tagalongs?"

"Tagalongs," Stewart said and hugged her.

So Stewart Hayes and Nash were friends. The encounter sparked an annoying prick of electricity inside of me. Stewart didn't make mention of having met me. If he and Nash were moving drugs inside canvases, he wouldn't want Macy and me to know about it. I hoped she was sensible enough not to mention the artwork I'd found.

Clive wore a tie-dye t-shirt with a pair of ripped Levi's and crisp white canvas tennis shoes. Seeing his tanned face and arms, I guessed the sun had bleached his shoulder-length hair. His appearance masterfully blended elements of hippie prep, and he pulled it off without compromising his manliness. Taking the keys from Katie Lee, he said, "Let me help y'all unload."

Nash and Stewart helped Clive carry our bags into the house. As the three walked along the breezeway, I contemplated drugs, cash, and canvases. It wasn't any of my business, but I couldn't help myself. I didn't have solid proof, but a definite hunch that Nash and

Stewart worked together in some scheme, and by default, Katie Lee was entangled. If I could figure out what was going on, I'd clue in Katie Lee before she and I became accessories to something that would intimately familiarize us with the justice system.

THE ONLY PRE-PARTYING AT Katie Lee's house was the journey from the driveway to the kitchen, where I finished a wine cooler. Katie Lee walked and talked slower than I did, but when it came to organizing a get-together, she was miles ahead. My bags were still in the hallway when the pizza guy appeared, his face hidden behind the stack of cardboard boxes he carried. He'd led a parade of Katie Lee's friends into the Browns' kitchen. I'd set my empty bottle on the counter when I spotted the McCoys. Bathtub Dew and shotgun shells have a way of bonding people together, and both Patsy and Mitch hugged me as though I'd always known them.

Inside the house the air hung with salty river and tobacco. The first floor became standing room only with open doors awaiting a gust of relief from the Trent River. Word had gotten around that the Browns were out of town, and a respectable number of locals showed up. By respectable, I mean more than I could count, and I had a hard time keeping tabs on Nash and Stewart. I needed to stay alert, to overhear anything pertinent to their business venture.

Patsy stood by Clive. "Raz, we have something to share."

I had no idea what she was talking about.

She nudged Clive's arm. "Don't we? Come on outside."

Clive wasn't a man of many words. He gave Patsy and me a head nod in the direction of the water. The three of us snuck away to the covered dock where rhythmic sloshing washed the rocky shore. The sun had disappeared, and a night mist crept up the bank. Hovering low, it disguised the water below the dock.

Pulling out a crumpled plastic baggie from his jeans pocket, he said, "This is local. None of that import crap."

"Have you smoked before?" Patsy asked.

"Not unless inhaling fumes counts."

Curiously, I watched Clive pack a small wooden pipe with dried grass, flick a lighter, and inhale from the side of his mouth. I'd been in a mob on Halloween, and now I could tick another item off my "to-do" list. The only problem was I wasn't checking the items off in the order of importance I'd listed them. If I continued at this rate, I'd be lucky to lose my virginity by Thanksgiving of senior year.

Clive held smoke in his lungs and spoke like Mr. Mouse. "Pretty good batch. Go easy."

Patsy coached, "Suck, hold, blow."

I'd been smoking cigarettes since I landed in North Carolina, and I didn't think this would be much different. Imagining the pipe was a Benson & Hedges, I inhaled a throaty burn, and abruptly exhaled a choking hack.

Patsy handed me a beer, and the three of us moved to the grassy slope beyond the water's edge. Clive couldn't stop talking. Between giggles, Patsy and I acted intrigued at his analysis of the distorted psychedelic blues roots of heavy metal.

"Do you think Axel Rose would still look hot in spandex if he was doing step-aerobics?" Patsy asked.

"Patsy," Clive said, "Axel Rose doesn't wear spandex; he wears leather."

She closed her eyes. "He'd look hot just marching up and down."

A pesky irritation that started behind my knees brought me to my feet, and I began swatting at my legs, bare ankles, and the night air.

"I've never seen hooch have that effect," Clive said.

"I'm being eaten alive, and I have a soggy bottom."

"Raz, calm down, smoking weed doesn't have any bladder control side effects. You were sitting on wet ground."

"Maybe you got chiggers," Clive said.

"Chigger? I'm not dancing the chigger. I'm busy killing what's biting me."

Patsy went all serious. "If you have 'em, you'll need to use medicinal soap to remove 'em, and just to be safe, wash your clothes."

"Preparation H," Clive said. "It's the only way to stop the itch."

"That's disgusting." I suspected mosquito bites and guessed the chigger scare was a bunch of southern hooey, but neither cracked a smile that I could see. I'd seen these two bump knees and share flirty touches when passing the lighter. If they wanted to be alone, their tactic had worked.

Weaving through the back garden path, I brushed against grassy mounds of sea oats and bumped into another McCoy. "Mitch."

"Hey you, I was just comin' to see what trouble y'all are causin'," he teased in his throaty accent.

"I have a potentially fatal case of chigger bites and a soggy bottom."

"Now that sounds serious. I've seen many a case of chiggers, even experienced the little devils myself. Those bites require immediate, expert attention."

Mitch was a natural flirt, very cute, and still driving with a permit. A combination of wine coolers and "local stuff" weakened my normally sensible judgment, and I flirted back. "Tell you what," I said. "I'll make you a deal."

"Go on, let's hear it."

"If you get two cold drinks, I'll address my chigger situation, get into a dry pair of pants, and meet you on the porch in five minutes to hear your medical advice."

He held the back door for me. "Darlin'," he said, "you have yourself a bargain."

The antique cottage kitchen table was an overflow of elbows. Rolling dice pinged across the planked pecan slats, and when they stopped, a ricochet of hoots and heckles erupted as someone shouted, "Drink up."

We parted ways, but before I went upstairs, a threesome that huddled against the kitchen sink caught my attention. Macy, Bridget, and Nash stood in a tight circle, and I poked my head between shoulders to see what they were doing.

"I'll give you one," Nash told Macy, "as long as you don't tell Katie Lee." Opening his hand, he held a fistful of assorted pills. "Do you want a blue, pink, or white one?"

Her red nail poked at them in his palm. "Which is the best?"

I stepped into the circle. "Macy, you don't know what he's giving you?"

Nash's voice sank into a slippery whisper. "They'll just give her a nice buzzin' feeling is all."

"What are they?" Bridget asked.

Checking behind his back, Nash lowered his voice. "The blue is Mr. Happy, the pink is Ms. Silly, and the white is I-can't-remember-what-happened."

Before Bridget or I could protest, Macy said, "I'll try Mr. Happy," and slipped the blue pill into her mouth, using saliva as a wash.

Wondering if I should give her the Heimlich before Mr. Happy dissolved, I lectured, "You realize you could die tonight."

Nash pushed the pills back in his pocket. "She's not gonna die."

From behind, Katie Lee clutched Macy's wrist and gently pulled her out of the group. "Stewart told me he thinks you're a doll."

"I want you to tell me exactly what he said," Macy instructed Katie Lee, and the two moved away to privately discuss Stewart Hayes.

Bridget followed them with her eyes, and her face wore an unsettled grimace. I scratched behind my knees thinking I'd missed something. Maybe she'd wanted Mr. Happy for herself, which reminded me of Mitch. "Gotta get out of these pants," I blurted.

"Sounds promising," Nash mouthed.

As I moved away from the sink, I overheard Bridget say, "I guess it's just you and me."

BESIDES A BOTTLE OF MIDOL and some bandages, the medicine cabinet in the upstairs hallway was as worthless as Geraldo Rivera in Al Capone's vault. Desperate for something to stop the itch, I moved into the master bath and locked the door behind me. One of the light bulbs above the vanity made a pop noise, and then darkened when I flicked the switch. Under the soft glow of the remaining two, I dropped my pants and twisted around to see my reflection in the vanity mirror. Swollen red bumps mapped my continental divide. Fleshy sensitive places under my knees, on my hipbone, and just above the crack of Gibraltar had been ravished. I held an antibiotic cream in my right hand and Preparation H in my left. Deciding which to use, I heard the master bedroom door shut and the click of the lock.

At first I didn't detect voices, only party noise pulsing from the first floor, and I wondered if I'd been mistaken. Pressing my ear to the door seam, I heard a zipper open and the clank of a belt buckle. *Crap, someone was fooling around in the Browns' bed.* Shuffling to the toilet, I lowered the lid and took a seat. One-word exclamations and an impressive orchestra of moans complemented the bang of the headboard. *I couldn't exactly sneak out without being spotted, could I?* My only choice was to wait this one out. Wondering how long they'd be, I checked my Swatch and busied myself by rubbing both creams on my bites before putting my pants back on.

Six minutes passed before silence. I hoped there wouldn't be an encore. In my head I chanted, *leave, leave, leave.* My concentration must have been off. Someone jiggled the door handle.

"It's stuck," said a voice I recognized.

"Duh," I mouthed from inside the locked door.

"I know this house," Nash said. "The locks are an easy pick with my pen knife."

"Maybe someone is in there?" the female voice said.

"Someone probably locked themselves out."

Shit, shit, shit. If Nash found me, I'd be labeled as the pervy listen-in-er, and as panic blossomed, I looked for a place to hide. There was the shower, but that was a stupid idea. Everyone looks in the shower. I checked the cabinets under the sink, but there was no room between the towels and toiletries. My options were climbing out the window onto the roof or hiding in the oversized wicker laundry hamper. Counting on the party to drown out any noises I made, I removed three pairs of Mrs. Brown's khakis, her button-down Liz Claiborne, towels, and Dr. Brown's black undershirt and matching bikini.

Inside the basket, I sank under the soiled clothes and wore the lid like a floppy summer hat. The bathroom latch clicked, and the female voice said, "So you think I could have a territory and get a commission."

I held my breath.

"Can't make guarantees. I'll need to talk to the boss."

In a sultry purr, Bridget said, "You know I'll make it worth it for you. It'll be our secret."

What a shit!

The conversation I'd overhead doused my happy buzzed state. As the sinks ran and the toilet flushed, I waited in the basket until I was positive they'd both left. The blood in my feet and in my ass had stopped circulating; those bits had gone numb. Cracking the lid open, I could see the Browns' rumpled comforter beyond the bathroom door. As I walked into the bedroom, voices from the staircase startled me, so I dropped to the floor, and something hard and square lodged into my knee. I picked up a silver butane lighter and ran my fingers over an engraving, *NW*. What an ass.

Resting at the foot of the Browns' bed, I wondered if there were any studies linking local stuff to hearing distortion? I wanted to be wrong about what I'd overheard.

A glint of light from the hallway streaked across the king-sized bed, and a gold loop earring stuck out from a pillow. I picked up the snake-head clasp. Katie Lee only wore silver jewelry. Bridget and Katie Lee were pals. Nash had hooked up with Bridget. Katie Lee adored Nash. I didn't like killing bugs, but given a choice, I'd squash one of the hard-shelled palmettos we found in our dorm under my bare toes before breaking Katie Lee's heart.

I DIDN'T WANT TO be privy to any other intimate information, so I rushed to my room to change my pants. Walking down the stairs, I took a deep breath and debated when I should tell Katie Lee. Now or when the party ended?

Making a scene wasn't my style, but I didn't know if I could stomach seeing Nash and Bridget. Past the foyer, the open basement door blocked my path through the hallway. Light glowed around it. The clicking of a Ping-Pong ball and poker chips echoed up the steps. I edged around the door and squeezed through a group of bodies. "Pardon me," I said, but before I was able to push past, a purple sleeve grabbed my arm and pulled.

Billy Ray was dressed like a jar of plum chutney, and his breath had fermented. "Razzle, come here and give me a hug," he said and blasted me with an air puff of whisky.

I intended to make as little physical contact as necessary, but his embrace was iron tight, and he planted a slurpy kiss behind my ear. Snapping out of his lingering clutch, I wiped my neck dry. He held tight on my other hand and asked, "Have you been hiding from me?"

Katie Lee didn't need to worry about her cheating boyfriend because I intended to kill her for inviting Billy Ray. Why did I attract the flamboyant thirty-year-old who didn't have any friends his own age? Someone reached between us, tipped a bottle of vodka, and held up a twenty.

Besides being the bootlegger for underage youth, I couldn't figure out why Billy Ray wanted to hang out with a bunch of teenagers. When he let go of me to snag the money, I didn't stick around to find out. I made a note to avoid him. If he caught me a second time, getting away might not be so easy.

The kitchen table dice game was still in play, and I moved past the overflow of bodies intending to find Katie Lee without knowing what I'd say. On the dark screened porch, I heard footsteps. Spinning around, I nearly crashed into Mitch. He held two cold cans of beer and handed me one. "Where have you been?"

"You'll never guess."

He motioned to a hammock. "Well, sit down and give me a try."

As we swayed with the feathery wind gust, I sipped my drink. Eliminating the headboard-knocking, bathroom-hamper-hideout incident, I shared a slightly exaggerated version of being cornered by Billy Ray.

Mitch slipped his arm around me. "I'll protect you from Billy Ray."

My heart rate quickened with a mixture of guilt and lust. He leaned forward and brushed his lips against mine. The warmth of his body sent tingles up my spine. Passion overpowered any sensible thoughts I could conjure up. We were in lip-lock for under a minute when his hand crept under the back of my shirt, searching for my bra hook.

"It's a front clasp," I mumbled, and he pulled his hand off my back. Mitch shifted his weight, and I rolled back. The hammock creaked then snapped in a flip, landing me on top of Mitch, and all hell broke loose.

A loud boom thudded as though someone had thrown Mrs. Brown's skillets down the stairs. The noisy commotion from inside escalated, and a steady fire of shouts and curses followed. I slid off Mitch. Guiltily we scrambled to our feet. He grabbed my hand, and we raced inside to see what the ruckus was about.

"Was that gunshots?"

"No, Raz, no gunshots. But definitely a fight. Probably broken glass, a mirror, and a lamp or two."

A crowd had gathered at the top of the landing that led down to the basement. Mitch and I pushed past to see for ourselves.

From the bottom step, Mitch asked, "What the hell's going on?"

Shoe scuffs and bloodstains streaked the country-blue floral wallpaper. More disturbing, my eyes fixated on Bridget's consoling arm that was wrapped around Katie Lee's shoulder.

Careful to avoid the moving pileup of bodies and swinging fists, Katie Lee yelled, "Knock it off! I'm gonna call the cops."

Weaving through the gawkers on the perimeter of the fight, Mitch and I made our way to her. Rows of wooden wine racks filled with bottles of wine and champagne lined the basement wall. Before our eyes, tangled limbs barreled backward, toppling the racks into a pile of bonfire scrap. Katie Lee spoke in monotones. "I'm—dead. My ass is—deep fried."

Billy Ray held Stewart Hayes in a neck lock. "You come back from college with a degree in asshole?"

Stewart grappled out of the hold, his face reddened. "You sound better with your mouth shut."

"Come on," Nash instructed Mitch and Clive, and the three moved in to break up the fight.

Staring at broken glass and spilled wine, I told Katie Lee, "On the plus side, there's no carpet." I didn't mention that red wine probably stained linoleum flooring.

Blood leaked from bruised noses, and Stewart's shirt had split down the side seam. As the fight lost its gusto, the punching momentum slowed, but insults still raged. Katie Lee, Bridget, and I stepped back to make room for Nash. He seized Billy Ray's arm and dragged him up the stairs.

Destructive grand finales have a way of clearing a party atmosphere, and only a handful of us stayed in the basement to assess the damages.

"Where's Macy?" I asked.

Bridget tilted her mouth to my ear. "Upstairs, passed out. The pill she took wasn't Mr. Happy. It was Mr. Sleepy."

Nash was a busy boy. He'd had a hand in making this a memorable evening for Macy and Bridget and, unbeknownst to her, Katie Lee.

"Who started the fight?" I asked.

"Billy Ray," Bridget said. "Stewart accused him of cheating."

"At what?"

"It started at the poker table. Stewart said something that pissed Billy Ray off, and he flipped the game table."

"There's a lot of toppling going around, and Katie Lee is the one who has to deal with the mess."

Bridget held my gaze, giving me the silent answer to what I knew. Local stuff does not impair hearing or cause hallucinations. Nash was a douche bag, and Bridget rated as a conniving bitch who pretended to be Katie Lee's friend. Tempted to tell her off, I held back out of respect for Katie Lee. It wasn't something that should be leaked in a room full of people. That would only spiral the evening into torrential drama. I'd wait to expose my roommate's cheater-pants boyfriend and double-crossing frenemy.

Patsy and I went upstairs to find some cleaning supplies, and I spotted Mitch and Clive outside. The basement brawl had replaced my lust hormones with sobered-up sensibilities. As adorable as I found Patsy's younger brother, it probably wasn't a brilliant idea to become involved with a minor.

Holding brooms and buckets, Patsy and I heard loud gasps in the family room. Katie Lee sat hunched on Nash's lap. "It was supposed to be their twenty-fifth anniversary celebration champagne. The bottle was from a vineyard in France where they spent their honeymoon."

Patsy kissed the crown of Katie Lee's head. "We'll help you clean up."

"Some of the bottles on the floor aren't even broken," I said. "Maybe it's not as horrible as it seems."

Katie Lee smiled at us and blew her nose. "Billy Ray is a prick. Who the hell invited him anyway?"

"Come on," Nash said, gripping Katie Lee's hand. He led her out the kitchen door and thought I'd barf.

MITCH AND PATSY HUGGED me before they left. I turned off lights as I made my way upstairs. More tired than buzzed, I determined I needed a clear head before I mentioned anything to Katie Lee and decided to wait until morning.

The second floor was dark and quiet. Before settling into the front guest room, I checked on Macy, fast asleep in Katie Lee's bed. Shutting the door behind me, I moved down the hall and bumped into Bridget.

"What a night," she said.

"For you."

"What are you talking about?"

"You've been busy trashing Katie Lee's relationship. Why did you screw Nash?"

Before she could hide the truth with lies, she froze.

I brushed her hair off her left shoulder. "Missing an earring? I heard you in the master bedroom."

She pulled me into the sewing room. "It's not what you think."

I didn't speak. I wasn't going to help her explain.

"Katie Lee is an amazing person. I did her a favor."

A squeaky bark erupted from my throat. This was going to be good.

"Nash isn't right for her. She deserves better, and I sacrificed a few minutes of my time to prove it."

"That's big of you. Have you told her what you've done?"

"Not yet, but I intend to."

"And you think she's going to thank you for your sacrifice? Do you plan on charging her for your time?"

"Rachael, come on. I know it was unconventional, and she may lash out initially, but Nash Wilson is not boyfriend material."

"I'll agree with you there."

"So you won't tell her? You'll let me?"

"You're the one who graciously offered yourself to prove a point. You tell her. But if you don't, I will." Spinning around, I left her in my dust. Slamming the bedroom door, I locked it.

My blood pumped, and I felt jittery. This was not the scheme I had wanted to uncover. It was late, and the house smelled partyfied. I lifted the blind and cranked open the double-pane window. The blanket of vapor that had snuck up the riverbank now draped its cloak over the magnolia trees. Nash's voice carried from somewhere in the night. Flicking the switch on the wall plate off, I kneeled at the window and waited while my eyes adjusted to the dark. The mist gave Billy Ray's purple shirt a ghostly aura. I pressed my ear to the screen and wondered, *What was Billy Ray still doing here? And where was Katie Lee?*

Billy Ray's feet staggered, and he windshield-wipered a thick finger in front of Nash's eyes. "Ten thousand." Poking Nash's chest, he said, "I want it, now."

Nash gripped Billy Ray's wrist. "Keep your voice down. I told you, it's tucked away."

Billy Ray shook loose and leaned into Nash's face. "Don't lie to me, pretty boy."

NOTE TO SELF
"Small get-together" is code for bash.

Nash drugged Macy and slept with Bridget. There's gonna be trouble when Katie Lee finds out.

Nash must have stolen money out of the suitcase, and Billy Ray wants it back.

19

Someone Please Tell Me What Happened

Toilet flushing and pipe-rattling noises woke me up. With Frankenstein precision, I shuffled to the bathroom sink and drank from a Dixie cup before sticking my head under the running faucet. Blinking the foggy haze from my eyes, I pretended not to recognize my reflection. My matted hair stuck to the side of my head, smeared mascara circled my eyes, and I wore my t-shirt inside out, back to front, with the wash instruction tag hanging under my chin.

The sensible thing to do would be to go back to bed, but my armpits stuck together, and I wore an avid outdoorsy scent. Sitting on the edge of the tub, I rotated the shower knob and waited for hot water. Inflamed red bumps covered my sensitive areas, triggering my memory to rewind. The only thing I'd figured out last night was that it's entirely possible to be in the wrong place at the wrong time more than once in an evening. I'd been attacked by a swarm of chiggers, kind of made out with a minor, witnessed a basement brawl, and hadn't gotten around to telling Katie Lee that her boyfriend had slept with Bridget and owed Billy Ray ten thousand dollars.

As I rinsed away last night's party funk, knots tied inside my stomach, and an inner turmoil regarding Katie Lee's reaction to Bridget's forthcoming confession manifested inside my chest. Before today ended, Katie Lee was going to freak. Bridget would probably get a purple eye and be paying for a one-way ticket on a Greyhound back to Greensboro. I needed to brace myself for the verbal outburst and tears that would be forthcoming.

When I turned off the water, I heard shouting and wrapped my head in a towel turban. I hopped on one foot to unplug the water in my ear. Definitely yelling. Mostly profanities with a southern drawl. An engine revved outside the bedroom window. I threw on clean underwear and a fresh t-shirt before kneeling under the billowing shade.

Near the carport, Nash's stationary truck was missing both rear wheels, and the axle rested on cement blocks. Wearing only jeans, he ran into the street and launched a rock at a red turbo Mustang that sped away. "You speed on home and climb back in bed with your mama. You pickled chicken shit."

If he was trying to wake the neighbors, he was doing a great job.

Slipping into clothes, I brushed out my hair and checked outside the window again. Walking up the driveway, Nash smacked unsuspecting foliage with a stick he'd found.

I hustled downstairs to find out what was going on. At the kitchen table, Macy adjusted the sleeves on her black dragon kimono robe, and then nursed a can of Mountain Dew through a straw.

"You aren't looking so good."

Macy dropped her head into folded arms. "I feel like dog doo."

"Where's Katie Lee?"

"Outside."

"Bridget?"

The door to the garage slammed shut. Out of breath, Katie Lee said, "Still asleep, in my parents' room."

So Bridget hadn't rushed down to have a heart to heart with Katie Lee over toast and coffee.

"Why is Nash's truck on cement blocks, and did I just see him in a shirtless sprint, shouting obscenities down the street?"

Katie Lee shook her head heavenward. "Billy Ray's pissed that Nash kicked him out last night. As revenge, he stole a couple of wheels off the Dodge truck."

Macy lifted her head. "That's fucked up."

"Where's Nash now?" I asked, wondering if he'd gone to fetch ten thousand from under his mattress.

"He took Big Blue."

I torqued my head. "You let him have the keys to your car?"

"How else would he get his wheels back?" Macy said.

"Guess we'll all be bussing it back to Greensboro," I mumbled.

Katie Lee poured a bowl of dry cereal and picked out the colored marshmallows. "So, Macy, did you fool around with Stewart Hayes?"

Macy lowered her eyelids. "He nibbled on my neck, and I was into him." Her raspy voice sounded like she'd been screaming at a concert all night. "Before we went upstairs, I needed to take pregnancy precautions, but I'd left my safety gear in my travel case, inside Big Blue."

Stiffening my hand in the air like a stop sign, I asked, "Do we really need these details for this story?"

"Yes," she growled. "Now where was I?"

Katie Lee reminded her, "You'd secured your diaphragm."

"Before I found Stewart, I bumped into Nash and Bridget."

Macy was getting to the juicy part when the phone rang. "Hold it right there, y'all," Katie Lee said. "I don't want to miss anything."

Softening her voice, Macy confessed, "That blue pill Nash gave me knocked me on my ass."

"Really?" I snarked.

"Nash is a terrible pharmacist."

"He's a prison sentence waiting to happen," I said.

Katie Lee walked back into the room. "That was Patsy. She's on her way. Keep goin'."

"I was headed upstairs to fool around with Stewart when Nash offered me some pills, and I took one."

With a mouth full of milky cereal, Katie Lee asked, "What kind of pill?"

"One that put me to sleep," Macy groaned.

Abandoning her cereal, Katie Lee pressed and hand to her forehead. "Nash thinks he has emotional anxieties. Even though I wish he wouldn't, he relies on meds."

As Katie Lee confided in us, I hoped she felt queasy from being spun by Nash's tilt-a-wheel of lies and deceitful behavior. If she was near her breaking-up point, maybe Bridget's confession would convince her to make the leap.

"His family life hasn't been the greatest. He escapes with drugs and alcohol." Her eyes clouded with tears. "He's never straight with me. When I ask him what's going on, we end up fighting. Last night was another big blowout, and we didn't make up until early this morning. Y'all, I love him, and I know I can help him."

That did not sound like a prebreakup statement.

Blowing her nose, Katie Lee turned to face Macy. "Did you sleep with Stewart or what?"

"Sleep with him. Yes. Have sex with him, I don't think so."

"How can you not know?" I asked.

Footsteps creaked a floorboard, and Macy closed her open mouth. A few strands of Bridget's blonde hair fell out of an otherwise flawless ponytail. Her makeup looked fresh, and her eyes avoided mine. I hadn't forgotten her plea. I intended to make sure she told Katie Lee that she'd slept with Nash. She didn't have to worry. I'd drop her off at the bus station.

"Hey, Bridget," Katie Lee said.

Bridget acknowledged the morning with a meek wave before staring inside the open refrigerator.

"We started fooling around upstairs," Macy said. "But that blue pill kicked in, and I passed out. I woke up naked, but everything seemed in order south of the border."

"Good Lord," Katie Lee said.

Macy stood up to get another soda. She asked Bridget, "Did anything exciting happen with you last night?"

A BRIGHT GLARE DRENCHED warm rays on the kitchen patio and streaked past the French doors' hourglass curtains. The sunlight blinded my vision, and I switched kitchen chairs. I didn't need any more heat radiating on me. Bridget's twisted deceit had charred my internal organs like a blackened marshmallow on a fire pit. She was an idiot to have slept with Nash. Katie Lee would never forgive her. I didn't attempt to grasp either one's interest in Nash, a guy who laundered money and was involved with God only knows what.

The audile grunts of their bedroom romp that I'd heard from behind a bathroom door had distracted my sleuthing focus. Bridget's excuse was überlame, and I guessed Nash's wouldn't be much better. Being the recipient of deception sucked. I knew that firsthand, thanks to my mother. The only positive about last night's tryst between the sheets was that once Katie Lee found out, our connections to Nash would be history.

As soon as Katie Lee disappeared into the laundry room off the kitchen, I plastered goldfish eyes on my face while repeatedly clearing my throat. Bridget glanced at me for two seconds before moving away from the refrigerator. Holding a pitcher of juice, she raised her voice to ask Katie Lee, "Where do you keep the glasses?"

If she felt remorse, I didn't see it.

"Bridget," I said, "I heard something happened to you last night."

Her mouth contorted, and her face drew a brain dump expression.

Katie Lee returned and bounced a glance from me to Bridget. Grinning, she asked, "Did you fool around?"

Bridget took a sip of juice. "I wish."

I wished I had a blowgun with venomous needles to shoot at a blonde target. *You flaming liar* rested behind my teeth. A primal grunt shot out of my mouth, but a rat-a-tat-tat sidetracked my impending verbal assault.

Patsy muffled, "Hey, y'all," around a powdered Krispy Kreme that clogged her pie hole. She pulled three-quarters of the donut out and asked, "How's the basement?"

"After some cleaning up, the damage is minor," Katie Lee said. "Nash and I used wood glue. The racks are standing. I'm just waiting for them to dry."

"I didn't hear a damn thing last night," Macy said.

"How many bottles broke?" I asked.

Katie Lee held up six fingers.

Bridget relaxed on a counter stool. "Can I pitch in to buy replacements?"

Katie Lee's shoulders dropped. "You are so thoughtful to offer. The whole incident wouldn't have been so horrible if the assholes hadn't broken Mama and Daddy's commemorative champagne. I'm beyond mad at Billy Ray. Now I'll have to fess up about the get-together."

The skin under the seams of my jeans felt dry and inflamed, and I couldn't stop scratching my hip. Squinting, Macy asked, "Do you have fleas?"

Lifting my shirt, I showed the girls a portion of my bug bite rash.

Macy backed her chair away from mine. "Eugh. How did you contract that?"

Patsy answered for me. "Rachael sat in a chigger patch down by the river."

Katie Lee visually inspected my red marks. "There's oatmeal soap in the master bath linen shelves. Do you want me to get it for you?"

I locked eyes with Bridget. She barely stirred, enjoying the morning as if this was any ordinary day, not the one where she was going to turn Katie Lee's world upside down.

I TOOK SHOWER NUMBER TWO with an oatmeal bar and afterward applied a heavy application of pink calamine lotion, which helped cool the inflamed bumps. After last night's alcohol consumption I needed air, the outdoor kind, and trod downstairs with the intention of walking to the dock while avoiding the chigger-infested grassy bank. Wondering if Nash had returned Big Blue, I heard hushed tones in the family room and froze. "I was drunk," Bridget whispered. "I don't even like him."

"Don't be so hard on yourself," Katie Lee replied.

I didn't have boyfriend experience, but if I'd been dating the same person since high school, I would've reacted with some emotion and made sure Bridget had a reason to visit a chiropractor—weekly. Maybe Katie Lee intended to break up with Nash and had moved beyond caring. I needed to find out for myself. Clearing my throat, I made a casual entrance and plopped into Dr. Brown's reading recliner. There weren't any noticeable signs of distress, boxes of tissues, or weaponry pointing at Bridget's head. *Was Katie Lee in shock?* The two stopped the conversation, and I asked, "Are we cool?"

"Yeah, Rach," Bridget said. "We're cool."

"Everything's okay?"

"As okay as it can be," Katie Lee said, "Y'all, we need to get ready to go to Jackson's."

"Wait a minute. Who's Jackson?" I asked.

"Jackson's a great guy," Katie Lee said.

Sinking back into Dr. Brown's chair, I pulled the recline lever. Unable to believe Katie Lee was okay with sharing Nash, I watched her closely for any signs of a mental breakdown. Not detecting anything out of the ordinary, I asked, "Do we have transportation?"

"Not yet, but Nash'll be here."

She could say his name without flinching.

"Where is Jackson's?" Bridget asked.

"His apartment is above the Marina Supply Store. Patsy got the clambake invite. He's expecting all of us this afternoon."

NOTE TO SELF

The sticky fluff inside Bridget's head has hardened and cracked. Since when is sleeping with a friend's boyfriend to prove a point considered a sacrifice?

Is Katie Lee really okay sharing Nash? I won't be borrowing him, ever.

20

One Bad Clam

The sky was cloudless, and intermittent gusts of warm air tossed my ponytail. I rested in a front porch rocker while Bacon, Katie Lee's tabby, wound figure eights around my legs. Patsy's turquoise Chevy Nova streaked up Katie Lee's driveway before it clambered to a halt. Clive rode in the front and Mitch in the back. Before she'd cut the engine, Nash coasted Big Blue in behind them. Patsy rolled her window down. "Wanna ride with us to Jackson's?"

"I'll grab a sweater and let Katie Lee know."

As I returned, Clive fiddled with the cassette case, and Mitch hopped out of the back, resting his arm on the roof. "Hey, Raz," he said, "it's been a while."

Mitch's hair was wet, and he smelled freshly showered. He held the back door open until I buckled myself in. Despite being considerate and cute, he wasn't a big-enough distraction to ease my mind about Katie Lee's lackadaisical reaction to Bridget's confession. And then there were Nash and Billy Ray. I didn't have a fuzzy feeling about being at a party with those two. I went through the motions of conversation as Patsy drove us across town, but my mind spaced. I needed to get a handle on what was inside Katie Lee's head. Maybe she'd concealed Bridget's admission under a smokescreen of self-preservation. But tonight, she could very well pop her top. And when she did, I didn't know if I could guarantee my own self-control. Bridget could be wearing two purple eyes at the party.

In less than fifteen minutes Patsy was cruising a quaint street of retail stores with scalloped awnings over storefronts. New Bern, with its postcard-perfect shops and marina alcove, had a Norman Rockwell charm. Searching for somewhere to park, she glided into an unmetered space near the pier.

A block-paved sidewalk with evenly spaced willow trees framed a dozen shops. Digging deep into her canvas purse, Patsy took her time getting out of the car. When Mitch and Clive spotted a docked Hewescraft fish trawler, a magnetic force reeled at them to take a closer look.

She found what she'd rummaged for and paused to light a cigarette. I leaned against a black streetlamp and waited for her. Across the street, a small art gallery nestled on a corner next to a restaurant outdoor patio. The brick exterior had been painted periwinkle. Glossy black paint trimmed the display window and the Dutch door. Together we walked to the front, where a handwritten note read, *Be back soon.*

Inside, the lights were off, but I could see an eclectic mix of southern-inspired paintings, sculpture, and pottery. The backlit window display illuminated an oil painting called *Baptism*, by Clementine Hunter. Patsy offered me a cigarette. I declined. I'd resolved not to smoke until I had a buzz. Pointing to the painting, I told her, "My dad is restoring some of her pieces for a museum in New Orleans."

"Cool," Patsy said, more interested in her drag than the art. Happy to lean against the brick-clad exterior, she waited while I scanned a framed biography that rested on a plate-sized easel.

Clementine Hunter, a self-taught artist, specialized in African American folk art. Born outside of New Orleans in 1886, Hunter was the granddaughter of a slave. Having never learned to read or write, she didn't sign her paintings but instead overlaid her initials. She chose to paint simple landscapes of early 20th century plantation life, depicted in bright colors on scraps of wood, doors, and even fabric blinds. Once established, she transitioned to canvas as a medium.

I loved her primitive style, the free whimsy, the layered colors, and I couldn't stop staring at the creativity behind the raw talent. Then it hit me. Halloween. I honed my eyes on the signature. Shadows were cast on it, and I wished I was on the other side of the glass. The insignia rested about four inches up from the bottom right, the same as the one I saw in Stewart's frat loft. *Why did he have a copy of a Clementine Hunter and all those other artists?*

Stomping out her ciggy, Patsy turned her attention back to the small, unframed painting. "Eight thousand dollars. Hell, I'll paint something like that for a quarter of the price."

"Painting a work of art isn't easy. If it were, we'd all be doing it."

BOAT SLIPS JUTTED OUT from the pier, and at the end rested a captain's oasis, the Marina Supply Store. Weathered wide-plank siding gave the building vintage appeal. A briny film clung to the windows, and I could barely see inside. In addition to selling a wide selection of candy bars, beer, and cigarettes, the store also sold fresh and frozen bait. As far as I could tell, it was an overpriced 7-Eleven.

Beyond the dock, a fishing boat churned a chop. On its way out of the harbor, it puttered past Patsy and me. She led the way around the perimeter of the building. Behind the store, there was a set of Dumpsters piled high with cardboard boxes and a staircase that spiraled up to Jackson's second-story deck where barbecue smoke billowed out to sea.

Halfway up the steep climb, I leaned back against the wood rail and strained my eyes upward into the late afternoon sunlight. A snow-white seagull squawked as it hovered above the tin rooftop where the rest of a flock rested with their beaks facing the wind.

Mitch and Clive and dozens of others I didn't recognize were already on the deck and inside the apartment. The nautical location with a 360-degree view of the water was killer. Jackson's décor was less astounding and more of what I'd call beachy-bachelor mix and match. I never knew crab traps were multifunctional as end tables. An old buoy, rigged with a yellow flashing emergency light, added an alternative whimsical touch to one of the corners. Only a guy would have a plaid sofa piled with Mexican blankets instead of cushions. And only a guy would set up a clambake on a deck just outside his living room.

In the center of the elevated patio, six knee-high Smokey Joe charcoal grills snaked like a Matchbox track. The foil-lined grill tops heaved with mussels, clams, and fish fillets. Plumes of fish smoke wafted through every apartment door and window, permeating my hair and clothes with eau de clam.

"Where is Jackson?" I asked Patsy. "And does his apartment always smell like this?"

Patsy curled the corners of her mouth. "Jackson's tall, thin, and always has a pinch of Copenhagen under his lip. You met him at Billy Ray's on your last visit."

"Pre- or post-Bathtub Dew?"

Patsy giggled. "Pre. He ladled you a glass."

I wrinkled my nose. "Are you going to eat any?"

"The clams are amazing, but don't open closed shells or you'll be hugging the porcelain all night."

"Who are all these people?"

Patsy pointed at the doorway. "Two of my brothers are over there."

I hadn't met Patsy's parents, but from what I saw, they carried an extraordinary gene pool. She told me she was the only girl and second youngest of eight.

"Isn't there a fable about seven brothers with supernatural powers?"

"Did the superpowers involve burping, farting, and wrestling?"

Patsy and I secured spots on the Mexican blanket sofa, and I asked, "Are you and Clive an item?"

"He hasn't made a move, and it's starting to annoy me. I think he's worried if we fool around, one of my brothers may kick his ass. I can't wait until next year when I go to university. I've got to get away from The Bern." Without a pause, she asked, "Do you like Mitch?"

"Of course I like Mitch. What's not to like?"

"Romantically? Because he likes you."

"Patsy, the age difference flips me out. Besides, I like hanging out with the McCoys too much to screw things up."

"That's too bad, 'cause he's a terrific guy." Leaning into my ear, she whispered, "My favorite brother."

I heard familiar voices from outside the open windows before I saw the Grogan Girls' faces. Katie Lee led Macy and Bridget into the apartment. There was a brief delay, and then I spotted Nash, and Stewart, beyond the glass slider deck doors. If Katie Lee knew that Bridget had slept with Nash, they all were acting civil about it.

Patsy leaned in. "Looks like the mischief-makers have arrived."

Bridget spotted some guys holding a beer bong and asked, "Can I try?"

It was then that I knew I'd misunderstood her conversation with Katie Lee. She hadn't revealed "the favor" she'd done for Katie Lee. I broke my self-imposed rule of not smoking until I had a buzz and bummed a lit one from Patsy. Rewinding my memory, I chewed on what I'd overheard. Had Bridget confided having sex with someone other than Nash? I inhaled deeper. *Busy night.* It was petty, but it irked me that even she had slept with a guy or two before I had. Not that I wanted to be intimate with Nash—'cause I'd stay a virgin if he were my only option.

While demon-eyeing Bridget, I exercised my thumb on my beer can pull-tab. She was no southern delicacy. This beer bong connoisseur had a naughty habit of luring her friends' men into bed. Her competitiveness, especially where Katie Lee was concerned, had to be stopped. Unfortunately, no one else seemed to notice her devious tendencies. Her candy-coated blonde exterior was a deceitful illusion that hid rancid liquid goo. The game she played didn't have rules, but I knew one thing: Bridget Bodsworth wasn't going to win as long as I was around.

Red nails dangled two frothy cups of beer in my face. "Hold these," Macy instructed. Resting her backside on the sofa arm next to me, she said, "Stewart Hayes doesn't know it, but he and I are going to finish what was started last night."

Steadily downing liquid bravery, Macy prepared for a pounce, but she didn't swallow fast enough. Another cat, with a southern meow, moved in. Bridget ran her finger around the rim of her beer cup. "Hey, Stewart. Wanna join me in the back room for a game of foosball?"

Abruptly Macy stood. "Fucking-A." She grabbed me by my arm and pried me from my prime viewing spot. Leading me down a hallway, she halted short of a bedroom where Bridget and Stewart had disappeared. "You and I are joining them."

"Macy, I don't foos."

"This'll be a quick intervention. I just need to send Stewart some signals."

I waved my hand at the smoke-filled air that stung my eyes. "I hope you know Apache. In here the only signals you'll be sending are smoking ones."

Before I stepped into the bedroom, Mitch handed me a plate of assorted seafood. I would've stayed to chat, but Macy wouldn't let go. In passing, I told him, "Thanks."

A maroon sheet secured with duct tape hung over the only window. In addition to the budget-conscious curtain, the bedroom also featured three pieces of furniture: an unmade corner mattress, a barstool, and a foosball table.

Since when had Bridget become interested in Stewart Hayes? If she had penciled a spot for him on her "to-do" list, she wasn't going to get far. Macy knew what she wanted, and her moussaka was a bigger force than anything I'd ever cross. I wasn't a betting girl, but I would double down on Macy any day.

Twirling a wisp of dark hair around her finger, Macy transformed her voice. "Stewart, can we play?"

Palming a white ball, Bridget said, "Foosy is a two-person game. You and Rachael can have a turn when we're finished."

Pulling a wad of cash from his pocket, Stewart selected a twenty and suggested a wager. "Macy and me against Bridget and Rachael."

"Perfect," I said and moved next to a soured Bridget who pouted her lips at Stewart. As I set the plate of clams on a nearby stool, my brain did a cartwheel. Stewart's team idea was brilliant since I wanted to have a word with Bridget.

"How do we play?" Macy asked.

He reviewed the game rules and demonstrated everything from the proper stance to a wrist rotation technique for moving the rods that held the plastic blue and red players.

Across the table, Stewart personally attended to Macy, helping her get a feel for their blue men. While they practiced toggling, I drained my beer then asked, "Did you confess?"

She picked at a corner of toasted bread from the plate I'd set down. "Confess what?"

I took a long, hard look at Bridget, gritted my teeth, and unintentionally added squeak to my voice. "You screwed Nash."

Bridget cleared her face of expression. She handed me an extra beer cup that she'd brought in. "I'd never do that."

Stewart stood at the opposite end of the foosball table. "Which of you ladies is first?"

"I am," Bridget said. She took her time, challenging Stewart's toggle rods as she knocked the little white ball around his plastic players.

To settle my fury, I drank half the beer I held even though it tasted stale. When Bridget finished her turn, I turned my back on the foosy game and confronted her. "If you don't tell Katie Lee, I will."

Bridget poked at the clams with a dull-edged knife that rested on the plate. "What are you going to tell? How you stake out bedrooms at parties?"

Flames leapt inside of me. Her daggered threat immobilized my reflexes. "Pry the closed shells apart," I slurred. "They're fresher."

"Your turn, Rach," Macy said.

Motioning to move forward, my feet stumbled backward, and I bumped into the stool. Bridget laughed. Pointing my finger at her like a gun, I clucked my tongue and puffed air in her face before snaking out of the room to clear my dizzy head.

I didn't go far. Weaving through a crowd, I leaned against a wall in the hallway and closed my eyes. My insides were in motion, and I concentrated to find quiet. A spidery touch brushed against my cheek. When I opened my eyes, Billy Ray's fingernail drew an imaginary line to my forehead. "Your cheeks are the color of a rose petal, and your crooked eyetooth makes an endearing smile. Has anyone ever painted a portrait of you?"

"I'm no masterpiece."

"Let me paint you before you decide."

My brain was fuzzy and my responses slow. Billy Ray's face took on a striking resemblance to Elmer Fudd, and I jeered, "You paint?"

Billy Ray sipped his beer and looked across the crowded room. Nash stood behind Katie Lee and stared in my direction.

"I been paintin' since before I walked."

"All kids finger-paint."

Reaching across the hallway, Billy Ray slid a closet door open. He motioned me toward him. "Wanna see my work?"

I tripped on my feet, and he caught my arm. "Did you paint Jackson's place?" I giggled.

He looked right then left. No one paid him any attention. Reaching into the back of the closet, he slid a canvas out of a cardboard sleeve and held the edges in his palms.

"Damn," I shouted.

Billy Ray shushed me.

"You paint folk art?"

"I'm in business with my cousin in New Orleans. If you're good to me, I'll paint anything you want."

My ears stretched his words and muffled them in my head. Someone opened the deck slider doors. Black smoke began to fill the apartment, and I heard screams. Billy Ray handed me the painting. "Put this back," he said and ran toward the front door.

I dropped to the floor and fixated on something familiar in the painting, until someone from behind took it from my hands.

"I'll take care of that," a southerner I'd never seen said.

"What are you doin' down there?" Mitch asked.

A red life vest and an oar caught my attention, and I crawled into the closet.

"Who is she?" the man holding the painting asked.

"That's Rachael, Katie Lee's roommate," Mitch said.

"She's toast," the stranger said.

"I'll keep an eye on her while you call the fire department."

"Why would I call the fire department?" the southerner asked.

"Jackson, your deck's on fire."

NOTE TO SELF
Bridget is an überbitch with a short memory.

Tell or don't tell? Neither option is going to earn friendship points.

21

Clearing Cobwebs

Static cluttered my brain, and I'd have sworn cat whiskers sprouted in my dehydrated throat. I had no recollection of how I landed under the covers with Mitch. His soft arm hair brushed my shoulder, and he smelled of sweet cologne. His wristwatch glowed: 3:40 a.m. Outside the room someone hacked, and liquid splattered. Beyond Mitch waves of breath pulsed. Crimping the eyelet comforter tight under my chin, I found the courage to roll out from under his arm and sit up on my elbows. On the other side of him, a woman wearing a satin eye mask lay motionless. Waves of her hair fanned across a pillowcase. Macy!

Processing the three of us in bed, I drew a blank. Had I launched into a hidden stratosphere with these two? I whispered, "Macy."

She slid her mask onto her forehead and yawned. "Hey, Rach," she said as if we'd bumped into one another on campus.

Sinking back into the pillow, I pinched my eyes shut and concentrated on making this delusion disappear. I listened to breathing. The two didn't vaporize, and now Mitch was awake. He stretched his arms above his head. "Hey, y'all."

This was no dream, but an unsettling reality, and I wasn't sure if I wanted to know how I ended up in a threesome. Digging deep, I asked, "What happened last night?"

"I knocked Stewart's ball across the table after you left. He was surprised at how quickly I toggled all the sticks."

"Macy, I don't need to know what happened to you, I need to know what happened to me. The last thing I remember is foosball."

Inching up, Mitch leaned into me and ran his finger under a strand of my hair that covered an eye. "You remember leaving with me. Right?"

Debating the legitimacy of ignorance is bliss, I cleared my throat and opened a packet of bravery. "That part is a bit foggy."

Mitch smiled. "Are your underpants on? That's usually a telltale sign."

I'm a dot-the-i, cross-the-t kind of girl. So naturally I peeked under the sheets. "Very funny. They're on."

Hesitantly I asked Macy, "Are yours?"

She rolled onto her side, slid a hand across Mitch's chest, and whispered, "Unfortunately."

I breathed relief. Mitch McCoy was a treasure who made me sizzle on the inside. Because he was still in high school, I wasn't prepared to have sex with him. But I'd be lying if I didn't admit that I liked having his attention for myself.

The three of us listened to convulsing and consecutive toilet flushing. Macy held a pillow over her ears while Mitch gritted his teeth and announced, "Someone's going to break the handle."

Even though I knew, I asked, "Who is that?"

"Bridget," Macy said. "She said she felt sick at Jackson's."

Darkness veiled the satisfaction that I'm sure beamed on my face. Burying my head in my hands, I pushed my fingertips against my eye sockets. "Jackson's party is a blur. I think someone slipped me a mickey."

Mitch checked his watch. "Don't look at me."

"Come on, Rach. Who would do that?"

Climbing over me, Mitch made apologies. "I hope y'all don't think I'm rude, but my mom'll skin me if I'm not back before sunrise."

"That's it?" Macy asked. "Love us and leave us in the dark of night?"

He pulled on a worn shirt-jacket with a Coast Guard patch and slipped on his shoes. "Ladies, it was a pleasure." Squeezing my toes from the foot of the bed, he whispered, "See ya around."

I scoured through the parts of the evening I found in my head. Bridget. She must've put something she got from Nash into my beer. I remembered confronting her, catching an incredible buzz, and getting trapped by Billy Ray.

With Mitch gone, Macy, not exactly sober herself, filled me in on portions of the evening. "Rach," she told me, "midway through the foosy tournament you walked out."

"Did you follow me?"

She shook her head. "Bridget said you went to the bathroom, but you didn't come back."

"Where was I?"

Macy giggled.

"Oh God, was I naked?"

Gripping my arm she regained herself. "Don't worry, your clothes stayed on. On my way to get a beer, I noticed a glow in the hallway closet. Behind sliding doors, I heard clunking. You came out wearing a red life vest and gripping an oar. Mumbled some shit about 'the oil on the hunter' being wet. Before I knew it, you were off. You said you needed to collect squirrels. Mitch followed you."

"Macy, I was blitzed out of my mind. Weren't you worried that I'd do something I shouldn't?"

"Mitch said he'd handle you. He's a good guy. I didn't see any harm in letting him."

She wasn't responsible for me, and I didn't see a point in holding a grudge. "Did you and Stewart finish what started in the bedroom Friday night?"

In the dark room, a spark shot from her eyes. "We managed to rock an empty boat. Stewart dropped me off at the Browns' house on his way home."

"How did the three of us end up in bed?"

Macy lowered her eye mask and stretched into the space where Mitch had been. "I didn't want to sleep alone, so I joined you two."

So Mitch tucked me in and didn't seem to mind company. *Nice.* I wondered if he'd tell his friends that he'd slept with two college girls. It was the truth, although I doubted anyone would believe him.

I LATHERED DISH SOAP on my hands and used a Brillo pad to clean paint off my fingers. In front of the kitchen sink, I stared at rain that danced on the Browns' garden path. The water turned the wintered Bermuda grass and garden perennials a brighter tone. The dark sky rumbled, and the wind redirected rain droplets to ping the glass on the box window. Last night I'd blacked out, which was beyond unsettling since I hadn't drunk excessive amounts or smoked anything from a pipe, at least that I remember. Forgetting chunks of an evening had never happened before. Not being able to recall what I'd done and said scared the crap out of me. I didn't ever want a repeat experience.

Bridget slumped in a kitchen chair with her head tucked in her arms. The sight of her turned my stomach. She was an out of control manipulator, and I'd caught onto her warped games. She'd be sorry for handing me that laced beer. Trusting her to be true to her word wasn't working. To deal with her, I needed to summon some inner crafty kick ass.

Macy hadn't made a morning appearance. When I checked on her last, the only part I saw was a strand of hair peeking out of the comforter. I felt her vitals. She took in oxygen and had a pulse.

Katie Lee came in from the garage. She'd showered, blown her hair dry, and was dressed. "Bridget, I found the 7Up."

In a trance, Bridget didn't acknowledge me, Katie Lee, or the surroundings with any real words. I have to admit I liked her as a motionless blob. When she had to focus all her energy on breathing, she couldn't hurt anyone.

As she poured the soda in a glass, Katie Lee filled me in. "Bridget got sick from something. Mama always gives me clear soda when I'm not feelin' well."

Bridget lifted her head. Her wet hair looked more mousy than blonde. The ends dripped, leaving dark spots on the mustard-colored sweat shirt she wore. Normally her porcelain cheeks carried a healthy glow. The morning storm cast shadows in the house, replacing the effervescence in her face with a muddy hue that complemented her sweat shirt. I guessed she'd eaten clams from a few closed shells.

Waiting for the toaster, I listened to Katie Lee recap the party highlights. "I can't believe y'all missed the fire. At first no one paid much attention to the tipped Smokey Joe grills. Then some idiot doused the flames with vodka. Jackson's deck combusted like a torched crème brûlée."

Bridget sipped on the clear soda. "I didn't see any of that."

Margarine melted on my toast. *I hadn't seen the mayhem either.* "How'd they put it out? Dump water or cover it with a blanket?"

"Are you kidding? Flames shot up to the roof. Jackson called the fire department."

Gears inside my head clicked. "Wait a minute. His apartment is on the end of the pier. How did the fire truck get to the Marina Supply Store?"

"It was funny as hell," Katie Lee said. "A fire brigade tugboat showed up and shot harbor water onto the back of the building before anyone bothered to shut the windows and doors. Jackson flipped out. He started yelling, 'the art, the art!' like he owns any."

Wires inside my brain sparked, unleashing a dull ache. I stopped midchew and asked, "Does Billy Ray paint?"

"Paint what?"

"Canvas."

Katie Lee plastered a "what?" on her face. "Not that I know of. I can't believe y'all missed the shootin' flames. Unless," she said, clucking her tongue, "someone was makin' their own camp fire with a certain McCoy boy."

"I wish I could remember."

The left corner of Bridget's mouth twitched, and her eyelids creased. "Did you ingest something you shouldnt've?"

"If cigarettes, secondhand clam smoke, and downing the doctored beer you handed me count, I'm guilty."

"In case you forgot, that was my beer you drank."

I bit into my toast. "What'd you put in it?"

"What are y'all talkin' about?" Katie Lee asked.

"Rachael is delusional," Bridget said and dropped her head back into her arms.

WALKING IN THROUGH THE BROWNS' front door, Patsy released an oversized straw that connected her lips to her convenience store Big Gulp cup. "Hey, y'all," she called out. "I wanted to say good-bye before ya head on back."

"I thought you were upstairs, asleep," Katie Lee said.

Patsy shook the mist off her hair. "I woke up early, went home to shower, and changed clothes."

On this rainy day, Patsy resembled the Morton Salt girl. She had secured her hair with a yellow silk scarf, the tails draping along her neck. The cutoff shorts and knee-high rain boots she wore matched. She carried an air of "fuck you" that I envied.

The phone rang in an adjoining room. Katie Lee didn't have the self-control to leave a beeping device alone and darted across the kitchen. I slid into a chair across the table from Bridget. Settling into the seat cushion, I pouted my lips. "You don't look so good. Can I scramble you some eggs?"

Bridget threw her hand on her mouth, pushed her chair back, and bolted up the stairs. I should have felt more satisfied than I did. Barfing her guts didn't change what she'd done. Nothing would. She had a hidden agenda that empowered her to play puppet master with other people's lives. The drug she planted in my beer could've driven me to do something beyond stupid. She needed to be stopped.

"Hey, Raz," Patsy said. "You left the party early."

The rain slowed to a taper, and droplets plunked on the cobblestone path that separated drooping mounds of sea oats. Outside the French door windows, the weight of the water had pressed the grass blades toward the ground. "Will you walk with me to the river?"

She searched my eyes and nodded. Winding through the garden path, we kept quiet until a view of the murky Trent emerged. The storm had calmed the surface but stirred up the river bottom. Pulling two cigarettes out of her pocket, Patsy lit them and handed me one. Blowing her smoke heavenward, she asked, "What's going on?"

"Someone drugged me last night, and I know who."

Patsy didn't speak.

"Bridget put something in my beer."

She resisted a drag. "Why'd she do that?"

"Friday night, I overheard her in the master bedroom. She and Nash knocked the Browns' headboard around. Probably chipped the varnish."

She inhaled, and after filling her lungs, she waited a beat. Releasing her breath, she asked, "Are you sure?"

"Unfortunately. It's the chiggers' fault. I was in the master bathroom applying cream on the bites. Before I finished, the two rolled onto the Browns' bed. I was trapped."

"Does Katie Lee suspect anything?"

A dark cloud curled closer to us, and the sky rumbled discontent. "Not yet. I confronted Bridget Friday night. She bullshitted me. Said she wanted to tell Katie Lee herself. That's not going to happen. Now she's acting like I'm from planet nut-so. After last night's narcotic trip, I'm convinced that she and Nash are out to scare me so I keep quiet."

I flicked the ash that grew on my cigarette. A fish flipped out of the water, catching some flying insect before disappearing back under the surface. I wished I had fins so I could swim under something.

Patsy had known Katie Lee and Nash since grade school. She was part of their inner circle, and I valued her perspective. Somberness washed her face. "I knew he was shit. He's been getting into trouble since middle school. Petty stuff: stealing, fighting, practical jokes. In high school, he advanced to a proper criminal. Growing marijuana, selling a science test he stole from a teacher's briefcase. I'd thought his one redeeming feature was loyalty to Katie Lee."

"Should I tell Katie Lee when I get back to the dorm?"

Patsy stared down the Trent River as if the answer would float to her on top of a water crest. "Nash has Katie Lee's heart wound tighter than a yo-yo. If you or I tell her, I'm not sure she'll believe us."

"Has she mentioned ending it with him?"

"Katie Lee's in a full-blown addiction until she finds somethin' better."

"So what do we do?"

"For now, keep quiet."

"What? And act normal?"

"You don't have proof. Both Nash and Bridget can deny the allegations. You'll be lookin' like a trouble-stirrin' liar."

Pulling the souvenirs from my pocket, I showed Patsy. She took the lighter from my hand and rubbed her thumb over the *NW* initials. "He could have dropped it anywhere."

Patsy had been there for me on my first visit to The Bern. Without her, I would've spent the night in the field at Billy Ray's. She knew this town and the players. I'd entrusted a huge secret. I sank my hands into my jean pockets, "Nash and Bridget are two conniving fakers."

Patsy crushed her cigarette under her boot. "Don't worry, payback is a bitch."

NOTE TO SELF
Mitch McCoy is a slice of nice. Hopefully I didn't embarrass myself too much.

Bridget definitely doesn't play fair.

I'm not comfortable keeping epic secrets. Patsy and I need to come up with a plan soon.

I've nicknamed the New Yorker who wanders into occupied beds Macylocks.

22

Taboo Turkey

A toddler kicked the back of my airplane seat for two hours. The pilot announced the Ohio temperature, twenty-three degrees with snow in the forecast. The chill had sunk into my skin before we'd landed. Without Mom, the holidays were going to be different.

My nana had lived with her best friend, Gert, for twenty years. Even after Nana passed we continued to spend Thanksgiving at their bungalow. Gert wasn't my biological aunt, but Dad and I considered her family. Aunt G had called Dad two days ago with news. She'd won a trip to Las Vegas in the jackpot draw at the Bingo Bucket. She'd chosen free drinks, nickel slots, and the all-you-can-eat buffet over spending the holiday with Dad and me. I was less than excited with all the changes to tradition, but didn't blame her. If given a choice, I'd go to Vegas over Canton.

Without Mom and Aunt Gert, I resolved that I'd just have to embrace a quiet turkey day at home. I decided there could be benefits: wearing my pajamas all day, plenty of leftovers, and a VHS movie marathon. I'd made a grocery list and planned to surprise Dad by volunteering to cook the bird and homemade fixings.

At baggage claim, the man who greeted me was not the same person who'd raised me. When Dad had dropped me off at college, his hair was salt and peppered. The salt had disappeared along with twenty pounds. Before I hugged him, I asked, "What's up with the spandex bike shorts?"

"Just finished a step class. Relieves the stress from the day, works out the kinks." Lifting his chin, he said, "And I've been told it detoxes the pores for a healthy glow."

My father, a man who'd never purposely broken a sweat and didn't know an astringent from paint thinner, attending aerobics class?

As if this tidbit wasn't enough of a shock, he delivered a second zinger. "Since it's just the two of us, I invited a friend over for dinner tomorrow. We're going to start a new tradition. Fondue Thanksgiving."

"Friend?" I asked. "What friend?"

"Someone I met in aerobics."

For eighteen years, my father and I had had a surface relationship. We didn't discuss anything in the category of touchy-feely. My mom's astrological disappearance had turned my family mechanics upside down. She'd chosen a group of traveling mediums over Dad and me, and now my father had a "friend" whom he'd invited over for Thanksgiving. If I read the signals correctly, Dad had rebounded.

THE GOOP INSIDE THE FONDUE pots carried a striking similarity to what bubbled in metal pans at the cafeteria self-serve station. Dad's mystery guest had a name, Trudy Bleaux. I estimated Trudy's age somewhere between too young to be my mother and too old to be my sister. Wiping something drippy from her chin, she giggled and told Dad and me, "Everyone should turn the holidays into a fondue tradition."

Trudy looked nothing like my mother. She was tall and lanky with mousy thin hair that draped over her shoulders. My mother was petite with short, layered hair. Trudy cross-pollinated color combinations and my mother stuck to solids with an occasional check or striped shirt.

She wore a silky scarf blouse, draped and belted over mocha leggings. The printed pattern on her chest mimicked a turkey dinner that had pulsed inside a Cuisinart.

Spearing cubed meat product purchased from the refrigerated deli section, I eyed the spider plant on the sofa table behind Dad and calculated my chances of nonchalantly lobbing my portion into it.

"Rachael," Dad said, covering his mouth, "give this a try."

Dipping the mystery meat into thick brown semiliquid that simmered above a small flaming tin of gelled butane fuel made me squeamish. The sauce resembled gravy but tasted like sweet potato. I wasn't convinced that drenching processed meats into baby food concoctions out-gourmet'd actual turkey and fixings. If this became an American tradition, I'd move to England.

"You should really get your heart rate up at least four times a week for forty minutes," the fondue queen told me.

She kept touching Dad's hand, and I had trouble focusing on her babbling. I wondered how she and Dad had connected and, more importantly, when they'd disconnect. When she fed him from her skewer, the visual made me want to hurl.

"If you lose something in the sauce," she told him, "you have to kiss the person on your right."

If I lost something, it wasn't going to be in the fondue pot.

"Course number two," Trudy announced, and I wondered if she giggled in her sleep. "Squash and purple potato squares accompanied by chive cheese sauce."

Fried chicken was a close substitute for turkey, and I hoped the drive-thru would be open tonight.

"You and Trudy," Dad said, "have something in common."

"Really," I said, pouring myself a generous glass of chardonnay. I figured Dad wouldn't flinch at my heavy hand since we had company. Searching the positive side, maybe Trudy could be beneficial; with her in the room, I could probably get away with lighting a joint.

"You're both a whiz in the kitchen."

"Rachael," Trudy said, "you and I should enroll in scullery classes."

"You mean culinary?"

"Everyone has to eat," Trudy said. "Wouldn't it be fabulous to pre-pare those fancy layered cakes you serve with tea and éclairs?"

I washed down my cheese-coated potato with an entire glass of wine and looked at my dad. He had to be testing me for—hell, I didn't know what.

Dad couldn't control his smile and his eyes beamed over Trudy. She was the kind of person who provided inspiration for a cartoonist. Thank God we weren't out in public. The two of them having fits of giggles when no one told a joke was embarrassing. I hoped that whatever was going on was an ephemeral thing. Then I started to worry. What if I lost him too?

SLEEPING IN MY OWN BED was the best part of being home. Each night I cracked my window and held my elbow out, careful not to extin-guish my cigarette in the snow that collected on the sill. Spending break with Dad and Trudy grated on my nerves. I actually used the excuse of studying to get away from them. Although Trudy didn't sleep over, they were never apart for long, and I wondered when Dad got his work done.

What had happened to my family? For eighteen years we were nor-mal-ish. Now, Mom was off seeking a vortex to channel, and Dad had dyed his hair, exercised, and dated. Wasn't I the one who was supposed to be doing crazy things? Mom and Dad had forgotten who the teenager was. My family dynamics had skidded off the rails, and now I seemed to be the sensible one. That was not right.

Nightly nicotine helped relax me, and I counted the days until my flight back to school. With Katie Lee and Nash in The Bern over break, I wondered if anything had happened. Retrieving a crumpled piece of paper from my backpack, I dialed Patsy McCoy.

"Hey, Raz," she greeted me, and I couldn't help but smile. Patsy McCoy was up to something. I heard it in her voice. "Has Bridget tried anything lately?"

Lying on my bed, I rested my feet on the wall. "It's bizarre. Bridget's sickeningly sweet, especially to Katie Lee. She's on her best behavior, offering to do Katie Lee's laundry, buying her sodas, and laughing at all her jokes. Always at her side, like a puppy after it crapped on the carpet."

"Lord," Patsy said, "what's she up to? Trying to convince Katie Lee she hung the moon?"

"Is anything going on in The Bern?"

"Somethin's always goin' on in The Bern. Guess what twosome I ran into?"

"Nash?"

"And Billy Ray."

My back stiffened. "Wait a minute. Last I heard Billy Ray stole Nash's tires. Why are they hanging out?"

"It gets better. I'm decorating my denim jacket, and I went to the Hobby Lobby for supplies. Billy Ray was buyin' paint thinner and canvas boards. Took all the ten-by-twelves off the shelf. Weird, huh?"

"Did they see you?"

"Of course they saw me. I stood right in front of the two of them and said hey."

"What'd they say?"

"Said, 'Hey, how's it going?'"

"What were they doing in there?"

"That's what I wanted to know. I asked what all the canvases were for. Billy Ray smirked. Said he was makin' homemade Christmas presents for his aunts."

"Really?"

I heard Patsy flicking a lighter and wished I were with her. "Those two are inta somethin'. Their faces looked like they'd been caught peeing in the pool."

"Paint thinner? Do you think they're planning arson? Patsy, what are we gonna do about Nash?"

"After checking out, Billy Ray got into a car with Jackson, and Nash left in his truck. I have a few friends quietly checkin' on some things. We need to figure out exactly what's goin' on before we set Nash on the path of redemption. Katie Lee needs to know what Nash is all about— from Nash. You and I are gonna make sure that happens."

"I don't know, Patsy. Nash is a professional screw-up. I mean how are we going to pull something convincing off?"

"I'm workin' on it. Just trust me."

I MET DAD AT HIS RESTORATION SHOP on Saturday morning. He wanted to show me a painting before we went out to lunch. His business headquarters was a nothing-special brick building near an industrial park and train tracks. No one would ever guess that one-of-a-kind masterpieces valued at five, six, and even seven figures moved in and out of the sliding barn doors.

Dad wore white cotton gloves and unwrapped a portrait. "Your mother bought this at a garage sale before she left." He laid the canvas under a white light on a worktable. "What do you think?"

"French. Sixteenth or seventeenth century."

"Good," he said, which surprised me. Dad rarely gave me compliments. Then he clarified, "Sixteenth. It's a Quesnel. Your mother paid one hundred fifty dollars. I met my buddy at the Cleveland Museum and had him take a look."

"What's the estimated value?"

"The frame isn't original, and there's some damage to the canvas, but the signature is authentic. Once it's refurbished we could get three to seven thousand."

"Way to go, Mom," I said, wishing she were here.

"Rachael, would you work on it when you come home for winter break?"

"Really?"

"Really. I'll give you a ten percent commission when it sells."

"Deal," I said, and we shook on it.

After rewrapping the painting, he slid it into a metal drawer. Some chair frames, a stripped sideboard, and three paintings on easels were in the workroom. "Are those the Clementine Hunters?"

Placing a hand on my back, Dad gave me a second compliment. "There's that sharp eye of yours. I miss it."

I wasn't accustomed to his niceties and fidgeted my toes inside my shoes.

"May I?" I asked, taking a magnifying glass from a tabletop. "I saw one of her landscapes in a New Bern gallery window."

"That's surprising. Not many come up for purchase."

"Is this a series?"

Dad stood behind me with his glasses on top of his head. "No. This one's titled *Baptism*. What piece did you see in New Bern?"

My heart palpitated. The Clementine Hunter I viewed through the display window was labeled *Baptism*. I'd received two compliments from Dad and hesitated to tell him, in case I was wrong. "I didn't get a close enough look. She's an amazing talent."

"Considering the poverty she lived in, Ms. Hunter defied the odds."

"The oil looks watered."

"To make them last," he said. "Her earlier works didn't feature many reds or pinks. Too expensive."

"The signature's unusual. It's centered on the right edge on the piece."

"Her artistic choice."

I stepped back. "The primitive style of plantation life is unique."

"That's what sets her apart. Makes her work collectable. Come on, Rachael, let me buy you lunch, then we'll do some shopping."

"Do you even know where the mall is?"

"Yeah, I have an idea."

"And you're willing to step foot inside? I mean actually go into stores that don't sell tennis shoes or electronics?"

"Looking forward to it."

I gave him a hug. "Dad, you're the best."

"Come on, we'll swing by and pick up Trudy."

NOTE TO SELF
Clementine Hunter—swear I saw the same painting in New Bern. Maybe I've been inhaling too much nicotine.

Dad has a girlfriend. How could he have found someone before I did?

December 1986

23

'Tis the Season

Back in North Carolina, the dismal fifty-degree weather was like a sunny vacation compared to Ohio. Despite the climate change, my temperament hovered in an icy zone. My disillusioned mood didn't stem from a yearning to be back in Canton. Nothing could have prepared me for four consecutive meals with Dad and Trudy over the break. Up north, home life brimmed with uncertainty. Thinking about Mom, Dad, and Trudy his girlfriend was complicated, and I didn't know what I could do to make things right. Being an adult wasn't how I pictured it. I longed for my parents to be the stay-married, get-back-together type. Contemplating those odds landed me on Denial Island. I liked my old life, and I didn't want it to change. Surely Mom and Dad missed the way things were and would find a way to make up. It would just take some time.

I'd survived the first day of classes since Thanksgiving break. Under bright sun, gusty winds tossed my hair like a mixer's whip blade that peaks egg whites. All the more reason to speed-walk toward the dorm. I had big news for the girls.

Thinking someone is witty and cute when you've been drinking is risky. It's like choosing a donut in the afternoon. They look decent, and you pick one with lots of icing, but once you take a bite, you realize it's stale. Thankfully I confirmed that Clay Sorenson—a.k.a. green jacket guy—is not a stale donut.

Today I spoke to him, sober. He was southern and could carry a conversation, which was good since I choked on most of my words. He'd been in my psychology lecture all semester, and I'd been too much of a wuss to approach him. After class, I stood to pack up, and my loose-leaf notes spilled into the aisle. Bending down to gather them up, I locked eyes with him as he handed me a page.

"I don't think we've met. I'm Clay Sorenson," he'd said, and I hung on his every word until I remembered to close my gaping mouth. I barely managed to sputter, "Rachael. O'Brien."

"Were you in the class right before Thanksgiving break?" he asked.

"Yeah."

"I missed that one. Could I borrow your notes?"

He made me so nervous that I forgot how to take in air. Fumbling with my binder, I pulled out the notes and hiccupped.

"Is it okay if I return them to you next week?" he asked.

"Keep them as long as you like."

"Great. Thanks," he'd said and left.

On my way across campus, I scolded myself. I should've penciled my phone number on the pages, in case he wanted to deliver them to my dorm. Monster news has a short life expectancy, and if I didn't tell someone in the next five minutes, the words would explode out of me and into the ears of some stranger.

A half block from my dorm an arm engulfed my waist and a deep voice with a twang whispered, "Did ya miss me?"

I turned around and punched Hugh in the shoulder. "Don't do that to me. I almost doo-dooed my pants."

He tussled my hair and walked with me toward Grogan.

"How was your Thanksgiving?" I asked.

Bouncing a wood toothpick around his mouth with his tongue, he said, "Let's see, Dad never showed. He preferred to hunt elk in Montana, and Mom hit the bottle and passed out before one."

"Sorry."

He shrugged. "Wasn't all bad. I took the skiff out in the gulf and caught a red grouper. Twenty-one pounder. I cooked it on the grill and downed a partial case. How about yours?"

"Dad has a friend."

"What kind of friend?"

"Hopefully a short-term one."

Outside of the Grogan Hall lobby, a light rain spat out of the sunny sky. A droplet hit my cheek. Opening the door, he lodged his foot onto the corner. "You seem in a hurry. You got something goin' on?"

I walked backward. "Hopefully."

WALKING INTO MY ROOM, I was convinced I'd have a heart attack. I dropped my satchel on my desk ready to spill my newsflash, but Katie Lee distracted me. She was rifling through her underwear drawer, dropping the contents, piece by piece, onto the floor. A body lay stretched on my bed. Even with a towel turban hiding her hair and a magazine covering her face, I knew it was Macy. Who else in North Carolina would wear a "Mets" sweat shirt?

Tossing her magazine to the floor, she said, "Hey, Rach," and flipped onto her stomach.

Katie Lee didn't acknowledge me with her normal "Hey." Before I shared my scoop she asked, "Is any of my underwear in your drawer?"

"Is that something you two share?" Macy asked.

As challenging as it was, Katie Lee and I ignored her. "Rach, just check. I have a quiz today, and I'm missing my lucky purple-stripe bikinis. They haven't let me down all semester."

Opening my dresser drawer, I said, "Check for yourself. Are you sure you didn't leave them home over break?"

"They've been missin' since the trip we all took to The Bern. I thought I'd left them home back then, but I didn't find them over the break."

"Enough with the panty talk. After my psych lecture, Clay Sorenson introduced himself."

"Who the hell is that?" Macy asked.

"Holiday Inn, green jacket. My lust obsession."

She rocketed off the bed. "This is huge."

"O'Brien," Katie Lee said, "drop your pants. You must be wearing my lucky bikinis."

"That's gross," I said.

With crossed arms, Katie Lee eyed me suspiciously. I tugged a corner of a hot pink waistband from beneath my jeans. "Mine are solid pink."

Katie Lee pulled me by the arm. "Tell us what happened."

"When class ended, Clay walked up to me. He introduced himself and asked if he could copy my notes from a class he missed before break. My body went mashed potato."

"Did you butter your panties?" Macy asked.

"Macy," Katie Lee said, "that's nasty."

"When Clay enters my orbit, my hormones play havoc with my neurological system. If he sits anywhere near me, it'll be physically impossible to pay attention to Professor Hayes."

THE NIGHT BEFORE OUR first final, Katie Lee and I planned an all-nighter. Processed foods filled the brain-drain void, and soda cans and Doritos bags overflowed our garbage can. Bridget stood in our open doorway and asked Katie Lee, "Do you want me to quiz you on anything?"

Since Patsy and I were still working on formulating a plan to reveal the lies she and Nash hid behind, I faked tolerating her. The sight of her prickled my backside, triggering a recall of bathroom captivity. Sharing the burden of the secret with Patsy hadn't diminished the hurt the information would cause. If I'd slept with Nash, I'd have avoided Katie Lee. Not Bridget. She kept hourly tabs on my roommate, always complimenting her hair, what great colors of lip gloss she wore, blah, blah, blah. The two weren't even the same major, but Bridget wanted to know all about Katie Lee's classes. I had enough trouble keeping up with my own, let alone tracking someone else's. If Bridget felt remorseful, she tucked it under care and concern for Katie Lee.

As we studied under the hum of our fluorescent ceiling light, the night stayed quiet with occasional plumbing gurgles and floor creaks. Katie Lee sat at her desk with her head in a book and slurped something carbonated. My eyeballs ached, and I closed my lids to dull the fatigue.

I awoke panicky and thought I'd overslept a final. The digital clock read 3:00 a.m. Katie Lee heard me stand and rotated her head in my direction, but didn't say anything.

My fuzzy head clung onto my dream. *Bridget standing in the dorm hallway in high heels, wearing only a green jacket.* What grade would my psych professor give me if I filled a blue book analyzing relationships that cross a line of decency: "The Effect of Deceitful Friendships on the Inner Circle." I couldn't study psychology anymore and moved toward the built-in dresser.

"Rach," Katie Lee said from her desk chair. "Please don't tell me you're organizing."

"What are you talking about? I don't organize."

"You dusted and polished all your shoes, then arranged them from shortest to highest heel before the first time you used your fake ID. I watched you Windex the plastic containers of your cosmetics, lipsticks, and shampoos, then dry them with a Q-tip after the night you spent with Kentucky Travis. Now you plugged in an iron and pulled out your t-shirts and underwear. What's bothering you?"

On top of our dresser, I unfolded the smallest pieces of clothing I owned. "I'm freaked out about finals week, and smoothing the creases in my underwear makes me feel better." I didn't mention that her new best buddy had slept with her boyfriend a month ago. Knowing the secret I kept dodged the friend and roommate code of responsibility and ate at my core, but I'd waited so long and now I didn't have the guts to tell Katie Lee the truth.

"Everyone feels the same," she said. "It's one big cram session. You'll get through freshman year. We all will."

NOTE TO SELF

Clay Sorenson is hot, and when he talks, he's even hotter. I need a plan of action.

24

Sub-Zero Idling

The early rain had cleared and left puddles in the parking lot. I squinted against the sun that reflected off the wet asphalt. I'd finished my first semester at college, and to quote Macy, "What was done, was fuckin' done." Knots disappeared from my muscles, and my head had cleared. Now I'd wait. In a few weeks, my grades would turn up in the mail.

Bridget, Macy, and I helped pack Katie Lee's belongings into Big Blue. "I'm really looking forward to the break. Spendin' some quality time with Nash and seein' all my friends back in The Bern."

At the mention of Nash, Macy, Bridget, and I kept silent, each for our own reason.

I wished I felt the same about going home. Dad hadn't mentioned Trudy on the last phone call. Figuring *no news is good news*, I assumed the two had ended their thing, but avoided asking. I considered dating a nonsafe topic and didn't like delving over the line that he and I avoided.

"Promise you'll call me if anything monumental happens," I told Katie Lee. "And be sure to let Patsy and Mitch know that I wish them a fabulous holiday."

Macy cooed at the mention of Mitch.

"It's Christmas, the season of care and joy."

Katie Lee put the key in Big Blue. "I bet Mitch would prefer your gift of goodwill in person."

Bridget let out a sigh. "Should be interesting to see who I room with next semester."

"What do you mean?" I asked.

She shrugged. "My roommate isn't coming back to Grogan."

"What's up with that?" asked Macy.

"She's moving off-campus with some friends."

"That sucks," Katie Lee said.

"I just hate the thought of adjusting to a stranger. If anyone's interested, I have space available."

"I like my privacy," Macy said.

"Rach and I are staying put. Ask around and see if anyone is interested."

Bridget rolled a rock around under her shoe. "If none of y'all want to switch, the best I can hope for is that I don't get assigned a roommate."

"I'm sure it'll work out," I said, not caring if it did.

"But look at Mama," Bridget said. "What if I get a roommate like her?"

I'd seen Macy and Francine in the take down and wasn't overly sure who clinched that battle.

Clicking her red nails, Macy said, "If that happens, you'd have to kill her."

Katie Lee and I laughed while Bridget stared, not finding humor in the sarcasm.

Big Blue's engine turned over, and Katie Lee said, "Merry Christmas, y'all."

JUST AFTER CHRISTMAS, KATIE LEE phoned my house. "I'm havin' a fabulous break. Lots of parties, and I've been out on the boat a few times."

From under my electric blanket in Canton, I said, "I'm jealous."

"Guess who was askin' about you."

"I don't know."

"Billy Ray. Wanted to know your home phone number."

"Please tell me you didn't give it to him."

Katie Lee laughed. "Don't worry, I made up an excuse."

I closed my eyes in relief.

"I broke the news to my parents about the anniversary wine."

"Are you grounded forever?"

"Nah, they were cool. Didn't make too big a deal of it."

"You never cease to amaze me. What else is going on in The Bern?"

"Nash and I are spendin' a lot of romantic time together."

Romantic time with you and how many others? The thought made me want to yak. "Make sure you take precautions. You don't need a love child."

"Don't worry, we're careful."

"How are the McCoys?" I asked.

"Daddy reminded Patsy and me that we'll be muckin' barnacles off fiberglass when I get home from spring semester. I'd hoped he'd forgotten about that."

She didn't mention Mitch. Not wanting to seem overly interested, I didn't ask. When I hung up, I noticed that Dad had left a package in my doorway. A pint of Kentucky bourbon arrived from Travis. The note read, "Thought you could use something to survive the Canton winter."

Travis and I had spoken a few times since Halloween and become kindred hearts. I wished for more. If he ever became disgruntled with his current sexual preference, I'd enthusiastically volunteer myself to bring him back to team female. For now, we were buddies.

A postcard with an *I love NY* tattooed on a voluptuous ass arrived a few days into the New Year. Luckily Dad was at his shop and I'd brought the mail in.

Happy New Year!
Hanging out with the old crowd in Queens.
Rang in '87 with a ball drop (the one in Times Square).
Vaguely recall the night. Will share what I remember.
See you in a few.
-M-

OVER BREAK I PRAYED FOR divine intervention. Anything would do: a lightning bolt that erased Trudy's memory of Dad, a torn gluteus maximus to keep her in her apartment. I was open to options, but nothing extraordinary happened. The novelty of Trudy lasted the entire break. In addition to her, Dad found a new obsession. Locks. He rekeyed the house and the shop. Each night I heard him turn the dead bolts on the front door and slide the chain. Then he moved to the back door. I guessed he worried that Mom would just show up and let herself in. His worst fear was my wish.

Scumbling and glazing the Francois Quesnel portrait kept me busy. I spent more time with my father than I ever remember, and during the day the meticulous detailing kept my mind from overly obsessing about Mom, Dad's annoying girlfriend, and the North Carolina crew. In the evening, when I snuck in my room to sip bourbon and smoke ciggies, I pondered all of them.

The night before I was due to leave, Mom called. She and Dad didn't say much. I wondered if they'd spoken before about what she was doing, if she needed money, and when she was coming back, but Dad hadn't shared anything with me. Mom asked me about my first semester, and I gave standard answers to her standard questions.

After I hung up, I found myself staring at the clothes that still hung in her wardrobe. Dad didn't know what to do with her things, and neither did I. As much as she hurt us, it didn't seem right to throw them away or give her stuff to charity. Not yet. Gripping a handful of fabric, I pulled it to my face and drank in the only touchable thing left of the mother who raised me. Standing in her closet, I realized even though

I considered my dad overly neurotic and annoying, he loved me. I could easily read his emotions; they weren't hidden or complicated. Sometimes you don't realize what you have until it's gone. I wasn't ever going to let go of him.

NOTE TO SELF
Working in Dad's shop took off the monotonous edge of being at home and will fatten my wallet.

Trudy is like a rash—infectiously annoying.

I made zero progress with Clay. Not sure if I'll get another chance next semester.

January 1987

25

What the Tarnation?

Gray clouds collected in the Carolina winter sky, casting gloom onto the campus landscape. Handing the taxi driver a crisp twenty, I slid off the plastic taxi seat and stood in front of Grogan Hall. Having one semester under my belt, I'd learned a few things:

1. Avoid wet riverbanks—breeding grounds for chigger patches. And chiggers can lead to a whole lot of trouble.

2. Don't fool around with Mitch. Despite his cute looks and smooth-talking southern, he's too young.

3. Never sip a drink Bridget offers.

4. Avoid contact with Nash Wilson and Billy Ray.

5. Refocus on Clay Sorenson.

Being a seasoned freshman, I was ready to navigate my way through semester number two. Carrying a duffel on my shoulder, I raced down the twenty-six steps toward the lobby. I'd missed the girls and wanted to hear details about their holiday breaks.

Inside the dorm elevator, I pressed number seven and wondered what my chances were of having another class with Clay. Probably the same odds as winning the jingle bell scratch card jackpot.

With a jolt the metal doors opened, delivering a rancid stink. Holding my hand on the door, I poked my head into the hallway and hoped that it was the wrong floor. It wasn't. Hustling toward my room, I searched my database of disgusting to identify the smell. My best match: old tennis shoe inserts splashed with sapsago cheese. Some aspects of dorm life I hadn't missed.

Before I unlocked my door, I knocked on Macy's. Giving her a hug, I asked, "What's that smell?"

"It's not me. We're lucky we're on the far end of the floor. It's worse near the elevators."

From behind us, Katie Lee said, "Y'all are lookin' marvelous." Out of breath, she asked, "Can I get a hand emptying my car? Mom sent me back with groceries, and I got a new boom box for Christmas."

Near the elevator Katie Lee pinched her nose. "Good Lord."

"Gross Grogan," Macy said.

"Something is seriously decayed. Has anyone looked for a dead animal in the stairwell?"

"That's creepy," I said. "How would anything get past the lobby and into an enclosed stairway?"

"I don't do basements or stairwells," Macy said. "I'm certainly not checking."

Big Blue's back seat and trunk heaved. Katie Lee had brought back more than groceries and a boom box. Her stash also included an overstuffed upholstered chair, a beanbag, a coffee table, and all her sweaters, coats, and winter gear. The armchair, covered in a psychedelic stripe, poked out from a bungee cord lock system meant to keep the trunk closed. It took us three trips to unload. When we finished, you couldn't see floor in our room.

Making an excuse about a phone call, Macy said, "Good luck with all that."

Trapped behind a mound of stuff, I stated the obvious. "Katie Lee, we don't have room."

Leaving her coat on, she grabbed her car keys. "Rach, we need to build up."

I looked at my chest. "Mine will never look built up."

"Not boob implants, a loft. Come on."

BEHIND A QUICKIE MARKET, Katie Lee kept the engine running while I stuffed milk crates into Big Blue.

"Try 'n' get all gray ones," she'd said.

I ignored her and rushed to fill up the car. I just wanted this loft built so I could get to campus and look for Clay Sorenson. He had to eat, and I guessed the cafeteria was the best location for a sighting. I planned to linger there as much as possible, and building a loft cut into my surveillance work.

I'd filled the car with crates when the employee door of the convenience store opened. I leapt to the front seat. "If I'm going to get arrested, it better not be for this."

Katie Lee jammed the gas pedal. "Buckle in," she said and gunned us out of the alley.

It took three more trips to the parking lot to carry the milk crates into our room. Somewhere in the hallway, I heard Hugh say hey to Macy. A knuckle rap clunked our wood veneer, and we watched the door inch open a quarter of the way before it nailed the pile of furniture and crates.

Half of Hugh's face jutted around the door, and he shimmied in. "Y'all look hotter than jalapeño corn bread."

Not initially recognizing him, I squealed.

"Oh my Lord," Katie Lee said.

"You shaved it off!" I shouted, unable to resist touching Hugh's smooth upper lip.

"I like the look," Katie Lee said.

An appreciative grin raised his cheeks.

We gave him respectable hugs in exchange for help building the loft. By dinnertime, my bed towered above Katie Lee's on two four-by-six pieces of lumber that rested on a foundation of vertically stacked milk crates.

"Is it sturdy?" I asked.

Lifting me up by my waist, he said, "There's one way to find out."

A muffled "eeew" and a scream erupted from down the hall.

Hugh lowered me to the floor. "Someone got a birthin' goat?"

Macy bounded into our room. "That sounded like Bridget."

Already in the hall, Katie Lee said, "C'mon."

A herd of Lookie-Lous, including Francine, pinched their noses as they gathered outside Bridget's room. After a quick snoop, dorm residents made speedy exits. The open door released an aroma that overpowered what had lingered in front of the elevators. Francine waved her hand in front of her face. "Lord, girl, your room has more stink than the public park porta-potties on the Fourth of July."

Bridget's bags lay in a heap on her floor. Something I didn't want to identify had been splattered across her baby-blue cement block walls. The cranberry and donut cream goo had dried in a design that reminded me of my dad's painter's apron. Paralyzed, she cupped her hands over her mouth and nose. Under rapid blinking, tears welled above her reddened cheeks.

On tiptoes, I peered from behind Hugh's shoulder. "Your room is trashed."

Her drawers and closets had been hastily emptied. Clothes and bedding lay strewn across the room. Two twin mattresses spilled from their frames. When I noticed the slits in them, I wished I hadn't made the insensitive comment about her messy room.

Forgetting to turn on his word-filter device, Hugh said, "It looks like someone hurt themselves jackin'—ouch, Macy."

Macy hadn't smacked him quickly enough.

Bridget gasped. "Oh God, I'm going to be sick if that's what's on my walls."

Wondering whose boyfriend she fooled around with now, I asked, "Did your roommate do this?"

"She wouldn't. We were friends. Besides, she left for break before I did."

Katie Lee pushed buttons on Bridget's phone. "I'm calling campus security."

It must have been a slow night, because Tuke Walson arrived just minutes after Katie Lee hung up. Ironed creases ran down the center of his pants, and a white undershirt applied pressure to the buttons that held his shirt together.

"Any idea who could've done this?"

"No sir," Bridget said.

"Did you lock up before break?"

"Of course she did," Katie Lee said.

Asking questions, taking Polaroids, and jotting notes, Tuke poked around the room. He stopped in front of the electric heater and pulled a sweat shirt off an open container of calcium-fortified milk. "Leave an open container of milk near a heat source, and you got yourself a carton of nasty." He crinkled his face and put the sweat shirt back. "That there is one cooked quart." It didn't take him long to tell Bridget, "I'm finished. Someone from the janitorial staff will contact you."

Exasperated and looking at the disarray, Bridget didn't know if anything had been stolen. He sympathized with her and said, "If there's anything missing, you can file a supplemental report."

"Is this going around?" Katie Lee asked. "Has there been a rash of milk-bomb break-ins?"

"No, ma'am. This is the first I've encountered, but college kids never cease to amaze me. Exploding toilets, now that buggers things into a real mess. My guess is that you know who did this. An ex-boyfriend?"

Pulling a pen from his pocket protector, he scraped at the crud on the wall.

Hugh lifted his nose from under his shirt to say, "You're a brave man."

"That there's condiment," Tuke said.

"Is that what you call it?" Hugh asked.

He shrugged. "It's all-American. Everyone puts ketchup and mayo on popcorn shrimp and hush puppies." After placing a business card on Bridget's dresser, he said, "Ladies, be sure and lock your doors. And call me if you notice anything out of the ordinary."

Macy liberally sanitized the seventh-floor hallway with an entire can of Lysol, while Katie Lee borrowed fans, and I disposed of the foul milk in the outside Dumpster. When I returned, Hugh had refilled the mattress stuffing and placed them back in their frames. He motioned Katie Lee and Bridget outside the door, and I heard him offer his escort services to accompany them to the basement washing machines.

"I'm totally freaked out," Bridget said. She asked Katie Lee, "Can I sleep in your room tonight?"

Without asking me, Katie Lee said, "Of course."

Hugh huddled with the two, wrapping them in his arms. "If y'all feel you need extra protection..."

"Forget it, Hugh," Katie Lee said. "You're not sleeping in our room."

"I was going to say I have a Smith and Wesson snub nose you can borrow. It's compact. Help ya sleep soundly."

"Keeping a firearm in a dorm is so illegal," Bridget said. "You realize you could get expelled."

"Let's just say I take self-defense seriously."

"Where is it stashed?" Bridget whispered.

"It's not welcome in our room," I shouted.

Hugh was crazy to loan Bridget a firearm. She'd probably get wigged out with dorm noises and accidently shoot someone on their way to the hall bathroom. He lowered his voice and said something else to Bridget.

I moved toward the door to further protest the gun thing, but he distracted me when he said, "Hey, I know some guys who are throwing an off-campus party tomorrow night. Y'all wanna come?"

"Definitely," Katie Lee said before she left with Bridget to throw in a load of laundry.

Francine emerged from the room across from Bridget's. She'd put a relaxer on her hair and warmed the gelatinous conditioner under a Saran Wrap shower cap that was secured with a gigantic rubber band. Lingering in Bridget's doorway, she said, "Hugh, I need someone about your height to help me hang a shelf."

"That's what all the women say."

"Are you daft?" she asked. "If I needed somethin' personal taken care of, I wouldn't be dressed like this."

Francine dragged Hugh down the hall, and the two disappeared. Macy shut Bridget's door.

"Are you crazy?" I asked. "It still stinks in here."

Bridget's phone rang. We both looked at it, and on the third ring Macy picked it up. She told the person on the other line that Bridget wasn't around and asked if she could take a message. When she hung up, she wore a twisted and confused look I'd seen before.

"Who was that?"

Macy scrunched her nose. "The accent was thick. I think he said Billy Ray."

"You're kidding? Why would he call her?"

Macy shrugged, "Maybe I misunderstood."

"This vandalism thing is weird."

She stuck her head out the window. When she brought it back in she asked, "Who could get in here over break and do this to her room?"

"I don't know," I said. My mind went into overdrive, and Bridget's behavior toward Katie Lee nettled at me. Why did she continue to hover in a deceitful friendship with my roommate? Why not spill what she'd done or cut ties? It could only be one of two reasons: a cheater high—having gotten away with naughty sex—or Katie Lee had something that Bridget wanted.

NOTE TO SELF
Vandalism on the seventh floor. Completely disturbing.

Bridget is sleeping in our room. I didn't agree to a loft so our room could accommodate three.

26

Better Than a Bundt Cake

Standing around in long registration lines inside a stuffy, sweat-infested gymnasium lowered my blood sugar and put me into a vegetative state. I needed to snap out of my funk if I was going to enjoy tonight's party at the yellow house. Fresh air and searching campus for Clay seemed like a good break.

Rushing through the late afternoon chill, I dodged the spit of rain. I'd been gone all day and hoped that Bridget's stuff had been dragged out of our room and back into hers. For safety purposes, I'd slept with a curling iron under my pillow and still had a dull crimp in my neck. Clay wasn't in the gymnasium or the empty cafeteria. The North Carolina College campus covered 220 acres, and I started to become disillusioned with the idea of finding him on the off chance.

Last semester he'd asked to copy my notes, once. He hadn't asked for my phone number or what dorm I lived in. Sensibilities pointed to the exit sign out of fantasyland, but reality village could be dull, and I wasn't ready to give up just yet.

On a final detour through the halls of Moore dorm, I stopped to see Hugh. "Hey, Rach," he said, giving me a hug. Pulling darts out of the target that hung on his door, he handed them to me.

"How was your ho, ho, ho?"

"Don't ask."

"I take it your dad is still seeing Trudy."

I snarled my face as an answer. Standing behind a piece of duct tape adhered to the linoleum, I launched my darts and wondered why I'd come for a visit, 'cause it wasn't to talk about my father's girlfriend.

"God damn, you throw like a marksman. Did you hear from your mom over break?"

I hit two bull's-eyes. "Are you trying to distract me with unpleasant conversation?"

"Rach, your family doesn't come close to my family's wackadoo. I just figure that stuff is, you know, better out."

Releasing a sigh, I settled on his desk chair. "Mom sent a package postmarked from Sedona and called once."

Throwing a horrible round, he asked, "What was inside?"

"Tarot cards and celestial earrings."

"Do you think she's really psychic? 'Cause if she is, maybe she can tell me when I'll beat her daughter in a game of darts."

"Very funny."

He glanced at a wall clock. "Are you thirsty?"

"Parched. First, I need to grab a jacket from Grogan."

"We can collect the girls and head to the yellow house."

A brisk wind kicked up leaves, and I tucked my hands deep into my jean pockets. Hugh and I didn't pass anybody on our walk to Grogan. Things on campus were quiet. Too quiet. So I asked, "Are you ever going to make a move on Macy, or is she too much throttle?"

"What are you talking about?"

"Come on. It's obvious."

Hugh stared at a squirrel that raced past us. "Rachael, men don't discuss men moves. It's against code."

I scoffed. He didn't fool me. Early termination of the Macy discussion sent my bullshit meter swinging, and I wondered if tonight would be a game changer.

"Did you stay busy over break?" Hugh asked.

"Ate, drank, and slept."

"You must've done something interesting."

My teeth chattered against the chill that crept under my clothes. "I refurbished a Quesnel portrait at Dad's shop."

"How does it look?"

"Amazing. Cleaning and glazing the piece brought out the facial shadows and deepened the colors. My dad's going to give me ten percent commission when it sells."

Hugh opened Grogan's lobby door. "You saved a masterpiece."

"My first one."

THE TIPS OF HUGH'S COWBOY BOOTS were silver, and the soles scraped the asphalt with each step he took. He led Katie Lee, Bridget, Macy, and me through an eclectic neighborhood of 1950s two-story, vinyl-sided homes that bordered campus. Dormant grass had turned dull, and patches of brown butted against the street. Bridget now slept in our room, and as far as I could tell, she didn't have any imminent plans to move out. I couldn't tolerate living with her and had to say something.

"Almost there," Hugh said.

"None of these houses are yellow," Macy said. "Are you sure you know where you're going?"

"How far is this place?" Bridget asked. "My feet are killing me."

Hugh stopped and leaned forward. His black-and-red buffalo plaid shirttail dangled over his jeans. Offering a piggyback, he said, "Hop on," and Bridget accepted.

"Are you sure the house doesn't have yellow trim?" Katie Lee asked. "Like that one?"

"I'm thirsty," I said.

"Y'all settle down." He pointed. "The yellow house is just ahead."

"That color is revolting," Macy said.

Beyond a fence with missing pickets rested the yellow house. I had to agree with Macy. The yellow I stared at wasn't pastel as I'd imagined. The siding was golden while the shutters, gutters, trim, and front door had been painted chocolate brown. Buckled steps led us to a recessed door where I tripped over a raised floor plank. Hugh caught my arm before I ate wood. Tonight I'd be partying inside a collapsing sunflower.

After some random introductions, Hugh handed me a plastic cup. "Follow me."

We all tailed him along a hallway lined with framed Bob Marley posters. "Cool," Hugh said, stopping to look at the still-shot photographs.

"No pinholes or creases. The color hasn't faded, and they're signed with a Sharpie. That's key. If the signature is authentic, these are keepers."

Wrapping his arm around my neck, Hugh guided me to the back porch where someone had already tapped a keg. "My art connoisseur. How much should I offer for them?"

"Wait till the end of the year. Maybe they'll be tired of them. Start at seventy-five dollars."

The drinking started as it always did, slow and steady. Tapping a pack of Benson & Hedges on my palm, I relished kicking back without a thought of things in Ohio, looming papers, and Mom. My second cup chilled my throat and warmed my face. The guys in the house weren't cigarette smokers, so I ended up out back in a circle of empty metal-frame lawn chairs. Southern winters were more civilized than the ones in Ohio, and I didn't mind.

I lifted my heels onto a cracked plastic chair and wrapped my arms around my legs, trapping heat between my chest and knees. Mindlessly I pondered trivial things like getting a head start reading my textbooks and whether I should've worn socks. The squeaky storm door slammed shut, and Bridget appeared double-fisted, with a third cup clenched between her teeth. She mumbled, "Help."

Rescuing the two cups out of her hands, I set them down. If this was her peace offering, she could forget it. After blacking out in New Bern, I'd never drink a beer she handed me. She settled into the chair next to me, and I wished we weren't alone. Our relationship rested on the perimeter of a superficial friendship. Her agenda seemed complex, whereas mine was simple. She needed to remove herself and Hugh's gun from my room, and I decided to address the topic. "Looks like you have a single room this semester."

Draining one beer, she stacked the empty cup under another.

"Things seem to be working out."

"What do you mean?"

"Katie Lee called housekeeping. Tomorrow they're scrubbing my walls and bringing a new mattress. A crew is painting on Sunday. You and Katie Lee have been really sweet to let me stay in your room. Is it okay if I bunk with you two more nights?"

I thought no, but my lips said, "Yeah."

Bridget's camera hung on a strap around her neck. Setting down the beer, she adjusted the lens and peered through it. "The room trashing was the last thing I needed after a brutal holiday."

The froth relaxed on her second cup, and she nearly emptied it before setting it down.

"What happened?"

"Christmas hasn't been easy since my mom passed away."

A soft current blew over my face, brushing the strands of brunette hair that fell out of my ponytail. We both had lost our mothers, but there was a chance that I'd get mine back.

"I didn't know. I'm sorry."

She pointed the camera at me. "Can I take your picture?"

I shrugged.

It ground in a continuous click, four or five times.

She rested it on her chest and picked up her cup. "It's been ten years since she took all those pills. You never get comfortable with the hollow feeling. The last few years, my dad's become a habitual dater. Sharing

Christmas with someone who won't be around by Easter is annoying. If I could've stayed at school over break, I'd have done it."

My beer had gotten warm, but I finished it anyway. "I get what you're talking about." I didn't understand why my mom left. If she hadn't figured out who she was in forty years, the chances of having a cosmic revelation had to be slim.

"I think it helps being away from home," Bridget said. "Classes keep me busy, and I'm not around the reminders."

The back door creaked open. I didn't recognize the girls who came outside for a smoke.

"Reminders?" I asked.

Bridget stacked another empty cup under her third beer. "It's hard being around the objects that carry memories. The smaller they are, the bigger the trigger. I can't go near Mom's jewelry. She used to wear a locket around her neck. When I sat in her lap I always opened and closed it, peeking at the picture of her and Dad before they were married. It conjures images in my head, and I daydream about what she'd look like, what she'd say if she were still around."

Muffled voices inside the sunflower house grew louder as more people arrived, but outside the air hung still. Not sure what to say, I lit a cigarette. I liked denial and hadn't shared my internal raw with anyone.

Leaning toward me, Bridget whispered, "Do you think we can ever be who we were, you know, before we were abandoned?"

I crushed my empty cup. Abandoned wasn't a word I liked. All this time I'd told myself that Mom was on an extended vacation, exploring a hobby with a group of new friends. Bridget's comment stung my heart. I didn't want to talk about it anymore. I hadn't forgotten the betrayal Bridget had performed with Nash. She hadn't ever been interested in my family, and I wasn't going to open up to her.

Music blared, and the house brimmed with people. I stood to move inside when the screen door partially opened then shut. No one came out. It happened again. The third time a foot I recognized kicked the door off its bottom hinge. Katie Lee and Macy had arms wrapped around one another and stumbled toward us. I didn't know who led who until Katie Lee said, "Can someone help me out?"

Bridget and I escorted Macy to a chair.

"I found this New Yorker wearing a lampshade and holding a toilet brush torch, posin' as the Statue of Liberty at the top of the stairs."

"Is that the shirt you wore over here, or have you borrowed someone's?" I asked.

Macy pinched my cheeks. "You're so cute when you're drunk."

The Macy magic show climaxed when she pulled her bra out of her sleeve and threw it in the bushes.

I left the backyard burlesque show to find a bathroom. I had a feeling this was going to be a long night and looked forward to the rest of the evening with a "what's next" kind of curiosity.

Pushing past a hallway packed with bodies, I didn't immediately recognize the sexy southern drawl that said, "Rachael O'Brien, you weren't going to pass by without saying hey, were you?"

INSIDE THE SUNFLOWER HOUSE, speakers pulsed a Van Morrison song about a moon dance. I gawked at the guy who had called my name. Clay Sorenson's dark, tousled hair gave his good looks a boyish charm, and the green jacket he wore matched his eyes. As he closed the gap between us, my chest exploded as though Pop Rocks had been sprinkled into my vital organs. My mind went momentarily static, ruining any clarity I may have summoned for clever conversation. If Clay hit on me, I'd gladly lose my virginity on the spot.

Since he'd seen me and said hello first, I guessed he'd broken off whatever had been going on with She-Devil. The last I saw of her, she'd thrown a hissy fit, kicking her espadrilles under Clay's arm as he removed her from the Holiday Inn. I would've considered it heavenly if I never blinked in front of the redhead again.

"What classes did you register for?" he asked.

"Art history, literature two, biology, and—"

"Art history? Hope you don't have Professor Schleck."

"I do. What do you know about her?"

Clay choked. "I had her last year. Her blue book essays are notori-ous. She pulls questions out of the indexes and fine print footnotes. No one has ever gotten an A. You might want to drop and pick another elective."

"I can't drop. Art history is my major, and Professor Schleck is my advisor."

"Art history? Do you want to work in a museum?"

"For a few years."

"Then what?"

"I want to discover new artists."

"You want to fill the world with masterpieces? Rachael O'Brien, you're full of surprises."

We shouted above the party noise, and eventually moved into the kitchen. I thought modest amounts of alcohol relaxed you. It didn't work that way for me when Clay was around. My eyes darted, I shuffled my feet and fumbled with my hands, unsure where to keep them. With my back to the kitchen sink, he stood inches in front of me. When he rested his empty cup on the counter, his hand brushed my arm. "Hold still," he said, smoothing an eyelash off my cheek. I worked hard to settle jitters that threatened to sabotage the moment.

From behind, someone squeezed my arm. Turning, I held my breath and got a face full of Bridget as she flicked her highlighted blonde wisps. Her intentions concerned me. I didn't need company around Clay, and I didn't introduce her.

"Rach, we're leaving."

"Already?"

"Macy keeps taking her clothes off. Katie Lee and I are walking her to Grogan."

It had taken me an entire semester to find some quality alone-time with Clay, and I hesitated.

"Not sure if we'll make it back," she said.

"What about Hugh?" I asked.

"Haven't seen him."

"You're not leaving, are you?" Clay asked.

Not wanting to end my Clay encounter, I squashed the little voice that told me not to walk to Grogan alone. He possessed a magical force that I longed to experience. Gambling that I'd have a tall and heavenly escort, I told Bridget, "I'll see you at the dorm."

She began to step away, but backtracked. "If you see Hugh, tell him we left."

Clay and I still had to shout at one another above the party chatter. "I'm bummed," he said, "that we're not signed up for any of the same classes."

He didn't mention being engaged, betrothed, or having a steady girlfriend. Giving him every ounce of my attention, I soaked him in like a fragrant flower. Clay Sorenson embodied everything I imagined I wanted in a lover.

When I polished off my beer, a drip slid down my chin. This was not the way to get into bed with him. I needed to get a grip. Excusing myself for a moment, I left Clay to use the bathroom, check my hair, and reapply lip gloss.

My bathroom karma could have been better. Upstairs I waited in a long line. It gave me time to have a lengthy conversation with myself. I needed to jail my nerves. If this was how I acted around men, I'd die an old maid. Shutting the bathroom door, I sucked wind from outside the window. After touching up my hair and reapplying some gloss to my lips, I straightened my back, ready to conquer.

Crammed bodies in the kitchen made it impassable. It took a minute, but I spied Clay. Inhaling deeply, I unfastened button number three on my IZOD shirt and navigated past the partiers who cluttered my path. He stood alone, his back facing me. I cleared my throat before I moved forward, but froze when I spotted perfectly sculpted nails glide down his arm and onto his hip. The auburn hair on the girl wrapping herself around him triggered a warning. When the silhouette of her jaw turned my direction, my feet locked. A cold sweat erupted down my spine, and a round of rapid-fire hiccups erupted. The thought of confronting She-Devil without Grogan Girl backup scared me.

Pressing her chest to his back, she mouthed, "Hey, baby," into his ear. I held my hand over my mouth and pushed my way toward the nearest exit.

Partygoers had overtaken the backyard and stood huddled in groups. With my back to the house, I rested my hands on my knees and swallowed hard. Clay and She-Devil were more than friends. If I'd known that, I would've left with the girls. As soon as I stopped hiccupping, I planned to sprint the three miles back to the dorm.

Breathing deeply, I kept my head focused on the ground. With a tunneled view of dirt, the tails of a red-and-black-check shirt entered my peripheral vision. Before I saw his face, I knew it was Hugh.

"Hey," I hiccupped.

He squatted down and handed me his beer. "Where is everyone?"

I took a sip. "They left."

"What are you still doing here?"

Peering around his shoulder, I checked the back door.

"Rach, what's going on?"

"Do you remember the night we all met?"

"How could I forget? I wore a beer down my pants."

"I just spotted the redhead who delivered that drink."

The memory stiffened his legs, and he crossed them. "Here?" he asked, looking around.

"In the kitchen."

"Rach, I'd do anything for you, but I don't fight girls."

"I'm not looking for round number two. Wanna head back?"

Motioning for me to wait, he pounded the beer. Folding an arm around my shoulder, he led the way around the side of the house.

From the street, I glanced back. A pocket of light flooded out from the kitchen window. Getting to know Clay was like riding the twirly-whirly at the fair. My chest contracted, my nerves pulsed, and I wanted to scream until my stomach flip-flopped like I'd throw up. Was he a player, looking for a new harvest of flowers? Would I be just another conquest? I didn't want to be easily forgotten.

AT 11:00 P.M., AN AUTOMATIC timer turned the hall lights inside Grogan off, and only the exit signs near stairs and elevators glowed. Leaning against the wall just outside my doorframe, I felt like a numb-nut for being attracted to Clay. He was handsome, charming, and involved with a redheaded beauty who'd probably eat her young.

Why didn't I say something cutting to She-Devil instead of hiccup-ping? I'd ruined my chances with Clay. In the deserted dorm hall I sank to the floor, reinventing a better ending than the one I'd run away from, when the exit door at the nearby stairwell clicked, pulling me out of my head. Two shadowy figures, one short and plump, the other slim and tall, thumped against the wall. Suctioned together in a lip-lock, the two rotated toward me like soft serve ice cream filling a cone. In daylight, they would've noticed me, but in the dark hallway, I blended into the wall.

Patting my pockets, I searched for my room key. Why was it that couples got to naked business when I was around? Once again, I was trapped. If I stood, they'd notice me, and if I stayed put, I'd see an overprescribed amount of exhibitionism. Hoping they wouldn't chris-ten the hallway, I froze and did my best to meld into the floor.

Francine's late night dessert fumbled with her door lock. He held her hand and moved backward into her room. Before she had both feet over her threshold, she tilted her head and spotted me. Slinging her hand to her chest, she hissed, "Lord, girl, you look like a corpse that's gone stiff. How long you been sittin' there?"

"Is that a trick question?"

"Are you gonna report me?"

"About what?"

Francine sighed. "I owe you," she said, and slipped into her room. It was good to be back.

NOTE TO SELF
Abandonment issues? Bridget and I have more in common than I knew.

Difficult to control the urge to throw myself into Clay's arms. With She-Devil lurking, I couldn't.

Francine's found herself a little something, something.

February 1987

27

The Southern Storm

biting wind stirred campus, and by late afternoon the sky coughed wet sleet. I hadn't worn a pair of socks since my senior year in high school. During the Ohio winter, it drove my father nuts. I'd done it as a rebellious payback for keeping my curfew at ten. It had given me pleasure to irritate him as much as the curfew irritated me. Being four hundred miles away from Canton, with Mom gone, the things I'd done and said back home now seemed childish. *When you think you know it all, you really don't know shit.* I thought I wanted to sleep with Clay, but I had competition, and now I wasn't so sure. I wished I was as experienced as Macy. Maybe then my head wouldn't spin in analysis paralysis. To clear my mind and stop myself from obsessing, I needed fresh air and broke my self-imposed sock abstinence for the trek to a campus bookstore.

After half an hour, I abandoned my brain cleansing and retreated to the dorm. On the lobby sofas, a crowd of regulars munched popcorn and drank Diet Pepsi while they watched *Love Boat* reruns. The rain had soaked through my clothes and suctioned my socks to my canvas tennis shoes, forcing me to strip off my footwear. Dormitories are giant petri dishes. In an effort to contain any friendly fungus, I tiptoed onto the elevator and down the seventh-floor hallway. Before I made it into my room, Macy grabbed my arm and pulled, shutting her door behind us.

Wondering who she'd offended today, I asked, "What's going on?"

Sinking into her beanbag, she picked at her cuticles. "Lock it."

Something was going on, which caused my left eyebrow to lift. I stood with wet pants sticking to my skin. "Well?"

"I want your word that what I'm about to tell you will stay totally and completely confidential."

"What have you done?"

She pointed a red nail at me. "Promise?"

Strands of hair clung to my neck, and I blinked away a drip that fell into my eyelashes. "I promise."

"Last night at the yellow house when I went to use the bathroom, Hugh asked if I wanted to smoke happy grass."

I rolled my eyes and dropped my soggy socks and shoes. "Hold on." After removing my windbreaker, I made myself a cozy spot on her bed and stuffed a roll pillow behind my back.

"Are you comfortable?"

Crossing my legs at the ankle, I rested my hands behind my head. "Now I am. This oughta be good."

"We went into a back bedroom to light up. We smoked a lot of weed."

"Uh-huh."

"We were goofing around, wrestling over something stupid, when he kissed me. He gave me tongue, and his hand was on my left boob."

I sat upright. "Oh God. What kind of bodily harm did you inflict on him?"

"Sober, I'm not attracted to Hugh. Stoned, he reminded me of a juicy hot dog. The kind street vendors sell in Manhattan, and I couldn't help myself."

"Wait a minute, you're a vegetarian."

"A vegetarian that fell off the wagon. I've been sampling the kielbasa at Hugh's all-you-can-eat deli."

"YOU HAD STONED SEX WITH HIM?!"

"Rach, keep your voice down."

"Tell me everything."

Macy curled her legs under her and spoke to the lint balls she plucked off her bouclé sweater. "Sometimes when I drink and puff the magic dragon my clothing gives me a restricted feeling. Last night, Hugh and I ended up doing it."

Cupping my hand on my mouth, I released a hollow Darth Vader wind suck. Through parted fingers, I asked, "How was it?"

"Outside of this room I will deny it, but sex with Hugh was damn good. What am I going to do?"

"After taking a spin on the Hugh express, how did you leave things?"

"Before he stood, he kissed me."

"That was romantic."

"On the forehead, and went to use the hall bathroom."

"Ouch."

"Once I put my clothes on, I packed the pipe and took another hit. I looked for him, but he was gone."

"You probably tuckered Hughie out, and he went to take a nap."

She grimaced. "Rach, I don't know where he went. Katie Lee found me at the top of the stairs."

"I think you overpacked the pipe."

She rolled her eyes. "We went out back and hung out for a while, but I didn't see Hugh again."

Inside the sunflower house, I'd been disturbed by the visual of She-Devil pretzeling herself around Clay and hadn't noticed anything unusual about Hugh. I hadn't drilled him about where he'd been and with whom. He was drunk, but so was I. Underneath his sexual-prowess commentary Hugh was a good guy. I'm sure he had a legit reason for abruptly leaving Macy.

Macy wiped the corner of her eye and sniffed hard.

"Macy, are you okay?"

"Allergies," she said.

It was winter. Not a plant or bush flowered.

"When I woke up this morning, last night came back. Clearly. Except, I don't remember you coming home with us."

"That's because I stayed."

"Did you see Hugh?"

"He walked me back."

"Did he mention being with me?"

"About getting pent-up physical frustrations released?"

"He said that?"

"No. He didn't say anything. Are you going back for seconds?"

Macy stood and moved to her stereo to sort through cassette tapes. "Here's the thing. I like to play by my rules, and I decide when the game is over."

"Did you use him for his equipment?"

"Yes—no—maybe. It just happened. Last night Hugh took charge, and it was good. Better than good."

"Macy, you have me confused."

"Hugh started and ended it. I think he used me."

"So you don't want a second round?"

"I've avoided his come-ons all year. The crazy thing is that it was good. But what if he didn't think it was? I mean why else did he leave? I need you to find out what he wants."

"Me? I've never had a boyfriend. How am I supposed to figure out which way his lusty pendulum swings?"

Her eyes softened. "Please, Rach?"

OUTSIDE, THE WIND HOWLED, and the metal frame of our single-pane glass window clinked as it flexed. Snuggled in the loft under my van Gogh *Starry Night* comforter, I cradled an open book. It was early February, and talk of Valentine's Day infested the dorm. Katie Lee had decided to surprise Nash with a romantic weekend getaway and bruised her fingertips calling bed and breakfasts across the state for weekend rates.

I'd been on campus six months and had a head full of unfulfilled fantasies about a guy who was guarded by a demon redhead. Besides shagging a three-step with a flamboyant redneck who showed up as regularly as a monthly period pimple, lip-locking a sixteen-year-old, and sleeping, literally, with Travis, who felt comfortable enough to profess his gaydom, I had zip. My attitude had hardened. Love, romance, relationships, and flirtatious teasing were for suckers. I gulped a pocket of air and held my breath before I exhaled the remnants of any emotional gobbledygook that festered inside me. Going forward, I decided I'd concentrate on being a sensible adult with focus—books and studies.

Macy covered my desk with her *Cosmopolitan* magazines and flipped pages like she was mad at them. "Hallmark holidays suck. Let me know when V-Day is over."

Knowing Macy was full of shit, I flashed a smartass grimace. The magazine she abused was upside down. Her love connection with Hugh had her wrecked, and I wagered they'd hook up again.

Pressed under my left thigh, my right foot went numb. I slid out of the loft and hobbled down the hall to work out the pins and needles. Carrying the thin booklet I'd bought at the bookstore, I read as I walked. I needed to choose an American folk artist and write a paper chronicling his or her craft. Making a navigational error, I ended up in the communal bathroom, alone with Bridget.

Her reflection in the mirror above the sink stared at me. Avoiding her would signal a blatant act of bitchdom. As much as I wanted to ice her, I couldn't. She ate meals and partied with us. Snuffing her out of the circle wasn't so easy and could backfire, leaving me as the loner. She hummed with a mouth full of toothpaste foam. I held one finger inside the closed pamphlet. "Does your mood have to do with February fourteenth?"

After spitting into the sink, she rubbed her tongue across her Chicklet-white teeth. Pulling a long string of dental floss from a container, she wound it around both index fingers like a garrote. "There is someone I adore. I could really see a future together."

"Nash?"

She snorted. "Please."

"I didn't know you were seeing anyone."

"I know this someone likes me; I'm just not sure how deeply."

She spiked my curiosity. "Who is he?"

"We're still in the discovery period. I don't want to say anything yet."

I couldn't decide if Bridget's cryptic response mostly annoyed or unsettled me. Could she be hiding an infatuation for bad boy Nash? *Who else had she slept with?* I figured she trusted me as much as I trusted her and that I was better off not knowing.

She sawed floss between each upper tooth four times, working left to right. Before she started the bottom row, she asked, "What are you reading?"

I backed up, inching my way to the door. "Eighteenth- and nine-teenth-century American folk art biographies."

"What is folk art?"

"It's when an artist ignores rules of proportion and perspective."

Bridget tilted her head and leaned her hand on the sink. "In paintings?"

"In anything. Metal, wood, a quilt."

She turned her back toward me and gathered her toiletries from the metal shelf below the mirror. "That doesn't sound artistic to me."

"Art isn't about a perfect sunset. It can be rustic and still tell a story."

"Who buys it?"

"You'd be surprised. My dad refurbished a couple of Clementine Hunter paintings for a museum in New Orleans. They're highly col-lectable and not cheap. If you know what you're doing, buying and sell-ing art can be lucrative."

Above us, the fluorescent bathroom lights flickered. Bridget wiped her mouth with a washcloth. "Did you hear? A big storm is forecast."

"If it snows, it'll stick for fifteen minutes, tops."

"We'll see," she said before ducking into a shower stall.

Conversations with Bridget left me off balance. She held eye con-tact uncomfortably long and got me to say more than I meant to. She never concretely responded to my questions, and I left feeling that she knew more about me than I did about her.

Back in my room, I found that Macy had left, and Katie Lee had chosen her Valentine's getaway location. I settled back into the loft with the art history pamphlet Professor Schleck had assigned. Gusts of wind knocked tree branches against our window. As the night wore on, the erratic pelting eventually subsided.

I awoke to a tap, tap. Then nothing. I heard it again. Tap, tap. Except this time, it was louder. A drool puddle saturated my cheek to a corner of my pillowcase. "What is that?"

Katie Lee stood, rubbing her eyes. "It's coming from the hallway. I'll take a look."

"It's six fifteen. Still dark outside. I may have to kill someone."

She opened our door a crack, enough room for Hugh to pounce in.

"Why are you holding a cafeteria tray?" Katie Lee asked.

I still hadn't gotten used to him without a mustache and didn't immediately recognize him. He wore his red-and-black-check shirt jacket, and a knitted black snow hat covered his shoulder-length blunt cut. He didn't see the resemblance, but I guessed Tom Petty was a relative. I'd asked if his mom was a groupie. He said he'd have to check on that and get back to me.

When he stepped into our room, I had a vision of greasy meat drippings. The kind you see spilling off rotating metal kabob skewers inside a street vendor's glass box. I worked hard to extinguish thoughts of him and Macy—naked.

"Have y'all looked outside?"

Katie Lee shut our door and climbed back under her covers. "Go back to bed."

"It's six sixteen," I said.

Hugh's shoes clunked across our floor. His eyes grazed over the top bunk, and he shook my ankle. "Look outside."

"Listen, boots. It's before visiting hours. You're gonna get us busted if you don't keep your voice down."

He grabbed the blind cord and yanked, crashing the metal slats to the top of the window frame. "Look!"

Leaning from my bunk, I squinted at a blanket of white.

"Ladies, we've got ourselves a snowstorm. Get your mittens 'cause Thursday classes are gonna be cancelled."

I rolled to the edge of my mattress and blurted, "You're kidding?"

Below me, Hugh fought to remove Katie Lee's covers. We all froze when a sheriff's knock rapped on the door.

"Hall monitor. Ladies, open up."

My eyelids ricocheted an alert. "Shit."

If we kept quiet and pretended no one was in the room, maybe the person behind the knock would go away. That didn't happen. A second round pounded our door. The voice behind the fist asked, "Do I hear male voices in there?"

Katie Lee called out, "Just a minute. I'm not dressed."

Hugh licked his lips and seductively eyed her.

He needed to disappear, and there was only one place to hide. Leaping down, I stuffed him inside my hanging clothes closet and shut the door. Katie Lee held her hand on our door handle until I climbed back into bed. She nodded, and I signaled a thumb's up.

Our hall monitor peered over Katie Lee's shoulder. "Hey, y'all. Sorry to bother you, but I got a complaint that male voices were comin' from your room. Do you have any boys in here?"

Katie Lee yawned. "No, ma'am. Your knocking just woke me up."

Our resident assistant took a half-eye look in our room. There was nothing to see. "Sorry for the interruption, y'all," she said, shutting the door behind her. A few footsteps later, we heard her bang on the room next door.

Hugh let himself out of my closet. His cheeks had reddened, and he wiped perspiration off his brow. Kicking his boots off, he sprawled on Katie Lee's bed.

After locking our door, Katie Lee mouthed, "Mama."

"Francine wouldn't bust us."

"Did anyone see you come up here?" she asked.

"I don't think so. I knocked on Bridget's door, then Macy's, but neither opened up."

I scoffed at Hugh. Where did he think this was? The seventh-floor stop-and-shop? "You're lucky Bridget didn't shoot your nuts off with the gun you loaned her. She's always fondling the damn thing."

He covered his privates. "She'd never inflict bodily harm. She has an easygoing temperament."

Katie Lee anchored her hands on her hips. "And we don't?"

"No. I mean yes," he stuttered.

Katie Lee pointed at the door. "Back the way ya came."

"On one condition. You both have to meet me outside."

A BLISTERY SHEET OF snowflakes blurred my vision, and I didn't see the snowball until it whizzed past my ear, smacking the glass door behind me. Campus Drive had disappeared under a cover of white. Nothing in the form of transportation moved. Cans of bug spray, not snow equipment, were standard down here.

The novelty of snow was like a limited-edition attraction, and students milled around campus at an ungodly early hour. Katie Lee saw someone she knew and disappeared into the curtain of white. I climbed to the top of the steps outside Grogan looking for Hugh. "Since I'm awake," I shouted to the dropping flakes, "I'll stay out here for ten minutes. Then I'm grabbing something hot to eat and tucking back into bed." Inclement weather had cleared my schedule, and I'd pencil in time for a nap, reading, and perhaps even write a first draft of the paper for Professor Schleck.

I hadn't brought winter gear to school and used a pair of socks as hand warmers. Cupping my palm along the rail, I sliced through mounded flakes like a jigsaw. As I clapped the clumps that stuck to my mittened hands, someone shoved my back, knocking me off balance. A second push launched me over the railing and down a slope toward the dorm. Powdered like a pastry, I'd lost a shoe. My attacker stepped in front of me. Heavy mascara framed crystal-blue eyes, and auburn wisps of hair poked out from the neck of her ski mask.

"If ya talk to Clay again, fallin' down a slope will be the least of your worries."

I knew this snow demon even though we'd never been formally introduced. Rolling onto my knees, I asked, "Who are you? His mother?"

She-Devil unmasked. Boring her eyes into mine, she hissed, "Clay and I are a thing, and I don't need you runnin' interference. Consider this your warning."

What was I? A magnet for the jealous violent type?

Pushing to my feet, I balanced on one foot and bunny-hopped to my rogue shoe. She-Devil hadn't budged. She stood with her hands on her hips. I pointed my water-stained leather flat at her and spewed fighting words. "Go plug your carrot head in manure."

Before I finished my weak verbal comeback, she shoved me again, but this time, I didn't go down without her. My aunt Gert was obsessed with Hulk Hogan, and over time I'd become a fan too. It didn't matter that she was six inches taller than me. She-Devil deserved to eat snow, and I wrestled her to make sure that happened.

Hugh slid down the hill in front of Grogan on a cafeteria tray and wiped out on top of us. "Can I play too?" Wiggling out from under him, I dusted caked clumps off my jeans.

"Get off of me, you lug," She-Devil shouted.

He rolled off her and stretched a hand. "Can I help you out of those wet clothes?"

Picking up her hat, she barked, "Stay away," and marched off.

Hugh pointed to someone sledding on a toilet seat. "Well, ain't that clever? That dude's ridin' with the lid down."

"Quit admiring snow vehicles." I smacked Hugh's thigh with my hand and accidently hit him a low blow."

He tugged his shirttails to shield his privates. "Watch it there."

If he'd known the details Macy had told me, he would've realized the specifications of his jingly jangles were about as big a secret as a billboard. I was pretty sure I could identify his manliness in a lineup.

"That girl's on you like a fly on poop. What'd ya do? Hook up with her boyfriend?"

The wind whistled, whisking powder off a drift. I held my sock mittens between my knees so I could smooth my hair into a ponytail.

"Not yet."

MIDMORNING THE HOWLING GUSTS gained momentum. En route to the cafeteria, Katie Lee and I dodged blowing snow that swirled in mini tornados around corridors of locked campus buildings. Sitting at our usual table, I held a warm mug of instant cocoa. "The ice queen appeared from nowhere. I wasn't even around Clay. I thought college would weed out the demented, power-hungry girl bashers." I started to giggle.

Katie Lee pulled an everything bagel apart and smeared it with cream cheese. "What's so funny?"

"She-Devil thinks I'll seduce Clay. Me," I whispered, "a virgin."

"Rachael, you don't need experience to seduce someone." Taking a bite, she garbled, "You may need a restraining order."

"I don't even know her name."

"Clay must like you, otherwise why would she care?"

"What if he's a player?"

"Do you want to play?"

"I want to be with him, but not if I have to fight a half-roasted nut."

Hugh slid on the bench next to me and reached across the table, helping himself to half of Katie Lee's breakfast. He draped his free arm around my shoulder. "What are your plans for the afternoon?"

"Taking a nap. For some reason, I woke up before the sun."

He squeezed me tight. "Daddy's here to make things better."

Katie Lee tsked, "Oh Lord, what do you have planned?"

Tucking blond wisps behind his ear, he knuckle-knocked the table twice. "Make yourselves available around two."

She stopped chewing. "Why?"

He interlocked his hands behind his head. "It's a surprise, and if I told you, that'd ruin all the fun."

SNOW CONTINUED TO FALL, and the blustery morning pattered into afternoon. Besides a shower, I hadn't moved from the top bunk until a man's voice shouted, "Incomin'. O'Brien, get some clothes on."

Katie Lee had disappeared somewhere and left our door cracked open. "Hugh, this better not become a habit."

His cowboy boots clunked nearer to me until he parked them next to the loft. He removed his snow hat and held it to his chest. "I'd love nothin' more than to wake you up every mornin'."

I knew he had already dined at Macy's. Desperate virgin or not, I wasn't open for his business. "I'm fully dressed under my comforter, and I'm not removing any layers, so get your mind out of the gutter."

He slipped his boots off before climbing onto the dresser. "Damn," he swore when he peered into my high-rise bed. Clicking his tongue, he said, "You, my dear, get to spend the afternoon with amazing company."

"If you're the surprise, I'm going back to sleep."

Unzipping his jacket, he used pickpocket fingers to remove a paper bag from an inside pocket.

"What do you have in there? A rabbit? Some pigeons?"

"Even better." He pulled out a bottle of dark golden firewater. "Rachael O'Brien, meet a good friend of mine, Jack Daniels."

"You want to spend the afternoon getting plastered? If this is a ploy to get me naked, forget it."

"Do you have any better ideas?"

The digital clock flipped. It was three minutes after two. "I'll get the cups, but I'm not getting naked."

Hugh took his jacket off and rubbed his hip.

"Did you injure yourself on the cafeteria tray?"

"Smartass. If you haven't had the pleasure yet, Macy's in a snarly mood. When I knocked, she opened her door and smacked me with her hair dryer. I'm guessing she doesn't want to play today."

It wasn't the way I'd greet someone I had sex with, but I wasn't as experienced as Macy. I figured she'd change her mind and join us. Seeing her and Hugh around one another would make for a fascinating afternoon theatre production.

Katie Lee and Bridget returned from a vending machine raid with 7Up and Coke. Spending an afternoon with Jack Daniels seemed harmless, and after a few sips of JD and Coke, I forgot to obsess that Clay hadn't asked for my phone number and that what could've been a moment in the sunflower house wasn't.

It didn't matter that the mercury was dropping outside. Perched on my loft while Katie Lee, Bridget, and Hugh hung out below, my twelve-ounce cup kept me warm. Handing me a refill, Hugh whispered, "Rach, I gotta get perspective."

"About what?"

"Macy."

"What kind of perspective exactly?"

Katie Lee and Bridget seemed distracted throwing ice cubes out the window at targets below.

He lowered his voice. "I might have slept with her."

"Y'all come over here and see if you can hit anything," Katie Lee said.

"I killed a dozen squirrels with a compound bow one afternoon over Christmas break. I should be able to peg somethin' down there," Hugh said.

Katie Lee drew a look of horror. "I'm going to report your ass to animal cruelty. Let them arm the squirrels with bows 'n' arrows so they can roast your savory bits in a nutty soufflé."

Uncontrollable giggles took hold, and I dropped my drink overboard. I didn't see it splatter, but heard Bridget shout, "O'Brien," which sent me into waves of hysteria. In my fit, I rolled near the edge of the bed where a gravitational pull swept me in a free fall to the floor. Bridget hopped back before I crushed her. Towering above me, she asked, "Are you alive?"

Like a bird that's flown into a window, the fall had stunned me. Unable to speak with open eyes, I shut them and sputtered, "Enough with Jack Daniels. I'm over him."

The next time I opened my eyes, Hugh sat on a stool to my right, and Clay stood to my left in blue scrubs.

I'D SWUM INTO NEVER-NEVER LAND until a familiar New Yorker's voice brought me back. "When can she get the fuck out of here?"

Bright lights seared my pupils and ice packs numbed my shoulder. I awoke fully clothed in a bed with railings and a clipboard resting against my bare foot.

Walls, bedding, and furniture were all mauve. The décor reminded me of a hair salon, except you didn't lie in a bed to get a perm and a trim. In a soothing drawl, Clay Sorenson told Macy, "Her right shoulder absorbed the impact from the fall. She has an anterior dislocation."

Maneuvering to sit upright, I pressed onto my dodgy left shoulder, where fireballs played pinball, and I whimpered. I wanted to be back in the dorm, in my own bed so I could slather myself in self-pity.

"Why am I here?"

Hugh tapped his head, as though we were playing charades. He waited ten seconds for me to guess. I gestured defeat. "When you fell out of the loft, we didn't know how hard you'd knocked your noggin. We brought you to the campus infirmary."

"What time is it?"

Hugh pointed at a clock on the wall. I squinted. It was just past ten. I recalled a still-image of our linoleum floor and another of Bridget's frozen face, but nothing after that. Embarrassed and groggy I scoffed, "I'm fine. It's just bruised."

Macy handed me a water. "You weren't fine. You couldn't get off the floor."

Defenseless, I grimaced. My shoulder, frozen on the outside, bubbled like hot lava on the inside. I was mortified by my klutzy mishap and that Clay had witnessed me in a self-induced comatose state.

Slouched in a chair next to my bed, Hugh tugged at Katie Lee's polka-dot scarf. She spun as he unraveled it from her neck. "Does she need surgery?"

Clay lowered the bed rail and shook his head. He reached in his pocket, unwrapped a peppermint candy, and lodged it in his cheek. "Since she was so—relaxed—the resident nurse and I popped it back into place. With ice packs, ibuprofen, and a sling, Rachael can leave when she's steady on her feet."

Even with dulled senses and slow reflexes, I felt tingly when I heard Clay's voice. A musk scent lingered around him, and greedily I drank him in.

A man with a beard peeked his head around the corner. "Alene needs you. Three C."

Excusing himself, Clay collected his clipboard off my foot and, before he turned on his heel, drew his hand across my ankle and lightly squeezed.

Like an actor in a play, Katie Lee whisked a privacy curtain aside. She'd secured a facemask and donned rubber gloves. Holding metal doctor implements, she arched her arms and crab-shuffled toward me. "Lay still. I promise you won't feel a thing."

"What's with the mask? And please don't come near me if you found those gloves in a garbage pail."

Hugh plucked the sharp scissors from Katie Lee's grip and tucked them in a drawer.

I whispered to Macy, "Why is Clay in scrubs?"

Macy adjusted my ice pack. "He's in the physical therapy work-study program. He's been taking care of you."

A chill swept through me. What had I said and done to embarrass myself and ruin my chances of Clay ever finding me attractive? I made air quotes with my fingers. "Explain taking care?"

Katie Lee flung herself across the foot of my bed, and Hugh stifled his giggles with her scarf. Hanging her head and feet off opposite ends, she asked, "Anyone hungry? Let's order pizza."

"And nachos," Hugh shouted.

"I tried to encourage Pixie and Dixie to go home," Macy said, "but Dixie wouldn't hand over the car keys unless I let her stay."

Katie Lee almost toppled Macy in a bear hug. She blurted, "Classes are cancelled tomorrow."

"Seriously?" I asked.

Clay stepped back into the room. "The storm has shut down Greensboro. How's the shoulder?"

"It's okay," I lied.

"You need to keep it on ice as much as possible for the next two days. When you're not icing it, wear a sling. You should have x-rays taken to make sure there's no fracture. With the snow 'n' all, our technician didn't make it to campus. She should be back tomorrow. I have some paperwork for you to sign. You can go when you feel up to it."

The potential of my shoulder being fractured wasn't as large a concern as my appearance. I didn't need a mirror to confirm that I looked closer to my worst than my best. Running my noninjured hand through my hair, I felt my cheeks warm, and I babbled, "I didn't realize you worked in the infirmary. Will I need physical therapy?"

Eyes down, he smiled as he concentrated on filling out a form.

Did he think I'd concocted this injury so I could see him? A painfully ingenious scheme I should have thought of months ago, if I'd known he worked here.

Katie Lee clutched Clay's arm. "Have you provided adequate medical attention? Have her wounds been cleaned and bandaged?"

Macy gripped an empty plastic pitcher and pretended to guzzle.

If the JD and Coke I drank had affected me the same as Katie Lee, maybe I wouldn't have been embarrassed by the dufus intellect she thought she'd acquired.

"Hugh, help me remove Katie Lee so Clay can have a word with Rach." A task not easily accomplished, Macy had to negotiate a vending machine visit to convince my roommate to leave.

Resting the clipboard under his arm, Clay sat on the edge of the bed. "May I?" he asked, adjusting my sling. His hand lingered on my fingers. "You have the hands of an artist."

"What do you mean?"

"Creative individuals, painters, potters, carpenters, have fingers that arc, like yours."

"And how do you know this scientific fact?"

"My mother is a sculptor."

Clay wore boyish good looks in a manly shell. He was different from the cute guys I knew in high school. Attention from girls swelled their heads, turning them into arrogant assholes. Clay seemed unaware of how his green-river eyes, strong hands, and tuft of chest hair that scurried out of his shirt collar affected me. "Seems you had some fun this afternoon. How come you didn't invite me?"

"I don't have your number."

Penning his digits on top of my paperwork, he said, "You do now. Listen, Rachael, I'd prefer to get you back to Grogan myself, but the infirmary is short-staffed and we're overwhelmed with snow-related injuries. I can't leave right now, but I'd like to stop by tomorrow. If that's okay?"

"Are you medically qualified to check on my injury? Or are you flirting with me?"

A loudspeaker asked him to report to the front desk. He laid my paperwork on a moveable table.

Unable to squelch a grin, he said, "Yes to both your questions."

MACY RANKED THE HIGHEST in the sane-and-sober category and drove Big Blue the half mile back to Grogan. No one had ventured where road, sidewalk, and lawn melded into one, and she crawled through the virgin snow, using streetlamp posts as a guide. The infirmary's vending machine selection of Ho Hos and stale pig rinds wasn't an adequate sweet-and-salty snack for Hugh and Katie Lee. The two fixated on creating a nacho pizza, and Macy dropped them off near the cafeteria. Under the cast of lamplight we watched them kick ankle-deep snow en route for a late night nosh session.

Beneath a veil of flurries, Macy parked Big Blue behind Grogan. I draped my coat over my shoulders, and the arms flapped like kite tails. Linking her arm in my free one, Macy guided me up the unshoveled stairs.

"Question for you. Did we just leave Clay Sorenson at the campus infirmary, or was that a hallucination?"

She clenched me tight. "That was Clay Boy."

"Recap please."

"After the fall, you couldn't move. Hugh and Katie Lee got you to the infirmary."

My shoulder pinged. "I'm with you so far. What about Bridget?"

Macy unlocked the lobby door. "She couldn't walk without crashing into inanimate objects. She went to her room to sleep off the whisky."

"Katie Lee and Hugh drove me—drunk?"

"They didn't drive you. They pushed you."

I shook wet snow off my hair. "What?"

"There was a racket outside my room. When I came out, your drinking buddies had you in a rolling luggage cart."

"Quit messing with me. How did I get to the infirmary?"

Macy tapped seven on the elevator keypad. "You know the yellow plastic bins on wheels?"

"The ones we used to move our stuff in the first day?"

She didn't bother to stifle a laugh. "The lunatics filled one with pillows. They loaded you in and wheeled you across campus. Your fantasy man scooped you out."

"Clay carried me?" My chest tightened. He had enveloped me in his arms, warmed me against his chest, and I didn't remember. "Did he check me out—medically? Wait a minute. How do you know all this?"

"Someone had to make sure they didn't leave you to freeze. I followed and caught up behind the three of you in Big Blue."

"Did he say anything nonmedical to me? You can tell me. Good or bad, just be gentle with the ugly."

"Rach, he likes you. He was overly protective and got you into a room right away. I managed Pixie and Dixie in the lobby while he and a nurse adjusted your shoulder."

"He said he wants to stop by to check on me."

"Make sure you're showered and have clean sheets on the bed."

"Macy!"

"A girl needs to be prepared."

"Speaking of being prepared, are you on friendly terms with Hugh?"

"Better than friendly."

"Do tell."

"I've decided to pretend what happened never happened."

"We need to talk this one through."

Macy yawned. "Tomorrow."

"Thanks for watching out for me."

I opened my door and noticed that our room had been rearranged. My bed rested on the floor. *Who pulled the loft apart?*

"What happened to you? Get caught playin' in a possum trap?"

I sank into the armchair and looked at the digital clock. It was midnight. "Nash, what are you doing here?"

NOTE TO SELF

Jack Daniels is no friend of mine. He must be related to Bathtub Dew.

28

That's Not a Speed Bump

Despite the frigid temperatures and snow on the ground, major highways had been cleared and classes resumed. Walking back from class, I longingly reminisced about the August heat and humming cicadas. I awoke to a room filled with shadows, and as lunchtime approached, the sky hung in an almost unnoticeable cast of light-hued pewter. Back in my room, I draped my legs over the arms of the upholstered chair, and I squeezed a palm-sized ball filled with dried beans. Clay had stopped by the day after the loft incident to check on my shoulder. He showed me a few arm flexibility exercises and gave the squeeze sack to me.

The way I toyed with it, you'd think I had a nervous condition. It was mental, but I liked placing my fingers on something he'd given me. Okay, so he didn't give it to me as a gift. It was supposed to help strengthen my shoulder, and the campus infirmary had charged me seven dollars. Regardless, it reminded me of his strong hands touching my shoulder and sent me into a dreamy fantasy of being with him in a hot and sweaty tangle. I had Clay's handwritten phone number, which

I kept in my pillowcase, and I knew where he worked. Now I needed a foolproof plan that didn't involve stalking or anything obviously psychotic to get some quality alone-time.

Macy popped into our room and asked Katie Lee if she could borrow her electric typewriter. "Hi, Macy," I said.

She ignored me and positioned her stance so I had a view of her back.

"I'm sorry I misplaced your hooded sweat shirt. If I don't find it, I'll buy you a new one," I said.

The back of her head faced me. "Thanks for reminding me. It cost forty-eight dollars," she said, then marched back to her room with the typewriter.

I shrugged at Katie Lee, looking for insight regarding Macy's chilly temperament, but she was preoccupied abusing the push-button phone. She'd mangled the cord into something that resembled a macramé belt I'd made at Girl Scout camp, and when she slammed it into the cradle, her left ear coloration glowed like an atomic fireball. She complained, "Where the hell is he? It's been five days."

The night I'd slipped out of my loft, Nash had shown up on his way to a "gig." Since I'd hovered in incoherence and Katie Lee was southern, our door had been unlocked. While I was at the infirmary, Bridget had let him into the dorm. He thought he'd surprise Katie Lee and waited. When I arrived without her, he'd paced around the room moving from the top of her desk to the dresser. My head pounded, I wore an ice pack under my bra strap, and my balance wasn't exactly stable. Katie Lee's boyfriend acted like the Energizer Bunny, and I threatened to pull out his battery. Once he anchored himself in a sitting position, I garbled semicoherent portions of an afternoon spent with my liquid nemesis. Nash half-listened. His eye wandered from the view of a passing student down below the window to our closed door. I'd sprawled on my bed. He'd offered me a soda. With the aid of a straw, I washed down three ibuprofen he'd fetched for me from a container of medicine in Katie Lee's drawer. He gave me an extra pillow and tucked a blanket around me, not leaving any loose corners.

"Nash, how do you know when you love someone?"

He'd pondered that for a minute then chuckled. "They sizzle your insides, and you do the same for them."

"Not sexually. I mean in your heart."

The heater under the window made a clicking noise before it kicked on and blew warm air.

He turned out my desk lamp. "You know you're in love when you do what's best for both of you."

My eyes felt heavy. Before I closed them, I said, "Katie Lee doesn't care about money, she cares about you. Whatever scheme you're in is going to backfire."

He stayed quiet. I wondered what he was doing, but was too tired to check.

"Whisky swillin' has you talkin' crazy. So where is Katie Lee exactly?"

Without opening my eyes, I whispered, "Making nacho pizza with Hugh."

I remember hearing our door click shut. When I awoke, shades of gloom streaked through open blind slats. Fully clothed, Katie Lee lay asleep on top of her bedding. Nash had vanished, and I wondered if I'd imagined seeing him, but Bridget verified that he hadn't been a figment of my imagination.

Katie Lee slept into the afternoon. After she drank a Pepsi, she crawled back into bed, and I asked if Nash had found her.

"Rach, I never saw him. He didn't tell me anything about a gig." Katie Lee pressed all ten of her fingers into her eyebrows as though they were antennae providing clairvoyance. "My boyfriend shows up unannounced then leaves without a word or even a note?"

For four days, I'd witnessed Katie Lee unsuccessfully phone-stalk Nash. Now, on day five, she slammed the handheld in its cradle, grabbed her pink ski coat, and tied a scarf around her neck. As she placed a hand on the doorknob, a tear escaped her eye. "That's it. I can't live like this. It's over."

Weighing the sincerity of her words, I waited a minute. I'd never seen her so rattled. She and Nash had fought before, but they never broke up. Nash, a professional smooth-talker, had always made nice before the breaking point. He'd have to dig deep in his bag of grovel to fix this one. Feeling that this was epic, I zipped across the hall before I lost my nerve.

Macy plucked typewriter keys with a single finger. I stood behind her and peered at the words she typed. *The Third Gender, somewhere between a man and a woman*, a paper for her sex and gender sociology class.

"Katie Lee is breaking up with Nash."

"I'm not talking to you."

"I'll give you the money, I promise."

"Rachael, I'm not mad about the sweater. I'm pissed that you told Hugh you knew we slept together."

I puffed an air blast, thinking that Hugh was screwing things up on multiple levels. "I did not. Who told you that?"

"Bridget."

"Whoa." I motioned my left hand fingertips to my right palm. "Time out. Who told her that?"

"No one told her. She overheard your conversation."

"Bridget needs to mind her own business or invest in a hearing aid. I didn't tell Hugh. He blabbed to me when we were snowed in."

"He's bragging?"

"He wasn't bragging."

"What did he say?"

"Macy, he likes you. He's having a hard time reading your signals and wanted my take."

"What did you tell him?"

"I lied. I told him it was news to me."

"Good."

I flopped onto Macy's bed. "He knew I knew. I told him I didn't have any idea what you wanted from him."

Macy pulled the paper out of the typewriter. "Shit."

"What do you want me to tell him?"

"Rachael, I don't want a boyfriend. I want to have fun. Being tied to one person puts a crimp on fun."

"How do you know Hugh wants a serious girlfriend?"

Macy slid a new piece of paper into the typewriter. "I can tell."

"Did he say something in your moment of passion?"

"Can we talk about something else? Is Nash dead?"

Pulling apart a mini Russian stacking doll that sat on Macy's windowsill, I confessed, "Not that I can verify."

"Then I don't believe they're breaking up."

"They haven't spoken in five days—a Guinness record. This time his dufusness has cracked her shell. She's a broken woman. It's our obligation to take her out and get her mind off him."

Poking her head in Macy's room, Bridget asked, "Who's going out?"

I hesitated to share, but figured she'd heard portions of the conversation. If I didn't tell her the news, she'd construe a tale that would make me look demented. "Jeez, do you wear a Miracle-Ear?"

"I have something for Katie Lee. Is she around?"

Macy plucked typewriter keys and hit return. "It's over with Nash. She's going to dump him, once she locates his ass."

Bridget's enchanted eyes grazed past mine. "Is she now?"

In that moment, we both realized that her secret had lost relevance. Telling Katie Lee that Bridget had slept with Nash would only be spiteful and result in one or both of us losing her friendship. The destruction of Katie Lee's relationship wiped the board clean between Bridget and me, and she grinned a wide smile.

BRIDGET AND MACY WAITED in the hallway. I zipped my coat, and Katie Lee flicked the light switch. We'd brave the cold to help my roommate dull the sting of her problematic soon-to-be ex-boyfriend at the tropical bar beneath the Holiday Inn. Nothing raging crazy. Just a few hours spent with friends, away from the dorm. My fingers encircled the door handle, ready to close it, when the phone rang. We all stood in a holding pattern and stared. On the sixth ring, Katie Lee asked, "Rachael, will you answer it."

A raspy drawl greeted me. "Hey, Raz, how's the arm?"

"Still attached."

"That's good to hear. Is Katie Lee around?"

I covered the receiver and mouthed "Nash." Our minirefrigerator chided in a low hum, but Katie Lee kept silent. I wasn't sure what I'd do if I were her. Ignore the call or give him hell and hang up. If she went soft and listened, girls' night would be ruined. What could he possibly tell her as an excuse? Maybe he'd pull out the old alien abduction to explain his five-day, couldn't-find-a-phone disappearance. It was the best explanation I thought of—at least the one with the most potential for flexible interpretation.

Katie Lee closed her eyes and moved her lips in a silent chant. Her normally bright lagoon blues turned murky, and she disappeared down the hall.

"Sorry, Nash. She left."

"Can you get her?"

"Are you okay?" I asked.

"Yeah. Why?"

"Maybe she'll talk to you later," I said and unplugged the phone.

OUTSIDE THE DORM LOBBY, night air levitated cold and quiet. I dusted off my shoulder, the good one, in case she broke down, and made a mental note to borrow a box of tissues from Macy. Despite my boyfriend inexperience, I'd help her sort through her emotional turmoil. But Katie Lee didn't break down into a distressed ball of goo like I expected and instead emitted serene calmness. Her demeanor conflicted with the person I thought I knew, unnerving my internal equilibrium. Inside, my nerve endings flinched, and I wondered, would she really end her two-year relationship?

Katie Lee cupped her hands over her nose and mouth. "It's too cold to walk. I'll drive us."

Bridget checked her camera film gauge and patted her pocket for an extra roll. As we walked to the parking lot, she brushed snowflakes off Katie Lee's coat collar. "If you drink too much, I can always drive us back."

Her accommodating offer jolted me with a dose of relief and annoyance. Relief that I could drink without chauffeur responsibilities—annoyance that she presented herself to be more considerate than the rest of us.

Except for the quick trip to the campus infirmary, Katie Lee's car had been idle since the winter storm rolled in, and her windshield glistened like an iced sheet cake. Since Bridget professed a predisposed case of backseat carsickness, she automatically settled into the front. Katie Lee turned the key over. Shivering like popsicles in a flimsy cardboard box, we waited for Big Blue to cough into a purr. Bridget busied herself snapping photos of icicles that dangled below the side view mirror. Macy didn't say much, and I guessed the cold had immobilized her inner smartass.

Katie Lee slid the defroster lever on high and flicked on the wipers. The plastic dashboard creaked, and the windshield blades complained as they swiped across powder and ice. Once vented air blew warmth, minipeepholes formed on the glass, eventually growing large enough to reveal the colorless landscape. I leaned forward between Katie Lee and Bridget. "I'm used to the white stuff. Maybe I should drive."

Bridget veered to face me. Creases formed across her forehead as if I spoke a foreign language.

Shifting the car into drive, Katie Lee said, "Don't be silly. Your arm is in a sling."

Before we left the parking lot, Big Blue fishtailed, narrowly missing a row of parked cars. Covering my face with my nonsling hand, I whispered, "Tell me when we're there."

THE CAROLINA COLD SNAP broke the longest record for a consecutive winter chill and jailed most cars that weren't kept in a garage until a plow or a thaw could rescue them. The Browns had given Katie Lee Big Blue because it was a large, safe vehicle—the kind that could take dings and scratches and not look the worse for it. She embraced the tank and mowed into unplowed snow that had drifted against the street curb, easily securing a prime parking spot in front of the Holiday Inn.

My door opened into a hard-packed snow wall. Unsuccessfully strad-dling the drift, my shoes plunged into wet. In an effort not to wipe out on the slick sidewalk, Macy linked her arm through my free one. Max, the bouncer, wasn't outside on his stool, and no one carded us.

Inside, students milled about, and we spotted Hugh at a corner table. He asked no one in particular, "What's goin' on?" and I had to respect him for holding back his inner puma from Macy.

Spreading her coat on a barstool, Bridget sat on it. "One of us has news."

He touched Bridget's shoulder and met her eyes. "I'm not the father?"

Bridget smacked his arm. "None of us are pregnant, you nympho."

Unstacking plastic cups, he said, "First pitcher's my treat."

Macy kept her coat on. Bypassing Hugh, she turned toward the bar. Katie Lee wasn't the only one with man problems, and I wondered if we'd have an early night.

"What's the news?" Hugh asked.

Katie Lee tucked herself on top of a stool next to him, and I stood. "Nash stopped by the night we made nacho pizza. He was in our room but didn't wait for me. He went AWOL for five days. Who does that? He only called tonight, right before we left. It's over."

Always available to deliver thought-provoking commentary, Hugh sipped his drink and licked the foam off his lip. "Whoa."

Since we'd driven, I hadn't worn socks, and my bare feet turned whitish. I danced a jig in an effort to warm my bones and to bring back circulation. Hugh motioned his head like an opening and closing drawbridge. "Got your thong on backward?"

"You don't need to concern yourself with my frillies."

Macy didn't return. She'd settled onto a corner stool at the bar. Stone, the bird-advocate bartender, chatted to her as he filled pitchers with beer and tipped liquor spouts into shot glasses. Tonight he'd trad-ed his stiff cockatoo for a rigid macaw, perched on his shoulder. Macy wasn't just pretending she'd never slept with Hugh, she iced him like he never existed, and I wondered whose feathers she ruffled the most.

Two beers therapeutically relaxed Katie Lee enough to tell Hugh how insensitive Nash was to let her worry for days on end. "After two days, his roommate wouldn't even answer my calls. That, or the phone got disconnected."

Hugh whistled. "Dump him."

Some guys from Hugh's dorm joined our table. He stood up, saying he needed to stretch his legs, and tweaked his head at me.

"What?" I mouthed. He waved for me to join him. Standing behind the table, he asked, "Is Macy avoiding me?"

"I don't have clearance to discuss whatever is or isn't going on."

"Rach, talk to me."

The creases around his eyes looked vulnerable, and I caved. "I'm going to have to speak anonymously. Anything I say, I will vehemently deny."

"Does Macy hate me?"

"Hate you? She doesn't know what to do with you."

"What do you mean?"

"She's conflicted."

Hugh guzzled his beer. "Women. Too much damn thinking."

"She's complicated."

"What am I supposed to do? Play along with her childish deny-and-neglect game?" Shaking his head, he reached for the pitcher and refilled his cup.

Katie Lee had an audience and took an opinion poll on the callousness of Nash's disappearance. Having been on the front line of her manic phone-dial-'n'-slam maneuvers, I backed away from the table of spectators who were about to hear the unabridged audio version and moved toward an empty barstool next to Macy.

Minus the psycho mind game play, I envied Katie Lee's and Macy's romances. I'd blown three encounters with Clay and had an unromantic dorm visit that amounted to a bundle of nothing. Hoping for a chance at redemption, I imagined batting my eyelashes, engaging him with witty conversation, and hoping that we both drank enough to disregard any inhibitions. Maybe I should have invited him out. I had his number, but I didn't want to chase. Who was I kidding? Clay was smart, gorgeous, and just being polite when he jotted down his phone number. Sipping cold beer only dulled the ache that had relocated from my shoulder and settled into my heart.

Having had a conversation with Hugh about Macy, I determined silence would result in bad juju, so I decided to keep things honest and tell her. I pulled a cigarette and a pack of matches out of my back pocket and watched Macy spin a shot glass in small circles. Sliding onto a seat next to hers, I asked, "What are you drinking?"

Pink dribbled down her wrist on the way to her mouth. She smacked her lips. "Sex on the beach." Pulling her head back, she assessed me. "You don't look so good."

"You look better than good. How many have you had?"

She motioned for another. "I gotta stay warm."

Stone placed a napkin in front of me and poured another. "Hey, Rachael, been a while. What happened to your arm?"

"Freak accident. I should have the sling off in a week. Where's Lolita?"

He hustled behind the bar, giving some glasses a quick wash in an upright bristle contraption. "She's molting. I brought Lester instead."

I turned my attention back to Macy. "Why are you avoiding Hugh?"

She bent back and looked to the table where he sat. "He's still over there?"

"His ear is busy listening to all things Nash."

Macy stiffened her back. "If she's not careful, he may want to date Nash."

I stared at Macy.

"Hugh is probably the type to explore all sides of the tracks."

"That's ludicrous. Hugh is as ungay as they come. He likes women, especially you." For emphasis, I raised my pointer finger. A trick I learned from my father—scary. "If you want to end what started, you're doing a fantastic job. But if any part of you likes him, you need to admit it before it's too late."

She downed the shot that rested in front of me.

"You should be warm enough for sex in the snow," I said and turned to look at Hugh for myself.

She gripped my arm. "Don't look. They'll see you."

"Who will see me?"

"Hugh and Katie Lee are putting coats on."

I waited a respectable three seconds. "I'm looking."

Macy drummed her nails. "Well?"

"They're gone. Probably went to move the car. It's just Bridget and the guys from Hugh's dorm."

Staying put, we pondered everyone's relationships: Katie Lee and Nash's demise, if I'd ever hook up with Clay—or anyone—and what Macy should do about Hugh. I scanned the bar at regular intervals for their return. "They've been gone over an hour. They should be back by now."

Pretending not to care, Macy said, "Maybe they're doing it inside Big Blue."

I didn't bother with a response to her silly speculation.

Bridget shared a pitcher with some guys neither of us knew, and we speculated whether she navigated the more-than-friends trail with any of them. At last call, I helped Macy stand, and we made our way toward the table.

Bridget pointed her camera at Macy and clicked. "Well, lookie who showed up."

Macy wrapped her arms around Bridget's neck and shouted more than whispered, "We didn't want to disturb your private conversation."

"Where did Katie Lee go?" I asked.

"She's upset about Nash. Hugh walked her back to the dorm."

Macy's shoulders sagged. "How are we supposed to get back?"

Bridget slid her hand into the side pocket of her purse and retrieved a set of car keys. "I'll drive us."

"Haven't you been drinking?" I asked.

"Only a few."

Cupping Bridget's face, Macy asked, "Do you know how to drive in snow?"

She pushed Macy's hands away and slipped on her coat. "The dorm is four miles from here. How hard can it be?"

The lights inside The Lounge flashed, and Stone jiggled keys as he locked up. We were the last to leave. Bridget asked, "Do you need a ride?"

Stone looked at the bleary night outside the basement window. "If it's not too much trouble."

A little voice inside my gut spoke to me. The older I'd become, the less often I paid attention. If my arm hadn't been in a sling, and if I'd worn boots and mittens, I may have listened to myself. *Walk home*, it said. *Walk home.*

We climbed the stairs to the sidewalk that exposed us to a winter wind that ripped through our clothes and nipped at bare skin. Shielding my eyes from the elements, I deduced that the quickest way back to my warm bed sat on four wheels.

Macy curled into a fetal position on the industrial-gray interior of the frozen backseat and rested her feet on my lap. Stone sat in front, and Bridget adjusted the driver seat. Before she started the car, Bridget said, "Smile," and blinded Macy and me with a flash. Immune to her photo compulsion, I never bothered to pose.

The night was desolate. Bridget took the empty road slow and center. I didn't care as long as I got home. As she approached a four-way intersection, she slowed, and below us, Big Blue's tires ground and puttered in a sluggish slide motion until the car collided with a snowbank.

"Bridget," I asked, "why'd you hit the brake?"

She pointed to a stop sign with only the letters *OP* peeking out from the white. Idling in front of an empty corner lot, the dark night rested still and cold. Big Blue revved and the tires spun, but the dormant branches of a snow-covered elm stayed in view.

Turning to Stone, Bridget said, "Somebody needs to push."

I pegged Stone at the type that used his mind more than his muscles. His frame was more suited for speed and agility than pumping weights. A mound of snow pressed to his window, clouding his view. "The snow is deep. We may be legging it."

Walking back to campus in sockless flats didn't hold much appeal. "I'll push too," I said and got out of the car with him.

The cold had snared the night soundless. No traffic, no trees rustling, no night creatures. I took my arm out of the sling so I could better balance myself to heave the bumper. Bridget gunned the engine, and the Oldsmobile's tires screamed resentment, spinning rubber deeper into the bank.

After tromping along the side of the car, Stone rapped on the driver's side. Bridget jammed the electric window switch. It did nothing more than click when she pulsed it. Without sitting up, Macy unwound her window.

His breath sent fog clouds into the car. "I'm going to rock her. When I count to three, gas it."

Crouching behind Big Blue, my numb feet stung when they flexed. Stone began to bounce the car and counted, "One, two, three," and we pushed our weight forward. The force of my shove rippled down to my feet, and the plastic soles of my flats skidded from under me. In a swift motion, more complicated than an ass-drop, I landed facedown and embraced the wet, white stuff. Chunks lodged beneath my shirt and stung my cheeks. When I contorted my body off my shoulder, it twanged, and I knew I'd jacked it. I heard the crunch of snow under tires before a death-gripping weight pinned my leg. Unsure of what had happened, I howled in pain.

"Stop the car. My God, stop the car!" Stone shouted. It was too late. Big Blue had rolled on me, flame-broiling my lower leg on a snow grill. It took too much effort to scream, and I moaned between erratic breaths like a dog delivering a litter.

Above my head, the rear passenger door opened. Trancelike, Macy locked eyes with me. Throwing her hand over her mouth, she stuttered, "Sh-shit."

Snowflakes descended like a swarm of bugs. I drifted into a dreamy corridor, pushing away from the pain that skewered my calf. Stone shouted against the frozen driver window, "Move the god damn car. Rachael's under the tire!"

Bridget's words stuck on her tongue. "My camera strap got tangled. Is she conscious?"

"She's blinking at me," Macy said.

My mind crackled as if an electrical storm passed through it, and I felt the searing burn until Big Blue rolled forward, releasing the knotted pressure. With opened eyes, I hovered between reality and unconsciousness. Seeing, listening, unable to speak.

White dotted Stone's dark hair like sprinkles on ice cream, and the frosty air had reddened circles on his cheeks. He threw his coat on me and gripped my hand. "Call 911! We need to get her to the hospital."

"If we call an ambulance," Bridget said, "the police'll show up, and we'll all get busted. Let's get her to the campus infirmary. It's closer."

Stone began digging around in the trunk. He found a squeegee stick and some old towels that he used as a splint on my leg.

A car door slammed. "Macy. Macy!" Bridget yelled. "Where do you think you're going?"

RACING IN AN AMBULANCE with a roaring siren through the streets may seem thrilling, but speaking from experience, it's overrated.

A buff medic with tanned skin, high cheekbones, and thin, straw-streaked hair took my blood pressure. She wore orange lipstick and in a German accent asked my name, age, and address before she severed my jeans with a swift splice. My paramedic had to be The Terminator's sister. When I told her I was a student, she asked for my parents' phone number.

Tears welled in my eyes. "My mom's out of the universe, and my dad has a girlfriend."

She nodded sympathetically.

At the hospital, she pulled the rolling stretcher out of the emergency vehicle and wheeled me across the Surgeon's Medical loading dock. Stone trotted behind, and I asked, "How did you get here so quickly?"

He rubbed his hands together and blew on them. "I rode in the ambulance front seat."

I signed some paperwork, got x-rayed, and swallowed two oversized codeine pills. Behind an encircling curtain, I lay on a mattress the same thickness as the one in my dorm, only this one had a remote control. Stone fidgeted with the buttons. "How about here? Or here?"

A beige blanket, all foam and no cotton, covered me. My feet had defrosted, and my plum-preserve-colored calf with a torn muscle rested in a Velcro contraption. Nurse Terminator said it would heal, and a doctor confirmed that'd I'd be released when the paperwork was completed. For eighteen years, the most injured I'd been was a skinned knee from falling off my bike. I'd only had the flu a handful of times and never had an injury that landed me in a doctor's office, let alone a hospital, until now. Having been stupid-lucky, I said a heavenward thank you and promised to be more careful after I kicked Bridget's ass.

Lester the macaw's mangled body hung by one foot from Stone's shoulder. His feathers had been considerably thinned. I could relate to the stuffed bird's state of disarray. "Stone, you don't need to stay. This is above and beyond customer service."

"I wanted to make sure you're okay."

Squeezing his hand, I asked, "Your mother didn't really name you Stone R, did she?"

His eyes twinkled. "The Holiday Inn issues every employee a name badge. My last name is Rogers. Someone screwed up, and I never said anything. The name gets me attention, interesting confessions, and way better tips."

Stone barely knew me, but he watched over me as though I were on an endangered list. If there were more Stone Rs around, the world would be a nicer place.

I'd drifted into a fitful sleep and awoke when Macy and Katie Lee arrived. Katie Lee held a bag of clean clothes and a box of donuts. Behind them, Bridget cradled a bouquet of flowers. "Rach, how are you doing?"

"How do you think!? Were you trying to kill me, or are you a really horrible driver?"

Bridget's voice crackled. "You think I drove over you on purpose?"

Macy sat on the foot of the hospital bed and rested a hand on my ankle. "It was an accident."

"Accident?" I said in a squeaky pitch.

Silence gripped the air and Stone whispered, "Awkward."

Katie Lee wrapped her arm around Bridget. "Come on, Rach. You don't seriously believe that Bridget would purposely hurt you."

Rage bulged my veins. I couldn't look at Bridget's sorrowful mask. Between clenched teeth, I seethed, "Get her out of my sight."

NOTE TO SELF

Macy is the glue in a crisis. She walked two blocks to call an ambulance. I owe her.

Not speaking to Bridget, obviously.

Stone R. One rare bird.

The only silver lining of my leg having been a speed bump—physical therapy with Clay.

29

Romance, Flowers, and Fraud

Katie Lee's phone warmed my ear. Travis had called to catch up. He said he'd been to the Ackland Museum in Chapel Hill for a new exhibition on local artists. After hearing the highlights, I'd vented for an hour about the freak runneth-over incident and kept coming back to the same question. "What was Bridget's motive?"

He offered perspective. "Do you know how much she drank? Or maybe she is a really bad driver? Have you looked in her wallet? Does she even have a valid license?"

"That's completely outrageous, but plausible."

"Are you speaking to her?"

"In Tarzan phrases."

"Has she apologized?"

"Daily, in her sickly sweet, deep-fried southern drivel."

"Hey now."

"Sorry, I'm bitter. I have to wear this contraption on my leg and use crutches. After that, I'll have physical therapy through the spring."

"That sucks. Any plans for Valentine's Day?"

I scoffed. "You're talking to the girl with a bum arm and a Velcroed leg. If I had romantic plans, I'd hate to think what could happen. This holiday is a wash. What about you?"

"Sorry, nothing for you to chew on."

"I should go and study or something."

"Me too," Travis said. "Be careful around Bridget, and take care of your limbs."

At least the Grogan Girls aligned on the upcoming Hallmark holiday. Katie Lee wasn't speaking to Nash, Macy continued to ice Hugh, and as for Bridget—I didn't give a shit if romance did or didn't orbit her planetary dome. Valentine's Day had absolutely no appeal. Misery does love company, and having Katie Lee and Macy without relationships made coping with the wretched day bearable.

After calling for a van to take me to class, I slung my book satchel diagonally across my chest, locked my door, and hobbled toward the lobby to wait. When I exited the elevator on the first floor, my chin paid a visit to my neck in an open mouth gawk. Nash held a bouquet of assorted red, pink, and white carnations. "Damn, girl. What the hell happened to you?"

"Nash?"

He nodded to his left. "You remember Billy Ray."

Nash's sidekick held a flat package wrapped in brown shipping paper. Dressed in an untucked white oxford with missing sleeves, Billy Ray had polished the look with a pink bow tie. His thighs were fire hydrant thick, and he wore his pink chinos fitted. It was a country boy's twist on preppy that had gone down Easter-candy-vomit alley. Normally I'm all about the shoes, but his were something even Elvis wouldn't have approved of. He shuffled his feet and constantly twitched his shoulders. Before I could protest, he wrapped an arm around me and kissed my cheek as though I was dessert.

"Hey there, Raz," Billy Ray stuttered.

I lost my balance on my crutches, and he steadied me without letting go of the package he held.

"Come to woo Katie Lee?" I asked Nash.

He adjusted the flowers. "Good guess?"

"You know me. Always observant."

"So how'd ya jack your arm and leg?" Billy Ray asked.

I squinted at the streaked bands of light that glinted past the front glass doors in the hopes my van had arrived. It hadn't. Sighing, I told them, "Fell out of a loft and got run over by a car."

"God damn, Razzle," Billy Ray chuckled, "you are an original."

In daylight, I estimated Billy Ray to be nearer to thirty than I'd remembered. He darted his eyes all around the lobby but rested them on me. When he licked his cracked lips, I decided to wait for the van at the curb. "I'd love to stick around and shoot the shit, but I have a lecture to get to. I'm not sure when Katie Lee will be back from class."

"Don't worry," Nash said. "We buzzed Bridget. She's coming down."

AFTER CLASS, I MADE a tactical pit stop at the library and inhaled old paper smell for two hours, giving Katie Lee enough time to deal with her surprise visitors. I hoped Nash and Billy Ray had left town by now. Billy Ray's prowl for anything female, specifically me, gave me shivers. I never wanted to see him again.

Back at the dorm, the seventh floor buzzed with girls getting ready for make-out sessions disguised as dinner dates. Every open door I passed had something floral resting inside. A hedge of fragrant carnations and fern sprigs hogged Katie Lee's desktop. I didn't need to see the card. Since the assorted flowers weren't in the garbage can, I huffed a baby tiger growl. She'd made up with Nash, and Bridget's standing had most likely been elevated to cloudlike since she'd let him into the dorm.

I spread a mixture of tuna and mayo onto a slice of bread and topped it with soft American cheese. Setting the timer on the toaster oven for four minutes gave me a sinister joy. My snack permeated the air, overpowering the delicate floral scent. After my first cheesy bite, a dozen long-stem pink roses glided into my room, hiding Macy's face. Her bright red nails clutched a glass vase. "Ah Jesus. Not you too?"

Placing the behemoth arrangement on my dresser, she clucked her tongue two times. "Lookie what I found with your name on it."

"You're kidding?"

Like a fox chasing a rabbit, Francine followed the scent into my room. She sniffed a rose and stepped back. "Whoo-wee, whoever sent those must have dropped a hundred dollars." She anchored her fists onto her hips. "And look at that crystal vase. Waterford?" Francine stiffened her neck, turned her head toward me, and rolled a throaty, "Um-hmm."

"Where did they come from?" I asked.

"Front desk," Macy said. "I brought them up for you."

"Is there a card?" Francine asked. "It'd be a shame if someone didn't take credit for those."

"Who would send me flowers? This has to be a mistake."

Macy reached for the vase. "Finders keepers."

Francine slapped her arm and plucked a card out of the center.

When I saw the handmade envelope, my head pounded, and I had to sit.

"Have you been flirting with someone over at the infirmary?" Francine asked.

"Maybe they're from Kentucky Travis," Macy said.

I hadn't told anyone Travis's secret and didn't intend to. These definitely weren't from him.

The envelope had been fashioned out of a gum-candy wrapper. The word *Razzle* centered on the front. When Macy saw it, she put her hand over her mouth. "Billy Ray."

The handmade sleeve was too bulky to hold just a note. I pulled out a hand painted miniature landscape no bigger than my palm. Under a pencil-thin wood frame, a handful of people, the size of paper clips, drank from plastic cups and clapped hands as they encircled a dancing girl. I turned on my desk lamp and pulled a magnifying glass out of my drawer. The brunette in the center of the portrait held a lit cigarette and reached for her partner's hand. "I think this is me."

Francine stood behind my shoulder. "Everything's so small."

"Is there a note?" Macy asked.

I flipped the painting over. Taped to the back was a piece of paper that had been trimmed with pinking shears. "Hope you're back on both feet soon. Looking forward to our next shag. Billy Ray."

Flopping onto Katie Lee's bed, I buried my head under her pillow.

"That boy sure must like you," Francine said.

Katie Lee stepped into our room. "What boy?"

"Billy Ray sent Razzle flowers and a painting," Macy said.

"Did he?" Bridget commented from our doorway.

"Oh my Lord. I just left him and Nash in the parking lot. He didn't say anything about it."

I held out the miniature portrait and showed Katie Lee. "I had no idea he could paint real art." She tilted the painting. "Maybe he bought a kit for this."

"They don't make paint by numbers this small. He used special brushes with a couple of bristles. Miniature artists paint under a magnifying glass. The man may be a creep, but he's a talented one."

"Maybe you can sell it," Bridget said.

"I'd burn it before I sold it."

"Wait till Patsy hears," Katie Lee said.

My stomach churned. Why did he have to pick me for his muse? It would be a long time before shag innuendos stopped. The only redeeming feature of Billy Ray was the two hundred miles that separated us.

THE DORM EVACUATED AROUND DINNERTIME. Francine had a date with her squeeze, whom we now knew as Roger, and Macy had retreated into her room. I wasn't speaking to Bridget, and I didn't ask about her plans. I didn't want anything to do with her and kept my distance whenever possible. Unfortunately, Katie Lee and Macy stayed friends with Her Royal Annoyance. It maddened me that they didn't see the rotting compost beneath her sweet exterior.

Katie Lee filled a ceramic vase with fresh water and arranged her carnations on the dresser. I verified what I already knew. "So you're back together?"

"He drove all the way up here and took me to lunch. I gave him a chance to explain."

"Did Billy Ray help him with his story?"

"It wasn't like that. Billy Ray ran an errand. Dropped us off while he took care of business."

"What kind of errand?"

Katie Lee shrugged. "I didn't ask."

"What happened to Nash for five days?"

"Sometimes he can be absentminded. He went to Winston-Salem to play a gig. Intended to come back the next day. Last minute, Billy Ray asked him to make a couple of deliveries. He drove to Asheville, then down to Charlotte before heading back to school. With the winter storm and all, it took him an extra three days."

"What kind of deliveries?"

"He didn't ask what needed transporting, just couriered some packages. Every delivery he makes, Billy Ray knocks five hundred off his new truck."

"Five hundred! Katie Lee, what's he delivering? Drugs, puppies, body parts?"

"Nothing like that. Nash says the parcels are light. The size of clothing gift boxes, wrapped in shopping bag paper. Billy Ray told him he doesn't need to know the specifics, and Nash doesn't ask."

"Katie Lee!"

"I know. I told him to stop, but he doesn't see any harm."

"Why didn't he call you?"

"Left without his address book and forgot our number."

"And you believe him?"

"Why would he lie?"

"For the record, I have a bad feeling about Billy Ray and these deliveries."

"Rach," Katie Lee said, "you're just freaked 'cause an older guy is sweet on you."

Our phone rang, and Katie Lee answered it. "All right. We'll be over." After she hung up, she said, "Get your coat and ID. We'll swing by Bridget's on the way to the cafeteria."

I'd never speak to or eat with Bridget alone, but in a group I could mostly ignore her. Macy joined us, and on the other side of the elevators, Katie Lee knocked on her partially open door. None of us could miss the porcelain vase filled with at least two dozen pink roses. *Nash—a two-timing, lying prick giving Bridget roses and Katie Lee carnations.* I broke my rule of icing her and asked, "Who are the flowers from?"

"I don't know exactly."

"How can you not know?" Macy asked.

"The note is signed, A Secret Admirer."

"Do you have any idea who it might be?" Katie Lee asked.

"None," she said, reining back glee.

I uncrossed my arms and clenched my fists together behind my back. "I hate to put a damper on your floral euphoria, but aren't you concerned that the roses are from the same person who used condiments to decorate your room over break? You may want to dial Tuke."

Bridget reached for her jacket that hung on the back of her door. "That's overreacting. The vandalism was a random incident. I'm starved."

In the elevator, Katie Lee told Bridget, "Those roses are as beautiful as Rachael's. And so many of them. Someone is into you."

Macy and I stood at the back of the elevator, and her elbow nailed my side. Bobbing her head at Bridget, she mouthed, "Who?"

I bit my lip and shrugged my good shoulder. I didn't know what I knew anymore.

NOTE TO SELF
Katie Lee and Nash are back together—no comment.

Billy Ray. Is there no losing that man!

March 1987

30

The Big Easy

My shoulder had healed. I'd retired the sling and could carry a book bag with one or two books. It felt pre-Jack Daniels, except in stormy weather. When clouds thickened and the air grew damp, it turned into a barometer. Instead of rising mercury, my joint ached.

I'd avoided the infirmary and hadn't seen Clay since my freak leg mishap. If he spotted me with the Velcro contraption and the sling, he'd think I was an accident-prone train wreck. Exploring the unknown naked avenues would have to wait until my dodgy leg healed.

After dinner, we hung out in Macy's room. I pushed her beanbag out of the way and began a set of leg strengthening exercises. I didn't have firm spring break plans, but when I did, I wasn't going to pack crutches.

"The last place I want to spend my time off is Canton, but I'm broke, and if I ask my dad for a loan, he'll insist I restore something to earn money. I'll be stuck working in his shop."

Macy stood in front of her dresser and turned her head around. "That's fucking ridiculous. No one spends spring break at home. Let's party somewhere outrageous, like Daytona Beach."

Katie Lee rested on Macy's bed. "Mexico or the Texas Gulf are supposed to be crazy."

"So you're cool with a girls-only vacation. No Nash?" Macy asked.

"Of course," Katie Lee said, which surprised me. I thought she'd want to spend the week rekindling the flame with him.

When a light sweat broke out around my hairline and at the small of my back, I gave my leg a rest. "I have two criteria, cheap and warm."

Sunshine and Kool-Aid-colored drinks garnished with umbrellas had more appeal than a Canton, Ohio, thaw. I had to avoid going home. Spending a week with Dad and Trudy had as much appeal as processing chickens at a slaughterhouse.

Dad hadn't sold the Quesnel I'd refurbished over Christmas, so the commission wasn't in my pocket. A reasonable excuse and some creative financing needed to surface to make a beach vacation happen.

Katie Lee lodged a Gobstopper candy into her cheeks. "If you need money, you could always donate plasma. You can get twenty dollars for an hour-and-a-half sittin'."

I started another set of leg lifts. "How do you know these things?"

She shrugged. "Confucius says ideas are like assholes. Everybody has one."

"I'll pass on the plasma donation. If you think of anything that doesn't involve an exchange of bodily fluid, let me know."

"Y'all, we need to ask Bridget what her plans are."

I walked Macy's garbage can over to Katie Lee. "Spit it out."

"Why?"

"That Gobstopper is messing with your head. You know my relationship with Bridget is barely tolerable."

Macy alphabetized her vitamin bottles. "Rach, you're so dramatic."

"Me? Dramatic?" I scoffed. "She attracts trouble."

Pinching the Gobstopper between her fingers, Katie Lee asked, "What are you talking about?"

"She spiked my drink at a party and drove over me in Big Blue. Her room got trashed over Christmas break, and she has an anonymous, mostly likely mental, Valentine admirer. And..."

"And?" Katie Lee asked.

I so wanted to blurt out that Bridget had slept with Nash, but Patsy and I were still working through that bit of information. "And spring break falls on Saint Patrick's Day."

"Rachael, what are you saying?"

"I'm saying I'd like to live to eat jelly beans on Easter. Someone is stalking her. Whoever it is saves their ambushes for holidays. She's not safe to be around, let alone accompany us on a vacation."

"She didn't try to kill you," Katie Lee said. "And you can't honestly believe that some nut-job sent her those flowers."

"A nut-job sent me flowers, why not her too?"

"If Bridget joins us we can split the hotel room in four instead of three. Can't you make nice for a week?" Macy asked.

I growled.

Making big eyes, Katie Lee stared at me. "We won't be driving. You won't even know Bridget's there."

I'd notice her, but their guilt tactic chipped at my sensibilities and quieted my inner voice, the one that told me Bridget attracted more trouble than Katie Lee's boyfriend, whom, coincidently, Bridget had slept with.

"As long as I don't have to sit next to her on the plane or share a hotel bed."

"You won't," Katie Lee said.

"And you have to promise me that Nash and Billy Ray will not crash our girls' vacation."

Katie Lee wore a look of shock. "Rachael, that's ridiculous."

"Then I'm in."

KATIE LEE TOOK IT upon herself to make a few phone calls. She searched for vacation deals and made destination suggestions that none of us could agree upon. Spring break was quickly approaching, and it looked as though I'd be tortured in Ohio for an entire week. Completely bummed, I hadn't said anything to my dad about coming home. I hovered outside of reality, not wanting to confront no chance of a tan.

When I returned from an afternoon lecture, Katie Lee popped out of our room. "Rach, get in here. I have news."

Macy lounged on Katie Lee's bed, and Bridget stretched across mine. "Hey, Rach," Bridget said. "Hope you don't mind me on your bed." I drew my thumb and motioned for her to vacate. She relocated her butt on top of Katie Lee's desk.

"What have you done now?" I asked Katie Lee.

"I found our spring break destination."

"Where are we going, and how much will it cost?"

"We're only two and a half weeks away," Macy said, "which is good."

Katie Lee lowered a blind slat with her finger and looked at Campus Drive below. She released her finger, snapping the metal strip. "Bridget just got off the phone with JR."

"Who's JR?" I asked.

Bridget purred. "A friend of mine."

"Don't tell me. He lives in Dallas."

Reaching into our minifridge for a soda, Katie Lee popped the tab top. "Who cares where he's from? All that matters is that he found us a last-minute package to New Orleans."

"It's a killer deal," Bridget said.

"How much?"

Bridget stiffened her polo collar up. "Airfare and hotel for six days and five nights, four hundred eighty-six dollars each."

I had to admit, it sounded almost doable.

"We leave on Sunday, return on Friday," Macy said.

"My sister lives near the Raleigh airport," Katie Lee said. "We can stay at her apartment the Saturday night before we leave, and the Friday night we return."

"I'm not sure. New Orleans? What's in New Orleans?"

"Come on, Rach," Macy quipped. "Bourbon Street, booze, hot college guys."

"It's an artistic town. Jazz bands, street performers, and galleries. You may even be able to finagle extra credit for art history if you write about some painting or sculpture you find."

"That's cheesy," I told Bridget. "And bars?"

The three stared blankly at me, not tracking with my train of thought.

"Last time I checked, none of us are twenty-one, and my doctored college ID isn't going to get me into Bourbon Street bars."

Pulling me to my feet, Katie Lee wrapped her arm around my shoulder and took me for a stroll around our room. "The beauty of this entire trip," she said, "is that Louisiana, God love 'em, still has a legal drinking age of eighteen."

"We can drink legally in New Orleans?"

"Until March twenty-first," Macy said, "at midnight."

"The drinking law is changing to twenty-one the last night we're there," Bridget said.

"This sounds like an intoxicated Cinderella fairy tale. Are you sure?" I asked.

"Positive," Bridget said.

Louisiana was not on any of my must-visit lists. "Isn't New Orleans a swamp that's below sea level?"

"A sunny swamp that lies on the mouth of the Mississippi, so bring your suntan lotion," Macy said.

Bridget clicked the ink on one of Katie Lee's Tar Heel pens. "Upper seventies to lower eighties with some humidity."

Releasing my shoulder, Katie Lee clapped. "The Big Easy will never be the same after it sees the likes of us."

There were two items to sort through in order to commit to the trip. The small matter of figuring out how to ask my dad's permission and scrounging up the money. My checking account only had three hundred dollars left from Christmas. Dad sent me a monthly allowance for incidentals. If I combined the two, I still didn't have enough funds.

Katie Lee and Macy called their parents right away. For them, New Orleans was a done deal. Bridget said she wouldn't have a problem getting an okay from her dad. My parental dynamic required a more tactical approach. Experience told me Dad agreeing to and financially filling the holes for a week's vacation in New Orleans was highly unlikely. There would be two reasons for him to pooh-pooh the trip. Reason one would fall under the dangerous umbrella. Reason two would be money.

I wanted to meet cute college guys, get a tan, and drink rum a hundred and one different ways. For now I pushed thoughts of those details aside. "Seems we're goin' to New Orleans."

LATE IN THE DAY, the sun skirted behind clouds, and a bone chill enveloped the last shreds of warmth. I shut our window and pulled a sweat shirt over my head. Leering in my open doorway, Bridget held a bag of microwave popcorn and two sodas. "Spring break is going to be fabulous."

Since she'd driven over my leg, she had worked hard to win some sort of friendship badge. She set a cold can of Dr. Pepper on my desk. The pull tab hadn't been opened, so I accepted the peace offering and spoke before I censored. "I'm worried about coming up with the money."

She munched a handful of popped kernels and washed them down with her soda. "Get a refund on your meal plan."

"Can you do that?"

"The girls down the hall just did. What plan do you have?"

"What do you mean, what plan? I eat three meals a day."

"You have the high tier. I'm pretty sure you can cut back to one or two meals a day and get a check for the balance."

"How?"

"The registrar's office. You show your student ID, and they write you a check."

I clicked the tab top open and slipped a straw in my Dr. Pepper. The last time I visited that place, I paid for a new student identification that added three years to my age. "I don't know. My ID has the wrong birth date. What if they notice?"

"How would they?"

The next day I'd bitten most of my fingernails down to raw edges. When I cashed a check for six hundred ninety-eight dollars, I rationalized, who eats breakfast anyway? Bridget had actually provided a useful piece of information. With my finances in order, I just had to figure out a way to tell Dad I'd be in New Orleans for a week.

NOTE TO SELF
Am I too hard on Bridget? She did help me figure out how to finance spring break.

Positive Dad will not approve of New Orleans. If I ask, the answer will be no. If I tell him, the answer will be no. Dreading that conversation.

Plan to spend spring break in a swamp.

31

Busted

Macy special-ordered a cheese sub with extra cheese. Behind the cafeteria stainless steel service station, a woman in a hairnet curved her mouth into a down grin and scrunched her eyes into an eat-shit-and-die expression. Macy ignored the goblin-esque stare and waited. The two had had a heated conversation early in the year about why she couldn't just remove the slices of meat she didn't want instead of having a cheese and lettuce sub specially made. Macy had explained that she could taste meat sweat on the bun, which made her violently ill. Special orders were not met with warm salutations. While Macy drummed her nails on her tray, I envisioned the foodservice lady secretly massaging slices of meat over the bun but didn't share my thoughts.

"Have you told your dad yet?" Macy asked.

"I'm not going to tell him anything."

"You're just going to disappear for a week?" she asked.

I zoned out at the sunlight cast through the floor-to-ceiling windows and didn't immediately answer her. Students seated at tables near the windows held a hand to shield their eyes, and a few wore sunglasses while they ate. "Kind of," I said, wondering if I'd received the "avoidance" genetic strand from my maternal gene pool. "He hasn't mentioned spring break. I think he forgot."

"That's convenient."

"The pieces are falling into place."

We joined Bridget at a table where she'd placed books on chairs to save them for us. Standing, she cheerily said, "Gosh, Rachael, you look good in that color."

"I'm wearing denim. Everyone looks good in blue jeans."

I wished she would get some emotional etiquette into her head. It didn't take a rocket scientist to understand that when you cause bodily harm that requires a hospital visit and physical therapy, even if it was a nitwitted accident, it takes time for the injured party to speak to you on pleasant terms.

"You're not wearing the Velcro contraption," Bridget said. "Are you in pain?"

"What do you think?"

"Sorry," she whispered.

"Rach, have you heard from Travis lately?" Macy asked.

I'd actually been talking to Kentucky Travis every week, and Macy had overheard the end of a recent call. She figured he and I would be hooking up, and she wanted to reconnect with his roommate, Ryder Ridgemont. Lately, she fixated on me arranging a double date. I avoided her eyes and concentrated on my lunch, the only meal I'd eat at the cafeteria today on my new plan. Bridget yammered on and on about spring break and her classes. When she ran out of material, she finished up with, "I have to stop by the bookstore. Anyone need anything?"

Macy pushed her tray aside, leaving half her sandwich on her plate. "I'll come with. I could use a couple of blue books."

"See you back at the dorm," I said and scooped a puddle of refried beans and processed cheese on my nachos. Francine came out of the self-serve line, and I noticed Clay behind her. My heart pattered. I hadn't seen him since I'd been on crutches. Now I just had a slight limp. I waved at Clay. He didn't see me. Instead, Francine met my gaze and moseyed toward me.

"How's it going?" I asked.

She put her tray down across from mine. "It's going."

"That doesn't sound like sunshine and happiness."

"I came here for a bit of peace. Y'all missed a big ruckus in your friend Bridget's room this morning."

"Bridget is not my friend. She is an acquaintance by association."

Francine cut into a ham steak. "Wait a minute. Aren't ya going on spring break with her?"

"Against my better judgment, yes."

"Your acquaintance had a surprise visitor."

"What guy is ogling over Her Royal Perkiness now?"

"An older one. And I wouldn't describe it as an ogle."

"What's going on?"

"I was in Chantel's room this morning, and she'd left the door open to get some air flow. Wait till you see her. She went and got a Flock of Seagulls cut."

"Like the band?"

Francine nodded. "She splurged on some new mousse and jojoba oil."

"Why?"

Francine pursed her lips. "Black hair isn't like the fluffy chinchilla coat you grow. Our scalps get dry and our hair breaks."

"It does?"

Instead of rolling her eyes, Francine circled her head. "You aren't well-versed in ethnic, are you?"

I shrugged.

"We were conditionin' and styling my hair. I'm plannin' on meetin' Roger for a dinner date."

"The guy you've been hot 'n' heavy with since you two made out in the hallway last semester?"

Francine unleashed a smirk and arranged mashed potato to look like a gumdrop on top of her neatly cut ham slice. "Three men knocked on Bridget's door. One was a City of Greensboro detective."

I stopped chewing my nacho and stored it in my cheek. "Are you serious?"

"I don't make stuff this good up."

"What did they want?"

"The detective asked Bridget to verify her identity. Told her they needed to discuss a matter in private."

As Francine spoke, I extinguished my peripheral vision and tunneled my focus on her voice.

"Let me tell you, that girl didn't look so good. Her face turned pasty white, more so than usual."

I pushed my tray aside. "You have my full attention."

"The bacon boys stepped inside her room and shut her door."

"And?"

Francine took another bite from her plate. She chewed that morsel twenty-seven times. After she swallowed, she bent across the table and lowered her voice. "Now I don't want you to get the wrong idea about me and Chantel."

"What did your bayou ears overhear?"

"Chantel and I took to studying in the hallway, outside Bridget's door. We didn't purposely snoop, but they talked so loudly."

I patted Francine's arm. "You may have some penance time on your hands."

"What do you mean penance? I did nuthin' wrong."

"Francine, tell me what went down."

"Settle your jitters," she said as she wiped the corners of her mouth. "Seems some shoes, mail order clothing, flowers, and cash advances totaling over seven hundred dollars had her room's phone number and address on the shipping details. Ordered over the last month, on a stolen credit card."

"No!"

Francine pouted her lips. "Um-hmm."

"What did she say to the police?"

"Said she knew nuthin' 'bout the merchandise or the stolen plastic."

"Maybe they made a mistake."

Francine raised a finger in the air while she sipped sweet tea. "One of them men asked if she'd retrieve her wallet and show what credit cards she carried. In a crackly voice that *bonne a rien* said she would not."

"Bonne a rien?"

"Someone who's good for nuthin'."

I nodded. Of all my friends, Francine was most aligned with my perspective of Bridge. "And?"

"We heard sniffling before that girl's wits came out of her storage files."

The sun shifted and softened the inside of the cafeteria. I shut my eyes and mouthed, "Oh Lord."

"Amen," Francine said. "The detective said Visa would be pressing charges that could amount to prison time for fraud."

"Oh—my—God," I barked, drawing unwanted attention. In a hushed tone, I said, "This is serious."

Francine motioned for me to lean into the table. "No one talked behind her door until one of the men offered an out. If she confessed and handed the Visa over, they'd arrange for her to pay for the purchases."

"No!" My mind went into overdrive. Did Bridget steal the card, or did someone give it to her? Nash had a suitcase of money and owed Billy Ray ten thousand. Then there was Nash's new Dodge that he drove off in after Halloween. Was this how he and Billy Ray made money on the side? Had Bridget become involved?

Francine snapped her fingers in front of my face. "Earth to Rachael. Come in."

"Sorry, what were you saying?"

Francine tipped her chin. "It got real quiet in there, but that girl is slippery like a swamp eel. I heard a drawer open. I have a hunch she found that Visa and handed it over."

"Does Bridget know you know?"

"How would she? We moved out of the hall. It wouldn't have looked so good if they came out and we were sitting there."

"How did it end?"

"We seated ourselves on Chantel's bed. We'd forgotten to shut her door, and we watched Bridget leave with the officers. I'm guessing they took her tooloulou ass to the station to fill out paperwork."

"Tooloulou?"

Francine rolled her eyes. "Stay with me. Fiddler crab—the kind with one big pincher. Sneaky buggers. They clank that claw, show-off-like, to lure smaller crabs to their tunnel. Chantel told me Bridget was gone for two hours."

"Did she say anything to Bridget?"

"Chantel's got gumbo. That's why we get along. She flat out asked what the police wanted."

The tables around us emptied. "And?" I asked.

"That nitwit waved it off. Said it was a misunderstanding. No big deal."

"Unfucking believable!"

Francine, a staunch Baptist, cringed.

"Sorry, France, I've been around Macy a lot and it just slipped."

We put our trays away and walked back to the dorm. Before we parted in the hallway outside our rooms, she offered some advice. "You can bet I'm not leavin' any unattended valuables around, and I suggest y'all do you the same."

I watched her disappear and heard the sharp click of her lock.

Katie Lee was at class, and Macy's door was shut. Closing my dorm door behind me, I hung my book bag in the closet. It slipped off the hook and landed on top of my duffel bag, where I noticed a lump. It was the Bible Dad had handed me back in August when we unpacked the van. Kneeling down, I feathered my fingers across the worn cover. I'd already paid the nonrefundable spring break money and would spend a week with Bridget in New Orleans. Even though she'd slept with Nash and had driven over my leg, she didn't act pick-pocket criminal.

I didn't know if I could believe Francine and didn't want to forgo my spring break plans, losing my deposit because of a rumor. Bridget didn't complain about money and never seemed short on cash. When I rested the Bible on its back binding, it opened to Thessalonians, the page marked with a hundred dollar bill. Dad must have tucked it in there when he dropped me off that first day. Sometimes people surprised me, in a good way. I hoped that Bridget and my mom would do the same.

The phone rang. It was Dad. I didn't want him to call and worry while I was away. After a back and forth "How are you? I'm fine," serenade, I spit out, "We have some time off from classes in a couple of weeks."

"I didn't realize you had a break," he said, confirming he'd forgotten.

"It's no big deal. I was invited to hang out with Katie Lee, Macy, and Bridget."

He must have been distracted because he said, "It's fine with me if you want to stay at Katie Lee's."

A prick of guilt twanged inside me for not clarifying where I'd be spending the time off, but I really wanted to get away for a vacation with my girlfriends. Timing and luck unexpectedly spun my way. I decided not to repeat the rumor about Bridget. What good would it do? I'd secured funding and had Dad's tacit approval for a relaxing break.

NOTE TO SELF
Not sure what went down in Bridget's room. Neither she nor Katie Lee has said anything.

Thessalonians, a good read?

32

Things Better Left Behind

I tapped the face of my Swatch. The little hand was on the seven, and the big hand was on the nine. Seven forty-five a.m., and daylight had emerged. Macy, Katie Lee, Bridget, and I stood curbside at the Raleigh-Durham International Airport. We thanked Katie Lee's sister for letting us spend the night before she drove away.

Macy didn't speak in the morning. She never scheduled a class before noon. I didn't let her grumpiness irritate me. Flying to a warm destination for a week of partying put me in a happy place, and I couldn't wait to get there.

Passing through automatic doors, I was surprised at the hordes of people and luggage that littered the check-in counters. "Katie Lee, are you positive we can drink?"

"We can legally consume alcohol in Louisiana. The only dignified state as far as I'm concerned. I mean, really, we can drive a vehicle, vote, join the military, and fight for our country, but we can't be trusted with a beer? I consider this a direct violation of my rights."

"You just had to get her started," Macy grumbled.

"What do ya mean, get me started?"

Bridget mimicked Katie Lee: "The drinking laws in this country are hypocritical."

"Settle down," I said, "we're in your camp. I'm stoked for break. I want to lay by the pool during the day and lounge in jazz bars at night."

We checked our bags, and I glanced at my wrist. "Eight fifteen. We're making good time."

"Stop with the time checks," Macy said. "You're disrupting my co-matose state."

After discarding a to-go sweet tea, Katie Lee motioned to visit the restroom, and we followed.

Bridget leaned on the wall outside the entrance. "I'm okay. I'll watch the bags."

From inside my stall I told the girls, "It's eight twenty-four. Did you see the security check line? It looks as if half the state is evacuating for spring break."

In a zombie stance, Macy lathered her hands. "Our flight doesn't board until nine forty. We have over an hour to go through that line and get to the gate."

Slugging behind a maze of people to get to the x-ray machine, I checked my watch at every corner. Macy and Katie Lee chose lines to the left while Bridget and I went right. When my turn came, I hesitated as the man in front of me fumbled to find his ticket in his briefcase. Bridget stepped in front of me and tilted her head back. "It's ten after nine."

While security passed my bag through a second time, the girls waited for me under the flight monitors. "Miss," one of the workers said, "you need to come with me."

"Why?"

"Miss, come with me."

I followed him to a door that read, *Airport Security, Private.*

Macy shouted, "Rach, what's going on?"

A tall man wearing blue pants two inches too short, motioned his hand at a gray plastic chair. "Take a seat."

Dumbfounded, I followed orders. "What's this all about?"

Two others joined us in the room. Then a fourth gentleman, gray at his temples, entered. He wore an airport detective badge that said *Grady*. He pushed the door, but before it shut, Katie Lee shoved her sandaled foot in the crack.

"Can we help you, miss?" one of the security men asked Katie Lee.

"I'm traveling with her," I said.

She let herself in, followed by Macy and Bridget. Katie Lee wedged her hands on her hips. "What's going on, y'all?"

In a voice that vibrated the flimsy drywall, Airport Detective Grady asked, "Where you ladies headed?"

"New Orleans, sir." Katie Lee glanced at her naked wrist. "Our flight departs in—"

"Thirty minutes," I said.

The security employee who had handled my bags gave my leather travel case to the detective. Unzipping it, he asked, "Do you have anything to say for yourself?"

I thought this was some kind of joke, but no one laughed. "Can you be more specific?" I asked, darting my eyes from him to the girls.

The detective began placing items on the table: lipstick, concealer, eye pencil, cigarettes. Pushing the items to the side, he made room for a small wood pipe and two tiny plastic cylinder containers the size of my pinky fingernail. "Do you call these nothing?" he asked.

My voice squeaked, "A pipe?"

"Miss O'Brien, this is drug paraphernalia. Illegal in the state of North Carolina."

You aren't going on spring break.

"They're not mine," I blurted.

Grimacing, Detective Grady managed to refrain from rolling his eyes. He didn't have to ask questions to scare me. His presence ignited my nerve endings into a series of pulsating shocks. I started to hiccup, and as an added bonus I thought I'd hurl.

Katie Lee went on the defensive. "She's not in possession of drugs."

Hearing her words plunged me into an out-of-body experience. That was my toiletry case with my makeup, but the drug stuff I'd never seen before. I hadn't packed them. They weren't in there this morning, or maybe they were. We awoke so early. I had dressed and left.

How in the hell would I get out of this? Would Macy, Katie Lee, and Bridget hop on the flight, leaving me to be booked on drug charges? *That's what Bridget wanted. She was sabotaging me.* The conversation in the room garbled around my eardrums, and my vision went out of focus. I could only form grunts and one-word answers to the questions being asked as my mind wrapped around the ramifications of wearing an orange jumpsuit in the women's penitentiary.

Bridget batted her lashes. "Can't you let her go with a warning?" *She'd already helped me enough.*

My roommate's eyes sparked with electricity. Katie Lee lived for these moments. Standing tall, she interjected some of her best bullshit scare tactic commentary. "Y'all can't charge her. You never read the Miranda Rights. Rachael, don't say anything until you have counsel." Slamming her hand on the table, she said, "Y'all are harassing her, and that is a state violation."

I believed in mind over matter and chanted, *this can't be happening.* Surely the earth had stopped rotating and I'd been flung into someone else's problem.

Katie Lee tapped a foot. "Y'all don't have anything on her, and our flight leaves in under twenty minutes. If we miss our plane, we expect reimbursement on the ticket and hotel accommodations—and being inconvenienced."

She dug my hole deep and wide.

The detective knitted his eyebrows together and glowered. "This is a serious offense. Possession of a drug apparatus is prosecutable in the state of North Carolina."

I stroked the face of my Swatch with my thumb, hyperaware of my saturated armpits and the ticking secondhand. We had fifteen minutes to get to our gate. I'm risk averse. Not the kind of lunatic who craves the adrenaline rush that goes with carrying a pipe and drug vials through airport security. I needed to set everyone straight. It was a setup, but how could I prove it? "This is a misunderstanding."

The detective opened the door and motioned to Macy, Katie Lee, and Bridget. "Step outside for a moment. I need a word with Ms. O'Brien."

From outside the door, Katie Lee raged, "They can't do this to her. We need to find a pay phone. My daddy can call in a favor from Judge Husk Driskell."

"There's no way we'll make our flight," Bridget said.

When the door closed, I told Detective Grady, "I didn't pack those. I've never seen them before."

"Who put them there?" he asked.

I struggled to fathom the logistics of the pipe and containers ending up in my cosmetic case. All I could think about was my dad and that he was going to murder me after he posted bail. Teary-eyed, I sniffled. "I don't know. Maybe someone in my dorm thought this would be funny."

The detective filled in some paperwork that rested on a clipboard. He didn't look at me when he spoke. "Since you are not in possession of any drug substances, I'm going to confiscate the pipe and vials. This time I'm sending you on your way with a warning."

I swallowed hard to suppress a hiccup, but my mouth wasn't producing saliva.

He set his pen aside and met my eyes. "I want to make it clear. These items are illegal and will not be tolerated. You're a very lucky girl. If there was even a speck of drugs in those vials, I'd have no choice but to arrest you."

My body slumped like a balloon with a leak. Detective Grady handed me my carry-on. "Ms. O'Brien, in the future, make sure you pack your own bags."

I acknowledged his advice with a nod. Before he changed his mind, I stood and waited for him to let me go. Outside the door, I saw the agitated faces of my girlfriends and willed Katie Lee not to make any additional commentary. Not bothering to check the time, the four of us turned on our heels and bolted for the B gates.

"Rachael," Katie Lee said. "Why did you pack those?"

"I didn't."

"We're going to miss our flight," Bridget said.

"I can see the gate," I said. "The door's still open."

The sign above gate B24 flashed *New Orleans, delayed twenty minutes*. The woman behind the counter picked up the handset and announced, "Flight 1326 to New Orleans is now boarding first class."

Plunking down in a chair in the boarding area, I dropped my bag and let my head sink between my legs. Sweat dripped down my neck.

Out of breath, Macy's eyes welled with tears, and she wiped them with her polished fingers. "The pipe and containers are mine."

I popped my head up and spewed words like dragon flames. "Jesus, Macy, why the hell did you put them in my luggage?"

"I'm lost," Bridget said.

"I keep them in a wooden box in my underwear drawer. I didn't pack them."

Tongue-tied, I had trouble constructing sentences, but managed to ask, "How did they get into my cosmetic case?"

"I've been racking my brain. I don't know."

"What were those tiny containers?" I asked.

Macy darted her eyes. "Old coke vials."

"You do coke?" Katie Lee asked.

"No. I mean once. Over New Year's Eve. In Little Jamaica."

"Wait a minute," I said. "You sent me a holiday postcard. You were in Times Square, not the Caribbean."

Macy rubbed her forehead. "It's a neighborhood in New York City. You drive through and pick up what you want."

Bridget put a new roll of film in her camera and wound it into place. Securing the lens cap, she looked up to scold Macy. "So Rachael just wangled out of a drug bust with your pipe?"

"Rach, I hope you believe me. I get buzzed, but not enough to forget putting my pipe and vials in your bag."

Katie Lee moved toward the line of people waiting to board. "Let's just try and get to Louisiana before the cops change their minds."

NOTE TO SELF
Someone in the airport almost got me arrested. I think she's blonde and slept with my roommate's boyfriend. Evil Bitch.

33

Hurricane Cocktails and Crawfish Kisses

The taxi drove past the muddy Mississippi where container ships and riverboats churned the water in a swift chop. Darkening clouds threatened rain on the delta swamp, and the moisture hanging in the air would've taken wrinkles out of linen.

During the eight-hundred-mile airplane ride, at baggage claim, and inside the taxi, I kept physically and verbally distant from Bridget. Despite vacationing with her, I planned to converse in no more than one-word grunts.

Situated on Decatur Street near Jackson Square, the Chateau Hotel was in a killer location. The cabby piled luggage for four onto the sidewalk that separated the front door from the cobblestone street. The hotel brochure boasted a cozy forty-five rooms. Katie Lee called it boutique accommodations, which was a fancy way of saying small and cheap.

Cupping my hands around my eyes, I peeked inside the front door. The intimate lobby walls screamed zim-zam-va-va-voom. Floor-to-ceiling petal-pink-and-gold-damask wallpaper and oversized tassel tiebacks, the size of a mini Nerf footballs, held eight-foot-tall silk

draperies. A tufted sofa with dainty legs, two eighteenth-century replica armchairs, and large vases with silk arrangements dotted a sitting
area by the front desk. Seeing the décor, I realized that no straight college guy would intentionally book a reservation in this boudoir. I still
held hope for meeting cute men, just not much of a chance inside here.

"What are we going to do first?" I asked.

In unison, the girls shouted, "Bourbon Street."

Katie Lee disappeared to check in, and Macy hunted for a luggage
cart. Bridget sat on a suitcase and tilted her eyes on her wristwatch.
"I'm so glad to be on break."

I ignored her.

"Is there a line inside?" she asked.

I didn't reply.

Bridget held her head in her palm and anchored her elbow on a
knee. "Why are your feathers ruffled? We're on vacation."

The ringy-rhyme purr of her voice snapped something inside
of me. She preyed on vulnerabilities, and I'd had enough. I had to
end her twisted game before someone, *most likely me*, got hurt. My voice
rasped low and steady. "I'm not stupid. I know you planted the drugs in
my suitcase to get me arrested."

She stood up and moved toward the hotel doors. "You're crazy."

I pinched Bridget's wrist and held tight. "You're not very careful,
are you? I know a lot more about you than you think. I'm wondering
if the detective at the Greensboro police would be interested in your
latest ploy?"

Bridget shook from my grip. She neither confessed nor apologized.

"Forget about pulling any more crap. You and I are done."

Katie Lee exited the doors and joined us on the sidewalk. "Our
rooms aren't ready. We can leave our bags in a closet behind the desk."
She unfolded a tourist map of the surrounding area. "The hotel man-
ager says Bourbon Street is a short stroll."

Macy came out of the double doors with a cart and a bellhop who
began to load our luggage. He handed Macy a numbered ticket, and she
gave him a five.

Bridget followed him, "I have a headache," she said. "I'm going to stay in the lobby until our room is ready."

"Come with us," Katie Lee said. "A walk might do you some good." Without looking back, she moved inside the hotel.

"Were you two arguing?" Katie Lee asked.

"I wouldn't call it arguing. More of a position statement."

"What's going on?" Macy asked.

"I told Bridget I know she planted the drugs in my suitcase."

"Why'd you say that?" Katie Lee asked.

"Because she did. It's the only explanation, and I'm not amused by her sense of humor."

"How'd she manage that?" Macy asked.

"In the airport, when we went to the bathroom. She stayed outside."

Macy processed what I said. "God, I was still asleep and didn't pay any attention to her."

Katie Lee had a hand on the hotel's door handle. Her thumb stroked the fleur-de-lis etched in brass. "Y'all, I know Bridget, and she just wouldn't do that. Let me go get her, so we can set things straight."

"Why would Bridget steal paraphernalia from me to put in your suitcase?" Macy whispered.

"My theory. She's mental."

"No, seriously?" Macy asked again.

"I don't know," I huffed.

Ten minutes later Katie Lee came out, alone. The three of us barely spoke as we crossed uneven cobbles, past a bustle of musicians and tourists who congregated in the French Quarter. We stopped in t-shirt souvenir shops, watched street performers, and Macy posed for a pencil character drawing of herself while extending her middle finger in front of her face.

The Louisiana air drugged us with a perfume of fried kitchen oil and olive tree blossoms, while the heat basted us like chickens in a rotisserie. I looked up and down Bourbon Street. "Let's get a drink."

Katie Lee clutched a handful of New Orleans tourist attraction brochures and pointed at a terra-cotta building with green shutters. "How about Pat O'Briens Bar?"

I approvingly nodded.

THE OUTSIDE OF PAT O'BRIENS was a green-shuttered, salmon-painted two story that possessed a colonial charm. It was always happy hour in New Orleans, and inside the building thirsty out-of-town revelers stood shoulder to shoulder. Katie Lee moved along the narrow bar and looked for seating. Wall mirrors reflected steins hanging from the ceiling, and a lit-up vintage shamrock cast a dim green glow on the bartenders.

I scanned the crowd for cute college guys and told myself not to let Bridget ruin my vacation. The one-way conversation I'd had with her had been long overdue. I felt stronger for having confronted her, and I was sorry I'd avoided it so long.

Ahead of me, Katie Lee abruptly stopped, her head craned to her left, and she pointed. "Is that Bridget?"

"Where?" Macy asked.

"They say everyone has a double," I mumbled.

"The table in the corner. She's sitting across from an older guy in a tropical shirt. Her back is facing us."

Before Macy or I confirmed Bridget's identity, Katie Lee wove toward the table. "Bridget?" she shouted and waved at us to follow.

A half-empty punch drink and a beer sat on O'Brien paper napkins. Bridget stood up, her cheeks reddened as she glanced at us.

"What are you doing here?" Katie Lee asked.

"I got bored and decided to explore. I thought a drink would relieve my headache."

A man I'd never seen brushed his hand across Bridget's back as he stood. He reached out toward me. "L-Jack."

"Rachael," I said, with Katie Lee and Macy following on introductions.

"How do you two know each other?" Katie Lee asked.

"Funny thing," Bridget stammered. "Small world. L-Jack is a family friend."

"Really," I said.

Prematurely grayed, L-Jack had the creases of an outdoorsman branded around his eyes. He motioned to the empty chairs. "Please sit and join us."

Bridget took a long swallow of her drink.

"What is that?" Macy asked.

She slid it across the table. "A hurricane."

"What's a hurricane?" I asked.

L-Jack arched his brows. "It's a rum drink that's this town's signature cocktail. Guaranteed to send you spinning."

"Like Dorothy in Kansas?" I asked.

A server dressed in a green-logo polo stood by our table and clicked a ballpoint pen. "That was a tornado."

Bridget plastered a smile on her face. She didn't offer explanations or show any signs of the headache she'd claimed to have. "Three hurricane cocktails. My treat."

"And another lager," L-Jack said.

"Can I see y'all's IDs?"

Bridget's offer to buy the first round bubbled uneasiness inside my veins. Was this her way of making nice? Her behavior was like a light switch that she flicked from naughty to nice. *I wished we'd left her in North Carolina.* I wondered if she'd use a stolen Visa to pick up the tab and made a mental note to watch the name she signed on the carbon copy.

Three twelve-inch blown glass vessels filled with twenty-six ounces of liquid arrived at our table. A fruit salad of cherries and orange slices bobbed on top of the ruby-red cocktail. Being buzzed for five days was one way of getting me through the break with her.

L-Jack carried the conversation. Said he'd fallen in love with the city on a family vacation and kept coming back. He told us about some of the local must-see attractions. A swamp tour, carriage rides through the garden district, and after-dark ghost walks.

Initially I'd been unsure of this destination, but zydeco and lively bar chatter melded in my ears, encouraging me to seize the addictive rhythm of this town. Each fruity sip I took left me feeling thirsty for more. When I neared the bottom of the rum concoction, any lingering post-travel airport anxieties had dissolved. Deciding to embrace the local cuisine, I ordered a crawfish appetizer.

"What does the L stand for?" Macy asked.

"Lucky."

"Your mother named you Lucky Jack?" I asked.

"Not quite. I own a gallery in town, Lucky's Art Consortium. Most people call me Lucky Jack, LJ, or L-Jack for short."

Southerners play a game called "Do you know?" They delight in finding somebody's great-aunt's cousin who knows the electrician two streets down. It didn't surprise me when Katie Lee nudged my shoulder. "Maybe you've heard of Rachael's dad, John O'Brien. He restores fine art back in Ohio."

L-Jack took a sip of his drink. "Now does he? What kind of art does your daddy restore?"

Pride swelled inside me, and I told him, "His last commission was a pair of Clementines."

The girls laughed at the mention of the small orange fruit, but Jack tipped his chin. "Hunter?"

Nodding at L-Jack, I noticed my body was slumping off my chair.

Our server landed a plate of crawfish and palm-sized packets of wet wipes in front of me. "There's enough to go around."

"They have eyeballs," Macy said. "I don't eat eyeballs."

Bridget pinched her nose. "Those are disgusting."

Normally I like seafood: shrimp, lobster, crab, flounder—but these red-shelled crustaceans stared at me from under antennas, and I swear one blinked. I reached out my hand then pulled back. "I don't know how to eat crawfish."

"Ladies," L-Jack said, mostly to Bridget, "let me teach you the Louisiana pinch and suck. May I?" he asked and lifted one of the creatures from the platter. "Watch closely."

L-Jack's hair looked like it was slicked back with Dippity-Do. His three-button shirt opening drew my eye to a chunky gold chain that held a weighty anchor charm. His laugh boomed, and compliments tumbled off his tongue. I guessed his agenda was hooking up. I didn't believe this smooth talker was an art dealer. He looked more like a carnival caller at the nickel bottle drop, and as far as I was concerned, he could get lost. I wasn't that desperate, and I didn't plan to carry the memory of his sleaze appeal with me to the grave.

Like breaking a graham cracker down a perforated center, he snapped a crawfish in two. Juice splattered on Bridget, and she squirmed to her feet. Offering his napkin, L-Jack dabbed the front of her leg.

What kind of "family friend" does that?

"Now the fun part," he said, and with the power of a Hoover, he sucked meat out the antenna portion of the crawfish.

Macy posted her hand like a stop sign and looked away. "That's fuckin' barbaric."

He smiled as though she'd paid him a compliment. His tanned fingers peeled the body of the other half. Dangling the dismembered crustacean above his head, he applied pressure to the tail and launched a morsel into his open mouth. Keeping a watchful eye on Bridget, he licked the leftovers from between his fingers.

Katie Lee clapped. "Rach, your turn."

Picking up a crawfish, I gave it a kiss and dropped it on my lap. Covering my mouth with my hand, I said, "My God, they're spicy." With my lips ablaze, I rushed to the server station and plunged my face into a water pitcher. It didn't help. My mouth was still an inferno.

From behind, someone pushed wet hair out of my face and handed me a towel. "Your mascara's running," Bridget said before cradling my elbow to escort me back to the table.

I didn't trust her and twisted out from her grip.

Voices in the bar grew louder. Back at the table, L-Jack patted his tearing eyes with a napkin and slid a basket of breadsticks toward me. "It'll dull the heat."

I pressed two on my lips and began to hiccup.

Sweeping a hand over the appetizer, he said, "Crawfish are as southern as cotton."

My relationship with crustaceans began and ended with one kiss. "Forget it," I garbled. "I can't feel my lips."

Hanging around with Lucky Jack wasn't attracting any cute guys to our table, and we needed to lose him. Ready to move on, I told the girls, "I need to walk this off."

Giving a heartbroken look, Lucky Jack handed the waiter his credit card. "Y'all can't leave. We were just getting started."

I clutched my hurricane glass and said good-bye to Lucky Jack. Hugging me, he slipped a business card into the back pocket of my Daisy Dukes. His boozy breath tickled my ear as he whispered, "Stop by my gallery."

Had my crawfish kiss turned him on? Outside the bar, I inhaled deeply and banished him from my mind. Experimentation with anything Jack was a terrible idea.

NOTE TO SELF
Kissing crustaceans, don't go there.

Hurricane = recipe for messed up.

34

Beware of Men Wearing Green Tights

Sunshine streaked through the slats of the faded vinyl window blinds onto two double beds. The window air-conditioner strained a grinding hum as it battled the clammy air that threatened to overtake our room. Staring at red-polished toenails reminded me that I hadn't landed a hot guy, but instead shared a bed, for a second time, with Macy. There wasn't a speedy remedy to recovering from hurricane cocktails and crawfish. So I laid still for the rest of the day in an effort to quiet the construction noises inside of my head.

The following day, March 17, I'd snapped back. Deciding to pay homage to my Irish heritage, I planned to eat the green breakfast of champions at the pub across the street. My morning menu selection would include green onion bagels spread thick with mint cream cheese, washed down with a frothy green beer.

"If you eat that," Macy said, "you'll pee green for at least two days."

"I'll risk it."

Louisiana humidity brought out waves of uncontrollable crazy in my hair, and I'd determined a ponytail would have to be my signature vacation hairstyle. Midmorning, the cobbled streets were still mobbed with partiers from the previous night and others like us who were getting an early start on Saint Patrick's Day. We waited over an hour in a line that snaked outside the pub, giving the muggy air ample opportunity to coat my skin in a film of perspiration. The girls and I took our time eating a late breakfast before moseying back to the hotel. The consensus was to work on our tans until we came up with a better idea. Behind the hotel, a kidney-shaped swimming pool rested in a lush garden. Framed by a high wall, moss baskets dripping with ferns and ivy cascaded downward in a tangle with hot-pink bougainvillea. Flipping over every half hour put me in official vacation mode. I'd embraced spending my break in a swamp.

"What do y'all wanna do later today?" Katie Lee asked.

"How about shopping?" I said.

Bridget slid her sunglasses onto the top of her head. "We can do that anywhere. Let's do something unordinary."

Macy sat up in her lounge chair. "I've been wondering about those transsexual bars."

"We can do that too," Bridget said. "But I was thinking of a tombstone crawl."

"What kind of drink is that?" I asked.

"It's not a drink. I thought we could visit the local cemeteries. They're filled with Civil War soldiers, courtesans, and vampires. Since New Orleans is below sea level, the tombs around here are above ground."

"That's creepy. Why do they do that?" I asked.

"So the bodies don't float away when it rains."

"Eugh," Katie Lee said.

Bridget fluttered her fingers in the air. "We may even witness a gravesite voodoo ceremony."

"I'm already cursed," I said. "I don't need someone dancing around me, chanting magic words and sprinkling herbs to reinforce my losing streak with men."

Katie Lee tipped her straw hat up. "Y'all, I prefer to party with the living, not the dead."

"Agreed," I said.

Sliding sunglasses back over her eyes, Bridget huffed, "Fine. But we'll be missing out. There aren't any other cemeteries in the country like the ones here."

"You've got your holidays mixed up," Macy said. "It's Saint Patrick's Day, not Halloween. My vote is for the transsexual bar. We'll see more oddities than you could ever hope for at a voodoo ceremony."

From outside the walls that enclosed the hotel pool, we heard a drumbeat resonate. "I bet that's a Saint Paddy's parade."

Leaving our towels and Panama Jack suntan oil behind, we threw on tees, shorts, and flip-flops to investigate. Two blocks away, floats with green fringe glided toward us and horns began to trumpet "When The Saints Go Marching In."

Green beads and plastic trinkets flew over my head as tourists and locals danced to an infectious rhythm. Weaving through the crowds, we followed the parade until we found an opening for viewing. A person the size of a leprechaun, painted from head to toe with body glitter, marched under a rainbow balloon arch. He sported a thong unitard and kicked his pointy boots with square green buckles like nobody's business. He wasn't bashful about spinning to show off his shamrocks, and I wondered if his mother knew he performed this trick.

"Nice ass," Macy shouted, and he galloped toward us.

I imagined leprechauns as antisocial and focused on hiding pots of gold. The New Orleans variety didn't fit that cake mold. The one in front of me found his tornado and wasn't shy about gyrating his treasure. Snatching my hand, he spun me around and led me onto his Emerald Isle float.

Lost in the moment, I climbed aboard and danced between giant-sized origami tissue paper shamrocks that had been speared into plastic turf. Being wooed by the cheering crowds that lined the streets made me feel famous, and I waved to strangers from the self-propelled party on wheels.

The "YMCA" song blasted from speakers. I was cool with that. Familiar with the hand motions, I joined a pack of green men who idolized The Village People until someone in high heels with torpedo boobs, an orange wig, and beer stubble squeezed onto my four-leaf clover. This androgynous person—I'll describe as a Vengeful Pat—shoved me off my shamrock and snarled, "Find another ride."

"Hey," I said, looking for the leprechaun who had lured me with his pot of gold. Unfortunately for me, he was intimately shimmying with a Dolly Parton blow-up doll, and I didn't have the heart to interrupt.

Floats move a lot faster than you think, and my leap to solid ground produced two skinned knees. Limping to the nearest sidewalk, I searched to find a recognizable face, street, or building. Nothing registered, and an uh-oh, sickish feeling harbored inside my stomach, which quickly morphed into a lightning bolt of panic that constricted my chest.

As the parade music drifted into the distance, so did the dispersing crowds. Wandering along the side street, I saw only a handful of locals, including a soulful clarinet player, who rested on a wooden street barrier. Turning corners, I speed-walked in the direction I thought was Bourbon Street. Vertical iron bars jailed broken glass panes on abandoned shops, and empty bottles and snack food wrappers littered the corners of boarded doorways. Muggy air and suntan lotion beaded on my skin. Not seeing horse-drawn tour carriages, street magicians, or historical-looking buildings, I realized I was directionally challenged.

Shadows stood in entryways, and hidden faces stared from behind screen doors. The street I hoofed along wasn't Louisiana's finest. My eyes darted, and I searched for a friendly face to ask directions. A man slight in stature with sullen cheeks leaned on the side of a one-story brick building. His shoe polish face didn't have enough wrinkles to warrant his shoulder-length gray hair and rubber-banded Santa Claus beard. He held a crumpled paper bag in one hand and a lit cigarette in the other. Rotating his head from left to right, he asked, "Where's a thing like you headed?"

He stood too close to avoid, so I asked, "Can you tell me how to get to the French Quarter?"

His smile opened the tunnel to tobacco-stained teeth. "The French Quarter," he repeated, as though he chewed marbles.

I tilted my ear, ready to head in the direction that he'd suggest. With a gruff laugh, Santa dropped his bag, and liquid trickled from it. Instead of reaching for his spilled beverage, he lunged for my arms. Pressing my back against the building, he pierced his jagged nails into my forearms. In a troll voice, he growled, "Show me your tatties."

Being scared shitless can paralyze. For me, it evoked a knee-jerk reaction, and I hooked my scabby right into Santa's dilly pickles. In a free fall, he keeled to the ground. Clenching my wrists tight, I had no choice but to topple down with him. A cocktail combination of body odor and cheap beer fermented from his sweaty pores. The noxious scent encircled me in a dizzying cloud. Temporarily I'd immobilized his reflexes, but not his abusive mouth. From a fetal position, he groaned, "You piece of shit. When I get my hands on you."

Fighting to align my wits, I wangled from under his clutch and scampered my flip-flop feet as fast as I could. Something metal clattered off the pavement close to my ankles, and I gazed down. Seems Santa had a rusty knife.

Not daring to look back, I turned corners and crossed deserted streets. Adrenaline pushed me forward. An occasional car passed, but their inhabitants didn't look like the give-me-a-safe-lift type. Growing up, I'd watched *Star Trek*, and I would've paid Scotty a colossal sum of money to beam me up.

A stucco wall, too high to climb, loomed along the street in front of me. A chunky lock as big as my hand secured black iron gates. One side tipped due to a broken hinge, leaving a narrow center opening. Once I shimmied in, there was no mistaking where I'd landed. Stumbling on the uneven ground, my eyes focused on the raised cement tombs that dotted a snaking path.

Engineers did not build cemeteries. At least not this one. A maze expert had a field day with these plots. There was no geometric organization. A sick joke on the living. Once you were in, it wasn't so easy to find your way out. A bigger worry, one that threw a knife, hovered on my mind, and survival mode motored me deep into the graveyard. The more turns I took, the harder I would be to find.

Fear had sharpened my senses, and I listened to the noisy breeze dusting overgrown weeds and leafy shrubs. I didn't want to be a victim. Not that anybody chooses. Since my family had gone down dysfunctional alley, my life wasn't bad, as in horrible. It just wasn't what I'd imagined. Lately, though, I'd started to get a handle. So what if Mom wanted to discover her prophecy powers and Dad dated? They were on their own journeys, and I'd started mine. My "to-do" list was still full. I wanted to sleep with Clay Sorenson, ride a zipline through the rain forest, stay in a haunted English castle, eat a Cuban sandwich in Miami, and open my own art gallery—and no one, not this Santa creep, Bridget, or Nash, was going to stop me.

Dead-ended in the far corner of the cemetery, I stopped next to an apartment of stacked tombs that backed up against a decaying wall. There wasn't saliva in my mouth to swallow, and I held my palm on my chest to keep my heart from escaping. I hadn't brought money or worn a watch, and I didn't know how long I'd been gone. Beyond my noisy heartbeat and heaving breath, I listened for the crunch of gravel or a foot treading the tangle of undergrowth. Too tired to run anymore, I squatted between the high-tower tombs and a smaller building, like an outhouse, with a sealed, knobless door. Overgrown dandelions and thistles framed a cemented plate stamped *Marie Laveau, 1782–1881*. Mardi Gras beads, a tube of mascara, coins, and a plastic snake cluttered the step in front of the enclosed sarcophagus. Three *X*s were randomly marked on the exterior walls of Marie's tomb.

"Ma fille. Vous n'avez pas l'air bien. Etes-vous perdus?" A woman's voice spoke, and I gasped.

I didn't believe in ghosts, apparitions, or hocus-pocus, but the French accent scared the crap out of me, and I wondered if I was about to become a believer. A nearby dog erupted in a quick series of howls, drawing my attention to a portion of the crumbling wall that had collapsed. Beyond it, a dirt path surrounded by knee-high scrub led to a porch. With a full-length wrap adorning her body, a mocha-skinned woman rocked a high-back chair and shushed the dog. Next to her feet, an oscillating fan flapped a screen, and a weathered side table held a candle whose wick danced inside a lantern.

Shaken but grateful I'd spotted an earthly being, I stepped over the wall rubble and approached. Stopping at the bottom of the porch stairs, I stared at the woman whose age seemed timeless. Her hands rested on faded chestnut varnish, and her fingertips contoured into indentations that I imagined had been worn into the rocker's arm rails over generations. With each forward sway, the chair's joints jeered a creak. Her streaked graying hair had been gathered in a French twist on the back of her head. Still rocking, she stretched her lips in a welcoming smile.

"I'm lost. Can you tell me the way to the French Quarter?"

She motioned to a bench. *"Vraiment? Asseyez-vous et reposez-vous un moment."*

I guessed her words signaled an invitation to sit and perched on the edge of a metal glider. This wasn't right, my being here. What was I thinking, following that leprechaun? I bumbled, *"Je ne parle pas Français*—I do not speak French," silently cursing myself for being unable to articulate more conversation from the elective I'd taken in high school.

The woman in the rocker gazed toward the cemetery. Touching a lace fan to her chest, she met my eyes. "Ezora."

Like an international tourist, I nodded then replied, "RACHAEL." The next best thing to speaking French in New Orleans had to be loud English. "I'm-lost. May-I-use-your-telephone?"

Ezora stood and motioned me toward the door. *"Vous, les filles sont trop maigres, vous avez besoin de manger."*

I racked my brain for a translation, but her accent was thick. I didn't hear the word telephone in that sentence and wondered if telephone sounded like telephone in Cajun-French.

"Telephone?" I asked again. She held the door open. *"Venez à l'intérieur."* Her words I recognized. *Come inside.*

Hesitating, I weighed options. Inside this house, she could have jars of formaldehyde with floating stuff she'd retrieved from the graveyard. On the other hand, a healthy population of poisonous spiders and slithering reptiles were at home in the hidden nooks of the crypts. And somewhere beyond the shadows, Santa lurked. My odds were better inside.

The kitchen sink light bulb threw a glow on the narrow hallway's faded carpet runner. The handloomed floral design I guessed to be as old as the terrace row house. Her decorating style embodied an island feel with the Caribbean blues and yellows that washed her walls. Ceramic trinkets and handmade figurines covered flat surfaces. A wood bench with carved symbols stretched the length of the hallway she led me through. Piled on it were newspapers, magazines, jars, and vintage coffee cans.

Ezora's ballet-slippered feet silently glided into a dining room. I followed her, mindful of the noisy floorboards below my flip-flops. At a table draped in an antique lace cloth, she tapped the back of a chair with the underside of the rings she wore. Opening a china cupboard, she selected two plates with a dainty posy pattern before pulling the knobs of a drawer where she reached inside to retrieve polished silver forks, spoons, and knives. The stems of the scroll flatware were engraved *EL*.

Helping set the table, I worked to quell my imagination, but the image of Ezora poisoning me so she could pack me into a crate and send me down the Mississippi wouldn't fade away. I considered bolting out the door, but if I backtracked through the cemetery, there was a high probability that I'd rest there permanently.

Disappearing into the kitchen, Ezora hummed in a deep alto, and I figured she could belt out an "Amazing Grace." She returned holding two cast iron pots. Adjusting potholders against the handles, she placed the cookware on silver trivets. Steam escaped the outer edges of the lids, filling the air with an aromatic blend of onion, garlic, and the sweet smell of fish.

"*Riz et étouffée*," she said.

I'd seen *étouffée* on the menu at the hotel restaurant. It was a seafood stew.

She scooped red rice onto my plate then smothered it in a dark brown sauce with flecks of green onion, herbs, and shrimp. I held a spoonful in front of my mouth and lightly blew.

My mother was a remarkable cook, and when I tasted that first spicy bite, I wished she were here. Ezora's étouffée sent fireworks of gourmet goodness into my mouth. Mom would not have left until she had this recipe. As I savored another spoonful, a shrill ring echoed from the hallway. "Telephone," I said, and she waved it off, signaling me to concentrate on the meal. As much as I wanted to dial 911, it would've been rude to let this home-cooked meal go cold, so I waited.

Ezora's French was as thick as my English, and we struggled with conversation. I pointed to the *EL* engraving on the spoon. "Ezora Laveau," she said.

I recognized Laveau. The name was etched in front of the raised grave I had hidden beside.

"Marie Laveau?" I asked, and she nodded a look of sorrow and pride. I thought it odd, and at the same time honorable, that she kept a daily watch on her deceased relative's eternity.

When we finished, I stood to help clear the dishes, but she pushed my hand away and pointed at the hallway bench where I'd heard the ringing.

The house clutter was one empty soup can away from hoarding. Prodding around boxes of newspapers and clothes piled on the black mahogany bench, I found a wall plate with a phone plugged in. I traced the plastic-coated cord until my hand rested on the receiver of an old-fashioned rotary phone. Without money or a phone book, I couldn't exactly call the hotel or a taxi. Stuffing my hand into the shorts pocket that I'd worn the first night, I pulled out a business card. Lucky's Art Consortium.

In less than ten minutes, my ride parked in front of Ezora's house. Sherbet pinks and oranges had settled in the sky before the sun bid goodnight. Squeezing my hand, she motioned for me to wait. I watched her retrieve a key from her apron pocket before moving to a corner of the room where a small wood box rested on a shelf. I heard the click of the lock, and when she returned, she dropped a trinket in the palm of my hand and closed my fingers over it. I hugged her. "Thank you for saving me."

"*Etre sûr et vivre long,*" she said.

Outside, L-Jack held the passenger door open to his idling Cadillac Deville.

NOTE TO SELF
Men dressed in green spandex pretending to be leprechauns will lead you astray.

Southern hospitality continues to amaze me.

35

Fake in the Grass

A few miles from Ezora's house, Lucky Jack parked next to his art gallery. Inside the historical walls of Lucky's Art Consortium, the bricks were the only thing original. Glass pendant lights hung from the exposed twenty-foot ceiling, and eight-foot walls painted bright white divided the gallery into alcove spaces to display artwork.

Wrestling out of a drunk's arms, dodging a knife, and racing through a cemetery in the New Orleans humidity had turned my shoulder-length hair into a poof ball. I ran water over my hands from the small vanity faucet and pressed my palms against my frizzy waves that escaped my ponytail. I'd begun decompressing in the safety of Lucky Jack's car, suppressing the possibility that my last breath could have been in the New Orleans Delta. I'd never been so glad to see someone I recognized, and LJ seemed pleased to have rescued me.

My story about a leprechaun and a demented Santa was out there. I hoped he didn't think it a ploy for sympathy sex, because I had no intention of remembering him as "The One." As soon as my heart stopped hyper-beating, I'd say a warm-felt thank you and recover back at the hotel.

Customers moseyed around his gallery, and he answered a question about a local sculptor. Seeing me handle a glazed ceramic three-dimensional amulet no bigger than an inch, he asked, "What do you have?"

Cupping the piece in my palm, I showed it to him. "Ezora gave it to me."

Lucky Jack put on a pair of black-framed glasses. "Ezora Laveau is something of a local voodoo maven. May I?"

I handed him the talisman. "The engraving is an eye."

He focused on the piece. "I've studied the Mayans and Hittites, but this appears to be..."

"Egyptian. It's the eye of Horus."

"You know ancient symbols?"

I shrugged. "A lot of crazy stuff comes through my dad's shop, and we end up doing research. Once, someone brought a stone with hieroglyphics. It looked authentic, and Dad called a friend. Turned out to be from the Valley of Kings."

"How old were you?"

"Nine."

Peering over his glasses, LJ's words caught me off guard. "You have an expert eye and a photographic memory."

Not many people knew. Only family. I hadn't told the girls. I don't know why, but I confided in him. "I can recall stuff. Symbols and signatures. If someone dots an *i* center, left, or right, size of loops—that kind of thing."

His staring made me uncomfortable. I figured he thought I was full of shit or something. "Do you paint or sculpt?"

"No, I leave that to artists. I mend works damaged by time and mishandling. Give portraits facelifts—make them look young again."

"What about sales? With your knowledge and keen eye, it could become a lucrative living."

His gaze lingered, and I didn't respond. Handing the charm back to me, he asked, "Do you know what the eye symbolizes?"

"Strength, wisdom, spiritual guidance."

The tourists left the shop, and Lucky Jack excused himself to lock the door behind them. "There's something I'd like to show you."

Guiding me through a dark corridor, he placed an arm around my shoulder. A voice inside my head pricked a warning. Although he hadn't done anything wrong, his invasive touch made me uncomfortable. I'd kneed one groin today. I didn't know if I would be accurate a second time.

After unlocking a door, he switched on a light in a windowless storage room where large metal drawers were stacked to the ceiling. A worktable sat in the center and a desk in the corner.

Hesitating to step inside, I asked, "What's this?"

He retrieved a key and a pair of black gloves from a desk drawer and motioned for me to sit. "I want to show you something."

Piles of paperwork cluttered the desktop. While he searched the art drawers, my finger aimlessly fanned a pile of invoices. Midstack, one caught me breathless. Lucky's Art Consortium had paid Billy Ray $46,000 for six primitives. The invoice had a New Bern address, and Lucky had signed his real name under a *received* stamp. There was nothing lucky about Jack Ray.

As I rewound my memory, I strung the pieces of an epiphany together. Billy Ray, a talented artist, partnered with his relative, Jack. The pair moved fakes south of the Mason-Dixon. Nash had to be involved. What about Katie Lee? Was she involved? Jack Ray—initials JR. Shit! Bridget's contact to arrange this trip. What did he want? To recruit me, or keep me quiet?

With an art drawer unlocked, he slid his hands into the black gloves. "These fireproof cabinets are airtight and indestructible."

Retrieving two wrapped canvases, he placed them on the white lacquered worktable and turned on overhead lights before unwrapping the artwork.

I thought Bridget had drugged me at Jackson's clambake, but maybe it had been Katie Lee or Nash. They both had access to pharmaceuticals.

Then there was the airport. Was sending me to prison her backup plan since she blundered not putting me out of action when she ran over me in Big Blue? *Why is Bridget after me? Is it because I know about art?* My heart drummed in a bad way.

No one would believe that Bridget had it out for me. I didn't want to believe me. Did I stand in the way of her and Nash? Did she pretend to like Katie Lee only to watch her fall once she dropped the bomb? I needed proof and protection. Sliding the invoice onto my lap, I asked, "What ya got?" and coughed to cover the noise I made folding it into a note the size you'd pass to the person sitting behind you in study hall. Alone in a room with an art forgery ringleader who wore black gloves, I stuffed the paper into my front pocket for safekeeping.

Lucky Jack drifted his eye to me. Curling his lips, he winked. With the artwork unwrapped, he stood back and motioned for me to join him.

Flee or fight. Personally I leaned toward flee, and was ready to run, but remembered he'd locked the front door. Reluctantly, I joined him at the worktable.

He watched me scan the paintings. Like a hunting cat holding back a pounce, I sensed that he was waiting for me to twitch or blink out of sequence. So I leaned forward and casually remarked, "Two Clementine Hunters. *Baptism* and *A Funeral.*"

"She's the hottest artist to come out of Louisiana. Just turned a hundred years old. When she passes, the value of these will soar."

What a sleaze.

The buzzer on the front door rang, and LJ excused himself. I scurried over to the desk and rotated his Rolodex to *A*. Methodically flipping the cards, I scanned each one. When I got to *B*, there was a card for B. Bodsworth and a Greensboro area code. "Jesus," I swore, but kept turning the cards. Lucky Jack was still talking out front when I got to the *H* tab. There was a phone number for S. Hayes. Halloween weekend, the beefcake. He had artwork in the Alpha Delta frat house. Did half of New Bern profit from the forgeries? As I flipped the *W* tab, I realized the voices in the gallery had gone silent. I went through that letter forward and checked a second time. Had I missed the card for Nash Wilson?

When Lucky Jack returned, I was leaning against the worktable. He apologized for the distraction and moved close, invading the space etiquette between people who are acquaintances. I'd seen the *Baptism* before today. In a New Bern art gallery, at my dad's shop, and a third I don't clearly remember in Jackson's hall closet. Stepping back, I asked, "Are these authenticated?"

Curtly he quipped, "Why do you ask?"

I wondered if LJ had locked the front door.

"Because they're amazing. I'm sure you'll get top dollar."

Lucky's Art Consortium was in a touristy section of the French Quarter, and I guessed it was no more than a five-minute walk to the Chateau Hotel. He'd left the gallery lights on, and we both heard the bell above the door chime again. "I should go," I said, swiftly moving out of the back room toward the front showroom.

"I can drive you back to the hotel."

No way was I riding in a closed tin can on wheels with him.

A large group entered, and LJ greeted them. As he shook hands, I waved, thanked him for picking me up at Ezora's, and left. Even though it was dark, a wash of relief settled over me as I set off on the foot journey through the bustling French Quarter. That was the last time I ever planned to lay eyes on Jack Ray.

I asked directions from a lady inside a souvenir shop. When I arrived in the hotel lobby, I borrowed a pad of paper and a pen from the front desk. Plunking down on a tufted sofa, I wrote down every contact I'd memorized from the Rolodex.

SHARING A HOTEL ROOM with three others for five days in a town that used to be a swamp, on a budget, without a car, was a lot of together. My lips had been tattooed a shade deeper from the crawfish encounter, and scabby bruises decorated my knees and arms from the Saint Paddy's Day altercation. I decided my run-in with demented Santa wasn't as nerve-racking as being in a small fireproof room with the head of an art fraud scheme.

On the cab ride to the airport, I emptied my carry-on and inspected my cosmetic case to ensure the flight back wouldn't be a repeat offense. I had to be careful around Bridget. I knew what she was capable of, and I wondered if her antics were a warning, or if her real plans had gone off the tracks. And Katie Lee. I couldn't trust my roommate until I figured out whether or not she was a player.

I had a phone call to make. He wasn't going to be happy that I crossed state lines without telling him. I didn't have a choice. I needed Dad.

NOTE TO SELF
New Orleans, not the most relaxing vacation. Next year my vote is for the Florida Keys.

I don't know who I can trust besides Dad.

April 1987

36

Encounters and Confessions

'd fessed up about being in New Orleans for spring break,
minus the airport security bungle. The space between my
ears kept replaying the phone conversation I'd had with Dad.
Both New Bern and New Orleans were enamored with Clementine
Hunter. If my father hadn't received the commission for her artwork, I'd never have noticed the duplicate paintings. But I'd studied
the brush strokes in the *Baptism* at his studio, and now I'd seen the
same artwork twice after that. I feared Dad had refurbished a fake.
Not recognizing a reproduction was career suicide. Even worse, the
museum could accuse him of switching out the original. Somehow I
had to set things right.

I wished he would've shouted at me for being vague about my break
destination. He didn't even ask how I'd paid for the trip. It shouldn't
have surprised me. Both he and Mom had a gift of administering blame
without raising their voices. In my family, self-guilt worked as an effec-
tive means of discipline.

Dad had listened to what I told him. When I finished, he said, "Tell me again about the *Baptism* painting you saw in New Bern, and then the one in New Orleans."

"The monogram signature, bottom right on both, not right center like the one in your shop. The circumference inside the curve on the *C*, on both, was tighter. The oils on the two here weren't watered down, the colors were more vibrant. The backs of the canvases were off-white with some staining, thinner than the piece you worked on."

"What makes you think the two you saw were painted by the same person?"

"The scenery was identical, brushstrokes consistent, but on the paintings in New Bern and New Orleans, there was one less person standing outside the church. Four, not five, ladies in white."

Blowing a curt huff, Dad said, "I'm going to make a phone call to my colleague at the New Orleans Museum of Art. I'll ask if he knows of Lucky Jack Ray. Find out if he has a reputation. But Rachael, if no one's complaining about being duped, there's no case."

Before we hung up, Dad asked me to mail him a copy of the invoice I'd nabbed and the Rolodex names I'd memorized.

"Masterpieces with a big price tag make people do crazy things. We don't know who the players are and what they're capable of. Don't tell anyone what you know. And stay away from New Bern."

MACY HELD UP THE CAFETERIA line while she decided what to order. "Baked ziti," she finally said to the lady in the red-stained apron who stood behind the steamy pans.

With a ladle in her hand, the cafeteria server stared at me. Even though it was lunchtime, she wore that end of the day, glazed eye stare. "What'll it be?"

Since I'd taken a cash payout on my meal plan to fund spring break, I'd been skipping breakfast and by lunch was starving. All morning I'd been craving a hot hoagie sandwich with all the fixings. "Steak sandwich. Extra onions and peppers."

Macy waved her pointer finger. "If I were you, I'd hold the onions."

"Since when are you concerned with my breath? It's not like I sleep with you—voluntarily."

She plucked a penne noodle off her plate and popped it into her mouth. "Since Clay Sorenson stopped me on my way to class to ask about you."

"If this is your idea of an April Fool's joke, I'm not laughing."

As we waited in line to have our IDs swiped, Macy lowered her voice. "I take your deflower quest seriously. You need to go big before you go home."

"I'm not sure I appreciate your special interest in my womanhood."

"Rach, Clay is perfect. I know you lust for him."

"There's a problem with Clay. He has a psychotic girlfriend who likes to threaten me."

Macy didn't move forward, and students surged past us. "He's single. I asked. I told him you were, too."

"Why'd you do that?"

"Because you are."

"He doesn't need that information."

"There's no time for games. The clock is ticking. I told him to stop by."

Inside my head, things went fuzzy. I scraped the onions and peppers into a garbage can and followed Macy to our corner table. Walking backward, she whispered, "It's going to happen."

I wasn't so sure about her prophecy. Proper southern children grow up with a strict code of manners. Whether or not their intentions are genuine is irrelevant. Being a New Yorker, Macy had probably cornered Clay and threatened him into saying what she wanted to hear. I'd been daydreaming about him since the first sighting at the Holiday Inn back in September. If Clay and I were meant to get together, we would've by now. There'd been opportunities. He was a blip that faded on and off my radar, and I wasn't convinced that we'd ever get our flight paths aligned. But a part of me still hoped.

BLOOMING HONEYSUCKLE AND DOGWOOD buds filled the warm air with sweetness. I hadn't found romance or met any cute guys worth staying in touch with on spring break. Besides Ezora Laveau, there was nothing lucky about that town. I'd officially crossed New Orleans off my annual spring break hot spot. My golden tan was the best thing I carried back from the trip, and to preserve it, I sunbathed between classes with an open book.

I tucked my knotted tee in my bra and hiked my shorts up my thighs to soak in the rays. Sprawled on a red-and-white-striped towel, next to me, Macy wore an itsy-bitsy-teeny-weenie black-and-white-polka-dot bikini. She looked like the optical illusion the optometrist shows you for an eye exam, but bigger, with a potty mouth and an aggressive foot that kept swatting my ankle.

"What?" I asked under closed eyes.

She rolled onto her side and faced me. "Clay may have friends, and God knows we all could use some cute guys to help get us through what's left of the semester." Tipping her sunglasses down her nose, she professed, "The dry spell on campus could be broken."

"Listen, you sex-crazed lunatic, do I look like a professional madam? I can't even find action for myself. The last thing I need is the responsibility of finding a selection of guys for you to invite into your cave for some rumpity-bumpity. If you're in need, you know perfectly well that Hugh is a walk across the quad."

Macy pushed her sunglasses back on her eyes. "I don't want to talk about him."

"Why not?"

She elevated onto her elbows. "He's seeing someone."

"I saw him yesterday. He didn't mention anything."

"I knew I shouldn't have told you."

I sat up on my elbows. "How do you know?"

Macy laid her head back down. "The last time I was in his room, I found a pair of woman's tortoiseshell-frame sunglasses on his bedside shelf."

"Wait a minute. I thought you only slept with him once."

Lifting up her new sunglasses, Macy rested them onto her head. She looked across the manicured lawn. "We've fooled around on occasion."

"You vixen."

"A relationship with Hugh isn't in the cards."

I suspiciously eyed the tortoiseshell-frame sunglasses she wore as a headband. "So you stole the sunglasses?"

"I didn't steal them. I'm wearing them to find the owner."

"Wait a minute, isn't this what you wanted? Not to be tied to one person?"

"After spring break, I changed my mind."

"I'm sorry," I said.

"I am, too."

THE BASEMENT WAS THE BEST-smelling place in the dorm. My wet clothes tumbled in warm air with a powdery-scented dryer sheet that promised to float me into the white, puffy clouds when I wore them. I set the timer for forty minutes and climbed the stairs to the lobby. Leaning by the elevator keypad, I watched Clay Sorenson stride through the glass doors toward me. His eyes creased in the corners, and his playful smile melted my insides. I didn't notice anyone else when his drawl sang, "Rachael O'Brien."

Choking on my breath, I began to cough.

"Thought I'd see if you were in." He took the laundry basket out of my arms. "Let me help you with that."

Clearing my throat, I asked, "How was your break?"

"Low key. I fished off a buddy's boat for a few days."

My hair fell out of a ponytail, and I wore a frayed t-shirt and shorts with flip-flops. Cursing myself for not looking more pulled together, I squeaked out, "Sounds relaxing."

"How's your shoulder?"

My lips tightened. I still didn't recall exactly what I'd said in my Jack Daniels state. There was a high probability that I'd rambled about how I wanted him to father my children. This was my chance to redeem myself; if I could remember how to speak in complete sentences, maybe I had a chance.

"It's a lot better. Only twitches when it rains."

"Are you busy? I mean is it okay if we hang out for a while?"

Breathe, breathe. That's it. Now think of something witty. Okay, forget witty and concentrate on something that's not stupid and more than one syllable. "Um…sure."

Inside the elevator we soared up seven floors, and I started to think that the dryer sheet promise of landing me in the clouds was true. Walking next to Clay made my feet feel airy. As we neared the end of the hallway, I willed Macy's door to be shut, but my karma was off. Making matters worse, she blasted the B-52's, which provoked Francine to shout out, "Whiney white music!" and slam her door.

It was easy to talk about Clay and lust for him from afar. In a dorm room, his close proximity made me nervous. I didn't have the practice to seduce him. Instead, I concentrated on not frightening him away.

My work was cut out for me. In under a minute Macy barged in, a wicked smile plastered on her face as she greeted him. I met her gaze and held it. We both knew she couldn't help herself. She was a mischief addict, unfamiliar with the word *imposition*. Settling into an armchair, she asked, "Where's Katie Lee?"

I reminded her, "Lifeguard certification with Bridget."

She pinched a grin. "Oh yeah. When do they get back?"

"Nine-ish," I said while mentally transmitting a different message, in case she tuned into my *exit your ass immediately* radio wave.

Right out of the gate, she asked Clay, "Why did you date that redhead?"

A wave of fret pinched my stomach, and I wanted to strangle her. She was like a puppet master; as quickly as she'd orchestrated our meeting, she was going to annihilate my chances with him. "Macy!"

"You know Sheila?" he asked.

She strummed her fingers on the chair arm. "Is that the psycho-bitch's name?"

"That's harsh," he said.

"Soda?" I asked, hoping to change the discussion to Coke versus Pepsi.

Macy glided the clasp of her gold rope necklace to the back of her neck. "She and a flight of demons ambushed us at the Holiday Inn, and during the snowstorm, she threatened Rachael with bodily harm for being near you."

Clay's mouth gaped. "Get out."

I searched for words to make the awkwardness go away. Before I thought of anything, Clay spoke. "I met Sheila last year. We stayed in touch over the summer and started seeing each other in August. It didn't go very far. She's on the controlling side."

A throaty guffaw slipped out of my mouth.

"Really," Macy scoffed.

"When it ended, I tried to stay friendly, but Sheila wouldn't stop calling. That kind of flattery has a short lifespan. She's been stalking me most of the year."

"Get a restraining order," Macy said.

"Maybe I should've. It got to the point where I avoided going out. She'd turn up wherever I went."

"Is she still stalking you?" I asked.

"Haven't seen her for a month. Either she got the message or met someone else."

Macy stood. "I should get back to studying. See you around."

"You will," he said.

Clay and I talked about classes, who we hung out with, and his job at the infirmary. Over an hour passed, and I realized I'd left my clean cloths in the dryer. Sharing the dorm with five hundred girls had taught me: never leave clothes in the machines. There wasn't a freshman manual, so I'd learned the hard way. Unattended laundry, wet or dry, can end up in a pile on the dirty basement floor, and select items can go missing. If someone is vengeful, an entire load can find its way onto the front lawn, in a stairwell, or ride the elevator until it's discovered. I grabbed my empty basket. "I need to check the dryer."

He put a mint in his mouth. "I'll walk you down."

On the lobby floor, the elevator doors opened, and I stood face-to-face with Francine. *I thought she was in her room.* Her head tilted sideways. Scanning past me she preferred to drink in Clay.

"Hey, Francine," I said. "This is Clay."

"Um-hmm," she said before meandering into the elevator.

Leaving her behind, we trekked down the flight of stairs to the basement. When I shouted, "Still in the dryer," he creased the corners of his eyes.

"Does some laundry elf rustle through your wet clothes and huck 'em into the bushes?"

"You'd be shocked at the things that happen in this dorm."

The washing machines and electric dryers clicked and hummed. Clay sat on top of a dryer next to the one I dug into. Electrodes sizzled inside of me, and one combusted when my arm brushed his. Straightening upright, I held a crumpled sheet, and he helped me uncrumple the ball of fabric.

"Rachael O'Brien," he said and paused.

The sheet folds drew him inches in front of me and I froze. Draping his arm around my neck, he delivered a kiss, and I realized that he had an uncanny talent to turn my brain off. It's one thing to be infatuated with someone from afar, but Clay's lips were no fantasy. They changed the game, and he had me flustered.

A dryer buzzed, and voices descended the stairs. We pulled apart, and he asked, "Do you have plans this weekend?"

"Not yet."

"Let's do something Friday night."

"What do you have in mind?"

He pushed hair off his eyes. "Dinner, maybe a movie."

I diagnosed myself with a serious case of infatuation flu. I knew the cure. Clay Sorenson was the medicine I'd been waiting for.

BOUNCING INTO MY DORM room, I dropped the laundry basket and flopped onto my bed. Smelling like pool chlorine, Katie Lee stood with a wet towel knotted around her waist. I didn't know if I should tell anyone for fear of jinxing good juju, but I couldn't help myself. "Clay asked me on a date!" I said, and squealed.

Ten seconds passed before Macy and Francine invited themselves in. Macy offered me a cigarette. All smiles, Francine and Katie Lee stood staring.

"O'Brien," Macy said. "We're here for a debriefing."

Francine settled onto a desk chair. "Speak, girl."

I started at the beginning. "He walked in the lobby unannounced."

"Nice," Katie Lee said.

"Nice? I nearly crapped my pants. He caught me off guard. I'm dressed in end-of-the-day tattered." I motioned a hand around my face. "Being polite, I invited him to our room."

"Of course you did," Francine said.

"Everything would have gone smoothly if Macy hadn't felt obliged to grill him about his relationship with She-Devil."

"Someone has to look out for you," Macy said. "In case you were wondering, I approve."

"Where's he from?" Francine asked.

"When are you going to see him again?" Macy asked.

"After he kissed me, he asked if I had plans this weekend."

"Wait a minute. Back up. Back up," Macy said. "He kissed you? Hello! Details!"

Francine synchronized a hand 'n' hip shimmy. "Girl, you spent two hours with that boy. If all you got was a kiss, you need to work on your technique."

"When are you going to sleep with him?" Macy asked.

Katie Lee pointed a hairbrush at me. "Make sure you protect yourself."

I couldn't sit still and hopped to Katie Lee's bed. "You people are gonna hex me."

Moving next to me, Macy said, "He'll call."

Since I'd returned from New Orleans, I'd kept the eye of Horus talisman in my pocket. I'd escaped Jack Ray, freaked out but unharmed, and considered the trinket good luck. I traced over the etching. "Even if he calls, there's the chance that things will go wrong."

Katie Lee grabbed her shower bucket. "Who are you kidding? Nothing is going wrong. It's all going right."

Our phone rang and I answered. "Hey, Dad."

He normally called me on Sunday afternoons, and I wondered if he'd heard something from Mom or about the fakes.

Lowering her voice, Macy asked Katie Lee, "Did you give any mouth to mouth?"

"Not tonight. You would be interested to know that Bridget and I are the only girls in lifeguard certification."

"Can I still sign up?" Macy asked.

"You could, but all the guys are in high school."

Macy whispered, "That's more up Raz's alley."

Motioning toward the door, I mouthed, "Out."

Macy flashed a toothy smile, like a kid who didn't want to obey, before leaving with Francine and Katie Lee.

"Rachael," Dad said. "We need to talk."

"Is it Mom?"

"No, it's not your mother, it's Clementine Hunter. The curator of folk art at the New Orleans Museum called me. One of her paintings they have hanging is a fake."

"Which one?"

"*Baptism*. Someone from the FBI is going to contact you."

NOTE TO SELF
Macy's direct approach is wicked. She's got nerve, and her strikes are accurate. God, she makes me nervous.

At least my hunch about the Clementine Hunter was right. If I'd been wrong, I would've looked like a dufus and tattled in vain about New Orleans when I should've kept the lip zipped.

Glad to be miles away from both the Rays.

37

Missing Masterpiece

F unny how when you're a kid, holidays and birthdays take forever to roll around. I'd just gotten back from spring break, and now Good Friday was weeks away. I met Clay on campus Tuesdays and Thursdays after lunch for an hour. He worked at the infirmary nights and weekends, and it was the only time our schedules crossed paths. My plan to lose my virginity in a meet-and-greet kind of encounter had become complicated. I liked Clay a lot and wanted him to like me, too.

Midweek, my art history professor ended class early. Outside the lecture hall, the sun was shining brightly, and the temperature sweltered as if someone had left an oven door open. Student traffic on campus was sparse, and I glanced at my Swatch. Twenty till one. Bodies would spill out of buildings on the hour. I stopped at a vending machine near the bench where I'd meet Clay and pondered Mr. Pibb versus Mountain Dew. I decided on Mr. Pibb, heavier on the cola flavor and less lollipop sweet. The can rattled down the chute. Before it made a final clunk, a tall gentleman in jeans, a navy polo, and tweed jacket asked, "Rachael O'Brien?"

"Yes."

Reaching a hand he said, "Storm Cauldwell, FBI."

"Jesus. Do you always show up unannounced?"

His sunburnt face gave him more of a ski enthusiast appearance than FBI. He flashed me his badge and asked, "Can you walk with me?"

"I'm meeting someone."

Smiling, he indented a dimple on his chin. "It'll just take a minute. Your friend can wait."

Since he said it would be quick, I agreed. "How did you find me?"

"Against policy to tell you."

"Really?"

He chortled. "I looked up your schedule and student identification."

I snapped my soda tab top open, and a fine mist spritzed from the can. "They keep black-and-white copies of student IDs?"

Storm nodded.

Shit, now the FBI knew I carried a fake ID.

I estimated Storm to be midthirties and six feet tall. He walked with a long, purposeful stride, and I hustled to keep up with his pace. He shielded his eyes beneath Ray-Bans and slicked his dirty blond hair with mousse that gave an all-day wet appearance.

"I've been assigned the case of the stolen Clementine Hunter. I'm coordinating the investigation with the New Orleans office and the IRS to inquire about the business dealings of Jack Ray. I need your word that you'll use discretion regarding our conversations."

"Of course."

"Tell me about the trip to New Orleans."

"You need to be more specific in your questioning."

He grinned. "How did you meet Jack Ray?"

"At Pat O'Briens. He and a girl I vacationed with, Bridget Bodsworth, were sitting together. He showed me how to eat crawfish and paid the tab."

"You like crawfish?" Storm asked.

"I thought I might, but I don't."

"Are you sure about that?"

"I'm sure."

"What else happened?"

"I got lost without money. I had Lucky Jack's business card in my pocket and called him for a lift. He took me back to his gallery. Showed me two Clementine Hunter paintings. Wanted to know my opinion."

"What was your opinion?"

"They were fakes."

"Did you tell him?"

"No. He's creepy. I told him he should get top dollar."

Storm retrieved a small pad of paper from inside his blazer and started jotting down notes.

"Did you have a more personal relationship with Jack Ray?"

"Please."

"Did he make a pass at you?"

"Is that question pertinent to the case?"

Storm tilted his head and kept writing. "How did you know the paintings were fakes?"

"My dad owns a fine art restoration shop. He worked on the same painting for the New Orleans Museum of Art." I paused and picked at a nail. "This is going to sound crazy, but I also saw that painting in a New Bern art gallery back in December and in a frat house at Chapel Hill before that. The New Orleans trip was sighting number four. That painting is reproducing."

"You're sure?"

I nodded.

"Do you have anything else?"

"I memorized three-quarters of Lucky Jack's Rolodex and borrowed an invoice that links him to New Bern."

Storm shook his head. "If he'd caught you."

"I know. Bad thoughts train tracked through my mind when I did it, but the coincidence is farfetched. Who'd believe me? I needed proof."

"Where do you have the information?"

"In my dorm."

"I need you to give it to me."

Students began to surge the campus. "Um, yeah," I said, looking at the time. "It's just that someone's going to be waiting for me."

Walking me back toward the vending machine, Storm glanced at his wristwatch. "I need to get back to the office. Can I stop by Grogan tonight and pick them up?"

"Sure."

After slipping a business card in my hand, he nodded his head and turned left while I navigated through the swarm of bodies to the bench where Clay sat.

"Who was that?" Clay asked.

"An art history aide. He's going to look over some papers of mine."

BEFORE THE SUN DISAPPEARED, bright rays ambushed our dorm room, and I twisted the blind cord closed. Katie Lee was on the phone with her mom. Macy let herself in and made her backside comfortable on my bed. She dug in a baggie of dried fruit and nuts and picked the almonds out. Having one day off for a three-day Easter weekend wasn't enough of a break to buy a plane ticket to go home. Since the dorms stayed open, both Macy and I planned to stick around until Katie Lee hung up the phone. "Would y'all like to spend Easter at my house?"

Macy accepted the invite, but I hesitated. Dad had told me to stay away from The Bern, and I didn't relish bumping into Nash or Billy Ray. Since Agent Cauldwell had asked me to zip my lip about the investigation, I couldn't tell Katie Lee the truth. Guilt prickled inside me, and I struggled to concoct a believable excuse. "Let me check with my dad."

Katie Lee and Macy had spent eight months in tight quarters with me, and both knew I'd skirted around the permission umbrella for spring break. They also knew the last place I'd spend a holiday was in Canton with Dad and his girlfriend, Trudy. Macy cornered me, and Katie Lee stood behind her. "Is there something going on that you haven't told us?"

An FBI agent had been assigned the case. Knowing there was a case trapped bubbles of nervous energy inside me. "Like I could hide anything from you two."

Macy was onto to me, and if I hung around Grogan, I didn't know if I could keep the secret. I grabbed my book bag and darted out the door. "I need a periodical from the library. I'll catch up around dinner."

INSIDE THE LIBRARY BUILDING the recirculated air smelled bland, like wearing an all-beige outfit. I veered beyond the double doors that led to the checkout desk and followed an adjacent hallway into an adjoining room with cathedral ceilings. The college used the space to feature seasonal art exhibits. Dropping my satchel to the floor, I sat on a bench and stared at contemporary black-and-white etchings by an unknown artist. I didn't want to lie to Katie Lee and Macy, but what choice did I have?

From behind, a woman's voice called my name.

"Professor Schleck."

"Rachael, I'd like to introduce you to the newly appointed curator of our campus gallery. Liz Stein. Rachael O'Brien."

Liz's flour complexion had a splatter of freckles. Dressed in a solid yellow tailored Jackie O dress, she shook my hand. "Have you heard? We received a federal grant to add a new building and acquire art for the university's permanent collection."

"I hadn't told the class," my professor said. "Has the funding been secured?"

"I expect everything to be finalized after Easter," Liz said.

"Who are you acquiring?" I asked.

"Tentatively I'm negotiating a Vermeer, a Rockwell, a Saatchi, and some local southern works, including Clementine Hunter."

I must have turned shades of sickly when I heard Clementine Hunter. Professor Schleck asked, "Rachael, are you okay?"

"Um, yeah." I cleared my throat. "Fine."

"It's going to be fabulous," Liz said. "North Carolina College is going to build a new wing onto the existing library to house the pieces acquired with the grant. Of course we'll work with other museums to borrow collections and collaborate on exhibitions."

"Did I hear you say you were purchasing a Clementine Hunter?"

"Two," Liz said. "If I can secure them. I'm working through a dealer in New Orleans."

Professor Schleck beamed. "Clementine Hunter is still alive. She turned one hundred this year."

Liz smoothed the creases in her dress. "Her great-granddaughter is a student. It would be a fitting tribute to have southern artists' work permanently featured at our gallery."

My little voice inside my gut spoke loudly. *Liz Stein was being swindled.* Lucky Jack was a busy man to be selling North Carolina College an original Billy Ray rip-off. If Liz acquired the painting from Lucky's Art Consortium, someone would eventually discover that she had purchased fakes, and she could kiss her job and any thoughts of an art career good-bye. Someone needed to expose the Rays before they skipped town to sip mai tais on some beach with their dirty money safe and sound in a Cayman bank account.

MEMORIZING FACTS AND INTREPRETING meaning takes concentration. I'd spread my books and notes across a chunky library table, then aligned my pens, pencils, and highlighters fattest to skinniest. My focus was zero. I needed to call Storm Cauldwell, but I'd left his business card in my room. Mindlessly staring at books wasn't exactly productive, so I dumped everything back in my bag and left. Mr. FBI would shit when I told him about this coincidence. What were the chances of North Carolina College buying a legitimate Hunter? Slim to zil. Did Liz Stein find Lucky Jack or did he target colleges? And how? Who was the middleman? Halfway across campus, I pulled a cigarette out of my pocket and stopped to light it.

"Don't you know those will kill you?" Storm said.

My hand flew to my chest. I looked over both my shoulders to see if anyone I knew was around. "Are you tailing me?"

"Stopped by to pick up the invoice and contacts. Your roommate said you were at the library."

"Wait a minute, you talked to Katie Lee?"

"Nice girl. And a guy."

"What guy?"

"Tall, dark hair. His name had to do with pottery."

"Clay?"

"That's it."

"What did you say to him?"

"Not much. Just that I was looking for you."

"Aren't you supposed to be, like, undercover while you flush out criminals?"

Storm motioned to a bench. Neither of us sat. He put a foot on it and leaned on his knee. "Don't worry. I didn't tell them anything. Said I had an extracurricular project you and I were working on."

"You didn't?"

"It wasn't a big deal."

"What did Clay say?"

"Didn't say anything. Excused himself."

"Great. Now I have to go on damage control."

"Settle down. I didn't blow the cover."

"Are you kidding?" I pointed at Storm's left hand. "A guy, without a wedding ring, asks about me?"

He smiled.

"Did you flash that dimple at Katie Lee? It isn't going to help the lies I'll have to tell. When I get back, you'll be the talk of the seventh floor."

"Something's come up that I need to share."

"Ditto."

Storm motioned his hand. "Ladies first."

I took a drag from my cigarette and nervously rubbed the talisman tucked in my pocket. "Get out your note pad. You'll want to pen this one."

Storm reached into the liner of his sport coat, and I noticed his shoulder harness and gun.

"You carry a gun?"

"For work."

"I figured you were a desk guy."

"Occasionally they let me out."

"You're not going to believe this."

"You'd be surprised what I'll believe."

"I just left the curator and my art history professor in the arts display room next to the library. North Carolina College has been awarded federal grant money to build a proper art gallery. Liz Stein is in charge of purchasing the collectables to fill it."

"I'm with you so far."

"She has some pieces picked out. A Vermeer, a Rockwell, a Saatchi."

"Sounds expensive. That must be some grant."

"And two Clementine Hunters from a dealer in New Orleans."

Storm stared at me. "You're not kidding?"

I shook my head.

"What's your news?" I asked.

"You know the Clementine Hunter in the New Orleans Museum of Art."

"Which one?"

"*Baptism*."

"The one my dad refurbished?"

"Not sure if the one in the museum is the one your dad refurbished."

"What are you saying?" *That my dad had a hand in stealing the original?*

"An agent from the New Orleans division met with the head of exhibits down there. We've done some checking. Matched the photos from the insurance file to the painting on the wall. It's been confirmed. The *Baptism* on the wall is a fake. The real one has gone missing."

Storm stopped talking as some students moved past. I rubbed the pulsing throb in my temples. Once we were alone, I asked, "Does my dad know?"

"He's cooperating while we investigate."

"Why did you tell me?"

"Because you keep turning up Clementines."

I stubbed out my cigarette. "Katie Lee has invited me to New Bern for Easter break."

"No, absolutely not. It could be dangerous."

"I need to clear Dad's reputation. I'm going."

NOTE TO SELF

Bumping into Billy Ray, Stewart Hayes, Bubba Jackson, and Nash over Easter weekend—highly probable.

38

Easter Eggs, Jelly Beans, and The Bern

atie Lee's promise of a fun-filled weekend drifted in and out of my head. "Low to mid-seventies and sunny is the forecast. We can take the motorboat out and do some ski-ing. If the wind picks up, there's always the sunfish to sail."

Holding an overnight bag, Macy locked her door. She stood in the hallway and asked, "You're comfortable leaving Clay for the weekend?"

"I guess," I said.

"Has something happened?" Macy asked.

"I don't know. I mean everything seemed fine. Now he's suddenly super busy with work or classes. I think he's avoiding me."

"I'm sure there's a reason," Katie Lee said.

"Did you sleep with him?" Macy asked. "They always get weird once you've seen them naked."

"If I'd slept with him, you'd know it. Is Bridget ready?"

"She's not coming," Katie Lee said. "She was up all night with the flu. Says she's bummed not goin' to The Bern."

The Bridget staying behind newsflash washed relief over me. I had an original masterpiece to flush out of the thicket, and I didn't need the added worry of watching my back for an ambush. The real *Baptism* could be somewhere in The Bern, and if it was, I planned to find it and clear Dad's name. After locking our door, the three of us walked down the deserted hallway.

Late in the afternoon, the parking lot seared heat, and Katie Lee opened Big Blue's doors to try and move stagnant air out of the car. Not feeling talkative, I offered the front seat to Macy. That way the two could plot our weekend while I devised my own plan. Katie Lee turned over Big Blue's engine, cranked the air on full blast, and pulled onto Campus Drive. She looked at Macy and asked, "Where did you find my sunglasses?"

"You've been screwing Hugh?"

A horn screamed, and a car swerved to miss us as Katie Lee plowed through a four-way intersection.

HOLIDAY INTERSTATE TRAFFIC was stop and go, adding plenty of extra time to delve into who exactly was sleeping with Hugh and how often. For the first leg of the drive, Katie Lee denied being intimate with him. Like a recording, Macy pushed. "Just admit it. You slept with him."

"Why are you so concerned with his personal affairs?" Katie Lee snapped. "Have you been sleeping with him?"

"I haven't slept with him," I said to deaf ears.

Once we entered Raleigh city limits, Katie Lee's eyes welled. She pulled off to the side and told us, "I've slept with him."

"I can't fucking believe this. That sneaky bastard's been sampling both of us."

WE'D DRIVEN THROUGH THE CRAVEN COUNTY outskirts under a starless sky in silence. Inside the Browns' kitchen, Katie Lee passed the island and followed the TV glow to the family room where Dr. Brown lounged with his slippered feet on the foot of a raised leather recliner. Sprawled on the sofa, Mrs. Brown lay beneath a fringed throw. Katie Lee shouted, "Hey, hey," to rouse her parents.

"Hey yourself," Katie Lee's mom said under sleepy eyes. "Was traffic horrible?"

Dr. Brown stood to hug us. "Ladies, it's good to have you all home. How's the schoolwork going?"

Over the shrill hum of a phone that echoed, Katie Lee said, "Oh Daddy, it's impossible, but we're managing."

Mrs. Brown yawned. "Go on and answer it. I'm sure it's for you."

Macy and I excused ourselves and carried our weekend bags upstairs. In the guest room, I went on damage control and told Macy, "This Hugh thing is not worth ruining a friendship. You both were blindsided. If you're going to be pissed at someone, it should be Hugh."

Unpacking, Macy didn't respond. I hoped the two could get over this. If I had to play referee all weekend to keep them civil, it would put a crimp in my sleuthing. The last time I visited Katie Lee's hometown, I'd avoided Billy Ray. Not this trip. I hadn't thanked him for the Valentine's flowers and miniature painting he'd left for me. He and I had a lot of catching up to do. I wanted to hear all about his interest in the arts and how he'd developed his craft.

Footsteps trotted up the staircase, and Katie Lee leaned in the doorway. "That was Meredith. She's having a party tomorrow night, and everyone should be there."

A MIXTURE OF BREWED COFFEE and sweet batter made the morning smell like the Pancake Hut. To commemorate Good Friday, I made a promise to give up the four-letter expressive adjectives through the holy weekend and prayed that I'd be able to shed clarity on the missing painting. Under closed eyelids, I searched for a solution. How would I make things right? I'd come to The Bern to confront a hunch that festered inside my head. At best, my plan was amateurish.

Sunlight brightened the guest room I shared with Macy. When I heard the shower in the attached bathroom, I flung the comforter off and knelt on the floor to dig in my overnight bag. Checking the batteries in my Sport Walkman, I unwrapped a blank cassette. There was a record button that I'd tested in a lecture.

I made a pile on the floor. The Walkman, a pair of black leather gloves, a bandana, a magnifying glass, a pen-sized flashlight, disposable camera, and mini binoculars that had had a travel mishap somewhere between my dorm and New Bern. Even though they had a ripped strap and a chip in the left lens, they still worked. I didn't own a purse. Carrying one was a nuisance. My coat would be bulky, but I had enough pockets in my army jacket to hold the gear. I pushed record. "Testing, testing. This is Rachael O'Brien. April 17, 1987. Good Friday. New Bern, North Carolina."

"What are you doing?"

With one sweep, I scooped my surveillance equipment into my overnight bag. "Nothing."

Macy wore a strapless Hawaiian floral bikini and, on top of her head, the tortoiseshell sunglasses she'd swiped from Hugh's place. After the realization in the car, Katie Lee had told Macy to keep the shades. It was a peace offering of sorts. Katie Lee, guilt ridden for sleeping with Hugh, was mortified that Macy and I had discovered her secret. My girlfriends needed time to chew through the revelation. Macy couldn't stay mad at Katie Lee, but Hugh I suspected would be in for a tongue-lashing. When we went back to campus, he'd be like a mouse with its tail in a trap, lucky if he survived with only a missing limb.

Macy collected her wavy hair in a scrunchie. Smelling like a coconut, she tapped her barefoot against the floorboards. "You've been acting weird since New Orleans. What's going on?"

I sighed.

"What really happened to you on that shamrock float? Did you do it with the little person?"

"Macy! I told you what happened."

Reaching in my bag, she lined up the binoculars, the bandana, the camera, the Walkman, the magnifying glass, and the flashlight. Like a hostess on *Wheel of Fortune*, her hand swept across the assortment. "What's all this?"

"Boating equipment."

"Yeah right. Do I look gullable?"

I smiled.

Arms crossed, she waited.

I sighed.

She drilled her eyes into mine.

"It's complicated."

"Anything worthwhile is."

"I've stumbled onto an art forgery scam. The fakes are coming out of New Bern. My dad's reputation and business are in jeopardy. I've lost my mom. I don't want to lose Dad too. Tonight I'm going to record a confession."

"Whoa, What? I'm not following."

"My theory. Billy Ray, Stewart Hayes, and Bubba Jackson are producing, storing, and moving fake masterpieces through Lucky Jack's Art Consortium. I think Nash may be involved. Dad refurbished two Clementine Hunters. One was titled *Baptism*. The piece is supposed to be in the New Orleans Museum of Art, but I've seen the painting in two galleries. Now the one my Dad refurbished has gone missing, and a copy is hanging in its place. I think the New Bern boys have the original."

"Billy Ray? The one who's hot for you? I thought he was just an eccentric redneck dufus."

"I wish."

"Tell me your plan."

LYING ON A BEACH towel all afternoon at the Browns' dock, I hardly relaxed. In a few hours we'd be going to Meredith's party, and my mind swept over tonight's best- and worst-case scenarios. Finding the original Clementine was the best I could hope for. Discovering nothing would be disappointing, but being found out could turn catastrophic.

Mrs. Brown served a meatless Good Friday dinner of stuffed flounder, seasoned collard greens, and, for dessert, she'd made blueberry crumble in a cast iron skillet. The days were getting longer, and from the dining room table, I watched the filtered rays of sun splash on the decorative grass mounds and spring annuals that had been planted in beds along the front path.

"What are y'all's plans?" Katie Lee's mom asked.

"Meredith has invited us over. I thought we'd take the boat. It'll be quicker."

Dr. Brown pressed his fork against his plate to gather the last of his crumble. "Make sure you secure her with a proper rolling hitch. Tide's going out. No wake near the dock."

Katie Lee stood to kiss him on top of his head. "Thanks, Daddy."

Macy and I helped clear the table. From the sink, Mrs. Brown asked, "Is Patsy joining you girls?"

Katie Lee picked up the phone. "She should be here any minute."

"Be sure to send her into the kitchen. I saved her a piece of crumble."

Salty mist, compliments of the river, hung in the evening air. Trying to center my nervous energy before Meredith's party, I slipped out to the Browns' front porch and methodically tipped the high-back rocker in rhythm with the croak of night frogs. I'd asked Katie Lee who'd be there. She'd replied, "Most everybody." With all the scammers in one place, tonight was my only chance to find out what the young entrepreneurs of New Bern did in their spare time.

Macy collapsed into the rocker next to mine. She took tonight's task of finding the Clementine Hunter seriously. Her attire said so. I couldn't decide if she leaned more toward a martial art professional or a caterer. Knowing her finicky food habits, I decided on martial arts.

"Pssst, Rach," she whispered.

I dug deep in the cavern of my chest for inner serenity. Since I'd clued her in, she used every opportunity to freak me out.

Standing to check the front door, she scurried back. "What if Billy Ray paid someone to paint the miniature Valentine he gave you and you have the wrong guy? What if Lucky Jack knows you took the invoice and told Billy Ray? They may know, you know."

Motioning for me to lean toward her, she wrapped an arm around my shoulder. In a quiet voice, a feat for a Queens, New Yorker, she said,

"I know how to get Billy Ray to talk. We can seduce him. Get his pants off, then tie his balls in a tight noose."

Her warped enthusiasm had me questioning the art forgery details I'd confided to her. I closed my eyes tight and pinched my lips together.

"What do you think?" she asked.

Concentrating to center myself, I selected appropriate words. "I'm not tying up genitals or participating in torture tactics."

After rolling her eyes, she rocked a few strides. "Why did Katie Lee let Nash back into her life if she's fooling around with Hugh?"

"My take?"

She nodded.

"Nash is a mixed bag of nuts. Like the Brazilian, he can leave a bitter aftertaste, and part of me wants Katie Lee to dump him. Other times he says something complicated and even insightful, like a macadamia. As much as I hate to admit it, it's hard to dislike Nash, and I am sympathetic with Katie Lee's conundrum."

"He must be fantastic in bed. It's the only explanation. I'm gonna ask her."

"Are you two back to normal?"

Macy clicked her polished nails. "She didn't know Hugh and I had a thing. I hid it, and he didn't enlighten her."

"You went ballistic when she asked where you found her tortoiseshell sunglasses. How did you know she was fooling around with Hugh? I mean she could've just stopped by his room and left them there."

"I have womanition. It's the seventh sense."

Squeezing my eyelids shut again, I braced myself for the hooey casserole she cooked.

"Ever since the snowstorm, Hugh backed off me. Not completely, but enough to notice."

"Define backed off."

"He wasn't as needy, and I guessed he was getting some somewhere else, but I couldn't prove it. Then he got sloppy. Forgot to meet me. Changed the location. Became careful about coming and going from my room. When I found the sunglasses on the shelf above his head-board, my womanition spoke to me. He was double-dipping."

"Are you freaked out that Hugh's been fooling around with both you and Katie Lee? That's a lot of sharing even for good friends."

"I'm mostly mad at myself for thinking I didn't want to be exclusive."

"Now what?"

"Katie Lee and I still have some talking to do. After that—we'll see."

A shrill whistle, some kind of birdcall, shrieked through the trees near the driveway.

"Y'all ready?" Patsy asked.

NOTE TO SELF
Never would have pegged Hugh for a thrill-seeking multitasker.

39

Hidden Treasure

The Bayliner rested in the water. When it wasn't in use, it hung on pulleys under a covered dock. Dr. Brown had taken the vinyl boat cover off and tied her to the end of the pier. Patsy, Macy, and I hopped into the boat, and Katie Lee started the engine. I had one goal. *Find the* Baptism.

"Raz," Patsy said. "Did you bring that lip gloss we talked about?"

"Lip gloss" was code for *blackmail items*.

Before we left Greensboro, Patsy had asked me to bring Nash's engraved lighter and Bridget's gold snakemouth loop earring. "I don't know what good it'll do us," I'd told her.

"It'll send a message. Nash Wilson is an ass, and I'm over him."

Time had dulled the enormity of the deceit. Sometimes I'd even forgotten that Nash had slept with Bridget. In my mind, Katie Lee's fling thing with Hugh had sort of leveled the cheating field. I could've been convinced to blank out that bit of old memory. Other things with bigger ramifications now consumed my brain space.

Nash hid his illegal activities from Katie Lee. If I found the painting, and if Nash was involved, he could be charged with conspiracy. That wouldn't be welcome news to Katie Lee and would have consequences on our friendship that I didn't want to think about.

"I brought it," I said, and Patsy nodded acknowledgement.

We didn't waste time, and Katie Lee quickly motored to deeper waters. The sinking sun sent the western horizon ablaze in pinks, and a lone, curved-billed ibis soared above our heads. Katie Lee skirted the ski boat across a still puddle, more like a lake than a river. Racing along, my hair blew like a sail with a loose rig. I buttoned my jacket partly to keep warm and partly to keep my bulging pockets still.

With decreasing visibility, Katie Lee turned on the headlight. Over the rumble of the motor, she shouted, "Y'all will probably recognize a bunch of people tonight."

"Will Billy Ray be there?" I asked.

Katie Lee shot me a duh look. "Probably."

From the seat next to me, Patsy shouted, "Katie Lee, where are you going? We passed Meredith's place."

"The marina, to pick up Nash. It'll only take a minute. We can get beer and cigarettes."

Nash wasn't welcome on the Browns' property; otherwise he'd already be in the boat. I thumbed the eye of Horus I'd fastened to my neck like a bead on a rosary. Let the games begin. First stop—sneaking around to pick up Nash.

I'd seen him over a half dozen times and easily recognized his signature stance. With both hands tucked in jacket pockets, legs crossed at the ankle, he leaned on a wood piling.

Katie Lee dropped the speed to a crawl and puttered between docks lined with boats. We passed a crabber dressed in a red flannel shirt and olive-green plastic pants. He wore mirrored sunglasses and a wool winter hat that covered his head down to his lobes. Messing around with metal cages, he waved as we passed, and something about him was oddly familiar.

Cutting the motor, Katie Lee docked in a slip just in front of the Marina Supply Store. Patsy threw a rope to Nash, and he moored the line to a dock cleat. "God damn. Don't y'all look fabulous."

"You're so full of it," Patsy said.

Scolding Patsy with her eyes, Katie Lee said, "Play nice."

Leaping out of the boat, Patsy asked Nash, "What do you need, cigarettes or beer?"

Nash had a track record of questionable decision-making, but around us he managed to ooze polite and easygoing. He didn't bite Patsy's bait. Instead he played her, pouting. Patsy held his gaze. "Beer," he finally said. She held out her hand, and he pulled a five from his pocket. "From the refrigerated section."

"Raz," Patsy said, "come help me."

Nash lent a hand to steady me out of the boat. When I touched firm footing, he tossed a black duffel and leapt behind it, taking my seat. After locking eyes with Patsy, I asked, "What's in the bag?"

He stored it under a bench seat. "A change of clothes."

PATSY AND I STOPPED in front of an ice machine. She straightened the bills everyone had donated for alcohol and cigarettes. As she counted, she asked, "Do you have it?"

Reaching into an inside pocket, I handed her a plastic baggie with the engraved butane lighter and gold loop earring. Reaching into her purse, she pulled out a folded note.

"What's that?"

"I penned a love letter to Nash. Katie Lee needs to detox herself from him. Once he gets this, it'll encourage him to wean himself from her company." She handed it to me. "Go ahead, read it."

It had taken Patsy a lot of time to cut letters from magazines. The note read, "Lying frauds deserve to be behind bars. Fess up or we will."

Snatching the paper from my hand, she refolded it. "It's not blackmail. It's advice."

Patsy's note read like something from grade school, and I had reservations about giving it and the evidence to Nash. He'd probably laugh his ass off and then say fuck you.

She slid the note into the plastic sandwich bag. "Nash needs to come clean, and we're aidin' his conscience." She put "the encouragement" in an outside pocket of her vintage bolero jacket and took her time securing a wood toggle button that closed the pocket flap. "Do you want beer or BJs?"

Besides a few fishermen, the dock and Marina Supply Store were deserted. I checked my Swatch and waved a hand. "Whatever you choose is fine. I need to use the ladies room."

"It's around back, near the Dumpster under Jackson's deck."

I didn't give Patsy a chance to come with me. I was supposed to be using discretion in this investigation and needed to do this alone. With urgency, I hustled to the back of the building.

At the bottom of Jackson's stairs, dusk had disappeared. Low-lit dock lights glowed on the slips that bobbed with the tide. Tonight I'd dressed sensibly: tennis shoes, belted jeans, and a T-shirt. From inside my jacket, I pulled out gloves and a flashlight.

Shiny silver screws held the new wood deck together. It hadn't been stained and smelled like hamster bedding. A window rested to the right of the door, and crevices behind partially closed vertical blinds glowed. I watched for shadows and listened for signs of Jackson or his friends. I didn't see anyone.

Climbing the stairs, I counted on Bubba Jackson's southern roots and prayed that he lived by the unlocked door mentality. If he didn't, I'd have to figure out how to break in. I lightly knocked. If he answered, I planned to use the old standby, "Can you tell me where the bathroom is?" I waited while the hum of a boat motor faded. Still no answer. Twisting the knob with my gloved hand, I pushed. Point for O'Brien.

Last time I'd been in this apartment, bodies stood on the stained carpet and beer cups covered the counter. Bubba wasn't the tidiest of bachelors; paper plates with moldy food cultured and multiplied a blanket of fuzz. The scent of hooch and sweaty socks had replaced clambake.

The space was small, and I estimated that I could scan it in under two minutes. First the obvious. I walked the perimeter looking for paintings on the walls. The only thing I found was a swimsuit calendar in the bathroom.

Next on my list, closet checks. The last time I'd been here, I'd blacked out. Macy said I'd come out of the sliding doors wearing a life vest and holding an oar while mumbling about a hunter. My head only carried snippets from that night, so I'd have to search everywhere.

There were two bedrooms. Only clothes hung in the foosball room's closet. The bathroom linen cupboard looked small, but I opened it anyway. Floor-to-ceiling shelves housed a few stacked towels, an unopened box of textured condoms, and a bottle of crap aftershave. *This Bubba Jackson character must be a real charmer.* Moving on, I flicked a light in the second bedroom. When I opened the closet, I inhaled a cloud of tobacco.

"Whatcha doing?"

I spun around. "Patsy. Don't do that."

Standing in the hallway, she held two plastic bags filled with beer and BJs. She put them down, took a drag, and asked, "Do what?"

"Make me mess my pants. How did you know I was up here?"

"You can't get into the bathroom without a key from the attendant. Why are you holding a flashlight and wearing black gloves?"

I heaved a breath.

"Speak to me, O'Brien."

Macy knew, and now I'd have to tell Patsy something. Unsure if I wanted to answer her, I opened the sliding door and flashed my light in the corners where lint balls collected and a pile of wet clothing wafted a sour smell. "I'm looking for something."

Patsy's cigarette ash grew, and she stepped into the bathroom. "Tell me what it is. I'll help you find it."

A bead of sweat tickled my neck. "A masterpiece."

Patsy's face creased with confusion. "That's vague."

"I'm looking for an oil painting. Roughly ten by twelve."

Pretending to smoke a joint, Patsy pinched her cigarette-free fingers near her lips. "Have you been partying without me?"

I poked the flashlight between fishing poles and inside an oversized tackle box. "Remember Jackson's party in November?"

Patsy chewed on her cheek. "Portions of it."

"Beforehand, you and I stood in front of an art gallery and looked at a Clementine Hunter painting."

"Oh yeah. Pricey thing."

"I'm looking for it."

"I'm not following you."

"I have a hunch that Jackson is moving fake artwork for a dealer in New Orleans. The dealer's name is Jack Ray."

"Any relation to Billy?" she joked.

A seagull screeched outside, and a boat horn sounded in the harbor. "I think so."

Absorbing what I'd said, she exhaled with force. "Holy shit. The canvases I saw Billy Ray buying at the Hobby Lobby around Christmas. Are you saying he can paint?"

I nodded. "He sent me a miniature landscape for Valentine's." I motioned for Patsy to follow me. "Come on, I haven't checked the hallway closet."

"So it's illegal to make copies and sell them?"

"Without the artist's permission, it can be a federal offense."

"I always figured Billy Ray would get arrested for growin,' not paintin'."

"He'll only be busted if he's been selling forgeries as originals. That's hard to prove."

"Why are you so interested in all this?"

The veneered door slid along its track. "My dad refurbished the *Baptism* painting. But now the curator at the museum says the piece on the wall is a fake. His reputation and livelihood are at stake. If I can find the original painting, I can sort things out."

Patsy twisted open a wine cooler. "It sounds complicated. Shouldn't you call the art police?"

I swayed the flashlight in the corners. "I just want to check...Bingo."

"You think paintings are inside those boxes?"

Handing her the flashlight, I said, "Hold this." Sliding my finger under a piece of tape that secured the top of a box, I could feel my insides charge with electricity as I broke the seal.

"What the fuck is taking so long?"

Startled, Patsy backed into me. Glancing at Macy, I said, "Shut the door behind you."

"You two are taking forever. Katie Lee left the boat to find you."

I had a framed painting halfway out of the box. "Where is she now?"

"Hanging on the dock with Nash. I told her I needed to buy Midol and tampons and that I'd bring you back."

"Y'all," Patsy said, "I gotta pee."

Macy dug in the plastic bag Patsy set on the floor and helped herself to a chilled BJ. "Any luck?" she asked.

"Jackpot." Each of the slim boxes I'd discovered had hand-addressed white shipping labels. Art galleries spanning the state from Wilmington to Asheville. Two boxes were postmarked to Tennessee and one to Alabama.

Reaching inside my jacket pocket, I pulled out the Fuji disposable camera. "I need to untape the boxes and photograph the contents next to the shipping label." A guilty pleasure, like holding a fork to a nine-by-thirteen pan of warm brownies, pinged inside of my chest.

Macy sprawled onto Jackson's sofa. "That's gonna take forever."

"Not if you and Patsy help."

Patsy emerged from the bathroom with a wide grin. She held a gallon plastic bag with duct tape around the center. "Y'all'll never guess what I found."

"Grass?" Macy said.

"Oh Jesus," I said. "Where'd you find that?"

"Taped under the toilet tank." She put her face into the bag and inhaled. "You realize I'm obliged to smoke this. Make sure it's not oregano."

I wound the camera film. "Patsy, don't. Put it back."

Under Bubble Wrap, I could see an oil still life of a dead duck hanging upside down from a shed roof and hoped it wasn't an omen. I didn't know the artist. On the back of the framed piece a sticker read *Terrell: Hanging Game.* I snapped a photo.

Patsy pulled out a small wooden pipe from her pocket. "Jackson won't notice if a little's missin'."

Macy rubbed her hands together. "I'll help you test it."

"Macy!"

She raised a red-polished nail to hush me. "Relax. Patsy and I'll be more productive."

Wrapping the dead ducks back up, I secured the tape and pulled out the next painting. A Thomas Richards landscape. Then a George Cooke. Some of the art in the boxes were duplicates with different addresses. I didn't know these artists. I'd have to look them up when I got back to campus. Choking on the smoke-filled air, I warned the girls. "When Jackson comes in here, he's gonna know someone was here, and the first thing he'll do is check under the toilet lid."

Patsy moved toward the bathroom and giggled. "It always smells like weed in here." Tripping over herself, she sent dried herbs shooting into the air like confetti. Picking through the carpet, she said, "Don't worry, I'm puttin' the bag back."

Bubba Jackson was part of the ring, but was Billy Ray? Had he painted these? The last package was the smallest. No bigger than five by six. When I unwrapped it, I recognized the artist. Heavy breath settled into my lungs. Macy bent over my shoulder. Squinting, she said, "It's a tiny watermelon and some fruit."

I snapped a photo. "It's a James Peale miniature."

"Is he famous or something?"

"Yeah, he's famous."

"That's the same size as the Valentine landscape Billy Ray sent you."

Before I answered her, the apartment door swung open. Fish-scented air blew in with Nash. He tipped his head up. "Ladies, what's going on?"

"Jesus Christ," Patsy said, "don't you know how to knock?!"

He inhaled. "Are you pre-partyin' without me?"

I handed Macy a ten. "I need another disposable camera. Can you go down to the store and buy one? And make up an excuse to Katie Lee. I need five minutes."

Nash walked behind me. "What have you found?"

Patsy locked the door behind Macy.

I slid the closet door shut. "Nash, we need to talk."

NOTE TO SELF

I was right. Not sure why I don't feel relieved.

40

Buggered

Nash parked himself on the Mexican-blanket-cushioned sofa. Patsy handed him a beer and me a BJ before taking out another for herself. I sat on the coffee table across from him. Patsy stood. We all took deep gulps. Besides the waves that collided into the boat docks, a silence elapsed.

"Nash," Patsy said. "We know."

He smiled. "What do you know, Patsy?"

"Don't be an ass. We know that you cheated on Katie Lee with Bridget."

He stopped smiling. "What are you talkin' ab—"

"Save the bullshit," Patsy said.

Moisture beaded on my green glass bottle. "I was in the master bathroom that night."

Patsy dug out the sandwich baggie from her front pocket. Reaching her fingers past the generous wad of Jackson's happy grass she'd confiscated and the note she'd created, she pinched Nash's engraved butane lighter and Bridget's earring.

Fingering the lighter he rewound his memory. "Bridget—she..."

The wind blew in the open window, clunking the blind cord against the sill. I looked out at the deck and below to make sure we were still alone. "You need to tell Katie Lee."

He tipped his beer can and guzzled.

"It was a one-time stupid mistake. It was nothing. Bridget seduced me."

Patsy scoffed, but I didn't. I knew Bridget.

Color drained from Nash's face. He looked sickly. "If I tell Katie Lee, I'll lose her."

I tugged a corner of the label on my wine cooler. "Katie Lee deserves to know. If you love her, you'll tell her."

Reluctant to make a promise, Nash crunched his empty can.

"You're kiddin' yourself," Patsy said, "if you think you can keep this lie hidden."

Childlike he said, "I'll tell her."

"Tonight?" Patsy pressed.

"Jesus, Patsy."

"Now tell us what you know about Billy Ray and this art scam."

Patsy dug in her purse for a pack of cigarettes. "And maybe we can keep you out of prison."

"Hand me another beer."

EVERYTHING IN JACKSON'S APARTMENT seemed as it had been, minus a little cannabis. I glanced at my Swatch. Ten till eight. I'd been dinking around for over twenty minutes. Even though I hadn't found the Clementine Hunter, my guess had been on target. Trotting down the deck stairs, I hoped Macy had told Katie Lee a believable excuse.

"Are we cool?" I asked Nash and Patsy.

"As a cucumber," Patsy said.

Turning the corner of the building, my feet locked. I still had something to find. I suspected it was near. "I'll meet you at the boat in two minutes."

Patsy dug in her pocket for cigarettes. She handed one to Nash. He put it between his lips, lit hers, then his. With his eyes on the lighter, he nodded his head. "We'll wait."

My adrenaline pumped, and I speed-walked with purpose. Last November, I'd only glanced at the Clementine Hunter through the window. It had been months since I'd seen it, or the original in Dad's shop. If it was an accurate copy, I wasn't sure I could pick out the inconsistencies, and I worried I wouldn't be able to tell them apart.

The last time I stood in front of the art gallery, autumn leaves danced with the wind on the sidewalk. The stark branches had undergone a rebirth, and beneath the streetlights, bright green buds had begun to open. Outside the storefront, I admired the Easter window display. Ceramic eggs dangling from silk ribbons hung over sweetgrass baskets and Edgefield pottery. The *Baptism* was gone.

The periwinkle-painted brick gallery was as I'd remembered. Only this time a pineapple doorstop held the Dutch door open. A woman dressed in a salmon sweater set and navy pants had turned out some lights and asked, "Can I help you?"

"On my last visit, there was an oil painting in the window. It was a southern plantation primitive."

She glanced at my jeans and army jacket then jangled her keychain. "The Clementine Hunter?"

"I guess that was it. Do you still have it?"

She peered over half-frame glasses. "Sorry, dear, I sold it before Christmas. Maybe there's something else I can help you with?"

"Oh, I wasn't going to buy it. It's just that I'd told someone about it. My roommate's mom, Cecile Brown."

Her face brightened. "You're Katie Lee's roommate?"

"Yes."

"You tell Cecile if she wants that Clementine Hunter she's gonna have to scoot on over to the McGees' and figure a way to talk Margie into selling it."

Thanking the owner for her time, I slipped her business card into my pocket. I didn't know who Margie McGee was, but I needed to find out.

Three businesses down, I spotted a pay phone. Inserting a quarter, I dialed the phone number I'd memorized. He answered on the second ring.

"Storm?"

"Yeah?"

"It's Rachael O'Brien."

"Are you okay?"

"Listen. I'm in New Bern, and I found some things I think you should know about."

"I'm listening."

"You need to get a search warrant for Bubba Jackson's place. He lives in an apartment above the Marina Supply Store. He's got a dozen forged paintings in his hall closet. They're packaged and addressed to art galleries."

"You've been busy."

"That's not all. The Clementine Hunter that used to be in the art gallery on Main Street was sold back in December."

"Do you know who bought it?"

"Margie McGee."

"Anything else?"

"Judge Husk Driskell is Dr. Brown's golf partner. He drinks bourbon. Woodford Reserve. It may help if you had a bottle before you ask for the warrant."

"Rachael, you've done enough. Get everyone back in the boat and head to the Browns' to tuck in for the night."

"How do you know we have a boat?"

"Rachael, you're not the only one playing a hunch."
"Careful with those crab traps. You never know what you'll catch."

NOTE TO SELF
Being followed by the FBI is both a comfort and annoyance, like being chaperoned on a date.

Patsy and Macy smoked weed from under the toilet lid—like drinking an open soda you found in a park?

41

Deranged Marshmallow Peep

ock lights reflected off the black water the Bayliner floated on. "Are you okay?" Katie Lee had asked me.

Macy zipped her purse. "I told her."

"Told her what?" I asked, feeling panicked.

"About your bathroom issues."

"What?"

"Don't be embarrassed," Macy said. "We all know you had the runs. Shit happens."

Leaving the explanation of why I was gone so long alone, Katie Lee started the engine and turned the boat around. On the cushioned backbench, I huddled between Macy and Patsy. The guy wearing the wool hat who'd been messing with the crab traps was gone. I knew Mr. FBI would be. Storm was a handsome agent. I'd be lying if I didn't admit that my adrenaline had surged when I gave him leads to help wrap up the case.

Katie Lee puttered out of the marina and then lurched the ski boat into open water. With the wind in our faces, the three of us ducked our heads and held onto our hair. An open BJ between my knees sloshed onto my shoes every time Katie Lee hit chop. Macy reached into her purse and pulled out a brown paper bag.

"What's this?" I asked.

"Camera."

I looked inside. "This is an underwater disposable."

"It's all they had."

My pockets were at capacity. Something needed to come out to make room for the camera. I handed Macy my Walkman. "Do you have room for this?"

She took it from me and slotted it into her purse.

Clustered tree canopies created monster blotches of darkness between sky and land. Beyond sloping banks of the Trent River, light from kitchens and family rooms shone through the bay windows of homes with water views.

It was a short ride, and Katie Lee slowed near a dock that jutted out from a clearing. A two-story boathouse with garage doors hung over the water. Wraparound picture windows provided unobstructed views, and inside I could see people throwing darts.

"This is some property," Macy said.

Nash leapt out with the line in his hand. "Mack McGee is the biggest developer in town. He's done well for himself."

Water slapped against the rocky shore, and the ski boat bumper knocked into the wood dock. I hadn't seen Meredith since Katie Lee's house party back in November.

"McGee?" I said, searching my memory bank. "Is that Meredith's last name?"

"I thought you knew," Katie Lee said.

My throat tightened. It couldn't be. Nothing worthwhile was easy. "Patsy, what's Meredith's mom's name?"

"Margie."

A whippoorwill called from the wooded thicket, and someone inside the boathouse let out a playful holler. Katie Lee stood on the dock.

She checked the knot Nash had tied. Satisfied, she looked to where I still sat on the bench in the boat. "Are ya comin'?"

Some things in life chase you. A familiar face, a destination, a building. It can be anything, hovering in your mind and sending reminders until you meet it, appreciate it, and give it the attention it deserves. I wanted Katie Lee to take me back to her house. Hell, I wanted to sip scotch and play a friendly game of Scrabble with the Browns. But there was no turning away. A painting needed to be found.

I stood, my legs swaying in rhythm with the rocking boat. "I'm coming."

Macy sipped the last of her wine cooler. Wiping the corners of her mouth, she asked, "Where are Meredith's parents?"

Patsy moseyed along the threaded dock planks toward shore. "Her daddy's on a business trip, and her mom's shopping with a client in Raleigh until tomorrow."

A flight of railroad crosstie steps led us up the grassy slope where we could see the main house. The lower level was ablaze, the second story dark. Submerged pool lights reflected upon the underside of a balcony. Below it, lion-mouth fountains spewed arcs of water that created circular ripples in the watery rectangular abyss.

Katie Lee opened the sliding doors where underage New Bern patrons filled the McGees' kitchen. Meredith was home from UNC-Chapel Hill. Stretching out her arms, Katie Lee greeted her, and she hugged all of us except Nash. "Hello, Nash," she said, drawing out the *sh*. She didn't show him any of the sixties' peace-lovin' hippie she'd dressed as on Halloween. Her greeting would have put my tail between my legs, but Nash ignored her, pretending his beer deserved his attention.

Scanning the kitchen, I didn't see Billy Ray or Stewart Hayes. I'd never set eyes on Bubba Jackson, so he'd be the most difficult to spot. Patsy had given me a description, but I didn't see a mound of dip in anyone's lower lip. Bubba continued to elude me.

I told Meredith, "Your home is killer."

She swished a hand in the air. "Daddy builds 'em, and Mama deco-rates 'em."

"This is some get-together," Patsy said.

Meredith steadied herself with a firm grasp on the counter top. "I know. I'm pissed. I invited a few friends over, and all of The Bern shows up. I had to wait in line to use my own bathroom."

Standing around in a huddle, I didn't pay attention to the con-versation but surveyed the home. Mrs. McGee had arranged antique blown-glass vases and bright ceramic canisters in uneven groupings. A lamp with a hand-painted rooster on the shade rested next to an ivy plant that grew out of a hammered copper ear-handle kettle. The chunky white kitchen baseboards framed sandstone-painted walls. A rustic table, upholstered chairs, and iron-rod cushioned barstools were scaled to accommodate the enormous room.

Framed oil landscapes matted in linen hung at eye level. The McGees had deep pockets to support their love of art. Maybe I didn't need to talk to Billy Ray, Bubba Jackson, or Stewart Hayes. If the Clementine Hunter hung somewhere in the house, I could just snap a photo. If I gave the film to Storm, he could cross-reference the photo with the curator files in New Orleans.

PATSY DIDN'T LIKE CROWDS and convinced us to retreat to the boathouse to play a game of pool. Oak trees lining both sides of the path thickened as we approached the water. The glow of landscape lights cast shimmers on the rocky bank, and along the dock. Across the river, twinkles blinked from the opposite shore like fleeting stars.

I trotted down the grass-covered railroad ties behind Patsy. Behind us, Macy, Katie Lee, and Nash lollygagged. Near the boathouse, Patsy pulled out her pipe and packed it with a clump of Jackson's secret stash and offered it to me. I raised both hands in a pass signal.

Macy startled me when she said, "You need to relax."

"I'll relax when tonight is over."

"Raz," Patsy said, "you got the photos. What else do you need?"

"I didn't find the right painting."

Patsy flicked a Bic lighter. "Maybe Billy Ray has it over at his place." I grimaced. "He might."

I didn't tell the two that I suspected the painting was somewhere here in the house. Dragging one or both of them on a scavenger hunt after they'd smoked Patsy's peace pipe a second time would slow me down and could draw unwanted attention. I'd do it alone.

The interior of the boathouse didn't have any of the fussy uphol-stered chairs and decorative knickknacks like the main house. Wide plank floorboards were underfoot, and simple molding framed the windows. I plopped onto a leather sofa and watched Nash. He'd been quiet on the boat ride. Nash wasn't a quiet person. Normally conversa-tion didn't lull with him in a room. He liked to ask the kind of ques-tions that made you roar or pissed you off. Tonight he didn't have any of us talking. His silence made me edgy. If he opened his mouth to the wrong people, I'd be screwed. He didn't have an honest track record, and I wondered if he'd keep his promise.

Patsy laid her chest on the table and spread her arms across it to claim dibs. "Ladies, pick your cues and prepare for a spankin'."

I stood to join her. The sooner I whooped Patsy in a game of pool, the sooner I could make an excuse and look for the painting. When I reached for a cue, I heard voices. My ears pricked, and I thumbed the trinket on my neck. We had company. Sneaking up behind Patsy, Billy Ray motioned at Stewart to keep quiet. Bending his knees into the back of hers, he collapsed her stance. "Hey, Patsy," he teased.

Patsy bolted upright and spun around. She crossed her arms and pierced him with cobra eyes, and I worried what she might say or do.

Dressed in sunshine-yellow denim pants, Billy Ray wore a matching picnic-table-check shirt and yellow leather docksides with white soles.

Adopting a demon eye sear, Patsy made a show of uncrossing her arms. She waved her index finger in his face. "You don't have the sense God gave a chigger. You so much as touch me again, and you'll be rest-ing in the marble orchard."

"Ah, Patsy, you're crazier than a hoot owl. You know I's just messin' with ya."

Under a laugh, Stewart tipped the lid of his UNC baseball hat. "Hey, y'all."

Katie Lee had joined Nash in the corner of the room while Patsy racked the balls.

At first Billy Ray didn't spot me, but when he did, his eyes widened. "Razzle Dazzle, we meet again."

I waved.

Spreading his arms, he moved toward me like a tractor plow. "Give Billy Ray a hug."

Midway across the room, he tripped over a chair leg, sloshing Bud on his hand. I stared at the overgrown human Marshmallow Peep that someone had let out of the cellophane package.

Moving to Patsy's side, I whispered, "Don't leave me alone with him."

She blocked Billy Ray's path and handed him a stick. "Are we huggin' or playin' pool?"

"Both," he said, scooping the two of us off the floor and into his arms.

A mounted wall case housed a dozen sticks and two extenders. Shaking off the powerful squeeze, I selected a cue with a dark maple inlay. From behind, someone covered my eyes, causing my back to stiffen. Billy Ray was too touchy-feely and in need of a hint to back off, so I prepared to ram his eight ball.

"Mitch," Patsy shouted. "Get your paws off my partner."

I relaxed my shoulders and turned around. "Perfect timing. We need another player."

He combed his blond hair with his fingers, and it lay in a perfect feather. "Using me for my gaming skills?"

A wisp fell over the corner of his eye, giving him a shy boy-next-door appearance.

"Mitch McCoy, I'm going to have to watch out for you."

Dragging a finger across the pool sticks in the notched velvet case, he said, "It's good to have you back in town."

As he chose one, I noticed paint stains under his nails.

Opening his palm, I asked, "What have you been painting?"
His cheeks flushed. "Model cars."

New Bern bred suspicion inside of me. I needed to get a grip. As I
channeled for an inner calm, Stewart distracted me. His Clydesdale
frame didn't push my buttons. Surprised to see Macy, he flirted,
and she acted interested. He took it upon himself to organize three
teams for a best-ball competition. "Losers have to shotgun an entire
beer."

I recalled his competitive streak from the foosball game at the clambake. Tonight, he had no chance of winning. Since I could remember,
I'd spent every holiday at my aunt Gert's, where she had taught me the
geometry and strategy of the game. She had an overflowing trophy case
from pool tournament wins. I wouldn't be shotgunning.

Heads angled down, Katie Lee and Nash stayed in the corner.
Between the noise of our pool game and people coming and going, I
couldn't hear what they were saying. Was he telling her he'd slept with
Bridget? Would she fess up about Hugh? This could be an early night.

Stewart paired the Marshmallow Peep and me together, which suited my plan. I wanted to know how Billy Ray busied himself in this small
coastal town.

In the first round, we played against the McCoys. Patsy took the
first shot and scratched a stripe ball.

Billy Ray was a drunken space invader. If I'd sipped the wine cooler
I held, I'd have knocked my elbow into his chin. Stepping back, I asked,
"Have you been staying out of trouble?"

He mirrored my movement and edged my arm with his. "Never," he
laughed, closing the space I'd gained. "What about you? Have you been
keeping safe? No more fractures or torn ligaments?"

"I've managed to stay accident free." I sipped my wine cooler. "Have
you painted lately?"

Tipping back on his heels, he polished off his can of Bud. "What do
you mean?" he asked before crushing it.

"The miniature you gave me for Valentine's was impressive. Have
you made any more?"

A Coleman cooler Billy Ray and Stewart had brought rested under the pool table. He reached for a can. "Need a drink?"

"No, I'm good."

He pulled the tab top off and pushed it inside the beer. "I paint when I can."

"Miniature landscapes?"

"I can paint anything."

"Anything?"

"Why you so curious?"

"I want to open my own gallery someday. Maybe I can feature your art."

Billy Ray's pie eyes enlarged. "Darlin', I have enough art to fill a gallery."

"Really? Where do you paint?"

"I work out of our barn."

"O'Brien," Mitch said, "you're up."

The balls had broken into a decent scatter, giving me options. We were solids. I sunk the one, five, and six.

"God damn!" Billy Ray shouted. "You're a shark."

Encouraging him to sing like a canary was proving tougher than I thought. Somehow I needed to loosen his vocal cords. Stalling, I missed the solid red seven.

Stewart's stature dwarfed Macy's. He leaned against a corner wall wearing faded jeans with an unbuttoned oxford over a T-shirt and a pair of leather loafers. The shoes looked Italian. Expensive. Macy knew I suspected he played a part in moving the paintings. I trusted her to be discreet and hoped she didn't reveal my suspicions.

On the corner sofa, Katie Lee hunched her upper body and dropped her head into her hands. Abruptly standing, she left the boathouse. Nash hung back a few beats and then followed. He had kept his word.

Mitch knocked a striped purple twelve into a side pocket. "Y'all took a while to get over here. Did you pre-party?"

Patsy high-fived Mitch for sinking a ball and then looked over her shoulder when she heard Nash slam the door.

"We picked up Nash and drinks at the Marina Supply Store," I said.

Billy Ray's keys jingled inside his pocket. "We were over at Jackson's. Must've just missed y'all."

Leaning against a corner Patsy asked, "Where's Jackson?"

Billy Ray pressed two fingers to his lips and sucked wind. "Went back to fetch his pipe."

A panic, like when you have a pop quiz you're completely unprepared for, jolted my nerve endings. I hoped Storm had gotten the search warrant and finished up. If the FBI lingered, Jackson would see them and bolt.

An oversized roman numeral clock ticked above the river stone fireplace. We'd been at the McGees' for nearly an hour, and I hadn't started my search. I needed to find that painting.

Handing Billy Ray my pool cue, I told a teeny, tiny lie. "I just realized that I left my purse at the main house. Will you cover for me?"

NOTE TO SELF
Billy Ray hides an aura of creep under sunny clothing.

42

Run Like you Stole Something

The McGees' home hid on a clearing between two large plots of wooded land. Cicadas hummed from the trees, and a swift breeze blew off the river. Outside the main house, a beach ball drifted above the pool, and I heard shouts and water play. Before I moved inside, I listened for Katie Lee and Nash, but they'd disappeared. I figured I'd find them when I finished my search.

There wasn't anyone I recognized in the kitchen. Since I'd already seen it, I moved on. I guessed a pricey Clementine Hunter would give dinner guests plenty of conversation, so I searched for the dining room. Silk balloon drapes with beaded trim flanked floor-to-ceiling windows. Turning on lights would've drawn attention. Sparingly I swept my travel flashlight across the walls. The beam reflected a family portrait inside a brushed gold decorative mirror above a sideboard, and a cluster of inked flower botanicals hung over the matte-and-shine wide-stripe-painted walls. I heard the jingle of car keys beyond the arched doorway. Switching the flashlight off, I hovered in a corner and froze. I was freaking myself out. The dining room was a bust.

The front foyer was a McGee time capsule with a decade of family vacation photo-ops.

"Hey, Raz," Meredith said. "Where is everyone?"

"Mostly in the boathouse." I pointed to an adjoining office wall with a series of bird dog charcoal sketches. "The artwork in your home is amazing."

"My mama doesn't like empty walls."

"Which is her favorite?"

"Hard to tell. She buys art like shoes." Meredith wrapped an arm around my neck. "I was looking for Katie Lee." Lowering her voice to a talk-whisper, she craned her head to see who was around. "You know she's forbidden to see Nash. He's not quality. He'll never amount to anything."

Alcohol had uncensored Meredith's tongue. I needed an excuse to keep searching and glanced up the stairs.

"You don't think they're upstairs?"

Shouting erupted over music that blared in the family room, and someone called for Meredith.

"Why don't I check? If I find Katie Lee, I'll tell her you're looking for her."

With a nod, she vanished around the corner.

I jogged up the staircase.

Car doors slammed, and from the picture window above the front door I saw more of New Bern arrive. I decided to start at the far end of the second floor and work my way backward. In the master bedroom, two carved Italian marble-top bedside tables anchored a mahogany four-poster bed with a silk canopy. A desk with French legs and a chaise lounge softened the room. Mrs. McGee had dressed her bedroom with needlepoint pillows of mangoes and pineapples. A series of tropical palm tree watercolors—a Cuban, a Bismarck, and a date palm—hung on the wall in a sitting area with a two-seater sofa, cushioned rattan armchairs, and a TV console.

My chest heaved as though my heart wanted to escape. What if Mrs. McGee had bought the painting for a client or had it stored? They probably owned a vacation home or two. I couldn't clear Dad's name until I found the Clementine. Needing to calm down and focus, I opened the balcony door for oxygen and listened to the party noise from below drown the night. Except for a beach ball, the pool was empty. The lion fountains still spouted water that spun the ball in a whirlpool it couldn't escape.

I slipped onto the balcony. My eye moved down the slope where the boathouse rested. The cloudy night had broken, and streaks of the moon now glistened on the surface of the glassy black Trent. I guessed that Katie Lee and Nash's relationship perilously dangled by a frayed thread. The relief I expected to feel with him out of her life didn't surface. I'd become accustomed to his screw-ups.

Back in the bedroom, I began to devise a plan to continue my search, but a noisy trickle of water drew me into the master bath. I eyed the faucet and ran a hand in the porcelain sink. It was dry. Thumbing the eye of Horus, I moved toward the water closet and gasped. The *Baptism* rested in a chunky wooden frame of elder wood on a wall above the bidet.

So we meet again. Turning the lights on, I emptied my pockets onto the vanity. I removed gloves, lip gloss, the used Fuji camera, a pack of gum, and the crumpled bag with the underwater camera. My mind surged in a rush as if I'd swallowed an entire box of dry powder cherry Jell-O. Steadying my hand, I snapped four pictures of the painting and tucked the underwater camera inside my jacket pocket.

Was this the painting Dad had refurbished or was it an original Billy Ray? Centering myself, I picked up the magnifying glass and took a deep breath. Closing my eyes, I retrieved an image of the painting in Dad's shop. The colors, the scale, the monogram signature.

"Funny place to find your purse."

My neck muscles stiffened, and my senses shifted into hypersensitive mode. In the tight space, stale beer breath permeated my nostrils.

Turning my head, I stared into cavernous black eyes rimmed in red. "Billy Ray."

He took the magnifying glass from my hand and used it to poke the items I'd scattered around the sink. "Disposable camera. Ain't that curious. What pictures have you been taking?"

"You know, making memories."

Picking up the camera, he moved toward me.

I stepped back. The master bath had one exit, and Billy Ray stood between it and me. The McCoys and Macy were in the boathouse, and Katie Lee and Nash had disappeared. The bedroom wing hung in a corner of the house, far removed from the downstairs party blare. Dread dripped down my spine. If I screamed my lungs out, no one would hear.

Billy Ray touched the end of the camera to my chest cavity and dragged it down, stopping at the bottom band of my bra. "I'm going to help you make a memory."

"Quit goofing around and give a girl some privacy."

Snapping the camera in two, he threw it at me. His throaty growl came from a dark place that made me think he was possessed. "You bitch," he said and gripped my neck with his sausage fingers. A towel rack pressed a welt into my back. "You've been snoopin' around Jackson's and now the McGees'. You think your shit don't stink."

My rebuttal was a hiccup.

He squeezed tighter. "I saw you and Patsy at the back of the marina."

His clutch constricted my ability to gather oxygen. As he leaned his girth into me, I squirmed, trying to push his bulk away. My stomach turned when I felt his hardness press against me. Billy Ray had worked himself into a fury. Keeping his viselike hold on me, he lowered his voice and whispered into my ear, "You think I'm so sweet on you that I wouldn't notice all your questions? It's because of you that this is my last night in town, and I'm gonna enjoy it."

The chokehold on my neck sent my brains on a journey toward my ears. The toxic combination of his sickly sweet aftershave and alcohol-laden breath made my eyes roll backward. I guessed I was blacking out when I felt the rancid rasp of his tongue drag across my face. When the light at the end of my tunnel began to flicker, my ears heard a southern man's voice say, "That's enough, Billy Ray."

He let go.

Gasping for air, I rubbed the welts on my neck.

Billy Ray spun to face the door. "Mitch, get the fuck outta here."

God it was good to see Mitch McCoy.

This wasn't part of my plan. I'd underestimated Billy Ray. I never thought him capable of violence. He'd crossed the line, and I wanted to crush him like a grape in a vat. In a swift maneuver, I jammed my heel onto his yellow leather docksiders and ground his toes. It felt good.

He hollered a loud grunt and then lunged for me. I jumped backward into the tub, putting a small elevation of cast iron between us. Billy Ray tripped on the throw rug, thumping forward, and Mitch tackled him from behind, grappling to lock his flailing arms.

Outside the picture window, I heard a low rumbling. The McGees' property wasn't visible from the main road. Through the wooded lot next door, a procession of headlights wound past trees toward the house. Storm had secured a warrant.

What advantage Mitch had in height, Billy Ray countered with his weight. Muscling out of Mitch's grip, Billy Ray rose onto one knee, and Mitch jumped back. Billy Ray bolted up and slung a punch into Mitch's gut, folding him in half, and followed with an uppercut into Mitch's face. I searched for something to help. Soap on a rope, bubble bath, a ladies razor, worthless. Billy Ray stood, pulling Mitch by the back of his collar. I couldn't wait for Storm.

With Billy Ray's back to me, I yanked the gold towel bar out of its brackets and stabbed him in the ear. My shot hit bull's-eye, and he went down flailing his arms for something to break his fall, but only managed to rip a water handle off the back of the bidet, creating a vertical fountain of pulsing water. Droplets splashed the Clementine Hunter before falling onto his dazed head that rested in the porcelain pot.

Mitch pulled at my waist. "Take your belt off."

"I owe ya, but—"

"Keep your pants on. I need to hog-tie him until we get help."

Obediently I handed Mitch my double-wrap leather belt.

Slumped on the floor, Billy Ray moaned. He'd cut his face when he hit the bidet, and his bloody ear resembled a dog's beloved rawhide bone. Using my belt, Mitch tied his wrists behind his back. I didn't feel any remorse for maiming his ear. It was self-defense, and I had a witness.

"He can still walk away."

"What do you suggest?"

"Take his pants."

"Raz, that's warped."

"It's a precaution."

Mitch slid off Billy Ray's shoes and winced.

"Are you hurt?"

"I'll be fine," he said and tugged at the banana-yellow pant cuffs.

"We need to get out of here, fast."

"Billy Ray's not stupid enough to chase us."

"You don't understand. The FBI is seconds away from busting this party."

"Since when does the FBI bust underage drinking?"

I pulled Mitch to the balcony and threw Billy Ray's pants and shoes into the pool. "Forged artwork. The bidet just watered one down."

"You and I don't have anything to do with artwork; why do we care?"

"They may do a sweep for drugs, and Patsy has a bag of hooch on her. We need to find her before they do. Jump with me. We can call my FBI contact from the Browns' and tell him what happened."

"Wait a minute. You have an FBI contact?"

Car doors slammed. "I'll explain later."

"Raz, there's something you don't know about me."

"What?"

"I hate heights."

"It's the quickest way to the boathouse."

Mitch and I stood at the edge of the balcony. He held my face in his hands and planted a kiss on my lips.

"What was that for?"

He backed into the bedroom and turned. "Hiccup remedy."
"The FBI may be downstairs."
"See you on the dock."

MITCH CHOSE THE STAIRS, and I debated joining him until I looked behind my shoulder at Billy Ray. He'd rolled out of the bathroom in a shirt and underwear, streaking blood across the McGees' white carpet. Climbing on top of the balcony, I aimed for the blue center and jumped. Plunging to the bottom, I pushed to break the surface, my heavy coat slowing my ascent. When sweet scented air filled my lungs I gasped. My underwater camera floated an arm's length away, but my binoculars sank toward the pool bottom. Reaching for the camera, I'd have to remember to thank Macy for her foresight. I didn't have time to dive for the binoculars and left them behind.

I heaved myself out and hauled my waterlogged ass down the slope toward the river. I wanted to get far away from Billy Ray and the McGees' property. But I needed to find Patsy, Macy, and Katie Lee. I inhaled nicotine before I spotted the lit cigarette. I knew the shadowy figure leaning against a giant oak. Out of breath, I blurted, "Bust. We need to get on the boat."

"Been skinny-dipping with your clothes on?"

"FBI is in the driveway. I'm guessing they're here for the painting and Billy Ray. They may sweep for drugs."

Nash stubbed out his cigarette and sprang into action. "Why didn't you say so?"

We sprinted to the boathouse. "If anyone has anything illegal in their pockets, their ass will be piled into one of the vans for a visit to the pokey. Where's Patsy?"

Nash threw something from his pocket into the bushes. "Inside."

"Katie Lee?" I asked.

"On the dock."

"Macy?"

"Foolin' around with Stewart."

My hand rested on the door handle. "Are you serious?"

Nash opened his mouth but didn't speak. From the main house, a voice echoed through a megaphone, "This is the FBI. No one move." That's when everyone scattered like hatching spiders.

"Get Patsy and Katie Lee in the boat. I'll find Macy."

There were four upstairs bedrooms, and I had mixed emotions. On one hand, I hoped to hell that Macy was in one of them. Then again, I wanted to kick her ass. She knew that Stewart was part of Jack and Billy Ray's posse. Was the attraction to him that magnetic? Had she tipped him off? I wondered how Billy Ray had found me so quickly in the main house and considered leaving her.

Three of the four bedroom doors were open, one closed. In spite of my apprehensions, I barged in. I found Macy and a compromised Stewart, who was wearing white boxer shorts with an allover UNC-Tar Heel stamp and nothing else.

"What are you doing to him?"

"Getting information."

"Macy."

"What? He's a prick."

A cord secured his arms and legs to the rustic bed's head and foot post. Despite being immobilized, he ranted abuse into the padded black lace bra that plugged his mouth.

"Where'd you get the cord?"

"Marina Supply Store."

Macy saw my eye fix on a long piece of fishing line, fashioned into a miniature noose that she was dangling across Stewart.

She smiled.

"I don't even want to know."

"The feds are here. We need to get on the boat."

Before following me out, she retrieved her C-cup from Stewart's mouth. "It's been fun."

"Bitch. Untie me." Stewart's southern had gone missin'. He'd forgotten how to charm a lady.

Macy and I heard the door below slam. Downstairs, partiers had scattered, and outside the window we saw the shadow of Nash with Patsy on his shoulder hustling down the slope toward the pier.

We sprinted outside and caught up to Nash. "Ladies," he said, "keep movin'."

Patsy perched her elbows on top of his shoulder. "What about Mitch?"

At the top of the railroad ties, we heard the shouts of men in FBI windbreakers as they searched the dark perimeter of the grounds and flushed out fleeing partygoers.

"He knows," I said. "He should be here."

Nash called out, "Katie Lee, get those boat keys ready."

She'd seen the bust unfold and relocated the Bayliner to the end of the dock. We were hustling the few yards left when Macy shouted, "My shoe!"

"Darlin'," Nash said, "forget the shoe and get in the boat."

Nash put Patsy down. She turned on her heel. "I need to find Mitch."

Her wobbly saunter wasn't hard to intercept. Before she made ground, Nash and I carried her back to the boat. She landed with a dull thud on the bench seat of the Bayliner. Katie Lee revved the motor, and we faded into the darkness just beyond the dock.

KATIE LEE CUT THE ENGINE. Swaying behind a curtain of black, we listened to the muffled shouts that intermingled with the current. From the boat, we watched the raid on the McGees' property, hoping not to spot Mitch being arrested.

Katie Lee swiveled the boat chair. "Y'all better tell me what the hell's going on." She pointed at Nash. "And skip the bullshit."

"So you're talking to me now?"

I didn't see it, but we all heard Katie Lee slap him.

"What was that for?"

"For screwing Bridget." She motioned for a second slap, but he caught her wrist. She struggled to lash at him and yelled, "How many others have there been?"

"Uh-oh," Macy muttered.

Patsy lit a cigarette and suggested, "Throw him overboard."

Pulling the keys out of the ignition, he dropped them down his pants. "Go ahead."

Katie Lee began sobbing.

Macy pushed her sleeve up. "Do I have to do all the dirty work?"

Katie Lee told Nash he could go to hell. Patsy offered a one-way ticket to send him there. As the abusive zingers flew, my mind sailed adrift. I shuddered to think what would have happened if Mitch hadn't shown up. *If anything had happened to Mitch...Where could he be?* A wave of heat shot through me, and I began to shake.

"Come on, Rach," Macy said. "You hold him down, and I'll dig for treasure."

I didn't answer.

She stared at me. "Rachael, Rachael. Nash, knock if off and give Katie Lee the keys. Something's wrong. Rachael won't stop shaking."

Katie Lee wrapped me in beach towels. "She's going into shock. We need to get her to the house."

Nash reached down his pants. I heard the jingle of keys and the start of the motor.

"Lord, y'all," Patsy said, "she seemed fine a minute ago. Did something happen back there?"

Like a fever entering my body, the damp air chilled my core and made my teeth chatter. Macy removed my coat, but my clothes were soaked. The towels helped slow the shakes, but every few minutes another set made me convulse. I just wanted to see Mitch unharmed, then crawl in bed, any bed, so I could end this night.

Macy spoke over me, filling Katie Lee in on the art fraud scam. Only Mitch knew about my near-deadly encounter with Billy Ray, and I didn't have the energy or inclination to recap what had happened. Nash skimmed the boat at top speed across blackness, occasionally bouncing the bow on a wave crest. The night wind ripped as though it would consume me.

As we approached the Browns' dock, Nash cut power. Lit like a Christmas tree, their house was an easy landmark to spot. The boat clunked wood slats. Katie Lee jumped out and ran. "I'm going to get Daddy."

The Browns' driveway had become a parking lot of blue and whites. "Nash," I stuttered, "the FBI may want you."

"I didn't do anything wrong. Just moved a few suitcases around."

Patsy secured the boat rope to the dock and took off toward the house.

"Did you find what you were looking for?" Nash asked.

I shook my head sideways.

Macy's eyes idled on him. She squeezed his shoulder. "Dr. Brown had better not find you here."

Grabbing his black duffel, he tugged the collar on his jacket. "Don't worry, I'm leavin'." He started to step out of the boat, but backtracked and leaned into my ear. "Bridget has it." Saluting us, he said, "See y'all around."

I wondered if I would.

NOTE TO SELF
My first instinct didn't lie. Billy Ray is a creep.

I can't believe I'm saying this—I'm going to miss Nash.

I owe Mitch McCoy.

43

How the Cow Ate the Cabbage

Outside the kitchen, Uncle and Sims began howling. Macy locked her arm in mine and guided me toward the house. Katie Lee and Dr. and Mrs. Brown hustled in a pack toward us.

Wearing a gray sweat shirt and matching drawstring pants, Dr. Brown held a flashlight and pointed it at Macy and me. Holding the light beam in my face, he said, "Rachael, you shouldn't be walking."

"Dear Lord, child, you're wet. Did you fall in the river?"

"Mama, she didn't fall in."

Dr. Brown looked into my eyes. "Are you dizzy?"

"Light-headed."

Handing his flashlight to Mrs. Brown, he scooped me up. "Katie Lee, get my bag out of the car."

Behind shadowed sea oats a walkie-talkie screeched. "Smith here. Over."

Beyond the thicket of trees, a tall, muscular man dressed in blue slacks and a windbreaker spoke into a device that he held in his hand. "Over."

The hand-held crackled. "We have two vans full. Taking one to Country Club Drive bear cave, the other to George Street."

Dr. Brown carried me up the path to the house. I looked behind him at the man near the garage. He drew a baseball hat low and spoke into the two-way, "Did you catch Peter Rabbit?"

Storm was still in The Bern.

The radio clicked. "Peter Rabbit and Baby Bear secured. Headed to the pokey with Smokey. Beaver Bait is still swimmin'."

"What happened," Dr. Brown asked.

"I was in the McGees' pool."

Mrs. Brown wore a cotton button-down and khaki slacks. Her hair was fastened in a ponytail clasp. She opened the slider to the kitchen. "Swimming in your clothes. You must have a death of a chill. Hayden, she needs to get into something dry."

The lights were bright, and men I didn't know, mostly cops—and Patsy—surrounded Mitch. Someone with a note pad asked him questions. I choked tears when I noticed his bloody nose and swollen cheek. He sat on a kitchen chair without his shirt. His arms had scratches, and his bare ribs had been wrapped in a white bandage.

As Dr. Brown carried me across the kitchen, Mitch stood and winced. An arm of someone I didn't know pressed his shoulder to keep him still. He pushed past and moved to clutch my hand. "Raz, you all right?"

I nodded. "Mitch, how did you know where to find me?"

"I overhead you say you left your purse in the house. Darlin', you never carry a purse. When Billy Ray left the pool game, I had a bad feeling."

My eyes welled. I mouthed, "Thank you."

Dr. Brown placed me on the sofa in the family room, "You can talk to Mitch once I make sure you're in one piece."

Katie Lee appeared with a leather medical bag. Dr. Brown took my pulse, looked into my pupils, and put a salve on the raw welts around my neck.

"Any pain, trouble breathing?"

My shaking had slowed into shivers. "I'll be okay once I get out of my wet clothes."

Leaning back, he looked at me. "Katie Lee, give me a minute with Rachael."

She turned the corner. His voice carried a low, confidential tone. "Rachael, Mitch told us Billy Ray assaulted you. Did he rape you?"

I fought the emotion that strummed inside my chest and stuck in my throat. I'd mistaken Billy Ray as harmless. A talented guy who'd misdirected his gift into forging paintings for profit. I never thought the pastel clothing he wore and the playful chuckle he chortled hid a rabid animal. "If Mitch hadn't shown up."

Dr. Brown put my hands in his. "Rachael, did he sexually assault you?"

"He would've if Mitch hadn't saved me."

"Mitch says you have a hell of a batting arm. You're a fast thinker. Rachael O'Brien, I'm proud of you."

"What are all these cops doing in your house?"

"Mitch showed up and rang the doorbell. Down here we have an open door policy. I didn't even remember what that bell sounded like. When I answered it, he gave us a fright. Said the FBI was raidin' the McGees' and that y'all were still over there. Told us about Billy Ray and that painting in the bathroom. He was frantic. I called Judge Driskell. Husk knew all about the sting, had approved the search warrant earlier this evening. Sent some officers from the department over to the McGees', but they didn't find you. We've been worried, waitin' for y'all to come home. Ten minutes ago, the FBI arrived. It's a god damn circus 'round here."

Mrs. Brown knocked on the doorframe. "How about some hot tea?"

"I'll have scotch, hold the ice," Dr. Brown said.

"Make mine a double."

UPSTAIRS, I PEELED OFF my wet clothes and tossed them into the bathtub. The eye of Horus chain caught around my head. Removing it, I was relieved it hadn't been lost during the pool plunge. After putting on sweats and combing out my hair, I plugged the sink. Filling it with hot water, I sank my pink hands in for warmth. When I looked into the vanity mirror, I saw Katie Lee's reflection.

I turned around. "Don't be mad at me. I didn't know everything would turn into such a monumental mess."

"Mad at you? I came to apologize."

"For what?"

"For almost getting you killed. I'm sorry I ever introduced you to Nash and Billy Ray. If I hadn't been so stupid about that suitcase full of money, none of this would have happened." Her eyes leaked. "I refused to believe that Nash could be involved in anything criminal."

Hugging Katie Lee, I said, "You're not responsible."

She wiped tears. "Oh, Rach, Patsy and Macy told me everything. How Billy Ray has been forging paintings. Stewart is the salesman, and Bubba takes care of shipping. All masterminded by Jack, who we met in New Orleans. The whole thing is crazy, and it all started here in The Bern. How did you figure it out?"

"I didn't figure anything out until New Orleans. That's when things clicked, but I wasn't entirely convinced of what I knew. After Jack Ray picked me up from behind the cemetery, he took me to his gallery and showed me a Clementine Hunter painting. The same one my dad had refurbished. I remembered seeing that painting in the New Bern art gallery near the harbor, and strung it together."

"Which one is the original?"

There was a knock on the doorframe.

"Come on in," Katie Lee called out.

Standing with his hands in his pockets, Storm Cauldwell wore his FBI jacket unzipped, revealing a leather shoulder harness and his gun.

"Ladies, hope I'm not interrupting."

"Storm."

He smiled, indenting the dimple on his chin. "Rachael O'Brien, I'm officially upset with you."

Combing her hair back with her hand, Katie Lee looked approvingly at Storm. "FBI? I thought you were a teaching assistant."

"Had to use discretion on this case. I hope you understand. I asked Rachael to keep what she knew to herself."

I asked Storm, "Did you catch Billy Ray, and have you found the missing painting?"

"We've taken Billy Ray to Craven County Medical, and then he'll be booked. We found a Clementine Hunter at the McGees'. It'll be sent to New Orleans for evaluation."

I recovered the underwater camera from my coat pocket. "I have something for you."

"What's this?"

"Photos of the *Baptism*, before it was splashed by the bidet."

Shaking his head, he pocketed the camera. I couldn't read his face and wondered if he was really angry.

Mrs. Brown shouted up the stairs, "Sausage biscuits hot outta the oven. Come on down."

"All right Mama," Katie Lee said, leaving Storm and me.

Storm put his hands on my shoulders. Sternly he met my eyes. "Rachael O'Brien."

"I know. I know. I shouldn't have snooped inside Bubba Jackson's apartment. I didn't break in. It was open. And honestly, I wasn't sure that Billy Ray and Stewart Hayes would show up at Meredith's. Billy Ray's a big guy. I had to hit him with something or he would've—"

Storm put a hand on my mouth, "Rachael, you went above and beyond what you should've—what was safe. You cut through bureaucratic channels and in one night busted this case wide open. I want to say thank you."

Storm's tanned face had a shadow of stubble. For being in his thirties, he still had it. Sliding his arms around my back, he sheltered me in safety, and I returned the embrace. Resting my head against the warmth of his chest erased the last few hours and cleared my head like a chalkboard wiped clean.

A shrill birdcall startled us. From the landing below, Patsy shouted, "Y'all need to come down before the biscuits go cold."

Storm released me and motioned with his hand for me to lead. "We're coming."

NOTE TO SELF
I love The Bern, but I need rest back at the dorm.

May 1987

44

Whipping Frayed Rope

"**I** caught Francine doing it with her door open. Her skin is tight and as smooth as butter. If it works for her, it should work for me."

Travis waited a beat. I wondered if the phone line had gone dead. "How often do you have to do it?"

"Every night, upside down, for thirty days."

"I don't know, Rach, that doesn't sound healthy."

My head tipped upside down off the bed, and I stretched my facial muscles to eliminate early aging. I'd already told Travis about finding the paintings in Bubba's closet, Billy Ray cornering me, and the raid at the McGees'. He thought we all were mad. Some people pay for a therapist, but I didn't need to. I had Travis. He was still gay. Instead of my lover, he'd become my confidant.

With all the crazy behind me, I could forget about the paintings, and I planned to coast through the last weeks of the term and concentrate on personal business.

"This weather dude sounds like a man of interest."

"His name is Storm. I was emotionally drained. It was probably nothing."

"An embrace like that is never nothing."

"I'm obsessed with Clay, remember?"

"I remember, but I wasn't sure you did."

Our lock clicked, and Katie Lee motioned for my attention. Interrupting Travis, I used our code, "Ice that cupcake," meaning I couldn't freely talk any more.

Flipping right side up, I hung up and handed Katie Lee the phone.

"I don't need to make a call."

"What was the hand motion for?"

"I need to talk."

"Have the police arrested Jack Ray or found Bubba Jackson?"

"Not that I've heard."

"What's wrong?" I asked.

She bit her lip.

"You're pregnant?"

"Rach."

"Hugh or Nash?"

"I'm on the pill."

"Then what's the problem?"

"It's Bridget. I confronted her with her betrayal. Told her I knew she slept with Nash."

The elephant fell off my back. Nash had told Katie Lee the truth in the McGees' boathouse, and now she'd confronted Bridget. I'd assumed this, but it just became official.

At the McGees', when Nash helped get us all in the boat, I'd glimpsed a part of him that Katie Lee had fallen in love with. I didn't have a crush on him or anything like that, but he had moved up a notch or two on my respect ladder. In my mind, Katie Lee's ex-boyfriend had taken a step toward redemption.

"How did that go?"

"Obviously not well. I thought she was my friend."

I watched her fiddle with a pink eraser. She wasn't as practiced as I was at keeping feelings hidden.

"What else?"

She moved to her bed, still dancing the eraser between her fingers. "Bridget said you're a vindictive liar for saying she slept with Nash. How does she know you know?"

Sinking into my desk chair, I spilled my guts. "I knew the night it happened. I overheard them in your parents' bedroom."

"Jesus, Rachael, why didn't you tell me?"

"I didn't think you'd believe me. I figured they'd lie about it, and I'd look like I was trying to cause a rift. It was wrong. I'm sorry."

She threw the eraser on the floor and walked out of our room.

INSTEAD OF STUDYING, I made a modern sculpture on the end of my pencil with my teeth. The only final I'd be passing was woodshop. Katie Lee hadn't spoken to me normal-like for two days, and I wondered if she'd ever trust me again. We only had a week before exams, and I couldn't leave the state to go home until I made things right between us.

Francine knocked on my door and let herself in. She fluttered an oriental paper fan in her face which was distracting, but I couldn't get past her neon-orange tank top and matching cotton shorts.

"Why are you dressed like a Fruit Chew?"

"Orange is mentally stimulating. Helps me study. Lover Boy stopped by."

"Clay?"

"Do you have more than one?"

"What did he say?"

"Said he was lookin' for you."

"That much I gathered. Was anything else mentioned that I'd be interested in knowing?"

"I asked the boy if he was stalking you."

I grimaced. "You make great birth control."

Sitting down on Katie Lee's desk chair, she flipped through the notebook that lay open on her desk. "He confessed that he was, and I told him I just wanted to make sure. Said he'd call you later."

I'd kept my promise to Storm about staying quiet about the forgery, and Clay didn't know what was going on. I owed him an explanation. But first I had some old business to settle. "Have you been in Chantel's room lately?"

"What do you mean by lately?"

"In the last hour?"

"May have. Why you asking?"

"Did you see Bridget?"

Francine feigned interest in Katie Lee's class notes. "Not sure."

"She and Katie Lee had a blowout. I was wondering if Bridget was okay."

She closed the notebook. "You and I both know that you don't give a baboon's ass about that girl after she ran over you in Big Blue and all. Are you plannin' a hair-pullin', fist-slappin' biscuit fight?"

"Me?"

Locking my door, she unplugged the phone and positioned herself like a construction zone roadblock. "Flap those lips if you ever want to see Clay again."

I bit the pencil.

She pulled it out of my mouth, and I unloaded the sorry tale on her.

NOTE TO SELF

Francine Battle = PP = Persuasion Perfectionist.

45

Bunny Boiler Goes Berserk

rancine left Chantel's door cracked open. A slice of her orange attire loomed behind the seam of the door. I had my hand on Bridget's door and whispered, "If you see her coming, divert her."

"Just be quick. My outfit is fresh, and I don't want to have to smear no Oreo filling on it."

Francine had seen Bridget leave with a laundry basket. I had maybe ten minutes, more if she started talking along the way. This was stupid. I knew it. I wasn't sure what details Katie Lee had told her about the Easter weekend. I should've left the snooping up to the FBI, but Nash's parting words haunted me. Bureaucratic organizations tended to act slowly, and I preferred immediate gratification. I didn't want to see or speak to Bridget. I just needed a quick peek in her room to satisfy my curiosity.

Out of habit, I called "Bridget?" as I walked in. The only person who greeted me was Lynyrd Skynyrd who sang from the cassette deck. Dorm rooms were small, and unlike the McGees' home, there weren't many places to hide things. Opening her dresser drawers, I slid my hands under her clothing and then checked the underside, in case she'd taken the painting out of the frame. Nothing.

Bridget's closet door rested partially open. My eyes drifted to a foil-covered shoebox on the top shelf. It was too small to hold a painting, and I should've moved on. It was probably some keepsake from her childhood. I pulled her desk chair over and reached for the box. When I lifted it off the shelf, the lid, plastered with photos, fell off. Some of the snapshots I recognized since I had copies. But in my set, all of us were in the photos. These photos were just of Katie Lee. I didn't know what I was looking at, and it seemed peculiar.

Stepping off the chair, I lowered the box. Inside I found a hairbrush, a Carolina Tar Heel pen, hair clips, and the half-used bottle of Lauren perfume Nash had given Katie Lee for Christmas. Gingerly I pinched the waistband of purple bikini underpants.

"What are you doing in here?" Bridget asked.

Throwing my palm to my chest, I gasped.

She yanked the altar box from my hands. "You aren't capable of keeping out of my business, are you?"

"You've been stealing from Katie Lee. What are you doing? Making a voodoo doll for some sort of sick vendetta?"

Bridget opened her top dresser drawer. When she spun around, a handgun pointed at my chest.

"What are you doing?"

"What I should've done a long time ago."

I shuffled backward until I became pinned at the foot of her bed. "This is mental. Put that down."

"Hugh was kind enough to lend it to me. A girl needs to protect herself from lurking vandals."

Not thinking that she'd really fire a gun at me, I scoffed. "Are you accusing me of vandalizing your stinking room? We both know you did that yourself."

"You can't prove it."

"Bridget, you're venting at the wrong person. Are you stressed over finals or something?"

She unlocked the safety. "I'm about to feel a lot less stressed."

"Don't you think someone is going to hear a gunshot?"

Keeping her eye on me, she turned up the stereo volume. If she was fooling around, she didn't show it.

Moisture beads of panic grew under my hairline. "Why are you doing this?"

"You've spent the entire year ruining my relationship with Katie Lee."

I squeezed my eyes shut. I wasn't tracking on the Bridget radio wave. "What are you talking about?"

"Like you don't know. I break up Katie Lee and Nash, and you keep them together. I give Katie Lee a reason to room with me, and you convince her to stay with you. She and I are kindred spirits. I love her, and we belong together, forever."

Locking her arms, Bridget held the gun with determination. My mind's lens retracted. I needed to stall, but couldn't think of a diversion. Her door swung open, and I was thankful that southerners didn't lock doors.

"That music is too damn loud!" Francine yelled.

Bridget turned to face her, and I imagined Aunt Gert giving me wrestling advice. *Leapfrog-body-guillotine would do.* I improvised. Kung Fu karate-kicking my foot into the back of her knees, I folded her like a crimped piece of dough, sending the pistol for a spin on the floor.

"Fry me a pickle. Blondie's gotta gun."

I launched to vise-grip Bridget's calves and feet, but she was a wiry kicker and wangled out of my grip. Snapping to her feet, Bridget charged the closet.

"The gun," I warned.

Francine barreled in front of the open closet and took an offensive lineman's blocking stance.

Weighing options, Bridget made a split-second decision. In a seamless motion, she walloped a smack across Francine's face.

Rage bulged from inside Francine, and her switch flipped to pissed-off-hornets-nest, she lunged for Bridget.

Undeterred and brazen, Bridget dropped to the floor and stretched her arms between Francine's legs.

Pinning Bridget between her knees, Francine squeezed her like a tube of toothpaste. "You late on your rabies shot?"

Popcorn rained in the air, and Katie Lee stood with an empty bowl. "Y'all stop that now, ya hear!"

"Bridget's got a gun. Dial 911!" I shouted.

"Jesus," Francine shouted, releasing her knee grip. "She bit me?"

I leapt for Bridget's ponytail, but before I pulled, Francine jammed her slippered foot onto Bridget's ass, pancaking her to the floor. Katie Lee shuffled her weight onto Bridget's legs.

Scampering over the body pile, I moved into the closet. "I got the gun."

Empting bullets into my palm, I pocketed them and picked up the phone receiver. As I dialed, Francine filled Bridget's ears. "Where were you raised? The zoo? Is that where your mama monkey taught you to bite?"

"This is Rachael O'Brien. We need a patrol car at North Carolina College. Bridget Bodsworth tried to shoot me with a pistol. Seventh floor, Grogan Residence Hall."

Katie Lee had left Bridget's door open. Catching my breath, I slid the snub nose pistol into a pillowcase. Macy and Chantel came in with our hall monitor followed by Tuke Walson from the campus police. They stood still, eyeing the pileup

I handed him the pillowcase and the bullets, and he tipped his baseball hat that read *Campus Security*. "Ladies, you can get up now."

Katie Lee stood, but Francine refused. "Houston, I've got a problem flattened beneath me."

Tuke pried Francine off Bridget and then offered his hand. Latching onto his middle finger, Bridget bent it backward. Convulsively, he jerked his hand away, but she held firm, dislodging the appendage from its socket with a loud pop. When he hollered, Bridget snapped to her feet and shot out of the room.

She was out the door, and I panicked that she'd be like the centipede you spot in your room. The one you lose sight of the minute you go to get a Dixie cup to trap it. Knowing it's still nearby, you can't relax, let alone sleep for fear all those legs will return to scurry across you in the dark. "Someone grab her," I shouted.

Francine led the chase down the hall.

Bridget sprinted for the staircase until she crashed into two police officers. Her cheeks and neck grew turnip patches. Pointing at Francine and me, she spewed vengeance. "They assaulted me. Those two. They're the ones you need to arrest. They broke into my room. It was an ambush."

"She's a liar. She was going to blow my head off."

Showing the whites of her eyes, Francine told the policemen, "This Wonder Bread loaf is missing her crust. She took a bite out my leg."

With his unharmed hand, Tuke dangled the gun by its trigger guard. "Ladies, ladies. Harboring a firearm is against dorm policy. We're going to need statements from each of you." He secured Bridget's wrist in his good hand, and the two policemen escorted all of us back to Bridget's room.

We waited around while the police interviewed us one at a time in the hallway. Bridget went first.

Tuke stayed behind with us, and Katie Lee asked where he was from.

He rocked on his heels and told her, "Hickory."

"What's in Hickory?" Macy asked.

His eyes glistened. "Furniture and hops."

While he mentioned the finer points of his hometown, I took the liberty of crawling onto the closet floor. Francine saw me and scrunched her eyebrows. I pushed past shoes and a dirty clothes pile. Running my hand against the back wall, I braved roaches and splinters.

More officers arrived in the hallway. "Greensboro police," I heard a woman say.

As I touched a slim cardboard box, my heart palpated with anticipation. Exiting ass first, on my knees, I tipped the box upside down,
and a painting encased in Bubble Wrap slid out.

Francine sidestepped toward me.

"Hey now," Tuke said, "what are y'all doing?"

In unison, Francine and I spoke. "Clementine Hunter."

"How do you know it's a Clementine Hunter?" I asked Francine.

Pulling the painting from my grasp, Francine said, "Don't you ask
me what I should be askin' you."

"My dad restored two of them, including this one."

Straightening her back, she lasered her eyes into mine as though
she was summoning truth detection powers to measure the sincerity of
my words. "Clementine Hunter is my great-memaw. She painted this."

MACY POKED AT HER baked ziti with extra cheese. "I'm not going
to miss this." I looked closely at a hair nested in her pasta.

"That's gross," I said, pushing my taco salad aside.

Slurping a Diet Coke, she asked, "When are you and Clay gonna
do it?"

"I've been distracted lately, and now the year is over."

Pointing a red nail, she spoke in a disciplinary tone. "You got a bad
attitude."

Katie Lee's backpack clunked onto the floor next to the cafeteria
table. "Look who I bumped into outside."

Tuke tipped his hat. "Ladies."

He focused on my untouched taco salad, and I pushed it toward
him. "Help yourself."

"Are you sure?" he asked, unfolding a napkin and tucking it in his
shirt neck. "Been busy this morning, and I haven't had a break."

Katie Lee nudged his hand. "Tuke, tell them what you know."

"You girls don't have to worry about your safety. Ms. Bodsworth has
been put on probation pending charges. The Greensboro police coor-
dinated with FBI in the Clementine Hunter art forgery. I have it from
a source that your hallmate coconspirited with Jack Ray. Phone records

show that she'd been in contact with him since November. Looks like she brought that painting back from New Orleans. Planned on selling it to Ms. Stein, the art curator, and then later, they'd switch it with a fake."

My brain ticked and hummed.

Macy clicked her nails. "Are you fucking telling us that Jack Ray knew Bridget before he sat at our table in New Orleans?"

Tuke swallowed a forkful of meaty bean mixture and nachos. "Look, I shouldn't say anything else until the case is closed. I'm sure the FBI will want to speak to all of you."

BIRDS CHIRPED OUTSIDE MY WINDOW. Not in a sweet, songful way but in a clatter that may as well have been New Year's pot-and-pan drumming. With only finals week left, I'd started to pull posters off the wall and pack some things in my suitcase. Macy lay sprawled on my bed with an open book. "I can't study with that racket."

"Call Hugh. He can come over with his bow and take care of things."

Macy and Katie Lee shot me evil glances.

"Sorry."

Macy started to click her red nails.

"What?" I asked, "Have I done something?"

"No," she said.

I looked from Katie Lee to Macy. "Is something going on with Hugh? Please don't tell me you had a threesome, 'cause if you did, I don't want to know about it."

"That's gross," Macy said.

"We've talked it over. We've given him up."

"Does he know that?"

"Katie Lee and I stopped by his room. I wore the tortoiseshell sunglasses."

"What else?" I asked.

Macy fidgeted. "There's something I've been meaning to tell you both. I'm transferring next year."

I stopped packing. "Why?"

"I need a change. I want to go to a university where they have a football team and bars."

"So you're just up and leaving us?" Katie Lee asked.

"I love you guys, but I've gotta get away from this place."

My chest tightened. I felt betrayed. "Macy, you're one of my best friends, and I seem normal when you're around. If you're gone, everyone will figure out how psychotic I am."

"You're not making this easy."

Summoning the guilts, I didn't respond.

CLAY HAD LEFT A PHONE message with Katie Lee. He'd invited me over around seven-ish. One final left and I'd survived my freshman year. Even ticked a few things off my "to-do" list, except for losing my virginity. I still carried that one with me. My stomach flip-flopped. Was tonight the night?

The evening was warm without humidity. Tree shadows crept against the lawn outside of Clay's dorm. I'd arrived twenty minutes early. I didn't care and raced up the steps then sped along his hallway. His door rested partially open, and I pushed it wide. His back faced me. Seeing his arms wrapped around Sheila Sinclair—a.k.a. She-Devil—I wondered if I stood in the wrong room. There was no mistaking his silhouette. My chest deflated and I realized that my fun-filled, romantic evening with Clay wasn't going to happen.

My voice trembled. "Clay Sorenson, eat shit and die."

Slamming his door behind me, I teetered on the verge of a tear storm and sprinted out of the dorm. How could I have been so wrong? The story about She-Devil stalking him was bullshit. If this was how I picked men, I deserved to be sexually inactive.

I'd bolted halfway across the grassy quad lawn when Clay shouted my name. I'd spent valuable energy working myself into a spiral of despair, and no one would talk me out of my emotions. As quickly as I had met Clay, I was over him. Until he tackled me.

"Get off of me," I hissed.

"What's wrong?"

"You're giving me grass burns. Please remove yourself."

"Not until you tell me why you left," he said, which only infuriated me more.

"You're sleeping with her."

"With Sheila?" He laughed.

"You're seriously sick. And Sheila-She-Devil is mental, which makes you two a great match."

"You've got it all wrong. Let me explain."

Since Clay sat on top of me, I didn't have escape options.

"Sheila stopped by to let me know she's found someone else. It's weird, but she wanted to break it to me in person."

"What?"

"She was about to leave. I was wishing her well when you came in."

"Really?"

He released my arms. "Really."

"You've inflicted a tremendous amount of emotional turmoil on me, and I'm not sure that I will ever recover to be the old Rachael."

"Rachael O'Brien, you're cute when you're mad."

He called me by my proper name when he flirted, and it didn't go unnoticed. Before I could protest, he nibbled my neck.

"Clay Sorenson, you don't play fair."

"You bet your ass."

"Hey, Rachael," Hugh said, towering above. "Everything all right?"

He had his arm around Sheila. She wore a strapless sundress, and Hugh rubbed his thumb on her bare shoulder.

"Yeah, I'm okay."

Clay unpinned me and offered his hand to lift me to my feet.

I brushed myself off.

"Haven't seen you around," Hugh said. "Thought you dropped off the planet."

"No, still here. You remember Clay?"

"Holiday Inn," Hugh said.

Sheila shaded her face behind a pair of John Lennon sunglasses. She reached her hand toward me. "Rachael O'Brien, I'm Sheila Sinclair." I limply shook her hand while I glared at Hugh.

"The police called me about my gun. I spoke to Katie Lee. She said Bridget tried to shoot you with it."

I nodded, downplaying the moment I didn't want to relive.

"Rach, I'm sorry I ever lent it to her. I'm completely gobsmacked. She was always so sweet." Hugh shook his head. "I had no idea she was crazy."

"Forget it. She's gone. A couple of days after the police searched her room, her mom drove up and packed up her things."

"Wait a minute. I thought her mom died when she was young," Hugh said.

Clay wrapped his arm around my shoulder.

"So did we, but she lied. Her mom divorced her dad last summer."

"How do you know?"

My hands rested inside my pockets. I was tired of the Bridget story. Katie Lee, Macy, Francine, Chantel, and I had stayed up all night after the gun encounter. We had analyzed everything, down to her dental floss routine. I'd already told Clay the whole sordid story. He thought I was making up a tall tale until Francine showed him her bite mark.

"Chantel introduced herself to Mrs. Bodsworth. Helped her pack up Bridget's things."

"Are you leaving Friday?" Hugh asked.

"Tomorrow, after my final. What about you?"

"End of the week, I'm driving Sheila home then heading to Florida. Are you working on masterpieces this summer?"

I stared at Hugh. The thought of spending a summer with Dad and his girlfriend shook my emotional balance. I hadn't heard from Mom in months and guessed she hadn't found her inner self yet. It was weird knowing that she was alive but not knowing anything about what she was doing. I rubbed the trinket on my neck. After nine months of freedom and independence, thoughts of leaving North Carolina for an Ohio summer horrified me. "Not sure what summer has in store for me."

"May I?" Hugh asked Clay before hugging me. "It's been a hell of a year. Don't be a stranger."

He and Sheila strolled away, and I wondered if he had a thing for complicated relationships. I whispered, "Good luck."

Clay folded me in his arms and led me toward his dorm. Finally we'd have some drama-free, quality alone-time.

The year was over. My last final was Professor Schleck's blue book written exam. I had tonight to refresh myself on a few facts. I was ready. A few hours spent with Clay would be harmless. Settling onto his futon, his leg touched mine. It took under a minute for us to maneuver into a lip-lock. A wave tumbled over me. His hands were crafty, and my bra disappeared. This was it, and I wouldn't have regrets. We both ignored the knock on the door, but Clay was a southerner and had left the latch unlocked.

Someone cleared his throat. "Rachael."

Clay and I detached our lips, and I wiped the spit shine with my fingertips. "Storm?"

"Katie Lee said I might find you here. I need you to come with me and verify a statement."

NOTE TO SELF
Southerners—do any lock doors?

Epilogue

eing home for the summer spun my emotional balance in a manic dance. Separated by hundreds of miles from the crazies who tried to kill me was a relief, but I missed Clay, my almost-boyfriend, who I almost had sex with, and the girls I'd befriended on the seventh floor of Grogan Hall.

I tried not to think about how wrong everything could've ended. Some decent juju had channeled my way, and I'd breathed a deep sigh every morning since. Clementine Hunter and the New Orleans Museum of Art had filed charges against Billy and Jack Ray, Stewart Hayes, and Bridget Bodsworth for heisting and forging artwork. The case files were in the hands of lawyers and courts to sort out.

There still was some open-ended business—namely Bubba Jackson. He had slipped through the cracks of the FBI raid on his apartment, which amounted to seizing a stockpile of forged paintings, invoices that linked New Bern to an art dealer in New Orleans, illegal fireworks, and a heap of cannabis.

Storm Cauldwell, the smoking-hot FBI agent in charge, confided that the confiscated marijuana was the largest North Carolina bust so far this year. Jackson's refrigerator, freezer, kitchen cabinets, and storage facility below his deck didn't contain household items and sporting equipment. Every inch had been stocked with blocks of cellophane-wrapped happy grass. No one in New Bern admitted to knowing his whereabouts. But once authorities found Bubba, he'd be facing an additional set of charges for possession and distribution.

Two weeks into the Canton, Ohio, summer, a certified package arrived at Dad's shop, addressed to me. A painting of a chorus group wearing white robes sang inside a country church. There was one vanilla face among the singers. Clementine Hunter had titled the painting *Awakening*. It came with a typed thank you note initialed in a Sharpie pen.

I called Francine at home in Louisiana to tell her I'd received the painting. She said it would make a fine addition to our dorm room in the fall. After I hung up, I flipped through the calendar and counted the weeks. I had ten to survive in Canton, Ohio.

An invitation from Paisley Ray

If you enjoyed this or any of my other books, I'd love to hear from you. I answer all my e-mails personally, and if you contact me, I will put you on my mailing list to receive notification of future releases, updates, and contests.

Online reviews of my books are greatly appreciated. By offering a line or two of opinion, you not only help other readers decide if this is something they would enjoy, you help me by giving perspective on the story.

Visit: PaisleyRay.com
E-mail: Heypaisleyray@gmail.com
Become a fan: Facebook.com/Heypaisleyray
Twitter: @HeyPaisleyRay
Pinterest.com/Heypaisleyray

For The Record

Hulk Hogan versus the Undertaker: there would not have been a televised match until 1991. The *Survivor Series III* took place in November 1987, where the big draw was Hulk Hogan versus Andre the Giant.

Fuji disposable cameras were developed in 1986, but had not been released in the United States yet.

Jelly shoes became really hot in 1983 and would have been "past trend" by 1986.

Acknowledgements

Many thanks to the fresh set of eyes, opinions, and valuable critiques provided by Marcel Bradley, Paige Kellar, Dorothy Vout, and the Tuesday night writers. And kudos to the Wikipedia community for their invaluable information on various subjects.

Sneak Preview

THE RACHAEL O'BRIEN CHRONICLES
SUMMER FLAMBÉ

A Novel
by
PAISLEY RAY

"A man's kiss is his signature."
~Mae West

Prologue

I began counting the days left in my freshmore break. Sixty-six. I wasn't a freshman anymore—hallelujah! I'd left that journey behind. The fall term hadn't started yet, so I didn't consider myself an official sophomore. Trapped in Canton, Ohio, limbo, away from my friends and potential boyfriend, I held low expectations for my first college summer at home.

Still intact, I considered my virginity to be like an unsightly mole that I needed to lose. But my entrance into womanhood would have to wait until I returned to North Carolina College. It wasn't likely I'd meet anyone lustworthy over the summer.

I was over knockdown dramas and hidden agendas. The best summer I could hope for was a quick one where I encountered as little face time with Dad's girlfriend as possible. I was nineteen, practically a twenty-year-old. I'd come to terms with the fact that my father now dated, but I hadn't warmed to the specimen he'd chosen. She was bound to materialize, and when she did, I planned to lay low and avoid her. My dad and Trudy Bleaux had nothing in common that I could see. The thrill of their tonic's fizz had to be receding, and I was betting that their tryst would go flat before the Fourth of July.

June 1987

1

Stale and Soggy

I needed a distraction, some sort of *flambé* in my SUMMER. Alone in my Canton, Ohio, bedroom the only light came from my lit cigarette. I amused myself by igniting a lone maple leaf that stuck to my window sill and watched the dark green sear yellow and orange before turning black and ashen. Sucking my cheeks in, I made fish lips in an attempt to blow smoke circles out the window. The stifling night air hung on me like a velvet curtain. I heard a screech echo from a tree, and I strained my eyes against the darkness to locate the feathery predator. Ignoring the distant ringing phone, I inhaled deeply and held a tobacco plume in my chest. With summer in front of me, I had loads of free time to learn how to make creative shapes from smoke.

Lately Dad got more calls from Trudy than I did from my girl-friends. That was not right! In defiance, I'd turned off the ringer on my bedroom phone. Contouring my lips, I released a controlled breath from my lungs.

The stairs creaked and Dad shouted, "Rachael, it's for you."

Quickly snubbing my cigarette out on the metal window frame channel, I hid the unfinished evidence in a wooden box that rested on my nightstand. "Who is it?" I shouted.

"Not sure. Someone with a southern accent."

Hoping it was Clay, I unwrapped a wintergreen Certs and placed it on my tongue. Last time I'd seen him, my bra was on the floor of his dorm room and my higher learning was progressing nicely until Agent Storm Cauldwell interrupted our end-of-the-year "study" session. When I'd left his room to give a statement to the FBI, things were awkward. Hoping to get back on the romance track, I mustered up my newly found sultry, picked up the phone, and whispered a sleepy, "Hello."

"Rach, you're never going to believe what's happened to me."

I waited until I heard my father hang up the receiver. "Katie Lee, what's going on?"

"It's Nash, he's left town for the summer."

"Wait a minute, you two broke up. Why do you care?"

She sighed. "I think I drove him away."

"How'd you do that?"

"I was in Big Blue with Gavin Snarks."

"Nice. Have I met him?"

"Maybe at Billy Ray's."

Hearing that name made me cringe. As much as I wanted to forget his thick fingers strangling my neck, I hadn't.

"After store hours we parked Big Blue in the Piggly Wiggly lot and moved into the backseat."

"Did you use protection?"

"We didn't get that far. The windows steamed up. When I cranked 'em down to let air in, I smelled cigarettes. Nash was lurking in the shadows. He'd parked his truck on the street and was leaning against it. He knows Gavin and I were fooling around. The next day I went over to his house to tell him to quit following me around town."

"Why'd you do that?"

"So he'd follow me around town."

"Katie Lee, that's mental."

"I can't help it. I miss him."

"So what exactly is the problem?"

"His mama told me he'd packed up and left. Gone to live with his daddy and work on the oyster farms in Mobile for the summer."

Outside my open window, a car door slammed, and I pried my curtain aside. The moon had set the night landscape aglow in crisp black and white. I watched a woman climb out of a Volkswagen convertible.

"Forget him. Why don't you pay more attention to the guy you had in the backseat of Big Blue?"

"Gavin's good looking, but his personality's as dry as a saltine cracker. When we're together, he never says more than two words, and I do all the talking. He's too much work to be around."

"Why were you with him anyway?"

"I don't want Nash to think I'm still sweet on him."

Even in the dark, I could see a leotard and tights carrying a pillow and an oversized shoulder bag. "Damn."

"Exactly," Katie Lee said.

The doorbell rang, and instinctively I knew I was about to ingest a higher-than-recommended dose of Dad's girlfriend, Trudy Bleaux.

"Katie Lee, I gotta go. Trudy just rang the doorbell. She's carrying an overnight bag. This can't be good."

"Oh Lord. Call me back when she's gone."

DAD HAD A SECRET and kept it hidden. Even though he's a staunch Cleveland Browns football fan, his favorite beer is made in their biggest rival's hometown. Dad drinks Iron City Beer, brewed and canned in Pittsburgh. I'd been in relax mode until Trudy's high-octane rasp rattled my inner ear. She had missed kindergarten 101 and didn't remember to keep a quiet indoor voice. She used an all-purpose, perkified frequency range, which I imagined she amped up when she taught her aerobic classes.

For Dad's sake, I'd promised myself to tolerate her and mind my own business. That task was easier when I was at school, separated from her by two states. I snuck down the stairs and turned a corner toward the garage to snatch a cold one from the fridge. I guzzled a quarter of the can to dull my sensitivity to her presence. Careful not to let the door into the house slam, I scurried halfway up the stairs and ducked behind the half wall where the railing ended.

I'd never witnessed Trudy's evening look. Whenever I saw her, it was in passing, and I mostly wished she'd disappear. She didn't have her makeup mask on, and a butterfly wing constellation of freckles splattered her cheeks. Her hair had been styled with a mixer. Not the dough or batter attachment, but the wire one for blending dry ingredients. She'd woven her hair in and out of the spaces between the beater blades.

"Trudy," Dad said. "It's near midnight."

"John," she blurted. "Someone broke into my apartment. Have you been reading the newspaper? There's been a rash of home robberies, and I've been victimized."

Dad wrapped his arm around her shoulders and guided her to the sofa. "Are you hurt?"

"No, I'm not hurt."

"Tell me what happened."

She grabbed a crumpled tissue from an outside pocket in her gym bag and blew her nose. "I taught the nine o'clock step class. Afterward I showered and changed at the gym. I needed flax seed, sardines, and spinach for my morning smoothie, so I went to the Valu-King. When I got home, I unlocked my door, and my apartment was—all tidied up."

Leaning forward, I peered at the two through the wood railing slats. They were oblivious to my presence. What a cockamamie story. Of all the bullshit things to say. Dad was not going to fall for this. It was the most asinine reason for throwing yourself at someone that I'd ever heard.

Dad tipped his head. "Tidied up?"

"You know. Cleaned, organized."

"I'm not sure I understand."

"You've seen my apartment. I live eclectically. I don't believe that kitchen utensils should be confined to drawers, and I like to style my hair and makeup by the entry closet."

I thought about interrupting to ask if she used the kitchen sink instead of the toilet, but refrained.

"Someone," she sniffled, "violated my apartment. Kitchen stuff is in the kitchen, and bathroom stuff is in the bathroom. Throws were folded, mirrors moved—you can see the furniture—and my bed's been made. My apartment smells like Windex."

Dad rubbed Trudy's shoulder, which made me want to hurl. These two were so opposite they couldn't possibly last. I told myself he was just rebelling against Mom's abrupt departure. Inside my head, I chanted the mantra, "Trudy's just a phase."

"I'm sure there's an explanation. Someone thought they were doing you a favor."

"Who would do that? I can't find a thing."

"Maybe Sky stopped by."

Trudy scoffed. "She'd never clean my apartment. She knows better."

"Give her a call. At least you'll know if it was your sister's doing."

Trudy puffed an anxious breath and turned her puppy eyes on my father. "I guess I could call her in the morning, but can I stay here tonight?"

Clearing my throat, I walked down the stairs. "What's going on?"

NOTE TO SELF
Katie Lee and Nash finally spending some quality time apart. Hoping it lasts so sophomore year will be drama free.

Trudy is weaseling her way into our house. Must come up with diversionary tactic.

Trudy has a sister, Sky Bleaux. Figures.

2

Bad Energy

ad was an early riser, and by default so was I. Trudy was not. Every morning before I left for the restoration shop, I warmed an icing-coated strawberry Pop Tart in the toaster. Working at the family art restoration business had pros and cons. On the plus side, I could wear whatever. On the negative, I carpooled with Dad, spending more hours in a confined space with a PU—parental unit—than recommended by a recent poll in *Seventeen* magazine. Luckily he and I didn't delve into any overly personal conversations. Mostly we focused on work.

In late June, someone flicked a circuit breaker, and the heat index soared to sweltering hot. Being sweaty in a house without central air-conditioning, and confined in close quarters with Dad's girlfriend, brings on irritability. I needed to convince Dad of two things: first, to install central A/C—admittedly dicey since our house is a fifty-year-old antique—and second, to ditch his Trudy habit.

To ease her visitor-imposition conscience, Dad's girlfriend initiated annoying acts of helpfulness. She'd step aside when I met her in the hallway, and in the evening, she patted the sofa with her hand in an attempt to lure me into the prime TV viewing seat. She preached the benefits of folic acid, fiber, and a slew of vitamins whenever I ate something from a box. She said she needed a new sports bra and wanted me to go to the mall with her. *Yeah, right.*

She was a master irritator, and by week two her overexercised, bounce-a-penny ass that still slept on our sofa grated under my skin. Leaving the kitchen table set for a cereal breakfast for me and washing a load of my laundry triggered menacing thoughts toward her well-being. I'd met an abundance of fakers my freshman year at college. Having experience with deviant unstable types, I determined her nicey-nice façade had to be a ruse. She wasn't right for Dad. He couldn't possibly be happy with her. She was just the first thing that came along since Mom left. Unselfishly, I decided to take it upon myself to crack her sunshiny shell.

Step one, surveillance. I kept a close eye on her and interrupted any potential lovey-dovey PDA—public displays of affection—she initiated toward Dad. I became a regular *Late Night with David Letterman* viewer and slept with my bedroom light on to give the illusion that I was still awake. I hoped this ploy would curtail after-dark alone-time between the two. The mere thought of her eggbeaters on Mom's side of the bed harmed my sanity. Step two, extermination. The sooner Trudy moved her jumping-jacked glutes back to her apartment, the less professional time I'd need to restore my mental health.

THE GRAVEL IN THE driveway outside Dad's shop crunched beneath his feet, drowning any early morning nature noises. I'd stayed up late the night before talking on the phone with Katie Lee and secretly smoking cigarettes. The conversation was one-sided. She wallowed over Nash, and I listened. It was no use trying to talk sense into my roommate. I knew better. Occasionally I interjected questions for her to ponder. "If he were behind bars, would you still want a relationship? Don't you think there is more than one person out there who you could be crazy-attracted to?"

She rebutted my second question. "You tell me. Is there another Clay out there? Or is he the only one?"

I hated when she did that. *Smartass.*

My father was a walking history book and rattled on about seventeenth-century ripple-molded frames in polished hardwoods. He appreciated repairing the pieces that had traveled through time. His size eleven feet stomped quickly up to the building. "We received a commission from the Canton Museum to refurbish twenty picture frames. Touching up stain and gold leaf, making sure the molding is intact. I said we'd have them completed in a week. I can really use your help."

After disarming the alarm, he headed for the coffee maker. I looked at him suspiciously.

"What?" he asked.

"Nothing," I said.

We both knew that Trudy preached the ill effects of caffeinated drinks. While the coffee pot finished percolating, he and I slid on our aprons and surgical gloves. He laid two of the frames on the worktable and pointed out where time, humidity, and mishandling had cracked the wood and damaged the carvings. As he and I worked, my mind morphed on the intricacies of the task, sweeping me away from time and place. He showed me how to apply an epoxy on chipped carvings, adjusting viscosity so it didn't ooze and dry in globs. Once we finished, we'd have to wait for the chemical bond to dry.

Dad removed a white sheet from a pair of Louis XIV armchairs. "Think you're up for repairing them?"

I gave him a nod-shrug. Moving toward the chairs, I admired the ornately carved frame. When I started a new project, I found myself wondering how many homes the piece had lived in. My fingers brushed over the curves of the arms. I guessed these hadn't been look-see antiques, chosen to be displayed as a tribute to acquired or pretend wealth. These had been owned by someone who didn't know what they had or didn't give a rip. Dings and chips around the legs had been delivered like a round of ammunition that lodged precise and deep. I imagined a child, unfairly disciplined, releasing frustration with a steady kick on the supple wood, while administering a sharp fingernail or the edge of a toy on the arm carvings. It would take a lot of work to make these look new, and I didn't know if I could piece the carvings back together without making it look amateur.

I fumbled with a corner square of sandpaper, and Dad interrupted me. He unrolled a felt case and offered me his woodworking tools. Dancing my fingers over the worn-handled chisels, I scanned the variances in shape and size of blades. I removed my favorite tool from his case. It looked like a paintbrush, except the tip held a piece of sandpaper no bigger than your thumb. I used it to smooth scrollwork and hard-to-get-at corners.

Dad smiled. "That's one of a kind, designed by your grandfather."

We used an array of stains and paints, but Dad recommended I use potassium dichromate. Toxic stuff—orange and red crystals that came in a tin. He taught me how to mix the right consistency and color. We tested it on a piece of scrap mahogany and watched it react with the tannins, producing a rich brown stain. Later on, Edmond, Dad's long-time assistant, would show me how to reupholster the seat.

Once I'd finished gluing loose joints on two chair legs, I plugged in a fan to speed up the drying. My stomach gurgled, and the bell on the door chimed.

Looking up, I did a double take. Dad had ordered takeout lunch, and I knew the delivery guy. Markus Doneski had gone to high school with me. While Dad went to get money, Markus moved toward me and muttered, "Well, well. If it ain't Arty Farty O'Brien."

I hadn't seen Doneski in a year and had actually fed his memory into my brain shredder. "Markus," I scowled.

"Miss me?" he asked.

"Ah, let me think. NO."

Dad returned from the office. "You two know each other?"

"Of course. I sat behind Rachael in trigonometry."

Dad handed him a twenty. "Oh, nice. I bet you two have some catching up."

I seared Markus with my eyes. I wouldn't be ordering anything from the Hoagie House anytime soon.

THE CANTON MUSEUM OF ART had a new exhibit, and my dad went over to help the curator, who was also a close friend of his. Figuring the chairs needed time to dry, and since the phone was not ringing off the hook, I took a leisurely lunch out back. After I ate my Italian hoagie, I closed my eyes and worked on maintaining my daily dose of sun-induced vitamin D.

Dad's assistant, Edmond, didn't hear me come back from lunch. Climbing onto a stool, I half watched him shimmy his hips in a dance around a worktable. He sang with Elvis about being all shook up. Swiveling his pointer fingers toward me, he softened the volume. His forehead looked moist. In a winded breath, he sputtered, "There you are."

I walked over and dabbed his forehead with a rag. "Is this what you do when you're"—I looked behind each of my shoulders—"alone?"

He chuckled, and his cheeks reddened, softening his badass biker look. His shoulder-length black hair had grayed near his face, and he pulled it all back in a ponytail. The denim shirt and jeans he wore, combined with his furniture-polish-stained hands, fit the mold of a grease monkey, not a sophisticated restoration expert. "You make a great spy. Sneaking up on people." He took the rag from my hand and hucked it in the wastebasket. "I don't reveal secrets that easily."

Lunch had landed hard. I rubbed my stomach. "Are there any Tums tablets around?"

"Check the Kittinger drawer," he said.

Stacks of client files and invoices rested on top of an antique walnut desk Dad had rescued. I sat down and dug in the center drawer. I didn't find Tums, but I did find a peppermint Lifesaver. I popped it in my mouth and leafed through the folders. For insurance purposes, Dad always took before, during, and after photos of commissions. The Canton Museum was a regular client, and files were labeled by department. Some private collectors' invoices also littered the desktop. Dad must have been working on billing before he left.

I was surprised to see a folder labeled *McCarty*. We did work for her, which was weird since she and Dad were icy. Geneva McCarty was a brazen eccentric whom I'd met a handful of times over the years. I flipped open her folder and leafed through some of the projects. Judging from the commissions we'd gotten, she had deep pockets. Mostly furniture repairs for nicks and scratches, gobs of painting restorations, some custom frames, a velvet jewelry box lining, and bookbinding. A Polaroid photo of a tattered, leather-bound book rested in the folder. I picked it up and looked at it closely. A string, wrapped in a figure eight securing two leather circles, held it closed. The title was engraved in gold lettering, the first letter of each word narrow and enlarged, the rest of the letters simple, not ornate. Fifteenth or sixteenth century, I guessed. *Nostradamus's Translation of Horapollon of Manouthis.* A French book of notes on Egyptian hieroglyphics. Funky. Jogging my memory, I swore I'd seen it somewhere before.

"Edmond, do you know how to bind books?"

"No, but your father does."

The date on the yellowed invoice was May 1968, the year I was born. Leaving the desk, I checked on the chair leg glue. "What do you think?"

He tapped the joints with a finger. "Let it dry overnight. Start the arms in the morning." He motioned with his head. "Give me a hand with the Tiffany chandelier?"

Sheets of glass and a box of pendants were spread out on a worktable. Edmond had suspended the lotus flower chandelier on a pulley. Shades of green ranging from emerald to mint gave the glass the illusion of tangled vines. Interspersed among the grassy-toned hues were delicate clusters of soft pinks. He and I traced cardboard templates for the missing glass and began cutting and grinding replicas. Once we finished, we'd apply copper foil and weld the pieces into place with a soldering gun.

A luster of light gleamed inside a coin-sized piece of leaded glass Edmond was inspecting. "How are things?"

I smirked. "That's a nonquestion question."

"Things in your life. I like knowing what you're up to, your plans."

"My plan is to work here for college cash and manage to survive summer without becoming mentally scarred by Dad's overzealous space cadet girlfriend." *There, I'd said it.*

Edmond smiled empathetically but didn't make a big deal of my Trudy Bleaux adjective outburst. He was like family, and I allowed him to pry into my personal business. He answered my questions on subjects that I didn't feel comfortable asking Mom or Dad. Topics like my paternal grandparents, who had died before I could walk. Dad went all ice cube when I'd asked about his mother's favorite color and if her handwriting was loopy or chicken scratch. Mom always pleaded the fifth, saying she didn't know. Edmond told me yellow and that her handwriting was like calligraphy, full of twirls and loops. Twenty years older than Dad, he'd known my grandparents when he was my age, and was the only source of information I had about my ancestry.

When Dad inherited the furniture repair business, Edmond encouraged an expansion into fine art. Despite Edmond's need to know my business, I categorized him under favorite, most trusted family friend.

I traced a template for a missing piece of glass in the Tiffany.

"Life doesn't stand still. Whether we like it or not, it fluxes."

The battered chandelier we worked on was testament to that nugget of wisdom. "Who brought in the..."

He turned on the grinder, drowning my words. I watched him smooth a piece of glass. Repairing the chandelier was like fitting a jigsaw puzzle, and I didn't look at the clock until the light streaming through the windows faded.

Removing his protective glasses, Edmond wiped the lenses.

I looked at the Swatch on my wrist. "Why hasn't Dad called?"

"He must be held up in traffic."

We tidied up the worktable, and Edmond turned off the lights. He wheeled his twelve-speed Schwinn Le Tour limited edition outside and set the alarm on the shop before he locked the door. The two of us sat in the mahogany Adirondack chairs, a barter trade from an artisan, that rested on a cement slab patio outside the shop.

He patted my knee. "I'll stick around. Make sure he shows."

A smoky haze of low clouds drifted across the sky, diffusing the sunlight. It was perfect weather for shorts, t-shirts, no shoes. At least for a few hours until the mosquitoes began to feast.

Chin up, he rested his closed eyes.

Watching the road for Dad, I asked, "Big weekend plans?"

"Planting snap peas and beets."

He had been on the planet three times longer than I had, but defied age. His brown eyes were bright; his skin had some roadways, but no potholes or loose guide rails. His picket teeth gleamed of youth. In junior high, I'd asked him his secret. He told me: eat colorful vegetables, run like you're being chased, Albolene cream on your face, elbows, and feet every night, and brush your teeth with baking soda.

Tilting his head forward, he asked, "What about you? Any plans?"

"Just hanging out. Hoping Trudy reclutters her apartment and deems it habitable. My opinion of her would move up a notch if she moved back to her own space this weekend."

Adjusting his graying ponytail, he suppressed a smile. "You don't approve of Trudy?"

Edmond was a perceptive guy. I grimaced, wondering why he'd bothered to ask. Then again, unlike Dad, he'd asked. "She's okay at a distance."

Made in the USA
Columbia, SC
30 March 2025